# The Sandman Inn

A novel by
JD Hall

ISBN: 1-60002-085-2

For You

"This book is cordially dedicated to you, the reader, who so ardently requested a sequel to A Light Cleansing."

## Acknowledgements

The author gratefully acknowledges the help of many people during the writing of the book. The lion's share once again going to my wife, Jean, for without her exceptional efforts as my editor, this book would not exist, or most certainly, never shared.

For words of encouragement, thanks go out to my family of friends who fed my motivation and never failed to ask, "how's the book coming?"

Last and certainly not least, the Author wishes to extend his gratitude to Ms. Holly Nethery for sharing her expertise during the final edits of, The Sandman Inn.

Cover: As envisioned and created by the Author.

JD Hall

Other books by
JD Hall

A Light Cleansing

# One

The morning air in the Appalachians was typically cool and this morning was no exception. It brought freshness unlike anything experienced in the city. Heinrich “Rich” Zeigler slowly inhaled the morning air that was free of smog but heavily tainted with farm scent. This immediately reminded him of the endless supply of fertilizer piled behind the barn. A pile about as big as the list of farm chores he detested as a child, and still disliked to this day. As he stepped clear of the barn Rich flipped the iron hasp that secured the entrance. Locks weren’t considered a necessity here simply because anyone was welcome to borrow anything at anytime. That was the way of the Amish.

Making the trip between the barn and house wasn’t far by farm standards, but then again, the gate at the back side of the lower forty acres wasn’t considered very far either.

Stopping next to the old water well Rich reached to his feet for the largest rock he could find, then held it at arm’s length just under the water bucket. He paused as he recalled how Grandfather often vowed to toss him down the well to recover all the rocks he’d dropped to their dark watery grave. Rich was never quite sure if Grandfather was serious, but he was sure Grandfather would have enjoyed tossing him down the well.

Immediately upon releasing the rock he began counting while listening for the splash. “Four…good table,” he said aloud. A count of six was bad news, for he could expect extra long prayers at the dinner table to include justification for rain. No sir, a six count was dreadful news.

Turning away from the well he looked west toward the Appalachian skyline that enveloped this section of the Amish community. A red-tailed hawk circled silently high overhead patiently scanning his breakfast menu far below. Rich would never argue that it wasn't beautiful here and that it held some happy memories, although most of the good memories were times shared with his mother.

Continuing his survey around the farm he noticed the desperate need for at least a hundred gallons of white paint and twice that number in hours for labor. His time on this visit wouldn't allow for such an effort. But he would promise once again to come back and paint everything that needed it, knowing all too well that it would never happen. Rich had long since placed farming at the bottom of his list of wants in life. That's why he'd been gone for years and only returned out of love for his aging mother, Imma. There was no doubt that within days of each other he and his mother would see this farm for the last time. She would leave in a horse-drawn hearse and he would leave in a hurry. His brothers and sister could have the farm and all that went with it…Grandfather included.

Grandfather Nikolas Orel Ziegler, once a bear of a man and twice as strong, had a deep dislike for his grandson Heinrich. Although never admitted, he often showed it when the two were alone. Rich could recall a list as long as your arm of blatant favoritism between himself and his two brothers. Actually, the fist sign of Grandfather's indifference toward him began as early as his eighth birthday. A child's birthday on a farm, primarily an Amish farm, was the single most personal day a kid could have. Grandfather never came to the table that evening for gift sharing or cake. In fact, Grandfather didn't even come into the house before Heinrich's bedtime. Mother made excuses for him and they were accepted, because Mother wouldn't lie.

Rich always believed that if his father hadn't died, growing up with Grandfather around would have been different, and any sort of difference would have been better. But Father did die and Grandfather never got over his son's death. He never stopped burying him. To this day Rich assumed Grandfather still held him responsible. It was in mid-September, the fall before Heinrich's eighth birthday that his father fell from the top joist during a barn raising. A barn raising was always a full-blown community event and everyone, but everyone, helped. The women prepared endless tables of food and the men raised the barn while the children worked as slaves, fetching whatever the elders of their gender demanded. Young Heinrich had a job as well. He was instructed, positioned and responsible for keeping the slack from the rope that stabilized his father high above. The inevitable questions were never clearly answered as to how his father lost his footing or why the rope developed slack. In truth, the young lad was just too small to counter a grown man's weight so high above.

Grandfather never saw it that way. He believed that his only son was dead because someone hadn't paid attention. Someone had neglected their responsibility. He never saw the rope burns deep in Heinrich's hands and never recognized the deep scares in his heart. Scars that he would carry for the rest of his life.

The three-sided iron dinner bell echoed throughout the farm as Rich took one last look at the mountains and whispered, "*Again the devil took him to a very high mountain and showed him all the kingdoms of the world and their splendor*…Matthew 4:8."

"Well, I was wondering where you ran off to, Heinrich. Wash up, Son, your breakfast is getting cold."

Surveying the table he quickly counted eight pancakes in the stack before the top cake leaned forward and concealed the rest. The fat on the bacon was still bubbling as it lay in a wrinkled pile next to a plate of sausage. The bread was expertly toasted and of course, homemade, as were the jams and jellies that had been cold-packed in small *Mason* jars. Rich took his chair just as Imma placed three eggs and fried potatoes in front of him.

"Thank you, Mother. This is more than I need."

"You need to eat, Heinrich, you look thin. Were you out helping your Grandfather?"

"Heinrich," he repeated to himself. Mother was the only one who called him Heinrich and she always made it sound so special. Everyone in his outside world knew him as Rich, but here on the farm he would always be Heinrich. Grandfather knew he preferred Rich but refused to use it. In fact, he most often just called him boy, if he called him anything at all.

"No, Mother, I don't think Grandfather wants my help."

"He's getting on in years, Son; you should try and mend your differences."

"Yes, Mother."

The back porch screen door banged closed announcing Grandfather Ziegler as well as creating an instant loss of appetite for Heinrich. However, he continued to chew on his toast and cut into a sausage link. While hovered over his plate he listened as the old man's boots hit the linoleum, one at a time, in unison with his grunts, coughs and wheezes. The shadow from this onetime burly farmer stretched across the floor as he slowly made his way into the kitchen. Heinrich looked his Grandfather directly in the eyes without offering a greeting but thinking that this man didn't look quite so dangerous anymore.

"I see thee still finds thy way to the table but not to thee chores, boy!"

"Good morning to you too, Grandfather."

It was a practice around the Ziegler dinner table for one to eat, not carry on idle chit chat, as talking was limited to please pass this, or may I have more of that please? All family conversation was done after the dinner meal, sometime before bible study, after bible study, or just before bedtime. Everyday of the week the children of this house were expected to commit to memory a new bible verse of their choosing. This was done religiously, so to speak, and Rich could not recall a single time when anyone got away with reciting a verse he or she had already quoted. Grandfather always knew. What Grandfather didn't know however, was that to this day Rich continued a daily study of bible verses and he had no intentions of telling him so. He didn't want to give Grandfather the satisfaction.

This morning's breakfast held to tradition. Grandfather became the first and only one to break the silence and make a request for seconds. Mother managed to anticipate Rich's needs by passing him things without requests. She was also bold enough to eventually ask a few questions at the table about her son's plans, which brought an expected grumble from her father-in-law.

"I'll be going into town later this morning, Mother. If you'll make a list, I'll be happy to do the shopping for you."

"Thank you, Heinrich; I do have a small list of things. Are you going to see Mariele? She's still unmarried, you know?" she added with a slight smile.

"She's a farm girl, Imma. The boy has no need for a farm girl."

Rich wasn't going to give the old man satisfaction for that one either and replied, "Grandfather is right, Mother. No, I'm just going into town."

Nikolas straightened his back and placed both elbows on the table before saying, "Thy brothers and I will be cutting hay in the west fields today. It must be cut, and in bales before the rains. Can we expect to see thee out there, or are ye going to stay inside and help with the women's work?"

"Nikolas, that will do!" shouted Imma. "Heinrich is my son, your grandson, and he does not deserve to be shamed that way in his home. I will not tolerate these insults any longer, do you hear me?"

"It's okay, Mother, really. It no longer bothers me." Turning to his Grandfather he said, "I'll see you in the fields when I get back, Grandfather."

"Thee car was blocking the hay rake, boy."

"I'll be moving it soon."

"No need, I already moved it."

"You! You moved my car, Grandfather?"

As Nikolas walked slowly in the direction of the mud room he added, "Wasn't no trouble. I hooked the team to it and dragged it out of the way. Thee will find your machine out by the hogs."

The days following Rich's homecoming improved as all parties began to relax and accept one another's existence. He never made it to the hay fields with his brothers and Grandfather as he had promised. Not because of the hard work involved, but mainly not to disappoint his Grandfather who didn't expect to see him out there anyway. Instead he made his way to Lancaster, found a booth in a discreet off-street tavern, and spent a quiet afternoon testing a variety of local beers while studying his bible verses.

Over the next few days he managed to put a nice coat of paint on the floors of the front and back porches, much to the delight of his mother. Grandfather, however, thought the steel gray was too dark and the paint needed a second coat, but that mattered little to Heinrich because Mother was happy. Making it a practice to steer clear of Grandfather when possible, Heinrich devoted most of his free time to his Mother or in the solitude of the tool shed. The tool shed had always been a favorite retreat for Rich by offering privacy that couldn't be expected in the house. As a young boy he often came here to study or simply be alone and work small pieces of wood with his hands. If Grandfather tracked him down it was to assign another chore, but never to share his skill of carving and changing the pine into art. Admittedly, Grandfather did have talent as a wood craftsman.

Rich received a cell call on his sixth day of vacation and a new work assignment was in the offing. The cell phone was not only his primary connection with the outside world, it was his only means. The lap top computer stayed in the SUV for it was useless without electricity, and this farm had none. He considered this the simple life, meaning it was simple to live this way. Initially, he had planned to stay ten days but leaving earlier wouldn't be the worst thing. He needed to get back to work.

The lunch chime had sounded twice before he made his way to the house. Although not accustomed to eating as often as this farm fed him, Rich made it a point to attend most meals out of respect for Mother's effort. Pausing near the back screen door to remove his shoes he overheard a conversation from the kitchen. He stood quietly out of sight and listened.

"I tell you, Imma, he's no good. I found a gun in his things. A GUN, Imma. On my land he brings the devil's weapon. A weapon used to take a man's life."

"I don't believe it, Nikolas. Why would Heinrich want such a thing?"

"Because he's no good! It was that war that taught him those evil things. You know he didn't have to go. He asked to go. Imma, none of our young men are obligated to fight in the English's wars. You know that. All Amish boys can be classified as conscientious objectors if they're drafted. But Heinrich, NO! The boy asked to go. And now he brings a gun on my land and into my home. I tell you he's no good."

"STOP, NIKOLAS, stop it! I cannot hear of such things. He's my son, a good boy, and you will not run him off again. Do you hear me? He's a good boy."

Heinrich could hear his mother's footsteps quickly leaving the kitchen, putting an end to this debate with her father-in-law. Turning from the door, he made his way to his SUV parked next to the hog lot. As his pace quickened so did his feeling of anger towards his grandfather. Not because his privacy was violated, but rather for making his mother cry.

Hurriedly he emptied the contents of his tote bag across the wooden work bench in the tool shed. The inventory was completed and nothing was missing. He actually was expecting to find that the Smith and

Wesson 44 magnum had been relocated to the bottom of the well or thrown in the center of the hog lot. But that would have required Grandfather to touch it, and of course he wouldn't. After inspecting the clip, he returned the weapon to its holster and closed the snap. Once all the items were secure in the SUV, Heinrich decided to inform his mother that it was time for him to leave. He had places to go and work to do. Perhaps he would even tell her that he'd stayed longer than initially planned.

Making his way toward the house, he was drawn to the old well like a magnet. Rich reached for the rocks at his feet and dropped a large handful into the bottom of the well. His anger began to surface with the ensuing splash as he tried to free the stones from along the rim and send them down the shaft as well. The old structure was as tough as Grandfather. With his composure regained he looked to the Appalachians for comfort and whispered, "*He set the earth on its foundations; it can never be moved...*Psalms 104:5."

Once on the porch Rich stopped and listened once again for voices, but heard none. With his shoes in hand he made his way past the mud room where he saw his mother standing next to a stack of dishes waiting to be dried. Grandfather Ziegler was seated at the table reading his bible.

"Heinrich, come in, you missed dinner, son, didn't you hear the bell?"

"Yes, Mother, I heard it, but I wanted to finish the painting and clean the brushes."

"Come now, sit down, son, and I'll put something together for you. You must be starved."

Rich noticed that his mother's thoughtful offer brought the old man's head up, for his law declared that if you missed the dinner hour, then you could expect food only at the next meal.

"Thanks, Mother, but I'm not very hungry. Actually I came in to tell you that I got a call today and need to go back to work."

Imma wiped her hands on the checkered dish cloth as she listened to his news, and immediately dropped it on the counter.

"But you just got here, Heinrich. Do you need to leave so soon? I've been thinking, why don't you quit your job with the English and come back home, Son? We need you here. You have been such a great help to me and Grandfather."

Rich glanced at his grandfather who never raised his eyes from the bible.

"I'll be back as often as I can, Mother. But look, since I don't plan to leave until after services this weekend, maybe we can plan a nice family get-together. We'll invite everyone. An old-fashioned pitch-in picnic, how does that sound?"

He could see the excitement growing in his mother's eyes at the thought of the family gathering once again, as they did so often years ago. The idea was accepted and Imma's menu was already beginning to form in her mind.

"I've noticed that there is one more little job I'd like to do before I go."

"Oh, Heinrich, you don't have to do anymore work around here. You've done enough for us just by painting the porches. Isn't that so, Grandfather?"

"Yes, Thee has done enough."

"Actually," said Rich, "from the first day I stopped by the old well and dropped my rock, I noticed that the rope and bucket need to be replaced. I don't think that old bucket would hold a cup of water after being pulled up from the bottom. I'm going to run into Lancaster and pick up a new rope and a nice new galvanized bucket. I shouldn't be gone…"

Grandfather's chair sliding away from the table interrupted Rich, but he continued as Grandfather rose. "As I was saying, I shouldn't be gone long."

"No need to be gone at all, boy. I've been meaning to get around to replacing that gear here in the next day or so myself. There's a new shank of rope in the tool shed and a new wood water bucket that Karl Yodder made. It's in the shed too. So ye don't have to bother with it at all. No need to hold thee up. You can go back to thy High People city and whatever it is ye do there when ye is ready."

Nikolas looked up at Imma's eyes that were giving him a chilling glare before adding, "Unless the boy really wants to fix the well."

"Yes, Grandfather. The boy really wants to fix the well."

The afternoon sun was at its best by offering both light and warmth to the work area around the original well on the Ziegler farm. Rich had intended to do this last little chore without the guidance of his grandfather. But as usual, Grandfather Ziegler was having his own way; however, it appeared that he had lightened up just a bit. Perhaps he was influenced by Mother's glare, or perhaps he was motivated by Rich announcing his plans to leave when this job was finished.

Nikolas began to recite the well's history without prompting. He spoke of how it was the first drinking water well on the farm, and the number of days it took he and his son, Heinrich's father, to dig it. He spoke with a great deal of pride as he detailed the number of trips he and his son made to carry the stone from the fields in order to line the walls of the well. Rich stood quietly as he watched his grandfather's wrinkled hands repair the damage to the spindle and slide a windsor knot through a slat to prevent the rope from falling free should its length become exhausted. Heinrich was impressed by the old man's skills, and if he didn't hate him so much he could have respected him.

"I believe the shaft should be replaced, Grandfather. It looks worn."

"No," he said while shaking his head, "no…your father carved that shaft from a hickory limb using just his knife and rasp. It stays. It's a part of this well as much as he is."

"I didn't kill him, Grandfather, he fell. That's all. He fell. It happens."

Grandfather Nikolas froze in place for a few moments before saying, "Bring me the grease from the shed, boy. The gears need greased."

Returning to the well with a pail of axle grease that looked as old as Grandfather, Rich found him standing on the ledge of the wall reaching forward to remove the gear's dust cover.

"You should get down, Grandfather. Let me up there to do that."

"I'll do it. Ye just hand me the grease."

"Do you want the pail or just a handful?"

"A handful will do."

Rich watched as his grandfather applied grease to the gear's bearings and a light amount to the gear's teeth. Once the dust cover was replaced, Grandfather Nikolas handed the screwdriver to his grandson. This project was finished. The well now had a new rope and a hand-crafted wood bucket, and all the moving parts had a fresh coat of lubricant. Watching attentively as his grandfather regained his position to step off the well's wall, Rich reached out to him saying, "Careful, Grandfather, let me help you down."

Without a survey, it would be safe to say that the majority of the 172,000 households in this Pennsylvania Dutch community had their own cemetery plots, each having a special location on a unique site overlooking their land. The Zeigler Farm was no exception. The site of this family's burial ground was atop a grassy knoll just to the southeast of the main house. A small gate defended the only access through the rusting black iron fence which surrounded the small cemetery. It was a peaceful and appropriate location for a loved one's final resting place.

Rich counted twenty-nine black buggies and an equal number of horses before losing count at the turn. Several of the elders were overheard saying that this was the longest funeral processions they could recall. Some in the procession moved slowly through the wheat crop before leaving their carriages and making the short walk up the grassy knoll. A moderate breeze from the southwest played with the black cloth of those walking as everyone gathered to pay their last respects and pray for the late Nikolas Orel Ziegler.

Heinrich Zeigler walked arm in arm with his mother followed closely by his two brothers, Wilhelm and Karl. Cacilia, the only surviving sister, and the only grandchild to show signs of grief, bonded tightly to her mother's free hand. The confines of the small family cemetery quickly became overrun by mourners. The iron fence had kept the number inside at bay, as those more removed from the family circled outside the three-foot iron wall. Prayers were said by anyone wishing to offer them, and there were many. Too many for Rich, but he continued his charade as the bereaved grandson out of love for his mother. In time the mourners began the slow descent down the grassy knoll and eventually regrouped at the Zeigler home where they again paid their respects and consoled the family.

There must have been over two hundred white bearded men, bonneted women and multiple-sized children in the backyard of the Zeigler homestead. The makeshift tables stretched as far as the need required, leaving very little space that was not covered by the pitch-in menu. The back yard was indeed a sea of black as family, friends and well wishers gathered after Nikolas Orel Ziegler's funeral services.

The county coroner investigated and officially determined that Nikolas Orel Zeigler's death was the result of suffocation, or death by drowning. Large amounts of grease were found on his hands corroborating the theory of loss of balance and loss of grip. The coroner also noted a four inch laceration located on the left base of the skull and several contusions about the forehead. It was speculated these were received from striking a rock or rocks along the well's lining. In conclusion: Grandfather slipped, struck his head on a rock and drowned in the well.

Heinrich "Rich" Zeigler sat quietly in his black SUV surveying the farm one last time before leaving. Mother and he had said goodbye in the house, but he could see her looking out from behind the curtain in the front room. "She'll be fine," he reassured himself. The siblings had met and agreed that it would be best if Wilhelm, the oldest, and his family would move in to look after Mother and farm the farm. After all, that's the way farms had been, and will be, passed on from generation to generation.

Rechecking his map and notes, as well as the compass attached to the dash, Rich was ready to leave. The driving time to his next assignment was estimated to be nine hours and nineteen minutes, or 600 miles due west according to OnStar. After drawing his lap belt tight he waved to his mother who was still standing at the window. A smile broke across his lips as he spoke to no one but himself, "Good bye, Mother. I promised I'd stay until after the weekend services, didn't I? And I also promised an old fashioned pitch-in picnic with all the family and friends didn't I?"

As he turned the ignition key he looked up once again and revisited the tree line of the Appalachian Mountains. The sun's reflection off the two shiny brass rings around the new water bucket brought his attention back to the well.

"No more rocks, Grandfather, no more rocks."

Looking into the rear view mirror as the black SUV made its way slowly down the gravel drive toward the blacktop he again whispered, "*Let them alone: they be blind leaders of the blind. And if the blind lead the blind, both shall fall into the ditch*…Matthew 15:14."

# Two

If you would have asked for more pleasant weather to spend an afternoon outdoors in Indianapolis, Indiana, you probably would have been told that it was not possible. The rain had moved out of the region and taken the humidity along with it. Directly above the Kramer's patio Jake could see nothing but a perfectly clear blue sky. This was complemented by a soft breeze from the northwest which capped the description of "a beautiful day."

Standing next to the patio table he topped two margarita glasses and sat the pitcher down between them. With glass in hand, he took a small sip to sample his concoction, making sure it was fit for human consumption, and nodded with approval. But just to be certain he made a second check before setting the glass down. He smiled as he watched Connie buzzing about the flower boxes removing dead petals and tossing them into the yard, only to have them float back to the patio with the gentle wind.

"Tossing rose petals at my feet, Connie?"

"Yes, your highness. What time is it?"

"Relax, Con. You're fidgety. Come, sit down and test your drink. They'll be here soon.

"I know. But it's not everyday our son brings his girlfriend home to meet his parents."

"Now, Connie, according to JJ she's just his friend. Girlfriend is your definition, not his. Did he say to what we owe this little get together?"

"Not really. I got the drift that Karen needs to arrange an interview of some sort for one of her class finals. JJ said he'd explain after they got here."

"An interview?" repeated Jake. "I'm a little surprised you agreed to that."

"Well, it was hard to tell him no. I thought it might be best if we take care of her project first, then we could have some snacks and visit for awhile before they head back to Terre Haute."

Jake nodded with approval and gave Connie one of his best devilish grins.

"Listen, Jake," she said as she walked to the table, "I don't want you to say anything tonight that would make JJ feel uncomfortable. This is uncharted territory for him."

"ME! Why would I do that? You're the one who's buzzing around like…"

"I know, but I'll never forget my first meeting with your folks and how awkward it was."

"Awkward? You were a downright nervous wreck."

"Okay, okay, let's not go there. Just be on your best behavior, alright?"

"I can still see my mom handing you a glass of tea, and you…"

"JAKE!" said Connie interrupting.

"You dropped that glass like it was a ten pound stick of hot butter. Splat."

"JAKE!"

"Anybody home?"

"There're here," said Connie, as she hurried from the patio. "Come on, Jake."

"You go; I'll stay here and guard the table."

JJ and Karen had made their way to the kitchen as Connie closed the patio door behind her to greet her son and his date.

"Hi Mom…this is Karen, the girl I was telling you about. Karen…my mother, Connie."

Connie shook her head at her son's attempt at introductions while extending her hand toward Karen. "How nice it is to meet you, Karen. Welcome."

"Thank you, Mrs. Kramer. It's nice to finally get to meet you too."

"Where's Dad?"

"Outside on the patio. Why don't you go keep him company while Karen and I get to know one another? Tell your Dad we're using his den and we'll be out in a little while. Oh, and JJ, tell your father that I said to go easy on the margaritas."

"Sure thing, Mom."

"That goes for you too, JJ," added Karen, bringing a smile to Connie's face.

"Thank you for agreeing to this interview, Mrs. Kramer. I'm sure you've done so many that it's becoming old hat for you."

"Actually, Karen, this will be my first, and please call me Connie."

"That would be nice, thank you," replied Karen. "You say it's your first interview? I find that surprising. I mean, considering all the notoriety and controversy Mr. Kramer has created. I just assumed that newspapers, women's magazines, or even talk shows have been hounding you."

"That's true, they have. But I haven't granted any interviews, not until now anyway. Frankly, Jake and I have been anxious to meet the young lady who has our son spending so much time around Indiana State these days. I must confess that granting this interview was a ploy to finally get to meet you. JJ thinks a great deal of you, Karen. I can tell."

"Thank you, Mrs. Kramer…Connie. I think he is pretty special too, but don't tell him I said so."

"So, how can I help you, Karen?"

"Well, as you may or may not know, I am working on a degree in journalism at State. One of my final exams requires that I interview one person other than a family member. I was hoping you would agree to my asking you questions surrounding your life in regard to Mr. Kramer's gift, and the changes in your family's lives as well."

"What kind of questions, Karen?"

Karen didn't immediately answer Connie's inquiry but instead took a moment to reach into her handbag and remove a Sony personal recorder. "Would you mind if I tape our conversation, Connie? We've been taught that it's the best and surest way to get quotes accurate."

"No, I don't mind. Just what kind of story were you expecting?"

"I am interested in doing a story with reference to the woman's side of your life. A sort of 'the lady behind the man' type of thing."

"I see." replied Connie. "Well, Karen, let's agree to this. You ask your questions and I'll do my best to give you a sincere answer, with the understanding that if I don't like the question, I won't give an answer. Is that alright with you?"

"That's fine with me, Connie. Let start with…"

Karen was not taking this opportunity lightly. Her dream of becoming a respected, dedicated investigative journalist was indeed sincere, and she was now sitting next to one of the most sought-after interviewees of the day. Perhaps even bigger than the First Lady herself. With Connie's reluctance to grant interviews, this journalism major was indeed getting "the exclusive with the elusive."

While doing her pre-interview homework, Karen had researched all the articles, film footage, and commentaries she could find. She had completed an intense study on Mr. Jake Kramer's near-death experience as told by Wesley Washington and Mitch Reinhart, the two persons directly credited with saving Jake's life, or more so, bringing him back to it. She had, laying before her, pages and pages of reference materials as well as an outline for her interview. Karen was totally aware that should her career develop she would most likely never again be in such an enviable position. She was in the Kramer's home, receiving a unique one-of-a-kind granted interview from the charming Mrs. Jake Kramer. Barbara Walters…eat your heart out.

"…what was your first reaction, Connie, upon hearing of your husband's accident? And how did you prepare to inform your children about the accident?"

Connie paused for a moment to collect her thoughts before answering. "I don't think anyone is ever prepared for news that someone they love has been hurt or killed. If we find the idea entering our minds most of us dismiss it immediately because no one wants to imagine such thoughts. But it does happen. People in our lives do get hurt, and we need to face it. Jake was involved in a terrible accident, but thankfully, he was spared and returned to us. As far as preparing some way to tell the kids, well, I can only say that I just went with my heart."

"Connie, when did you first realize that Mr. Kramer could recall the memories of the deceased, and what was your reaction to such astonishing news?"

"Well, that would have been back when Jake was in the hospital recovering from the accident. I remember he made a comment about a little girl named Jenni Lynn Meese during a news telecast. He said, 'she's been cleansed.' That was the first time I had heard him use that term, cleansed."

"And what was your reaction to his cleansed comment?"

"I didn't understand what he was implying at the time. Was she killed, or hurt, or just what he meant.

But he refused to comment any further on the subject. Let's say it was a confusing time for both of us."

"Thankfully, Jake recovered from his wounds and eventually came home to you, JJ, and your daughter, Margaret. How did his new ability change your daily lives?"

"Well, Margaret loved tapping her daddy's recall ability for her homework research projects. He was a natural, a talking encyclopedia. JJ, on the other hand, never said much about it one way or the other. You probably know the answer to that question better than I."

Karen smiled before asking, "And what about Mrs. Kramer?"

"What about Mrs. Kramer?" repeated Connie as she managed a smile, and paused before rushing an answer. "To be truthful, Karen, I guess my feelings were balanced between being proud, scared and envious."

"What do you mean by proud, scared and envious, Connie? Would you care to elaborate on that?"

Connie's response was interrupted by JJ bringing two cokes into the room and placing them on the table before the two ladies. Connie was indeed impressed. Not only with her son's manners, but because this was perhaps the first time she could recall him bringing a drink to his mother without being asked. She watched JJ and Karen exchange eye contact before leaving the room suggesting that their relationship was developing into more than just a friendship.

"I'm sorry, Karen. Where were we?" asked Connie after sampling the soft drink.

"I was asking how you felt proud, scared and envious of Jake's abilities."

Connie took a deep breath before answering and then said, "I am so proud of Jake for helping so many people. Those people had nowhere to turn, no one to count on, and in most cases, had lost all hope. Jake relieved their anguish regardless of the results. Good or bad, they could now put their lives in order. People like Tina Myers, Jennifer Sutton, Josh Driscoll, and Lilly something or other, just to mention a few. Oh, and June Grodey. How could I forget finding that woman standing in our doorway asking to see Jake. My heart was lost to her from the first sight of those tears as she stood in our foyer. She looked so frail and vulnerable as she rolled a tattered Kleenex between her fingers. Then she handed me an envelope filed with information concerning her baby. What a wonderful thing Jake did for her in locating her baby, Jimmy. I'm very proud of him for that."

"And scared?" asked Karen.

"I'm scared for him because of all the Walter Driscolls in the world."

"Walter Driscolls?" repeated Karen.

"YES, Walter Driscoll. He tried to shoot my husband right here in our own home. Right here in this very room," said Connie. "He and countless others fear Jake because of the information he may or may not know about their misdeeds. There are a lot of people out there with skeletons in their closets, and every one of them wants to keep those doors closed. So because of them, I'm scared for Jake. And I'm scared for us, too."

Karen looked into Connie's eyes and saw the genuine truth of her statement. She was scared. Perhaps more scared than she even admitted to herself. Karen had read the reported details concerning Walter Driscoll's attempted murder of Jake Kramer. She also read how Driscoll was found dead in the Kramer's front yard with a bullet hole through his head. The official investigation listed the incident as attempted murder resulting in suicide. But it just didn't compute to Karen's journalistic instincts. She had made some notes during her research to look into the possibility of a third party. A third party who may have been looking out for Mr. Kramer.

"And finally, what about envious, Connie? Are you jealous of your husband?"

Connie started to laugh before saying, "I was hoping you might have forgotten I said that, Karen. Oh, I guess there are times that I get a little jealous of Jake's popularity. But then I get over it. You see, what people don't realize is that Jake Kramer has always been a warm and caring person. His near-death experience didn't alter that. If I get a little jealous, it's only because so many people are demanding his time. That's time he and I enjoyed together, our time. Now that's being shared with others. Yes, I'll admit that makes me somewhat jealous. However, all the good he does by helping the oppressed, well, I can't be jealous of that, can I? There were many who had no one to turn to, and no one who could or would help. That was until Jake Kramer came along. But now they call and they write, or they stop by. Each one a bearer of his own burdens. Genuine and heartfelt as they might be, still they need my husband and that makes me a little jealous at times."

"And what about Connie Kramer?" asked Karen again, knowing there was probably more to that answer. "How does Connie Kramer feel?"

Connie's answer this time was immediate and direct, "Connie Kramer is numb."

Karen looked up from her notes at Connie's remark and paused for an explanation, but received none.

"I don't understand, Mrs. Kramer. Would you care to elaborate?"

As Connie readjusted her position in her chair, Karen became unsure if she was going to receive an answer. She watched quietly as Connie's facial expression lost the warm smile that she conveyed to this point.

"It's people, Karen. The people make me numb because of their constant demands on Jake and on our lives. As I mentioned, the phone rarely stops ringing. Would you believe that we've had our number changed twice, and still our latest unlisted number has been exposed? We've all resorted to carrying cell phones for a little relief. No one should have to live like that.

"The mail makes me numb too. Look at the boxes in the corner, Karen. The one on the left is unsorted, and the big one next to it is full of threats or phony requests. People have tried to use Jake for their own personal gain, or even worse, their vindictiveness. Some scared me so badly that I couldn't finish reading them. There are days that I tremble with each ring of the door bell, or every ring of the phone. Once I shook so badly while holding the mail that the letters fell from my hand. But now I'm numb to that, numb to them. I don't care if he helps them or not. In fact, I sometimes wish he wouldn't. I've prayed that he would lose this gift that has almost become a curse to our family, as we knew it."

Karen watch silently as Connie fought back her emotions and attempted to regain her composure.

"Connie, may I look at some of the mail?"

"Help yourself," she said while managing a smile.

Karen removed one of the opened envelopes at random and pulled the letter from the pouch. Connie watched as Karen's eyes widened with the words she read.

"It's okay. You can read it aloud. They don't bother me anymore."

Karen read in part…"Kramer…Say your prayers. You won't know who, when, or where, but I'm not waiting around for you to finger me. You're a dead man."

"My God, Connie, have you gone to the police with these?"

"Jake has a friend in the FBI that he often talks to. He's a good and dedicated man. It was his suggestion to keep the mail. That's the only reason I haven't burned them while envisioning it was Voodoo burning its writer in hell."

Karen smiled at her remark while selecting another envelope.

"Dear Mr. Kramer,
I know how busy you must be but I need your help in locating the killer of my son, Eric. He was killed on June 14, 1977…"

Connie watched Karen's compassion surface as she continued to read the heartfelt rendering of a mother's plea to locate her son's murderer.

"…yours in prayer,
Mrs. T.M. Burton."

"I can understand how these must really get to you, Mrs. Kramer. Did Jake help her locate the killer?"

"Yes…that letter was from the killer."

Karen was completely taken by surprise at Connie's answer and could only respond with an open mouth and blank expression.

"What?" she managed to say.

"That letter was from the killer, not Mrs. Burton," repeated Connie. "He was trying to learn if Jake could inform the authorities that he was Eric Burton's killer. Of course Jake could, and in fact gave the information to Inspector Pierson. They haven't located the man yet, so we kept the letter. See why it's necessary to become numb?"

"May I see an unopened envelope, Connie?"

"Sure…please, help yourself."

Karen reached deep into the box and removed a envelope simply addressed,

Jake.

919 Crest Street,

with no return address. Removing the paper Karen read aloud, "*Behold, I am coming soon! My reward is with me, and I will give to everyone according to what he has done*…Revelation 22:12."

Karen looked at Connie with puzzlement in regard to understanding the significance of the bible verse and asked, "Any clue what this is supposed to mean?"

"None. Just toss it in the box and hope for the best."

# Three

"Jake, if you're planning to read very long you should have more light," said Connie as she entered the den and found Jake studying the evening newspaper.

"I was just scanning the headlines while waiting for the nightly news."

"I saw you rubbing your forehead. Poor lighting can give you a headache you know, and you don't need that."

"Too late, babe," replied Jake as he continued reading.

"Did you happen to see this piece on the Burger Barn slayings?"

"No, I haven't seen a paper in days. Please tell me they solved the case?"

"I wish. Unfortunately, this article only reminds us that it's been ten years and the police are no closer to making an arrest."

"My heart aches for their families," said Connie as she approached her recliner. "One day those responsible will have to answer for what they've done, one way or another."

Jake looked back at the article while unconsciously rubbing his forehead with his fingertips in an attempt to soften the sharp pain.

"Jake, I was just thinking. Perhaps…"

"NO!" said Jake, as he cut her off in mid-sentence without looking up.

"What do you mean, NO?" snapped Connie. "You haven't any idea of what I was going to say."

"Yes I do, and my final answer is, NO."

Connie eased back in her recliner, forced the foot rest into position, and assumed her best sulking position as Jake returned to his paper. Relying on experience from years of marriage to Jake Kramer she knew he'd blink first. She could hear him rustling his newspaper while forcing a cough in their library-like atmosphere.

"Okay, Connie, What was it?"

"What was what?" she replied without moving.

"Look, I'm sorry, okay? I shouldn't have cut you off that way, but I have a doozy of a headache brewing and I knew what you were about to suggest. I just don't like being provoked into demand searching…you know that."

"Well, for your information, Mr. Kramer, I wasn't going to provoke you into anything, much less demand searching. I was about to suggest that we have JJ and Karen back for a barbecue next weekend so Margaret can meet her too."

"Oh," said Jake.

"I accept your 'oh' as begging for forgiveness."

Jake smiled and shook his head as he stood and made his way to his recliner near her. "Look, I am sorry, but I'm not begging for anything. I think you managed to exclude about half of what you were really going to suggest. So let's change the subject and you tell me how the interview went?"

"I think it went very well. At least she seemed pleased and must have thanked me a dozen times. I like her and I think JJ likes her too. Did he say anything about her to you?"

"Connie…we're guys. Guys don't talk about stuff like that, especially with their dads."

"No, I suppose they don't."

"I did learn something from him though, and I'm very happy that he is finally taking charge of his life."

"What?" asked Connie as she scooted forward in her chair. "What did he tell you?"

Jake's first instinct was to run with this one and string her along for awhile, but he decided it was too late in the evening for that type of amusement.

"He asked me if I would be disappointed in him if he didn't return to work at Kramer and Associates."

By now Connie had her recliner upright and was resting on her elbows as Jake had captured her complete attention.

"Not come back? But he's been studying for an apprenticeship. What does he want to do now?"

"It's okay, babe. Relax. He plans to finish his apprenticeship studies, but then wants to move into the electrical engineering field. I think he likes what he's doing and should go for it."

"Wonderful," said Connie. "So what did you tell him?"

"Just that. If he likes what he's doing then he should go for it. I also told him that he couldn't disappoint me by taking charge of his life in a positive manner. I'm really quite proud of him, Connie, and I suppose I should have told him so. You remember that there was a time when I expected him to become a master burger flipper?" Jake paused before saying, "I should have told him that too."

"I believe we're finding that things do have a way of working out for the best after all," she said.

"I guess so, but unfortunately not for everyone," he replied while rubbing his forehead and reaching for the TV's remote. "Let's watch the news, shall we?"

"You watch the news and I'll go take my bath. We can talk about a barbecue weekend and JJ's future later." She paused before leaving the den and asked, "Do you want me to bring you some aspirin?"

"Thanks, but it can wait until you come back."

Jake pressed the power button on the remote control and brought the late news to life. "…highs in the upper 70s with an 80 percent chance of rain late today and ending sometime early next week. Details later in the broadcast…Brian"

"Thanks, Tom. Also in our news tonight, the Indianapolis Colts' franchise is asking for a renovation on the newly completed Colts' Arena…we'll tell you why later in the program. And, on the tenth anniversary of the ill-famed Burger Barn killings, law enforcement officers are still searching for clues. These and other…"

The brutal pain in his temples was so severe that it forced Jake's head back against the leather covering his recliner. Pressing his palms firmly against his ears he attempted to neutralize the pressure that was trying to explode inside his head. Nothing he had experienced to date could mock this excruciating pain, and it didn't seem to be easing. Jake opened his eyes only to find blurred vision. The image of the newscaster on the screen began to stretch like a balloon, first horizontally, and then slowly began to distort itself vertically. As the throbbing increased, Jake watched everything before his eyes turn completely black then fade away.

An unknown number of voices began to echo with a canyon-style repeat in Jake's ears. Each voice tried desperately to gain notice until the blend finally became undistinguishable and formed a repetitive scream. He squeezed his eyelids tightly closed and stared into the darkness. Deeper and deeper he penetrated into the black empty space while listening to the cries from afar.

"This ain't good," he whispered softly, as the light particles were beginning to form. However, they were irregular and gave the appearance of a hand-held sparkler used on Independence Day. This image also appeared distorted and blurred. He watched intently as the ball of white sparks moved erratically around his dark world, dragging a glowing tail in hot pursuit.

Nothing was as previously experienced. Jake gripped the arms of the chair as the lights stopped momentarily then centered themselves in his vision before thrusting directly toward him. He felt the urge to jump clear but was unable to move. The high-pitched humming became louder and continued to echo until the light finally withdrew to what he considered a safe distance. Jake could feel his chest heaving and his heart racing as this was not the satisfying or relaxing experience to which he had grown accustomed. This needed to stop and the sooner the better, but the entire episode only continued to escalate. The shower of color failed to form a rainbow and instead continued in a harsh shade of white that now began to pulsate from bright to dim, bright to dim. As he looked into this deep space of flickering light he watched the particles gradually collect themselves into a tight entity that also plunged directly toward him in a sharp, stabbing motion. He was quivering now as small beads of perspiration began rolling down his forehead, with one pausing on the tip of his nose before falling to his chin.

"Something or someone out there wants my attention and they're definitely getting it," he whispered. "This is not good."

The ball of lights slowed slightly but maintained its pulsating rhythm until it suddenly erupted into a vibrant starburst that turned his black space into burning white. Then the raining candles from the starburst were snuffed out one by one. Jake jumped at the sight, then settled back in a rigid position refocusing on the shower surrounding the spinning ball. As unexpected as the first starburst appeared and fell, a second burst exploded. Jake again quivered at the shower of lights in this immeasurable dark void as horrifying cries echoed in his ears. With his fingers clawed deep into the leather of his chair his chest heaved in rapid rhythm and his heart raced at a deadly pace.

The next two light bursts were equally as incredible but less startling and allowed him an opportunity to watch more closely. As the last of the fading candles was snuffed and darkness once again prevailed, Jake managed to release his grip on the chair and press his palms against his ears in an attempt to lessen the cries. But the cries could not be silenced. Feeling his body's tension easing slightly he made an effort to open his eyes, only to find total darkness. If his eyes were indeed open, then Jake Kramer was blind. Quickly he forced his lids closed and reopened them again, but there was no change in the result. Nothing but darkness. Absolute black, laced with agonizing voices bellowing in his ears. Jake tried to seize this moment of inactivity to collect his emotions and come to terms with this new and undesirable experience.

The final burst was unprovoked and explosive beyond description, as it once again covered Jake's deep black space with a blinding white light that became so intense that it brought him upright in his chair. The white particles with conscious intent withdrew and formed a globe in the center of his vision. First, the globe revolved counterclockwise. Then in a slow, deliberate movement it rotated from vertical to horizontal until it began to spin like a wheel. Surrounded by complete darkness the bright white globe commenced rolling toward Jake and steadily increased its momentum. As the rolling became faster the globe grew larger and brought a deafening squeal to his ears. Jake sat captive in his chair, oblivious to his surrounding, while witnessing a totally new mystical light experience.

The globe spun to the point of becoming a blur before his eyes. As the rotation continued, Jake watched sparks begin to eject from the globe's axis as the dark background started to lighten into a pulsating red glow. This he enjoyed because the vision somehow managed to ease the pressure in his temples and the roaring in his ears. Subsequently, without prompting, an image of a young male appeared on the right axis followed by a second male emerging on the opposite side. The images gave the impression of pain and fear as both looked hauntingly into Jake's eyes. As if directed by the globe, the imagery began to rotate around the globe. The first image revolved around the equator as the second moved past the poles. Each in turn disappearing behind the light and reappearing without fail. Jake's heart rate accelerated as two additional facial images appeared from within the axis. This time one male and one female took their places navigating around the globe. The globe's revolution held steady as yet another young lady appeared and found her place among the group. Jake held his eyes fixed on the five young people before him for each expressed their own plea for help while committed to a unique presence around the globe. As they continued their orbiting, he studied their haunting imagery and tried to commit this supernatural phenomenon to memory.

The globe's rotation once again accelerated and the lights started to blend. The images began to distort and, without protest, were drawn in separate directions then disappeared into the globe. The light particles continued spinning until they again became a complete blur which created an amplified humming in his eardrums that seemed to last for an eternity.

The closing spectacle could only be compared to the Big Bang, followed by an implosion imitating the actions of a black hole in space. There wasn't time for the light globe to stop its forward movement and withdraw; nor was there time for the darting lights to return to multi-colored movement. There wasn't time to bathe in the soft illusion of the rainbow for the total scenario simply burst open with a flash of brilliant white light, then imploded and disappeared into itself. This magnificent spiritual event ended in a matter of milliseconds leaving Jake dazed and shaken.

He slowly opened his eyes to find only blurred vision brought on by the intensity of his headache, the blinding white light and the ruthless humming in his ears. He waited anxiously for his vision to return while making every effort to relax and get control of his emotions by taking long deep breaths. He quickly learned that trying to disregard the visions of those young people was impossible. If he had any regrets, it would be that this hallowed experience ended too abruptly and left no resolve. Leaning forward in his recliner he placed his elbows on his knees and rested his head in his hands.

"Who were they and what were they trying to tell me? Five kids, five young…of course, the Burger Barn."

Connie, having finished her evening bath and the customary nightly ritual of planning her next day's wardrobe, made her way down the hall with Jake's aspirin in hand.

"Jake, JAKE! Honey, are you alright?" she asked as she entered the den. Jake didn't respond but remained in his awkward position while shaking uncontrollably. Connie moved quickly toward him, knelt down at his side and placed her left arm across his shoulders.

"Jake, honey, it's me. Can you hear me?" she repeated softly. "Jake you're bleeding. Look at me, honey. What happened to you?" she asked while reaching for a tissue from the box on the end table. Connie reached out and placed her hand around his right wrist and pulled gently until she could see the side of his face.

"Honey, you have a nose bleed," she said as she gently placed the tissue against his nostril. "No…you have a double nose bleed," she added while reaching for additional tissues. "Tilt your head up a little. What happened to you?"

He didn't speak a word but responded to her instructions in a sedated-like manner. Gently turning his head toward her in order to wipe his face, Connie looked directly into his eyes and sensed an immediate cold chill throughout her body. She was, in fact, shaken with fear from her husband's glare; the glare of a man who had just returned from hell. She had to force herself to look into his eyes again, but was determined to do so, for this was her husband, the man she loved, the father of her children. She would not allow herself to fear him because this was not Jake's fault.

His face was damp from perspiration and stained with blood from the nosebleed. Using another tissue, Connie made an attempt to wipe his brow but he brushed her hand away.

"Jake, let me clean your face, honey, it's okay…"

He slowly turned his head to Connie and spoke scarcely above a whisper, "Connie, Connie, I…I can't make them stop."

"I know, honey, its okay." She repeated, trying to comfort him.

Jake was trembling now and Connie could see tears forming in the corners of his eyes that were the deepest shade of red she had ever seen.

He began to cry, at first softly, then uncontrollably. He was crying loud and hard. Crying not only for the kids who had lost their lives at the Burger Barn, but he was also crying for all the Tinas, the Lillys, and the Jennifers of the world. He was crying for all the abused, the oppressed, the forgotten, and undeniably, he was crying for Jake Kramer.

"I can't…I can't make them stop hurting."

Connie held him as tightly as she dared and whispered, "I love you, Jake, I love you. It's okay."

Jake cried until he could cry no more. He was completely spent, yet managed to straighten himself up and rest against the back of the recliner. Connie's heart ached as she watched from her kneeling position. His swollen eyes and grim expression gave the appearance of one who had aged ten years in the past hour. Thankfully he had stopped trembling, but he was nervously rubbing his hands together at his waist.

"Honey," said Connie, as she pulled herself to her feet. "I'm going to fix you something to drink. "I'll be right back, okay? Will you be alright?"

Jake never moved, leaving her to wonder if he had heard her at all. Nonetheless, she kissed him gently on the forehead and left the room.

Connie found the room deserted when she returned to the den with two small glasses filled with scotch and ice. The TV was muted as the screen flickered in the darkened room, casting a blue strobe effect on the walls. The only noise in the room was from the ice cubes rattling against the glasses she held in her shaky hands.

As she made her way down the hall in search of Jake she heard water running from the shower in their bath. The modest room, lit only by the soft glow of a night light, illuminated the silhouette of her husband through the distorted glass of the shower stall. As steam rolled from the enclosure he stood directly under the shower head taking the spray directly in the face. Placing his drink where he would be sure to find it she turned away, leaving Jake Kramer to cleanse his mind and body.

Although drinking scotch on-the-rocks was out of character for Connie, she managed to empty the glass without any problem and she was starting to feel its effect. After she had turned down the bed and dimmed the lights in his den she silently checked in on Jake once again. If he had moved at all during her absence it was barely noticeable as he remained motionless, facing directly into the spray. Connie slid between the sheets assuming that Jake would come to bed as soon as the hot water ran out. The small amount of scotch she consumed had indeed eased her anxiety thus allowing her to relax and become warm and comfortable as her eyes lids began to grow heavy.

# Four

*"Wake-up little Susie, wake-up. Wake-up little Susie, wake-up. The movie wasn't so hot, it didn't..."* Connie reached for the radio's snooze button to silence the Everly Brothers and rolled back on her pillow.

"Honey, its o-dark-thirty. I have the snooze on. Are you awake, Jake?"

Raising her head Connie turned to his empty half of their bed. He had either done a great job of straightening the covers or he hadn't slept in the bed at all. Dropping her head back on the pillow, she rubbed her eyes trying to awaken her senses. Her mind searched to recall any mention of an early appointment, but then, what's the big deal she thought, he often gets up before me. I'm a sound sleeper, besides, I was exhausted last night because...She quickly sat up in bed listening for any indication that Jake was somewhere about. "The water isn't running, so he either finished his shower last night or we ran out of water," she whispered.

"Good morning, sleepy head, time to rise and shine. I brought your coffee, lightly creamed as preferred, and I'm fixing breakfast this morning too, so no dilly-dallying around. It's going to be a great day. The weatherman says partly cloudy and pleasant temperatures, but that won't happen until it stops raining. Come on babe, up and at 'em."

Connie had never been accused of being an early morning sprinter, but she couldn't have uttered a sentence if she wanted to. The aroma of coffee and bacon made its way to the rear of the house and attacked her as she was finishing her hair. If she wasn't hungry when she got up, she certainly was now. Her senses were completely awake and able to hear the bacon popping in the skillet as she walked down the hall. Hovering over the stove, Jake was completely absorbed in his cooking as Connie went unnoticed as she entered the kitchen. Pausing, she watched him move about the counter while whistling to a tune playing on the radio.

"Hey, there you are. I thought I was going to eat this buffet alone. Grab a chair babe, and I'll fix your plate. Need more coffee?"

Connie pulled a chair from the table and took her seat, giving a smile as a response. She was completely involved in an emotional turmoil between bringing up last night's incident, or letting it go until he mentioned it. But she knew he would never readily discuss it unless forced to do so by yours truly.

"Is Maggie awake?" he asked.

"I heard her alarm. I'm sure she's up and getting ready for school," she answered.

"Good, because I've cracked a bunch of eggs and you're going to need some help eating all this…more coffee?"

"Jake, what time did you come to bed last night?"

"I don't know, I never thought to look, but it was late. You were out like a light."

"I was hoping we could have talked."

"About what?"

"Last night. You, me…us."

"What about you, me…and us?"

"Jake, did you come to bed last night?"

"Come on, Connie, what's this all about? So I had some trouble sleeping and I got up a little earlier this morning. What's the big deal? Now eat your breakfast, dear, before it gets cold."

"Good morning, Mom, Daddy. Something sure smells good."

"Morning, Maggie. Grab your chair and start with your juice. I'll dish up your breakfast."

"Thanks, Daddy."

"Mom, can you drop Becky and me off at school this morning? We need to get an early start. Becky and I are working on a computer science project together and if we don't get there early, all of the computers will be taken."

"Sure, honey, no problem."

"I can do it, Connie. I need to get to the office early too. I have a mound of paperwork piling up and I need to call Inspector Pierson sometime today. What kind of project are you girls working on?"

"We're doing a paper on the components of a basic home computer."

"Say, that sounds interesting."

Yeah, it is. We have a list of parts, you know, CPU, hard drives, modems, geek toys, stuff like that. This morning we're going to find information about how they work together."

Connie listened quietly to the father-daughter conversation, but still had questions of her own to ask Mr. Kramer when the opportunity allowed.

"Why do you need to call the Inspector, Jake?"

"Nothing important. I haven't talked to him in awhile so I was thinking about asking him to buy lunch. Say Maggie, I was thinking, why don't you give me that list of computer parts?"

"Why, Daddy?"

"Well, I thought I would slip down to CompuStore, pick up the items, and we'll build a computer as part of your project. That should give you girls an interesting experience and perhaps earn a little extra credit in the deal."

"WOW! Do you think we really could do that?"

"With a little help from the experts, I'd say we could definitely do that."

"Cool! I can't wait to tell Becky. I'll get the list and be right back," she said sliding her chair from the table.

Connie knew she had been cut short, and wouldn't have it, particularly now that Maggie had left the room.

"How are you feeling this morning, Jake? Is your headache gone?"

"I feel great…no headache. Would you like more coffee?"

"No, I would not like more coffee. What I would like is to know what time you came to bed. And I would also like to know that you're alright this morning. You had a terrible experience last night, Jake, and I'm worried about you. I'm also very curious about your meeting with the Inspector.

Jake placed his coffee cup on the counter before addressing Connie. "Look, I do not recall checking the clock for the correct time when I came to bed last night. I do not have a headache this morning. I do feel alright, and I was just planning to have a nice lunch with the good Inspector. Would you care to join us?"

Maggie broke a piece of crisp bacon between her finger and teeth while standing near the table listening to her parent's debate. The snap was loud enough to cause her parents to pause and regroup, after realizing that she had returned to the kitchen without their noticing.

"Are you about ready to go?" asked Jake.

"Anytime you are. Bye, Mom, have a good day."

"Thanks, honey, you too."

Connie returned her fork to her plate and placed her napkin aside as well, for she had managed to lose her appetite. Jake had cut her short again, but she was more determined than ever to revisit this subject later in the evening. He may be trying to forget last night's experience, but she couldn't. He needs to talk about it. If not to her, than to someone else. Someone professional, like that Doctor what's-her-name at the hospital…Harrison…Harring…Harrington. That's it, Dr. Doreen Harrington, the psychologist. She made a mental note to look for her number and make a call today. If not for Jake, then she would make it for herself. She also made a mental note not to have another heated conversation like the one this morning in Margaret's presence.

# Five

Jake was so totally engrossed in the girls' conversation about their upcoming computer project on the drive to school, that he didn't notice the headlights coming on the Chevy Tahoe that was parked on the street about a half block from the house. He also failed to notice that the SUV had made an illegal u-turn in the middle of Crest Street and was now tailing him at a reasonable distance.

As they approached the school zone, the girls gathered their backpacks and other belongings so they would be ready to exit the truck as soon as it came to a stop. They were on a mission this morning and the sooner they could get started the better.

"Thanks, Daddy, see you tonight."

"Thank you for the ride, Mr. Kramer."

"You're welcome, ladies. Behave now, and remember you're here to study books not boys."

"Oh, Daddy."

Leaving the school, Jake pulled into traffic and adjusted the tuner on his radio swapping Van Halen for the Carpenters' on the oldies station. As he made his way to the Kramer and Associates offices, he reminded himself that he should offer this shuttle service a little more often. For although he felt invisible to their conversation, he thoroughly enjoyed listening to it.

Traffic was light and Jake was lost in song as he pulled into Dunkin' Donuts for a dozen of their fresh glazed to take to the guys at the shop. By the time he arrived at work, the cab of his truck was filled with the fresh baked aroma from the box of eleven donuts.

The black Chevy Tahoe pulled to a stop in the gravel lot, roughly 25 meters north of the Kramer building and shut off the engine. The driver removed a memo pad and pen from his pocket and jotted down, Time-0735, Memo 4: Locate the Cushman Company's building. Memo 5: Identify the second Kramer girl. Upon returning the pad to his breast pocket he whispered, "*Behold, children are a blessing from the Lord. The fruit of the womb is a reward…*Psalm 127:3."

Being the first employee to arrive at the office wasn't unusual for Jake, as he enjoyed taking advantage of the quiet time, which only lasted until the crews arrived. The Mr. Coffee machine had completed its job and Jake poured himself a cup as he made his way to his office. While leaning back in his chair, he placed his feet on the window ledge, wrapped both hands around the coffee mug, closed his eyes and began to relax. He wouldn't have had any difficulty falling asleep if he dared to let himself, as he had very little the previous night. Connie was right about his not coming to bed. But that was a little fact he didn't care to admit, for he was just too upset with himself to lie still, much less fall asleep.

But today he had a plan and a good one at that. First and foremost, he would not dwell on last night's embarrassing state of affairs, for nothing good could come of it. Next, he would not allow Connie to prompt him into talking about it, for nothing good could come of that either. So for now, as far as he was concerned, last night didn't happen.

He allowed his eyes to remain closed and without any prompting the light particles emerged and slowly began to swirl in a normal counterclockwise rotation. This was better, for he never grew tired of the brilliant display of color or the tranquil feeling it offered. The light was in control once again and Jake had no desire to protest. He could see snow capped mountains forming in his mind and almost sensed the cool, crisp air as a light chill encompassed his body. The voices of the Parker brothers began to emerge from the distance as, once again, Jake Kramer became absorbed in the light and the entire mystic experience it brought with it.

With his eyes pressed closed, he easily placed his coffee mug on the desk while focusing on a mountain pass laden with snow-covered pines that lined the canyon walls. He envisioned a small column of smoke rising from the center of the pass…a black trail from the stack of an oncoming train.

"I can see it, Sam, she's about two mile away."

"How many cars are there?"

Jake continued looking at the large black and gray clouds as he unconsciously raised both arms and formed his hands around his eyes, giving the impression that he was holding a pair of binoculars.

"Four, I see four, countin' the caboose, Sam. Are you sure the gold shipment is on that train? We can't blow this trussel twice, you know?"

"It's on there, Sam. You can bet on it. From the Denver Mint to Sacramento and you can bet that car's full of soldiers guardin' it too."

"That's okay, Wil. Let's drop the tree about here. That should leave the mail car 'bout in the middle when she stops."

Sam watched as his brother dropped the forty foot white pine across the tracks just out of view from the bridge.

"Okay, that's good. Now let's get out of sight and wait for her to stop."

The Parker brothers knew the engineer had seen the fallen tree by the blast of steam that released the boiler pressure, followed by the screech of the steel wheels sliding along the rails.

"You in the mail car…throw out the strong boxes and nobody will get hurt."

No answer, only steam hissing from the engine.

"You got just one minute to throw out the boxes, or we blow the bridge. You don't have to die. That's a two-hundred foot fall, soldier."

"We ain't got no gold in here. Nothin' but mail. You want the mail, you can have it."

"Forty-five seconds," said Sam.

The door on the south side of the mail car slid open allowing one soldier to jump out and run toward the rear of the train. Before Sam could raise his rifle the young soldier stumbled on the rail ties and fell from the bridge. His fading scream was brief and final.

"Thirty seconds."

"You don't have this bridge charged. If you did you'd already blown it."

"Don't bet your life on it, soldier. Twenty seconds."

Sam saw a mail sack swinging outside the door before being tossed over the side and free falling to the cold stream below.

"That's all there is I tell you, just mail. Come on and see for yourself."

"I'm gonna do just that, soldier. I'm gonna sift through the wreckage at the bottom of the gorge and take the gold from you down there. You got ten seconds."

Even from a distance Sam and Wil could hear the men inside screaming at their Sergeant.

"Throw it out, damn it. Throw it out!"

"Take your hands off those boxes, Private."

"Let me out of here."

"Shut up! Get back to your positions."

"Five…Four…Three…Two…One."

The noise was deafening and the blast was bigger than the Parker brothers could have imagined. Some timber from the bridge flew one hundred feet in the air as the train started its two hundred foot fall in a twisting, grinding motion.

The Parkers hid behind the boulders to avoid the shower of debris, but they could see the train disappearing with the engine trailing the caboose. What appeared to be slow motion took less than ten seconds, although the screams, rumble and smoke seemed to last forever.

Sam looked at his brother but said nothing, for nothing needed to be said.

It took the two men the better part of an hour to get to the bottom, find their team and wagon, and make it back to the wreckage. The iron and wood were piled fifty foot high and scattered for hundreds of yards. The bodies bothered them more than either would have imagined, but they got over it. It was nightfall before they located the green wood siding of the mail car and the two treasured strong boxes that cost the lives of eighteen human beings. Tired, wet and cold the Parkers loaded the strong boxes onto their wagon in the dark.

"Let's get as far from here as we can before we make camp, Wil."

"Good idea. Hang on a minute, Sam. I think I see the mail sack over there, I'll get it."

"Let it go, we got enough."

Wil jumped from the wagon and ran toward the pouch. He leaped onto a pile of loose timber that shifted with his weight and started a reaction that brought a caboose wheel and axle rolling down across his back. Wil Parker lay motionless among the lifeless bodies of the engineer, fireman, and soldiers.

The moon was directly overhead when Sam rode away from the wreckage. He gave his brother the best burial he could under the circumstances, but the Army would have to bury their own.

The mountain trail was rocky, steep, and narrow, and it was the rocks near the edge that gave way to the weight of the wagon. The wagon, horses and Sam were all drawn down the side of the mountain and came to rest in a ravine thirty feet below. How long he laid unconscious Sam didn't know, but he did know that he was hurt. His right leg wasn't broken but the ankle was badly sprained as was his wrist. He was also bleeding from several wounds he received while sliding down the wall of rocks. He felt sharp pain around his ribs that throbbed through his chest with each breath or the slightest movement.

Looking around he located the strong boxes next to the broken wagon and a downed horse. How he managed to avoid being crushed under the weight of the wagon was a mystery but he wasn't complaining. On the ledge above, Sam could see movement from the second horse of the pair. Gathering all his will-power and strength Sam made it to his feet without passing out again.

With broken ribs, a swollen ankle and all his other injuries Sam managed to slide the strong boxes under an overhanging ledge and cover the bounty with stone. Just how he did it, or how long it took, he didn't know, nor did he care, because the gold was his and no one would find it. As the morning's sun began to remove the night chill from his tired, swollen body, Sam retrieved a miner's pick from the wagon. Then slowly and painfully he swung the pick while etching a large "P" into the smooth rock face above his gold.

Sam shot the horse with the broken leg, but the black one, though bleeding about the side from minor cuts, could save him. He knew from the blood he coughed up that he too was bleeding internally and needed help. Once on the horse and back on the trail, he paused to look at the surroundings and committed them to memory for his return trip. He took a long look to the northeast, noting the valley where two rivers joined at the foothills below. "That's Miner's Creek and Pine Run," he whispered.

It was midday when Sam Parker crossed the crest of the trail and began his descent to the small mining town about ten miles to the south. He was very weak, tired, wet, cold, and still coughing blood. He never knew if he fell asleep or passed out, but it was the impact of sharp rocks that awoke him. He felt himself sliding towards the ledge, grabbing desperately at loose stones and shallow rooted scrubs. Near exhaustion, Sam Parker began his free fall to the rocks some two hundred feet below. His fading scream was also brief and final.

# Six

When Wesley L. Washington arrived at the office he found the service door unlocked, the coffee brewed, and the lights on throughout the building. With a cup of coffee in one hand and a donut in the other, he made his way down the hall to thank Jake for breakfast. Wesley paused as he approached Jake's office after noticing him sitting by the window with his hands cupped around his eyes like a pair of binoculars. Not wanting to cause any embarrassment to Jake, he stepped back and stood quietly in the hallway. As he sipped his coffee Wesley watched his friend focus on something out the window that he himself couldn't see. Suddenly, Jake released his imaginary binoculars and began rubbing his face. He then reached out for his cup on the desk as Wesley cleared his throat and tapped on the door jam.

"Good morning, boss. Thanks for the donuts."

"Hey, morning, Wes. I didn't hear you come in."

"Just got here. I wanted to get some stuff together before heading out to the site. I'm hoping to finish up the Eagle Glenn project late this afternoon or first thing tomorrow for sure."

"Hey, that's great, Wes. Tell you what. I'll look in on you guys later today and if you can finish up by noon tomorrow we'll have a little celebration ready when you get back."

"The guys would like that. They have really been crankin' on this job ever since JJ left for school."

"I know. So let's have some lunch brought in and blow off the afternoon. Sound okay?"

"Yeah, that sounds great, but I won't tell them until we're finished."

"Wes, there's something I should probably tell you about JJ."

"He's okay, ain't he, Jake?"

"Oh yeah, nothing like that. But he was home last weekend and told me that he has plans to continue his schooling. Chances are he won't be coming back to work here."

"I see," said Wesley, sounding a little disappointed. "Well good for him."

"Yeah, I'm proud of him. So, the point is, we may want to scout around for a replacement. I know you can use the help."

"Okay, boss. I'll ask around. Well, I better get started. The guys are on the clock."

"Wes, how's Stacie and the kids?"

"Everybody is fine, thanks. Little Jake had a bad cold last week, but he's back to normal now."

"Good…what about Granny Fay and her daughter?"

"You mean my mother, Rosa?" said Wesley grinning at his question. "I think Granny Fay will outlive us all. As for Rosa, I'd have to say things are good between the two of us. She was able to take some classes on how to use a computer while she was in the big house and her parole officer has placed her with a temp agency. Now she works everyday and seems to be happy. Last week she found a small apartment on Marsh Street, so now she's trying to talk Granny into moving in with her. I think she really wants to try and make things right between the three of us."

"Things have a way of working out, don't they, Wes?"

"They do when I have you around, Jake. I know that I would never have accepted her as my mother if it wasn't for you. I'll never be able to pay you back for all you've done for me, Jake."

Jake had to pause and clear his throat before responding. "You can start by getting to work, big guy."

"See ya later, boss."

Wesley and crew left the shop for the Eagle Glenn complex as the office fell silent once again and Jake settled back in his chair. On his desk pad were two projects for the day. The envelope on his left contained information that would be shared with Inspector Pierson of the FBI. The other included the list of items needed to build a home computer that he received from Maggie that morning. Since it was still early in the day he knew he would have time to shop for the computer parts before meeting the Inspector for lunch, assuming he was available. But first he thought it would be best to do a little research in order to understand the confusing and complex world of computers. After all, he had promised to help the girls build one, but at this point in time he didn't even know where to find the gas cap.

Jake leaned back in his chair and assumed his favorite position. With his feet on the cadenza he closed his eyes and tried to relax. He sat comfortably for a few minutes before changing positions in his chair. Over the next five minutes Jake changed, altered, and rearranged himself at least a dozen times in the chair. This was not due to an upsetting light experience, but rather the fact that he wasn't visiting the rainbow of lights at all. The lights had never failed to materialize when he summoned them before. This thought bothered him more than he cared to admit because there were times he had prayed that this gift would go away. Perhaps his prayers were now being answered and that thought was upsetting as well.

Jake stood and made his way to the coffee machine but changed his mind, thinking that perhaps the caffeine could be to blame. He could feel his heart racing as the idea of not bathing in the light and visiting the shared memories of the cleansed began to weigh on his mind. Again he took his seat and pulled himself up to the desk placing his elbows on the monthly planner and his hands under his chin, as he asked, "What's happening to me? Where did they go?"

With his eyes squeezed tightly closed Jake sat motionless and tried desperately to locate a hint of color from a swirling rainbow in the black space before him, but such was not the case. Disappointed, he deemed it best to end the search, at least for the time being, and curb his frustrations. As he tried to relax and compose himself he began to feel a numbness and prickly tingling in his legs and feet. He immediately opened his eyes and raised his head, causing his hands to fall lifelessly to the desk top with a slapping echo. Anxiety began to overtake him as he fell back in his chair. This brought his hands sliding across the desk top until they fell free to his thighs, again in an unresponsive slap. Jake's heart was pounding at a dangerous pace as the word paralyzed entered his mind. He tried to stand but couldn't move his legs. He then attempted to place his hands on the arms of his chair to raise himself, but his arms also failed to respond.

Jake could feel the needle-like sting creeping up from his waist as it clawed through his midsection into his chest and invaded his body. His heart continued to race, but it did not outdistance his fear, as the thorny tingles moved slowly up his neck until his head no longer turned and he could not feel himself swallow. The numbing sensation continued upward above his jaw and mouth until the lips no longer moved. He sensed the itching as it engulfed his tongue and rendered it useless, thick, and dry. Helpless and alone, he tried to call out, but only mumbled like a mute.

The body of Jake Kramer had succumbed to the unyielding pursuit of the prickly needles as they swiftly crept above the ears bringing silence and fear. His vision was reduced to a blur before fading into darkness, as finally, without any means of defense, his brain surrendered to the invasion as he lost consciousness.

The deafening bang from a trash collector dropping a dumpster to the blacktop startled Jake back to reality.

He found himself leaning against the desk with his head resting in his left hand and the right hand gripping a lead pencil. He had no idea how long he had been there or why he had an excruciating headache because he never bathed in the lights. In fact, he didn't know what he had been doing or thinking about for the last… however long it was. He sat upright and rubbed his temples, then stretched his back muscles and attempted to stand on shaky legs that were slow to respond. He fell back in his seat as the memory of the previous events began to resurface. Jake rubbed his hands together checking for feeling and response. The reaction was slow and his fingers ached terribly. He quickly massaged his thighs in order to relieve the annoying dull pain. In fact his entire body felt like he survived a two-week bout with the flu. Placing his hands on the desk-pad he began to push himself clear in an attempt to stand, but abruptly froze in place.

Jake leaned forward and stared at the monthly planner on his desk noticing that a sheet had been torn free and flipped over. He also became aware that the back of the paper was no longer blank but instead contained a blueprint-style drawing. Pulling the sheet free for a closer look he stared in awe at a hand-drawn sketch to which he could only marvel in disbelief. Jake was holding a skillfully drawn computer schematic complete with illustrations of the working components, as well as identification of each particular item. As he studied the print closely he recognized yet another baffling fact. The writing was not of his own hand. Never in his life had he printed as neatly or clearly as what he saw before him. One could say it mocked a printer in clarity.

"My God," said Jake returning the paper to the desk. "I understand." He stood and rolled the chair to the cadenza behind him as he repeated, "I really do understand all of this. I know what it means. I know that's the mother board," he said pointing to the drawing. "That's the CPU. There's the hard drive." Sliding his index finger across the paper he paused and said, "This is the video card. That's a memory board and a dial-up modem. Here's the CD-Rom drive."

Jake fell back in his chair in a complete state of confusion. "I never saw the lights," he said. "I don't remember a thing…nothing at all about how the drawing got there. But I know how to build it and I know how it works…it's simple, nothing to it. But I don't know how I know for I never saw the lights."

He spent the next hour or so reviewing the computer schematic and compared the parts with the list from Maggie. He added a DVD burner, magneto optical driver and network cards to the list, thinking that if they were going to build one, it may as well be a keeper. Although today's specter-like experience may never be understood, Jake accepted it as good. Actually, he had found it refreshing to think about this new expertise of his and looked forward to building a super computer with the girls.

With the morning about half gone, Jake knew if he called Inspector Pierson and confirmed a late lunch date, he would have time to do a little shopping at CompuStore across town.

"Perhaps I'll just wait and call the Inspector tomorrow and mosey on down to the store now," he said to himself.

Upon speaking those words a sharp pain hit him squarely above the eyes before wrapping around his head and sending him back to the seat of his chair.

"WOW, what brought that on?" he asked himself. He sat quietly for a moment as the pain began to subside. Ever so slowly he made his way to his feet but was still shaken by the unexpected strike to the forehead. Jake realized that the past sixteen hours of his life had been less than predictable, but receiving unprovoked blasts such as the last one couldn't be tolerated very often. He convinced himself to shake it off and head out for CompuStore. Again the pain hit him squarely above the eyes, mocking the first attack, but this one added voices. Crying or moaning, he couldn't tell, but they were both male and female. After taking a few minutes to regroup, Jake spoke aloud, "Okay kids, you win, I won't put you off any longer."

With that said he reached for the phone and dialed Inspector Pierson.

# Seven

"Inspector Pierson speaking."

"Inspector, this is Jake Kramer. I wasn't sure I'd catch you in. Do you have a moment?"

"I always have time for you, Jake. What can I do for you?"

"How about having Uncle Sam buy me lunch for starters?"

"Uncle Sam's budget wouldn't get us much of a lunch, Jake, but I'll tell you what I'll do; I'll spring for it myself. That way you won't be embarrassed if the cashier turns down the Bureau's card for lack of funds. Where and when?"

"Manny's, in about an hour?"

"Manny's, in about an hour," repeated Pierson as they both hung up their phones.

Local traffic was unusually heavy for this time of day so Jake opted to take the back roads to Manny's. The rain had slowed to a few sprinkles and the sky hinted that the sun might have a chance to make a showing later in the day. The four-way stop gave Jake a break to turn up Hall and Oats singing, *Sara Smiles,* and he found the urge to sing along with the few stanzas that he knew. "Keep the day job, Jake," he reminded himself. "Keep the day job."

The black Chevy Tahoe began following him at once keeping a minimum of forty meters to the rear.

Watching the contour of the road, the driver kept pace not wanting any vehicle to separate him from his prey.

The short straight section of road ahead became clear, presenting an opportunity for the black Tahoe to accelerate and close the gap between the two vehicles. Jake's mind was focused on the closing verse of *Sara Smiles,* so he paid little attention to the rearview mirror and the pursuing SUV. The thud to the rear bumper interrupted Jake's singing rehearsal as he instinctively adjusted the steering to keep his truck on the pavement and clear of the embankment to his right.

He looked up at the mirror as the SUV steadily closed the gap once again. He didn't recognize the vehicle or the driver, and had no idea as to why this nut wanted him off the road. Nonetheless the car came at him again. Jake pressed the accelerator pedal tight against the floor in an attempt to out-distance the SUV while drawing at his seat belt and bracing for another impact.

This time the contact sent Jake's truck into the oncoming lane, but fortunately there was no oncoming traffic. Once again regaining control, Jake accelerated pushing his truck and driving skills to the limits on this county road. A quick glance in the rear view mirror showed no headlights from the black SUV. As Jake looked ahead to the oncoming left curve he wondered if he could take it at this speed, or if he should slow down since it appeared he was no longer being pursued.

It was the sun's reflection on the glass of the passenger's window of the Tahoe that caught Jake's eye as the back tinted window returned the sun directly into his cab. Where the SUV came from Jake had no idea, but it was directly along-side of him and swerving. Blinded by the sun's reflection, Jake promptly released the gas pedal and applied the brakes in an attempt to slow his truck.

The collision was both deliberate and forceful as it sent Jake's pick-up off the road and down the embankment towards a cattle fence. The barbed wire slapped against the windshield as the broken post smashed alongside the left fender. Working frantically to gain control Jake's actions were completely without thought. Then, after an eternity of downhill terror his truck came to rest two feet inside a large roll of cattle feeding hay. How long he sat inside the cab of his would-be coffin Jake didn't know, but he did know that someone deliberately ran him off the road.

Slowly opening the door he stepped free on uncertain legs and surveyed the area while reliving the event that just took place. His truck was damaged, although not seriously, but most importantly he wasn't. Retaking his place behind the wheel, he knew his four-wheel drive could accept the challenge of making its way back up to the blacktop, so he looked around for the path of least resistance. There, on the road surface above sat the black Tahoe with a male figure leaning against the left fender chewing on a blade of grass. No effort to assist, no attempt at an apology and no evidence of remorse. Who was this man?

While standing on the gravel of the road's edge watching his prey in the field below, he couldn't help but fell a sense of disappointment from being unchallenged. Returning to the driver's door he whispered, "*Fear him, which after he hath killed you hath power to cast into hell; yea, I say unto you, Fear him*…Luke 12:5."

Jake was seated in the rear left corner booth as Inspector Pierson made his way past the long counter. Jake stood offering his hand and motioning Pierson toward his half of the booth.

"Thank you for joining me, Inspector. I took the liberty of ordering our iced tea. Yours is from Indy, mine is from Long Island."

"Well, thank you, Jake. We'll have a dinner meeting one day so I might join you in your brand of tea. Was that your truck I saw in the lot? The one with damage to the fender and hood?"

"Probably."

"It looks fresh. As a matter of fact it looks like hay packed in your grill. What happened?"

"Nothing serious, Inspector; let's just say the road got a little narrow for two vehicles."

"Was it deliberate, Jake? You're to let me know about any attempts on your life, remember? That's one thing I can help you with."

"I appreciate that, Bob. No, it was just a tight curve on a county road, nothing more."

Inspector Person suspected Jake was withholding the truth from him, but decided not to cloud the atmosphere by probing. He instead made a mental note to keep tabs on his friend. They kept the conversation light as Millie buzzed around taking their orders. The Inspector sensed that Jake was somewhat tense, probably the result of his accident or perhaps over the subject for this lunch which hadn't surfaced as of yet.

"I'm glad you called, Jake. I have been wondering how you're getting along. We haven't talked in awhile."

"I'm fine, Bob, thanks. The phone calls have slowed and the volume of mail has also let up a bit. I've been reading most of the letters to censor the hate and junk mail, trying to spare Connie."

"Don't take the hate mail lightly, Jake. If you receive anything that appears to be threatening, remember I want you to save them and let us have a look at them."

"I believe the FBI is a little too busy to be looking into Jake Kramer's hate mail, Inspector."

"The Bureau may be, but I'm not. Jake, we owe you, and if you don't mind my saying, you've become more than an informant. I like to think of you as an assistant, or more so, a friend."

"Thanks again, Bob. I'll call before I get in too deep."

"See to it, Jake. I'm here for you and I'll use all resources available to me if need be. Now then, what's on your mind that brings us to this lunch?"

Jake reached into his pocket and removed a yellow legal sheet of paper and placed it between them, as he said, "Inspector, do you recall the killings back about ten years or so involving some kids working at the Burger Barn?"

"Recall it? Hell, Jake, that case haunts about every law enforcement officer in the state of Indiana. It was terrible in itself, but not solving the crime compounds the tragedy. I still have an occasional nightmare about those five young kids. All of them working weekends for a little spending money and then to be killed so senselessly during a robbery. All over a measly four-hundred and eighty-six dollars. Less than a hundred bucks a child. My God, what a waste."

"Perhaps this will help keep the ghosts away, Bob," said Jake as he slid the folded sheet of paper towards him. "I was reminded of it the other day by a newscaster reporting on the anniversary of the incident."

Inspector Pierson unfolded the paper and studied its contents closely. Then he placed it down on the table folding his hands across it. Jake watched him as he removed his handkerchief and cleared his nose. Inspector Pierson reached for his tea and emptied the glass before returning it to the table. With his composure regained, he spoke.

"Jake, do you have any idea how much effort has been poured into this case? The man-hours, the thousands of interviews, the countless dead ends, and you just handed me the names of the suspects."

"I'm sorry it took me so long to get it to you, Bob."

"What went wrong, Jake, why did they have to kill those kids?"

It was Jake's turn to moisten his tongue before speaking. "One of the employees, a Leroy Bennett, was actually involved in the robbery and it was he who unlocked the back entry, giving access to Thompson and Baker. The plan was simple enough, just tie up the kids, steal the Saturday receipts and exit. Unfortunately one of the girls recognized Jermaine Baker and called out his name. Baker became scared and furious. He dragged her into the back room where he beat her before having his way with her. Then he beat her some more. It was Leon Thompson, his partner, who eventually pulled Baker off her, but it was too late. The duct tape was wrapped tightly around her head covering her nose and mouth. The rest is as they say…history."

"With one dead, and Baker's name known, they couldn't leave the others alive at that point," said Pierson. "But why Bennett? You said he was in on the robbery."

"Well, Bennett fell apart. He became hysterical when he saw Lorie's beaten body. Then to make matters worse he looked at the tape around her mouth and noticed her big brown eyes staring back at him. He just lost it. He tried to run out the back door, but Thompson caught him and tied him up too. So much for honor among thieves."

Jake and Inspector Pierson sat quietly for a moment as Jake motioned for Millie and ordered another Long Island Iced Tea.

"Make it two," said Inspector Pierson.

"How are we going to prove this, Jake? We need to find those two men and put them away. Put them away forever."

"I have some good news and some bad news for you, Inspector. The bad news is…we can't prove it."

"And the good news?"

"The good news is…we don't need to find them."

"I don't understand."

"Well, we can't prove it because all of the eye witnesses are deceased. Jermaine Baker, the one who was responsible for three of the murders lost his life five years ago last May in an argument over who owed who, how much. But you can find Leroy Thompson any time you want at the Attica penitentiary in New York. He's now serving life without parole for an unrelated crime. So you see, Inspector, the only satisfaction you can get from this is knowing the details. It would be a foolish waste of taxpayers' money to bring charges against Thompson. He's caged."

Pierson shook his head in agreement and added, "You're right there, Jake. Besides, as you pointed out we couldn't prove it anyhow, certainly not without the murder weapons."

"After leaving the bodies in the woods along Midpoint Road they took a different route back to the city. The weapons were tossed into the West Fork of the White River, Inspector. Baker threw the guns out as they crossed the old iron bridge on County Line Road.

There's been a lot of water under that bridge, Bob; the weapons are gone."

Inspector Pierson took a drink of his iced tea and decided to take the second sip before setting the glass down. "Well Jake, I just hope the families find some comfort in knowing their children's killers aren't free to walk the streets anymore."

"You can't give them anything to support your theory, Inspector."

"Sure I can, I'll simply tell them that Jake Kramer confirmed it. That'll do it."

Millie stopped by the table once again to ask if they needed anything, but only the check was requested. In due time the check was placed in front of Jake, but Inspector Pierson was having none of that.

"My treat, Jake, I can't thank you enough."

"No need to thank me, Inspector. You know how to get in touch with me. Well, I better get moving. I have to pick up some parts for a school project."

"Now that brings back memories. What kind of project are you doing, Jake?"

"My daughter, her friend and I are going to build a home computer."

"Really? I had no idea you knew how to build a computer."

"Neither did I, Bob. But I plan to call on and get some advice from a lot of people who did."

Inspector Pierson smiled at that one as he stood and said, "Let's keep in touch, Mr. Kramer, shall we? If you can't call, you can send me an e-mail after your project's finished."

Sitting unnoticed across the street from Manny's pub was a black Chevy Tahoe with extensive damage to the passenger's side of the vehicle. From his stealth position, the driver watched Jake exit the pub and make his way through the parking lot. With the rear window down he could feel the relaxing cool air pass though the SUV. The head rest on the seat provided perfect support for his prized German PSG-1 rifle, as the crosshair in the telescope remained expertly fixed between Jake's eyebrows. Deliberately and ever so gradually his right index finger began to curl. The repeat of the rifle was drowned by the air-horn blast of a Mayflower moving van as it passed between him and his prey. The target across the street was replaced by the green panels of the trailer as the spent slug would one day be pulled from someone's belongings as they unpacked in their new home. Shaking his head in disbelief he placed the weapon on the rear seat as he watched Jake back his truck from its space and drive from the lot, followed closely by an unassuming dark blue Impala.

As he reached for the ignition key his movements were redirected by the ringing of his cell phone.

"Yes?"

"Please enter you PIN number followed by the pound key."

Without taking his eyes off Jake's getaway truck he pressed 0108 # on the key pad.

"We have a critical situation that needs immediate attention."

"I haven't finished my work here."

"We have a critical situation that needs immediate attention. Are you available? Press one for yes, or two for no, followed by the pound sign."

Looking at the phone unit the driver pressed 1# and returned the phone to his ear.

"You are booked on flight 2385…leaving Indianapolis at gate C7 in 90 minutes. You are authorized to use Immunity ID at security. Your seat assignments are 4A and 4B. A drop bag will be placed in the magazine pouch on the back of seat 3A. Be advised, the packet is a reverse open unit. Press one followed by the pound sign to acknowledge."

Again he looked at the key pad and pressed 1#, then returned the phone to his ear only to hear a disconnect tone.

Somewhat confused by this impromptu reassignment he tossed the throwaway cell phone from the window into a drainage ditch and watched it quickly sink out of sight. There'll be a new one with different codes in the packet he assured himself. He then made a mental note to remember and open the drop bag upside down to avoid destroying its contents. That would be a huge error, especially on an aircraft. Next he set the OnStar for the Indianapolis International Airport and merged into the traffic. Rarely did he accept such interruptions and never, but never, had he abandoned a mission. But a critical situation call is indeed a rare and lucrative troubleshooting opportunity.

As he watched Jake's truck disappear among the sea of city traffic he couldn't help but feel a sense of failure. He felt like a red-tailed hawk that missed his lunch by a hare. "Run, Kramer, run, for you have been given a reprieve, "*Wine maketh merry: but money answereth all things*…Ecclesiastes 10:19."

# Eight

It took Jake two trips to bring in all the boxes containing the computer parts for Maggie's and Becky's science project. His shopping list had increased to include a LG1910S monitor and a Microsoft J54 optical keyboard. Getting caught up in the assignment he also thought it would be nice to include an HP scanner, especially since it was on sale. His main reason for expanding the parts list was that he decided to offer the finished project, with Maggie's approval of course, to Becky Sanders in as much as she didn't have one and Maggie had unlimited access to theirs. He thought it was the least he could do for Alex's family after everything they had done for them. Surveying his collection he smiled at himself as he recalled his conversation with the sales-clerk at CompuStore. He must have thought Jake was an expert for he was never confused by questions, understood each suggestion, and asked for specific manufacturers, as well as the top of the line components. All in all Jake was probably more excited about this little endeavor than the girls.

The only thing unclear about this whole venture was how he had gained this new talent without seeing the lights, but he decided to dismiss the matter as trivial.

Jake located and set-up the card table in the den to use as a work table. He also arranged the chairs and found a shop lamp that would provide excellent lighting. "Tools," he said as he turned to make yet another trip to the garage. As he passed the patio door in the kitchen he noticed Connie sitting in a deck-lounger facing the sun.

"Connie, I didn't know you were home. Is everything alright?"

"You tell me, Jake. Is everything alright?" she replied without opening her eyes.

"Oh yeah. I got some great stuff for the girls' project. You want to come in and take a look?"

"That's not what I was asking, Jake. I mean how are you feeling today? We didn't get much of a chance to talk this morning."

"I feel fine. Listen, I went down to CompuStore and you should see…"

"Stop it!" she said as she pulled her lounger into an upright position. "I don't care about that damn computer and I don't want to hear about the CompuStore. I want to hear about you. I want to know what happened during your vision last night. I want to know what happened to make your nose bleed the way it did. I want to know if you came to bed at all last night. And while we're at it, I want to you to explain to me what in the hell happened to your truck. How did the driver's side get smashed? I want to talk with you, about you, and about you and me; so stop changing the damn subject."

Jake had been sitting on the front edge of a deck-chair when she lit into him, but he was seated well against the back of it by the time she finished. He wasn't really shocked by her outburst, for with all things considered, he had it coming. She was right of course. He had been doing his best to avoid talking about his recent vision experience and she was correct in assuming that he hadn't come to bed last night.

He looked into her eyes that showed more love than anger, as he said. "The vision was horrific, Connie. I would prefer not to describe it because I choose not to think about it. It involved the Burger Barn teenagers and today, over lunch, I gave the details to Inspector Pierson. Hopefully that will please those kids because they were becoming…let's say, persistent. Maybe now they can rest in peace.

"I don't know what caused my nosebleed. I didn't realize I had one until you pointed it out to me. I assumed it was caused by the intensity of the headache."

Jake paused while looking at Connie as she sat quietly, arms folded and looking out at the roses. "Those kids didn't have to die, did they, Jake?"

"No. They didn't have to die."

He could see a small tear leaving the corner of her eye as she continued to look at her prized roses. "This morning when I realized that you hadn't slept in our bed…I was hurt. That was a first for our marriage."

"When I got out of the shower you were sleeping," said Jake. "I picked up the drink you made for me and went to the den. I guess I wanted to be alone…nothing personal."

"Well, I took it personally this morning, Jake. Maybe I shouldn't have, but it made me feel unneeded."

"If you must know…I felt ashamed and embarrassed for the way I broke down last night, Connie. That's not the kind of thing a man is proud of, so I wanted to be alone."

She turned to look at him and said, "Ashamed? Jake, you have nothing to be ashamed of. It should make you feel proud that you can help people the way you do. My word, honey, those were the kids crying… not Jake Kramer."

"If you say so."

"I do say so. I know so. You have been crying inside for so many people that you couldn't hold anymore. Hell, Jake, you can't possibly know who you're crying for."

She saw Jake nod in agreement but she doubted that he was convinced. Sitting upright she turned and took his hands. "Honey, you know what I think you should do? I think you should have a talk with someone other than me. Someone professional."

"And I think I could use a cold beer. Would you like one?" he said leaving his chair and making his way toward the door.

He returned to find that Connie had retaken her original position in the lounger, so he retook his and placed their drinks on the table beside them. She was starring at her roses again.

"I can't wait for the girls to get home. I'm really looking forward to helping them build a computer. You know that…"

"I called Dr. Harrington this morning, Jake," she interrupted.

"Who?"

"Dr. Doreen Harrington, the psychologist. I called her this morning."

"I'm not going to see a shrink."

"Psychologist, Jake, she's a psychologist and I didn't call for you. I called for me."

"I don't understand?" he said before taking a long draw from the cold bottle.

"No, I don't believe you do," she said as she turned and looked directly at him. "I called her, Jake, because I don't know how to cope anymore. When I saw you last night I knew we needed help. You may choose not to recognize it, but I see it, and I needed someone to talk to. Someone who'll listen, and, God willing, might be able to help me. I called Doctor Harrington for me, Jake. But I guess that really means for us."

"When do you see her?"

"I already have. Her receptionist told me the earliest opening was in six weeks so I scheduled it. Thirty-minutes later, Doctor Harrington called and said she would make time for me today, if I was available. I took the afternoon off and I met with her after lunch. I like her, Jake. She is a very caring lady, and she is anxious to meet with you too, when you're ready. She has been following your exploits very closely. I think she can help us."

Jake finished the last of his beer and sat the bottle down before picking up the one untouched by Connie. He stood and walked to the edge of the patio before asking, "When's the next appointment?"

"Next Thursday afternoon at two-thirty."

He paused and stared up at a hawk circling effortlessly high overhead looking for its next meal as Connie sat motionless looking at her husband.

"Connie."

"Yes."

"Be careful driving down there."

# Nine

Alex Sanders held his cold stare at the reflection in the mirror above the bathroom sink. It returned an image of one who had spent days engaged in substance abuse, a life-threatening infection and even self-pity. He rubbed the stubbles from a two-day beard growth, then ran his fingers through his hair which looked unruly despite being closely cropped. He definitely looked fit for undercover work as a derelict, but that wasn't his intent at all.

It had been two days since he retrieved the sack filled with the details for his last troubleshooting assignment. This led to two days of self-imposed exile which allowed Alex to come to grips with his anger and his fear.

Needless to say, he had no intentions of taking the life of his friend, Jake Kramer, or allowing someone else to take it either. Now determined, he elected to end this powerless frame of mind and do something about it. Uncertain of his success, Alex knew that he didn't want to hear of Jake's execution while he sat sulking in his California condo.

He entered the kitchen to start the coffee maker before taking preliminary steps to improve his personal hygiene. As he walked past the dinette Alex looked down at the contents of his pick-up bag which were scattered on the floor where he'd left them two days ago. The photograph with the red circle clearly drawn around Jake Kramer's head remained on top of the pile of newsprint.

"Don't worry, partner," he said just above a whisper. "I'll take care of it."

When Alex returned to the kitchen he was showered, refreshed and determined. Knowing he had foolishly wasted two critical days he quickly retrieved his cell phone from the trash and placed it in its charger. Returning to the table Alex gathered all the newspapers and deposited them in the trash receptacle with the exception of Jake's photograph. That he placed aside for motivation. He could think of no conceivable need for the Canadian passport or the packet containing new identification, so the decision was made to run them through the shredder. The packet of money was a no-brainer and always welcomed, thus the shredder was never considered. A 9mm-hand gun and silencer was also saved, for one never knows when they may be useful. Alex felt an adrenaline rush as his optimism began to grow and a plan began to take shape. Agreed, it might not be the best of plans, but it was a plan nonetheless and that was better than none.

The computer was logged on and the search engine *Google* was ready to begin searching. Aware that Major Hudoff was the only contact he had with the club, this made his task clear. Find Hudoff and then cross each bridge one at a time. Alex Sanders dedicated the next five hours to his mission. The continuous dead ends were expected and frustrating, but failed to curb his spirit. For if he failed, Jake Kramer would surely die.

Using va.com and usarmy.com, Alex was able to locate several Hudoff's, but quickly found that the officers' addresses were considered to be classified information. Continuing his search he was able to locate sfahg.com; a Special Forces web site that proved to be most helpful. Alex felt confident that his best effort for locating Major Hudoff would be in the area of Ft. Bragg, NC. Hudoff, once an Army brat, and an Army professional himself, most likely remained close to home. If Ft. Bragg failed, he would then visit Ft. Benning, Ga., the home of the Airborne.

Alex stood up, stretched and then made his way back to the kitchen. Removing the cell phone from the charger he looked closely at the LED screen and selected caller ID. Quickly jotting down the last numbers from incoming calls he dialed the last one first.

"We're sorry, the number you have dialed is now longer in service. Please check your dir…"

Alex didn't hold-out much hope in actually reaching the live person who had confirmed his assignment, but he had to try. The remaining two incoming numbers were dialed and the results were the same. He then dialed the original contact number, 800-555-7878 and actually reached a recorded message. "Thank you for calling, please enter your pin number followed by the pound sign now."

Alex entered 147021# and waited for a response. The low tone was long and soft, then ended with a disconnect sound. Alex quickly selected redial and received the same message with the same results.

He poured the last of the coffee that had become scorched and bitter from sitting for hours on a hot burner. The clock reminded him that it was mid-afternoon and his stomach reminded him that he hadn't eaten today. He needed to get out, get some air, and get some food. But first he would make airline reservations to Raleigh, North Carolina. His plans were set and his confidence was mounting. He would complete the details for closing the condo tonight and drop the keys off to Mrs. Cummins before leaving tomorrow. He reminded himself not to appear hurried when he said goodbye to Rose for the last time.

It was 5:37 A.M. Pacific Standard Time and Alex had been up, showered, and dressed for over an hour. Not because he was rushed, but because he was anxious. Today was, as it is said, the first day of the rest of your life and he was ready to live it. All details with Valley Realtors had been completed for the sale of his condo and the leasing firm would pick up the furniture tomorrow. His itinerary was set for his travels to Ft. Bragg; his bags were packed, and all that remained was to say good-bye to Rose Cummins.

Mrs. Cummins gave Alex one of her warm grandma smiles as she opened her door and welcomed him into her home, but her eyes couldn't hide her suspicions for his visit.

"Alex, may I please fix you some breakfast?"

"No thank you, Rose, I'll get something at the airport."

"Oh no, I was afraid you'd say that. You're leaving aren't you, Alex?"

"Yes Rose, I must be going."

"Do you have time for coffee?"

"Perhaps a half-cup if it's not any trouble," replied Alex, remembering his promise to himself.

Alex and Rose Cummins exchanged small talk as he sipped his coffee, but the atmosphere was less than festive as he tried in vain to keep the subject away from his leaving.

"Rose, I do have yet another favor to ask of you, if you will?"

"Of course, what is it, Alex?"

Alex removed an envelope and door entry keys from his shirt pocket laying them on the table.

"Tomorrow the leasing company will be here to pick up their furniture and later in the day someone from Valley Realtors will stop by for the keys. I took the liberty of giving them your name and address as keeper of the keys."

"That's fine, Alex. Of course, I'll be happy to help you. What about the envelope? Who gets that?"

"You do, Mrs. Cummins."

"Me?"

"It's a little something for you as a thank you."

"Alex," said Rose, "If that's money…"

"No ma'am, it's not money. It's a gift certificate from me to you for taking such good care of me. Please don't open it until tomorrow after all your work is finished, Rose. Because if I hear of any complaints I'll come back after it."

Rose responded with soft laughter saying, "Thank you, Alex. I'll try not to mess things up for you.

"Alex, I know I'm just being a foolish old lady, but I do hate to see you move away. I always looked forward to your homecomings."

"Thank you, Rose, I'll miss you too. I should be going. Please take care of yourself."

"Just a moment, Alex, I have a little something for you," she said as she hurried to the counter and returned holding a small box. "I want you to have this."

Alex couldn't speak and had to look away as he accepted the gift from her tiny, shaking hands. He slowly removed the perfectly wrapped paper and raised the lid to expose an early nineteen-hundred vintage pocket-watch. He looked up at Rose's moist eyes as she said, "It was my father's. I never had a son to pass it on to…until now."

# Ten

American Airlines flight 192 departed Los Angeles, California, at 10:38 a.m. enroute to Raleigh/Durham, North Carolina, with Alex Sanders once again taking his customary first-class seat. He gazed out the small window to his right at the river far below winding through the terrain trying to find its way to the Gulf of Mexico. As he watched the tiny objects of the landscape disappear below, he remembered Jake's comment of how small our existence was in God's vast creation. He also remembered Jake's look of contentment as he hinted as to why the universe was so big and what's beyond. "Don't be afraid, Alex," he said softly. "There is nothing to be afraid of." Alex was, in fact, afraid though; not of Jake, but rather for Jake.

He reached into his shirt pocket and removed the small box that Rose had given him earlier in the morning. Carefully opening the lid and removing the delicate timepiece Alex found himself choking back the lump in his throat as he recalled Rose's comment that she didn't have a son to pass it along to until now. It was most likely the first time in his life that he felt a woman considered him worthy to be her son. Alex stared at the watch for a period of time before returning it to his breast pocket. Tomorrow, after assisting the leasing and realty companies Rose would open her gift certificate and learn that she must choose between a red, white, or blue Honda Accord from Mountain View Honda Sales. Alex was sure she would be excited, but the car would never be more meaningful than her gift to him.

Checking his wristwatch and realizing he would be confined to his air ride for another two and a half hours, Alex reclined his seat and attempted to nap.

The late afternoon sun was casting shadows across the parking lot as Alex Sanders gathered his overnight bag and made his way to his room. The green tag attached by a brass ring to the motel key had a large number 8 printed on the face and The Bunker Motel boldly printed on the reverse. Alex entered the modest room and tossed his small carry-on luggage on the bed. As he scouted the room, the motel's decor brought a smile to this former Green Beret's face. He noticed the lamps were made of spent artillery shell casings and their shades were crafted from parachute cloth. The closet was fashioned from used barracks lockers and at the base of the bed was a footlocker. "Definitely the proprietor of this bunker had to be a Fort Bragg retiree," he said to himself.

After finishing a priority-one stop in the bathroom he settled on the bed, grabbed the phone directory and began leafing through the list of H's. He located two Hudoff's, a Mr. Clayton E. and Major W. Robert. Alex jotted down the addresses on a house note-pad and placed the book aside. He had taxed his memory many times trying to recall Major Hudoff's first name for he had always addressed him simply as Major, or Sir.

However, he could recall a few chats with those who had a few too many, asking if Waldo ordered this or that. But that was the extent of it.

"Major Waldo Hudoff," he said aloud trying to convince himself that the name sounded right, the address seemed correct, and Mr. Waldo Hudoff would be easy to find. Nonetheless, deep down inside, he couldn't believe it.

It had been a long day, starting with his good-byes to Mrs. Cummins and hours sitting on an airplane getting to North Carolina. He was tired and hungry, but sleep was his first priority. So he slid down on the olive green camouflage bedspread and within moments, fell asleep.

By 0715 hours North Carolina time, Alex Sanders had found his way to The Bunker Motel's dining room, aptly named The Mess Tent. If this former Green Beret hadn't been so preoccupied with his mission he would have taken a little time to enjoy the Army artifacts placed around this establishment. He sipped hot coffee from a metal cup and leafed through a copy of the *Stars and Stripes* newspaper as he waited for his order of the #2 infantryman platter, complete with three eggs, grits, bacon, toast, a side of biscuits and gravy, and of course lots of hot coffee.

Alex tried to corral his optimistic attitude toward locating the address of W. Robert Hudoff and finding it to be the Major Hudoff he was looking for. Not surprisingly, breakfast was delivered on an aluminum metal tray, restoring more memories of the good old days, although the food here was much better.

By 0845 Alex had checked out of The Bunker and was enroute to 8131 W. Alvin Street, home of W. Robert Hudoff. The drive past familiar sights went unnoticed and he was somewhat unconscious of the lane and street changes he was making. His mind was preoccupied with how he planned to approach the Major.

Pulling to a stop in the drive, Alex noticed the curtains shifting from the modest breeze allowing him to see movement in the house. As he made his way to the front door he could feel the mix of anxiety and a rush of anticipation. The bell was answered on the first ring by a young lady in her early thirties, petite and very pretty.

"Yes, may I help you?" she asked offering a slight smile.

"Good morning, Ma'am. I'm not certain that I have the right house, but I'm trying to locate a Major Hudoff. We served in the forces together."

She studied Alex for a moment before saying, "I'm Mrs. Hudoff. Won't you step in please, Mr…?"

"Sanders, Alex Sanders."

"Won't you step in, Mr. Sanders? I'll get Robert."

Alex watched as she walked down the hall saying to himself, "The Major better stay on vitamins or he'll never keep up with that one." He stepped into the unpretentious but neat and clean living room of the one floor framed home. Alex paused to look at the photographs on the walls and sofa table, then picked up one of a platoon standing at parade rest, but was unable to recognize any of the faces in the frame.

"That's my platoon in Officer Candidates School," said a voice from behind him. "I'm Major Hudoff, how can I help you?"

Alex returned the frame to the table as he turned to face the Major who was also in his early thirties, well fit, and undaunted by Alex presence.

"I'm Alex Sanders, Major," said Alex as he offered his hand. "You can obviously tell by my expression that I have located the wrong Major Hudoff.

"And which Major Hudoff are you looking for, Mr. Sanders?"

"Major W. Hudoff was my CO in Nam. We served with the forces together there. I was passing through the area and had hoped to see him again. I thought we might get a chance to lie and cry over old times."

"When was your tour in Nam, Mr. Sanders?" asked Hudoff as he walked toward the picture collection.

"Numerous tours, sir, too many times. The first was in seventy-two, the last in late seventy-four."

"And you say that you served under Major Waldo Hudoff?"

"Yes sir, do you know him?"

"Bob…Bob. Lynn told me someone is here asking about Wally."

"Yes, Mother, that's right. Come in and meet Mr. Alex Sanders. I believe Mr. Sanders served in one of Dad's units."

"Dad's units," repeated Alex to himself, "Now this is beginning to fit into place." He watched as the neatly dressed and robust Mrs. Hudoff approached him and offered her hand.

"Mr. Sanders," she said, "How nice to meet you. I'm Charlene Hudoff."

"My pleasure, Ma'am. Please call me Alex."

"Very well, Alex. May we offer you something to drink? Coffee or tea perhaps?"

"Coffee please, if it's not any trouble."

"No trouble, Alex."

Young Hudoff responded to his mother's offer and moved toward the kitchen without a word.

"Your son favors the Major, Mrs. Hudoff."

"In many ways, Alex. He's a fine son. I'm proud of him. You met my daughter-in-law, Lynn?"

"Yes, briefly."

Robert returned with a tray and placed it on the table in front of the sofa. All was quiet as they watched him pass the cups and saucers.

"Are you still in the service, Alex?" she asked.

"No, Ma'am. I was telling your son that I was just passing through and hoped to visit with the Major. Do you expect him soon?"

The room couldn't have gone any quieter if Alex had turned deaf. Mrs. Hudoff's expression turned from pleasant to one of stunned as she looked to her son. Alex followed her gaze to Robert as he spoke.

"Alex, when did you last serve with my father?"

"Well, as I said, we last rotated out of Saigon in seventy-four, why?"

"Mr. Sanders, Alex," said Mrs. Hudoff. My husband Wally was killed in Vietnam on April twenty-second of seventy-five. We just assumed you knew."

Alex leaned back in his chair and found himself taking a deep breath before saying, "No, no Ma'am, I didn't know. I'm sorry. But then I also didn't know that the Major had a son. I never heard him mentioned."

Robert stood and walked to the rear of the room leaving Alex to think he had said something wrong again.

"Wally never mentioned a son because he never knew he had one, Alex. Perhaps I can explain. Back in January of seventy-five it was evident that the United States was going to pull out of the war in Vietnam. You may not be aware that Wally was among the first American combat troops to arrive in Vietnam on March eighth, nineteen-sixty-five. Wally, being the devoted career soldier that he was volunteered to go back and finish the job he helped start. I'm afraid I was a little more than unreceptive to the idea and life around home was very uncomfortable between the two of us. I pleaded with him to stay state-side and let someone else go. I told him he had done more than his share for his country. We argued for days and I sometimes wonder if I didn't drive him there…drive him to his death."

"Mother, that's enough. You know better than that."

Mrs. Hudoff regained her composer and added. "Sorry. I was going to explain about Robert, wasn't I? I learned of my pregnancy after Wally had shipped out in January. I was going to tell him after he returned, but he was killed before he ever knew. Just three days before the fall of Saigon. Just three days."

Robert made his way to Alex's chair holding a framed picture and offering it to Alex. "Do you recognize anyone in this photograph, Sir?"

Alex accepted the picture and immediately felt a quiver that engulfed his body as he looked upon the 5$^{th}$ group, special detachment of the Green Berets. He located himself kneeling to the right of Major Hudoff and to his left knelt Cityboy. He found Rumrunner, Hayseed, Steamer and Blackjack. They were all there. A bunch of young, foolhardy, gung ho mothers. Alex didn't need to answer Robert as his expression told them he had found his former group commander.

Alex slid his finger across the glass and stopped on the second soldier standing to his left and subconsciously tapped at the glass.

"Someone special?" asked Robert.

"No. Well perhaps in some ways, yes. He became known as The Gospel."

"The Gospel?" repeated, Mrs. Hudoff, "how did that come about?"

"His given name was Zeigler. Heinrich Zeigler, I believe, but he was mostly called Hinny. He was a Mennonite from the hard core Amish country up in Lancaster Pennsylvania, I think. No one ever understood why he volunteered for active duty for he didn't have to. But I'll tell you this, he was a natural-born shooter. He possessed the eye of an eagle, the stealth of a chameleon and the patience of a cat. And he quickly earned top-gun sniper status in the Beret force."

"But he was nicknamed, Gospel, and not Top Gun, why?" asked Robert.

"I would guess it was because he spent every free moment reading his bible. Not just occasionally, but every free moment. In fact, one Sunday he corrected the chaplain on a scripture quotation during a service. I suppose it was his way of finding forgiveness or peace of mind, I don't know which. He never said and no one ever asked. He carried a small pocket-sized bible with him when he went out on hunts and as Second Lieutenant Benning, who acted as Hinny's spotter told us, 'Hinny would recite bible verses just above a whisper as he laid waiting for his mark'. I think it was Cityboy who asked the LT if that story was really true and he answered, 'that's the Gospel.' One morning Gospel walked into camp carrying Lieutenant Benning across his shoulders. Refusing all offers to help, he carried the LT directly to the aid station where the Medic pronounced him dead on arrival. Gospel never spoke; he just stood there quietly looking at Benning. Then he turned and stared hard at every one of us one at a time. I'll never forget that look in his eyes, never. He went directly to the ammo dump, refilled his magazines and walked out into the bush. We never saw or heard from him again." Alex looked about the room at the audience that was absorbing his every word. Thinking he may have talked too much he simply added, "That's the Gospel."

It was Lynn Hudoff's first appearance in the room since she answered the door earlier. She was carrying fresh coffee in one hand and in the other a decanter that she handed to her husband. Alex watched as three cups were filled about half full with *Irish Cream* to which Lynn added coffee and then took her leave. Robert, picking up his cup and offering the gesture of a toast said, "Now, Mr. Sanders, if you will, tell me what you know about my father."

The wall-clock chimed eleven times giving Alex an opportunity to make his excuses for leaving. He declined two offers to stay for lunch, knowing he hadn't released any confidential information to this point and he didn't want to press his luck. Besides, he became fond of these people and he still had to find the Major. Robert and Mrs. Hudoff walked Alex to his car accepting his promise to visit should he pass through North Carolina again.

"I had almost forgotten how pretty the Carolinas were," said Alex as they reached his car, "but I do recall how much the Major loved it here."

"Yes, he did love it here, but not as much as he loved Washington."

"Washington?" repeated Alex.

"Fort Lewis, Washington. Wally's father was base commander there when Wally was a youngster."

"Well that's something else I didn't know," said Alex as he opened the car door.

"Yes, they all loved it there. His family owned a cabin in the mountains around Mount Rainier. Actually, they owned several hundred acres."

Alex paused to listen as she went on.

"They dubbed it Bivouac Mountain. His father took him up there to hunt, fish or just camp out in the wilds. When his father passed on, it became Wally's. He swore it would become our retirement home, but that wasn't to be."

Not wanting to appear overly inquisitive, Alex closed his car door while saying, "I spent time at Fort Lewis. Where was this Bivouac Mountain?"

"Oh Lord, Alex, that was years ago. I'm not sure I could find it now. I do remember taking Highway 7 south to Longmire, but Wally took so many back roads. I didn't always know how he managed to get us there."

Alex smiled and gave an understanding nod, "Do you still own it? It sounds like a place I might like to spend my retirement."

"You Army men are all alike, Mr. Sanders. No, I sold it. Actually about six months after we received news of Wally's death I got a call from a realtor in Olympia making an offer on behalf of a client. I could hardly refuse. It was quite a handsome offer. So I signed the deed and deposited the check. I was a widower with a new baby. You know how it is?"

Farewells were repeated and Alex Sanders backed away from the Hudoff's drive making his way back to Raleigh. Next stop…Olympia, Washington.

# Eleven

The ride south along Highway 7 was particularly beautiful to Alex and he had no difficultly understanding why Hudoff would like it here. The scenery was breathtaking and if a man wanted to be left alone this would be the place to do it. Two stops and two inquiries at the local Gas and Go's proved to be of no help in locating the whereabouts of one Bivouac Mountain. It was obviously a Hudoff family pet name.

Alex eased off the blacktop and brought his rental to a stop in front of the gas pump at Grady's Groceries and Gas. This station looked no different than the others and he found the results to be no different either.

"Lived 'round here lots of years young man, but I ain't heard of no Bivouac Mountain, here 'bouts.

After paying for his fuel and snacks Alex returned to his car ready to continue his search.

"Lookin' for Bivouac, are you, young fella?"

"That's right," answered Alex. "You know where it is?"

"Maybe. What you want there?"

"I'm looking for an old friend. Do you know how to get there?"

"Maybe. Your friend got a name?"

"Maybe."

The pause seemed longer than it was as each man sized the other up for the next round.

"The name's Grady. This is my place."

“Sanders, Alex Sanders,” said Alex offering his hand.

Grady took his hand but continued looking directly into Alex’s eyes. If he managed a smile it was ever so slight that it went unnoticed by Alex, who wasn’t going to be the first to break eye contact. It was Grady’s turn to start the next conversation.

“Yeah, I know where it is. It’s been a long time since I heard it mentioned though,” said Grady as he broke his stare and his grip on Alex’s hand.

“Probably not since the General died,” said Alex.

That perked Grady up. “You knew the General?”

“Not as well as I knew his son Wally. I served with the Major. He and the old man brought me up here years ago on weekend passes. I thought I would remember how to get back there, but I guess I don’t. Nothing looks familiar.”

Alex let it go at that. It was Grady’s turn to show if he was buying his story or not.

“You drink beer, young fella?” asked Grady.

“I’ve been told I do, but I don’t remember.”

That melted the ice and brought a toothy smile from Grady. “Pull your car over there next to that red pickup. You’re blocking my pump.”

It only took two beers for Grady to decide that he believed, trusted and liked Alex Sanders. This was one of Alex’s best areas of expertise, gaining the confidence of others and he played it well for he needed Grady. He needed Grady to open up and that was definitely beginning to happen.

"Yeah, I sure did like the General. He and me 'came good friends. We'd hunt together, fish together and get drunk together. I felt bad when he died 'cause I really liked him. Nothing was ever the same after that. Oh, I liked his boy too. Wally was okay, but he was a lot younger and a little different. I always thought he could be dangerous if a body crossed him."

"When was the last time you saw Wally, Grady?"

"A few weeks back. He never stops here for some reason or the other. Not that I need his business mind you, but that has always struck me as odd."

"You mean he just drives by?"

"Yep," he answered, as he finished the last of his beer and tossed the empty at the cardboard box in the back of his pick up. "He just drives by."

"Grady, you said you could give me directions to Bivouac."

Grady looked at Alex and smiled as he shook his head no. "Nope, I never said that at all. I said I knew where it was. I never said I'd tell you."

Alex tossed his empty at the cardboard box and pulled himself off the tailgate. "Well, Grady, thanks for the beer. I best be going. Got things to do before dark."

"Nope," said Grady, as he stood from the tailgate. "I didn't plan to tell you how to get there; I planned to take you there. Follow me. It's on my way home."

Alex shook his head at the old man as Grady slapped him on the back while pointing his best I gotchya finger at Alex's nose.

Although he hadn't given much thought to it Alex did consider himself experienced at surveillance and tailgating. However, he really didn't need much skill to keep up with Grady's red Ford, for according to Alex's speedometer his top speed was thirty miles-per-hour. Thankfully, this pace didn't last long as he noticed the taillight and turn signal indicating that Grady was pulling his truck off the edge of the road. Alex watched as Grady's left arm appeared from the driver's window and his index finger pointed towards the area directly across the pavement. With his commitment completed he waved his hand at Alex and drove off around the curve ahead.

Alex sat quietly for a few moments as he realized two important things. One, he had no idea where in the hell he was, and two, he sure didn't see a driveway across the street. "Did ole' Grady lead me down the proverbial path?" he whispered. That he didn't know, but he decided to look around at whatever it was Grady had pointed to. Parking his Bronco clear of traffic, although there was none, he walked across the road looking at the area indicated by his guide. He located a drainage culvert covered by weeds that offered access to a narrow lane between the pines. What gave the appearance of an abandoned logger's trail showed signs of recent light traffic. "Could be hunters," Alex reminded himself as he made his way into the trees. No Trespassing signs were posted on either side of the lane just out of sight of the main road. Alex walked another thirty meters before noticing bent grass in the lane as well as a few broken twigs on the overgrown brush. "I think I'll do a little off-roading," he said aloud as he turned to make his way back to his four-by.

About four steps into his about face Alex caught sight of a weathered board resting against a pine. Stepping through the brush he pulled the board free, turned it over and rubbed at the lettering to remove the moss. There embedded in the grain by a novice hand using a wood burning iron he read the words, Bivouac Mountain.

The excursion up the mountain trail was no challenge for his Bronco as he rocked and bounced his way to a crest before stopping about a half-mile up. This was his first opportunity for a lane change. To his left the lane went down towards the valley, while the path to his right disappeared over the crest above. He pulled the gear lever into low range and subsequently continued up Bivouac Mountain.

Alex slowed while looking ahead at the next challenge. The path narrowed between a rock wall to his right and a steep cliff to his left. He decided it would be best if he did a walk-up before continuing. As he stood under the rock's ledge Alex clearly saw the roof-line of a cabin about eight hundred meters beyond. The road would be passable and unchallenged once he mastered the ledge. However, the ledge was indeed a natural deterrent and most likely gave the General a good laugh when a guest walked on to the cabin from there.

Alex made no effort to conceal his approach or vehicle once he reached the cabin. A quick look around showed no evidence of another means of transportation or movement in or around the area. Still, a bold approach would be best in this situation. If the Major was inside, Alex didn't want to surprise him. After all, this was a social call, not an assignment.

"Hello…anybody in the cabin? Hello." No response. Alex stepped hard on the front porch and knocked firmly on the door as he repeated, "Hello… anybody in the cabin?"

Slowly he reached for the door knob then purposely diverted his attention to the door jam and gently ran his index finger around the surface. He felt foam in the seam between the door and its casing. A quick examination of both windows along the front porch revealed the same. Alex smiled as he nodded with understanding. The foam was intended to keep out the harsh north wind; or in as much as the Major was an expert in demolition, it may well have been a binary foam explosive to keep out intruders.

After completing a rather extensive reconnaissance around the cabin and the immediate area he made his way to the back porch and paused at the railing while looking at the surrounding country. It was unquestionably beautiful here. From this vantage point Alex could see the sun's reflection off a small lake about two hundred meters to the southeast. The tree-line and lush green foliage around the water's edge challenged a rainforest for color and density. Then, moving to the opposite rail, Alex could see miles of valley stretched out below. Yes, this was truly a beautiful, isolated and perhaps lonely place. Standing quietly he listened to the wind and an occasional call from the wild until a chill engulfed his body and awakened his sixth sense. He slowly turned and scanned the surrounding tree line.

"Someone is watching," he whispered. "Is that you, Major?"

Standing motionless, with the exception of eye movement, Alex continued his survey. All his instincts and training were at full alert. Then his peripheral vision caught movement off to his immediate right. Alex quickly turned, kicking a porch chair on its side in the process and frightening a small doe back to her cover deep in the trees.

"Getting jumpy are we, Alex?" he said aloud.

With the chair back in place Alex took a seat and checked his watch noting that he had accomplished nothing during the hour he had been at the cabin. More so, he also realized that a decision had to be made as to how long he would sit idly by, wasting precious time while waiting for Major Hudoff's return, realizing that it may not happen for days, or perhaps weeks for that matter. But he needed some evidence to find the whereabouts of the Major or clues as to who the Major's contact at the Club might be. Clues that could only be found inside the cabin. Alex rose from the chair and moved toward the back door. Again he checked the outline of the door but did not expect to find any foam this time, for the Major also needed an entry. Reaching for the door knob he again became aware that eyes were on him as his instincts remained on alert. He would not allow himself to turn his head or look back over his shoulder. Alex proceeded to open the unlocked door of Major Hudoff's Bivouac Mountain cabin and step inside.

# Twelve

Deep in the thriving green foliage, fifty meters beyond the lake of the isolated cabin, on what was affectionately dubbed Bivouac Mountain, he sat silently on a fallen tree watching an intruder recon the area. Occasionally, he raised his binoculars and tried to identify the man at the cabin, but a clear view had not yet presented itself. He watched as the intruder made his way to the back porch and slowly walked its length twice. He watched him turn too quickly and knock over the deck chair. "Getting jumpy are we?" he said with a smirk.

As patience delivers, he watched as the man paused at the hand rail and looked directly towards the lake. Quickly he raised the binoculars and rotated the focusing wheel for a clearer image. As the haze in the lens vanished, he whispered, "Sandman."

Alex paused in the center of the kitchen after completing a 360-degree visual check of the room. Absolutely everything was in its designated place. The main room and bath were also found to be in similar array. However, the bedroom proved to be the only room that seemed to offer any signs of a personal nature. Alex stepped to the dresser and picked-up an eight by ten framed photograph. He could not have rendered a guess as to who was in the picture if it wasn't for his recent trip to North Carolina. Now there was no doubt. The woman pushing a baby stroller along a neighborhood sidewalk was indeed the Major's widow, Mrs. Hudoff. Perhaps twenty-five years younger, but it was Charlene alright, taking their son Robert for a stroll. Upon replacing the picture he took a second. This particular photo was perhaps taken twenty years after the first. It showed Robert Hudoff receiving his Lieutenant insignia during a military ceremony. Alex then located a leather-bound photograph album on the night-stand next to the bed. It was also filled with a series of pictures spanning some twenty-odd years. Alex quickly fanned the pages and moved to replace it on the stand when the image of one picture resurfaced. Again he fanned the pages looking for whatever it was that had caught his attention. About half-way through the album he paused on a cracked and faded picture of two men in military fatigues, fully armed and shaking hands while standing amidst dead Viet Cong soldiers. It was Major Hudoff and Colonel Wilkinson of the 5th Detachment Command post. Alex recognized them both and thought it was odd that it was the only picture in the album that wasn't of the Major's wife or son. Replacing the book he returned to the kitchen while trying to grasp why Colonel Wilkinson would be in the book. Of all the people Hudoff knew or commanded, why did he see fit to have only Wilkinson in his mementoes?

Alex searched the cabinets noting a variety of canned goods and other non-perishables. The refrigerator contained nothing in the way of dairy products that could offer an expiration date or suggest an approximate time of purchase. However, there was beer, lots of cold beer, which Alex helped himself to as he continued his investigation.

He had managed to collect some peanut butter from the cabinet, a jar of jelly from the fridge and a loaf of bread from the freezer. "Good protein," he said as he started to prepare lunch.

It was the second time since his arrival at the cabin that his senses alerted him to the fact that someone or something was watching him. He had no explanation for it, just something he knew. Alex removed a carving knife from the wooden butcher block and drew it slowly through the bread creating two equal parts. Putting the knife down, he opened the refrigerator and removed two cold bottles of beer before making his way to the patio table on the back porch. As he made his way through the screen door, Alex's senses again went to full alert.

"A man could get shot sneaking around up here, Sandman," said a voice from behind. Showing absolute control and indifference, Alex casually pulled up a chair and took his place at the patio table without any acknowledgment. He removed half of the sandwich and slid the remainder towards the empty seat to his right, followed by a cold bottle of brew.

"Lunch is ready, Major. Sit down before your beer gets warm," said Alex without turning around.

"What are you doing sneaking around up here, Sandman?"

"I didn't sneak up here, Major. I drove. I hope you like peanut butter and jelly. I couldn't find any cold cuts.

Alex took a small bite of his sandwich, giving the Major time to show himself.

"How did you find me?" asked Hudoff, still standing out of eyesight.

Alex finished chewing and took a small drink before he responded.

"Sit down, Major. We need to talk."

The silence on the porch took control as Alex continued with his lunch and gazed out across the lake. It was now the Major's turn to volley.

"And just what do we need to talk about, Sandman?" asked Hudoff, as he pulled a deck chair free and took his place at the table.

Alex turned to Hudoff for the first time and looked angrily into his eyes. "We need to talk about the troubleshooting assignment you gave me, Major."

"I don't assign them, Alex. I only obey them as you do."

"I told you that I had planned to go liquid. I told you that I didn't have the heart for this work anymore. But you convinced me to take one final assignment. 'Get it behind you', you said. 'An Al Qaida terrorist camp director or a Columbian drug lord', you said. 'Two lowlifes the world could do without.'"

"And," said Hudoff as he paused between drinks.

"AND!…You know damned well that I've been assigned a hit on Jake Kramer," said Alex as he glared at his former Company Commander. “Kramer wasn’t on the plate when I agreed to take one last shot. You set me up, Major. You set me up and I don’t like it. You used me, knowing damn well that Kramer is a friend of mine. He’s a good man, doing good things for a lot of people and he doesn’t deserve this.”

Alex was standing now looking down at the major which he didn’t appreciate. He also didn’t appreciate Alex’s tone, but understood why he was using it.

“Grab us a couple of beers while you’re up, Sergeant.”

Alex stepped clear of the door allowing it to slam closed behind him while startling the wrens on the hand railing. The Major could sense that Alex had mellowed a little during his short absence. Setting the beers between the two of them Alex retook his place at the table.

“Thanks, Sandman,” said Hudoff, reaching for the nearest bottle. “Feeling better?”

“I want it cancelled, Major.”

“That’s not an option. You know that.”

“I’m telling you, Major, I won’t do it.”

The Major adjusted his position in the deck chair and placed the beer on the table before responding, “I never expected you to do it, Alex. As a matter of fact, I would have been disappointed in you if you had.”

Alex leaned back in his chair completely puzzled. “What in the hell are you talking about, Major?”

"What I am talking about is simply…I did you a favor here and you're too damned pig-headed to recognize it."

Alex sat silently for a moment trying to catch up with Hudoff's thoughts. "Am I to understand, Major, that you gave me an assignment to troubleshoot my friend as a favor to me?"

"Yes."

"Well, before I fall on my knees to give thanks, would you mind telling me just how in the hell you came to that conclusion?"

Hudoff moved forward in his chair and leaned on the table with his forearms while looking Alex Sanders directly in the eyes. "It's true that I knew Jake Kramer was a friend of yours. Hell, I saw pictures of you helping him to his feet when he visited The Wall, and pictures of the Kramers and you walking up the courthouse steps together back when he testified in that preacher's trial. Half the recon photos I saw in Kramer's folder were of the two of you. Hell man, if I didn't know better, I would've thought you two were queer for each other.

The Major paused and collected his thoughts before continuing.

"Alex, I'm sure this friend of yours…Kramer is a good man. I'm also sure he's helped many people in his own way. BUT, his problem is that he has a damn big mouth. He has managed to scare the hell out of a lot of very important people. Did it ever occur to you to advise this individual to use a little discretion? If anyone should know about that, it's you."

Alex reached for his beer and looked to the lake as he answered, "Yeah, I tried. The problem is that he has a soft heart for victims, especially kids. He just doesn't seem to think past that."

"That's all well and good, but it tends to shorten one's life cycle."

"And this was the favor you did for me, Major… giving me the assignment to make me aware of the troubleshooting?"

"You don't have to thank me, Sandman."

Alex stood, took his beer, walked to the railing and stood quietly looking out at the water. Major Hudoff also stood and walked toward the back door. "You think about it, Sandman, while I get more beer. This is a good day to get drunk."

# Thirteen

He hadn't changed positions since taking cover among the thick vegetation across the lake from the cabin, nor had he felt the need to stand and stretch his legs. He had adapted well to this fallen tree seating as he was accustomed to long periods of inactivity. Perhaps that's why he's still alive today. At one period, his keenness was complemented by two chipmunks, unaware of his presence, playing around his feet.

He had not sampled any of the nutrition bars in his pack, or so much as reached for a bottle of water. He simply sat and watched the cabin across the lake. The large ferns provided excellent cover making it difficult for one to spot him from this distance. He slowly brought the olive green set of field glasses to his eyes and began gently rotating the wheel.

"I see company has arrived, Sandman. But he likes to stay in the shadows. Let's just give him a little time my friend…he'll show himself. They always do. I'm in no hurry."

With the patience of a red-tailed hawk Rich sat on his log and leaned back against the tree, as he watched the activity on the porch across the lake.

Hudoff found Alex still standing at the railing when he returned from the kitchen. Taking a place to his right, he placed a cold bottle on the handrail next to Alex.

"How do I stop this thing, Major?"

"You don't," said Hudoff between sips.

"Who's your contact, Major; perhaps I could try to buy the contract."

"Listen to yourself, Alex. First, you can't buy out even if you had the money. And second, you're probably too late as it is."

"What do you mean…too late?"

"How long have you been sitting on this assignment, Sandman?"

"A week, maybe ten days."

"Well then, chances are the assignment has been piggybacked by now."

"Piggybacked? What in the hell are you talking about…piggybacked?"

"It's a term for a second troubleshooter…a back-up in the event the prime is lost."

"Are you telling me someone else may have this assignment too?"

"It's not uncommon on high profile assignments like this one. You've been a piggybacker on a couple of jobs yourself. Algonan, the sheik, comes to mind for one."

Alex thought for a moment and said, "I remember him. He died of a heart attack the day before my set-up."

"Exactly," replied Major Hudoff.

Alex looked back to the water as he said, "I've got to try, Major. He's my friend. Tell me who your contact is, sir. Who brought you in?"

"I could tell you, Son, but it wouldn't do you any good. Nobody talks, especially him."

"It was Colonel Wilkinson wasn't it?"

Alex could see that he had struck a nerve in Hudoff. He, in fact, brought a slight smile to the man's face. "Colonel John T. Wilkinson was instrumental in getting me involved…yes."

"Who else?"

"I don't know anyone else, Alex, as you don't know anyone else but me. That's the way it works and that's why we're all still alive today. Although that could change very quickly if you persist in probing around in company business."

"I'd like to talk to this Colonel Wilkinson. Will you tell me where he is?"

"It's a waste of time, Alex. He won't talk to you."

"It's my time, sir, said Alex, giving a desperate look.

"He was promoted to the rank of General and given a staff assignment at the Pentagon, in D.C. The last time I heard, he resides in Arlington."

"Thanks, Major. Arlington's a big city, but I'll find his address and locate the General."

"Arlington's a big cemetery too, and I'm sure he hasn't moved."

The Major could tell from Alex's expression that he felt helpless and desperate. He did withhold some information that Alex was seeking, but it would not have done him any good. It would have only alerted and made some very sensitive people angry. This they both could live without. Hudoff watched as Alex finished the second half of the bottle and sat it on the table before removing the cap on the fresh one.

"I could get Kramer into the Witness Protection program, said Alex. I know an inspector friend of Jake's. I'm sure he would help."

Major Hudoff shook his head smiling as he said, "Do you recall the Victorie Massino assignment?

"Victorie Massino? Yeah, I remember that. That was one of my early assignments in New Mexico."

Hudoff shook his head in agreement, but added nothing.

Alex thought for a moment then said, "He was in the program? Are you telling me Massino was in the Witness Protection program?"

"No one is safe, Sandman. Not if they're marked, and your Mr. Kramer has marks_all over him."

Alex was feeling really desperate at this point as he asked, "What would you do, Major, if you were in my place, I mean?"

Major Hudoff picked up his bottle before saying, "Buy flowers."

As much as he hated to admit it, Alex knew he had exhausted the amount of information Major Hudoff was willing to share. It would be pointless to go on, for the only thing that could be accomplished was damage to their relationship. A relationship that, to this point, was respected by both parties. Alex saw no reason to pursue the issue. He looked his former Commander in the eyes and asked, "What kind of flowers?"

Hudoff smiled and nodded but said nothing.

"Major, I think that once again you're right…it is a good day to get drunk.

The conversation turned light and the beer drinking became heavy as the two former Green Berets began to relax.

"You never told me how you found me here, Sandman."

"Grady showed me."

"Grady? That old bandit down at the grocery?"

"Yeah. He said he remembered Bivouac Mountain and led me to the turn-off down at the road."

Alex was immediately aware that he had struck another nerve in the Major as this one erased his smile and instantly created a sense of uneasiness.

"Bivouac Mountain?" said Hudoff.

Alex nodded yes. "He told me that he came up here with you and the General, years ago. He liked your old man."

"You've been to North Carolina. How did you find them, Sandman?" Hudoff asked abruptly.

For the first time Alex noticed a kill glare in Hudoff's eyes. He was angry.

"What did you tell them?" he asked sharply.

"Relax, Major. I didn't tell them anything. Your secret's safe."

Alex got up and moved back to the handrail, attempting to downplay the moment. With his back to the table he listened for a sign that the tension was easing. The Major's tone had mellowed as he asked, "Last time, Alex…how did you find them?"

Alex explained while the Major listened and asked questions about his recent visit with the Hudoff family. He could tell that the Major had deep feelings for his widow and their son. Whatever it was that drove him to fake his demise was not asked or explained. It was simply none of Alex's business.

"I bought this place from my estate you know. I gave her every dime I had saved and every dime I could beg, borrow or steal. I remember the realtor thought I was nuts to make an offer like that, but she had a boy to raise. My son. I never knew she was pregnant. I…oh hell," he said, jumping to his feet, "here's to what might have been, but will never be. I'll get more beer."

By the time Hudoff returned to the porch the sun was beginning to lower itself behind them which created a spectacular Kodak moment across the lake. "It is beautiful here isn't it, Alex? It is about the only place I've found that I can be without ghosts. My old man and I used to stand right here looking out at that lake. He'd say, 'When God took the seventh day off to rest he must have come here.' This is where I want to rest someday."

Across the lake, nestled deep in the dark green undergrowth atop a steep knoll, he scanned the Major and Sandman through the single eyepiece of a Hendsoldt 6 x 42 rifle scope. He estimated the distance to be a little over seven hundred meters to the porch railing. A distance he considered a little challenge for his expertise. The cross hairs made an exact plus sign in the center of the glass. He gently and deliberately centered the cross hairs between the eyebrows while alternating between the Major and Sandman.

The lake's surface couldn't have had less movement if it were frozen. The mirror-like reflection provided ideal acoustic for nature's own to echo throughout the valley. It was the single repeat of a rifle shot from the hill across the lake that interrupted this perfect harmony. The wildlife screeched and scattered in protest as the gunshot echoed down the valley walls.

The eyeglass gave a perfect account of the two men at the railing falling to the deck. Pausing a few moments for confirmation, he made a mental note that the body appeared lifeless, and with absolute confidence in his skill, he knew it was a kill. Directly, he adjusted the rifle sling on his prized German-made PSG-1 and slid it over his shoulder. Upon completing a quick policing of the area for personal litter, he made his way up the grade toward his awaiting ATV. He looked again at the majestic mountain skyline and said, "*But God shall wound the heads of his enemies, of those who love their guilty ways*…Psalms 68:21."

Mother Nature's chatter began returning to the mountain landscape as Alex continued to hold his opossum posture. His left hand lay inches from his face, giving a clear view of the second hand of his watch. After two minutes of being down he gradually rose to his right elbow. He knew he wasn't hurt, but he was unsure if the Major was still playing dead, or in fact, had suffered a direct hit.

"Major, were you hit? Major?"

Alex dared to raise his head above the fallen table, giving a clear target to the shooter if he was still around. However, instinct and training told him he was gone. Now standing, Alex looked down at the motionless Major W. Hudoff. It was a haunting sight that one never became hardened to. Standing quietly he looked at the Major's eyes that had been expertly dissected at the bridge of the nose by a rifle's bullet.

There was an uncanny calm around the porch as Alex surveyed the scattered debris prior to scanning the east slope of the mountain. He visualized himself on the opposite side of the lake and imagined himself in position for such a shot.

"That knoll…there…right there," he said while pointing to the southeast. "700…maybe 750 meters. There are only two people I know who could have made that shot and I'm one. That leaves only…" Alex nodded in agreement with himself as he said…"the Gospel."

Alex knew there was little he could accomplish by hanging around Bivouac Mountain, but there was an unexplainable tranquility surrounding the cabin. He felt neither the fear to run, nor the need to grieve. Obviously there was little he could do for Major Hudoff, other than bury him. After all, Mrs. Hudoff was widowed years ago and what purpose would it serve to have her and their son relive such an experience.

There was little time to waste with indecisions here, for the echo of a small engine's whine fading down in the valley made Alex fully aware that he was currently in second place in the race for Jake Kramer.

It wasn't the most Christian burial a man could receive, but a battlefield burial was not without respect. The grave was covered with brush and a variety of rocks with a small transplanted fern as a headstone. There would be no need for an identifying marker for this man who had died years before.

The sun had disappeared behind the mountain as Alex made ready to depart Major W. Hudoff and Bivouac Mountain. While standing at the foot of the final resting place of his former commanding office, mentor and friend, he snapped to attention and presented arms. Before making an about-face to take leave, Alex paused, stood at parade rest and then delivered a brief eulogy to all who had served.

"Nice shot."

# Fourteen

Neil Diamond was well into his hit song Sweet Caroline on the oldies station as Jake returned his coffee cup to the desk. After suffering through another somewhat restless night and pounding down three Advil earlier that morning, he had dismissed any thought of going to the office today and decided to take another floating holiday. Inasmuch as he was the self-appointed CEO of Kramer and Associates he had granted himself several of these perks over the last few months. More to the point, no one had complained or questioned his absence, so he assumed Wesley was taking care of business without any problems.

Jake was aware that he had all but formally announced his retirement from the everyday routine. Some of his loss of ambition might be attributed to his age or perhaps the fact that he was preoccupied with his new gift; but regardless of why, one could not dismiss the fact that Jake Kramer was a wealthy man. His Grand Cayman bank account had blossomed beyond his wildest expectations. This was entirely due to the combined treasure hunting ventures with his friend and neighbor, Alex Sanders, but that was another story. The fact remained that Jake Kramer had gone from a struggling small-businessman to a multi-millionaire in a very short period of time. The priority mailer he held in his hand, postmarked in New York, with Sandman printed in the return address would multiply his Cayman account by an obscene amount. Yes indeed,

Jake Kramer was a very wealthy man. With that thought fresh in his mind he took a pen in hand and made a note on his calendar to give his partner, Wesley L. Washington, another sizeable appreciation bonus. Jake lingered over his note for a period of time and then drew his pen through it until it was no longer legible. Smiling at his newest thought he wrote, "Memo: Check with accountant and lawyer to complete details for selling and transferring ownership of Kramer and Associates to Wes."

Jake leaned back in his chair, completely satisfied with his decision. In fact it was the most satisfying feeling he'd had since who knows when and he needed it. Things hadn't been so great between him and Connie in the last few weeks. They'd been pushing and pulling in so many different directions that…well to the point that neither one was happy with the other's opinion. Given that, Jake was sure Connie would be very happy for Wesley, Stacie and the kids. They were a deserving, hard-working family and she loved them as much as he did. On that subject Connie and he both strongly agreed. The right time would present itself and he'd tell her about his plan for Wesley, complete with all the details suggested by counsel. He'd suggest, once again, that she retire from Cushman's so they could travel and do the things they promised one another all their working lives. One thing however, she would have to lighten up on the psychologist bull. He didn't object to her visits but he wanted no part of that crap.

Jake recollected his thoughts before they ran too far in the wrong direction. There was a big difference between his retiring and his psychology views. He preferred to dwell on the former because working was no longer a part of his daily routine. In fact he only went to the shop these days to be alone. His office at Kramer's had become a great place to find quiet time and search the lights, play with his coin collection, or dream up new treasure-hunting trips for Alex and himself. Like a trip to Colorado to find the Parkers' rock face that he'd dubbed the "Chiseled P Gold." He certainly would need Alex for that little excursion. But he needed Alex for a lot of other reasons too, like having someone to sit with on the patio, shoot the breeze and share a bottle of beer or two. A true friend, called the Sandman.

Alex had been gone on his final assignment for several weeks now and Jake was becoming concerned about his cohort. However, if anyone could take care of himself in a bad situation it was Alex Sanders. Jake had been witness to a demonstration of Alex's self-defense skills and even brought home a black eye as a souvenir. The eye had healed, the swelling was gone and the only thing that remained was his personal humiliation over the whole incident. As Alex said, "Someday you'll look back and laugh about it," but for now he was still a little embarrassed.

On his third trip past the card table that supported Maggie's and Becky's computer assignment Jake stopped and visited the project. What a fine example of modern technology it was. The girls had received an 'A' for their efforts and were asked to bring the unit to the classroom, remove the cover and do a show-and-tell regarding the assembly process. This they did to the amazement of their instructor, which helped confirm that they indeed did the work on the project. Much to her disappointment Becky wasn't permitted to accept the computer from Maggie until Alex returned home and gave his final approval. Feeling a sense of pride and fulfillment Jake nodded and smiled at their accomplishment before making his way to the kitchen.

He was restless…much too restless to hang around the house. With a quick check of the clock, as old habits mandate, he decided it was time to make his way to Manny's Pub for an early lunch.

"Out kinda early ain't ya, Jake?" said Millie as she sat a frosted mug of his usual down in front of him.

"Yeah, you know how it is, Millie, I have a hard time staying away from you."

"Sure, honey, you lie and I love it. Say, where's you friend? He ain't been around here in a while."

"Which one, Millie?"

"You know…the cute one with the big muscles."

"Alex?"

"Yeah, that's him, Alex. Where's he been? You two were thicker than peanut butter and jelly."

"He's working out of town, Millie, but I'll be sure to tell him you were asking about him next time I see him."

"Good, you do that and bring him in with ya the next time. I'll buy the first beers. Whatcha havin' today, Jake?"

"I don't know, what sounds good to you?"

"I like the babybacks and the coleslaw is great."

"I didn't know you had babybacks here."

"We don't, you gotta get 'em down at Isaac's Ribs, on 3rd. They're great."

Millie, knowing she managed to yank Jake's chain started laughing at herself and quickly had Jake laughing too. A little humor was something he could certainly use.

"Okay, Millie, I give. Seriously, what do you recommend?"

"Eat at Isaac's," she managed to say before breaking out in another burst of laughter that echoed throughout the room.

Millie laughed and waddled all the way to the kitchen. Jake sipped his beer and admitted that coming here was excellent therapy for him. Who needed a shrink when he had Millie?

Walking unnoticed past the long row of wooden stools paralleling the bar at Manny's he selected an indiscreet booth in the far corner of the room. Taking the side that offered an un-obstructed view of Mr. Kramer he settled in and reviewed the menu and subsequently placed it aside.

"What can I get ya, honey?"

"Do you have ale on tap?"

"You betcha…can I draw ya one?"

"Please."

"Can I getcha somethin' from the kitchen?"

"No thanks, just ale for now. Is that Jake Kramer seated over there?"

"Sure is, hon," she replied while turning to look in Jake's direction. "You know him?"

"Only by reputation."

Millie smiled and cracked her gum as she placed her green order pad in the pocket of her apron. "I'll fetch your beer, hon. Be right back."

He could see the shadowed figure of a stout man walking in his direction making his way from the entrance. Tilting his head down toward his folded hands on the table he watched every step this man took as he drew closer. His face remained obscured and shadowed from the radiant sunlight that followed him from the entrance. Nevertheless, he knew who he was by the posture, the build, the poise, and by the confidence displayed in his stride.

"Sandman," he whispered under his breath.

Millie's timing was impeccable. By setting the mug of ale on the table before him she placed herself directly between him and the Sandman, creating a screen that few could see around if they wanted.

"Now that's a first," she said while wiping her hands on her apron.

"I beg your pardon?"

"A bible. I ain't never seen, in all my years of waitressin', a customer readin' a bible in a pub."

"Maybe they should try it," he replied without looking up.

Millie shook her head and cracked her gum once again before she turned to walk away. "If ya need anythin' hon…just wave the good book."

"This seat taken?"

"Alex. Alex, my God, it's good to see you. Sit down," he said as he extended his hand and pointed to the seat across from him. "I've been worried about you my friend. You've been gone a long time."

Alex smiled at Jake's enthusiasm as he said, "I had a lot of things to take care of. How about you, Jake, how you doing? Have you had any trouble?"

"Trouble…me? Hell no…no trouble. When did you get back?"

"Late last night. I stopped by your house this morning and then went to your office. When I didn't find you there I was pretty sure I might locate you here at Manny's."

"Well, I'm glad you did. Welcome home."

"I saw your truck parked in the back lot at the office. What happened to the driver's side? It looked serious."

"Oh, that. No big deal, Alex. I got cut off on a back road that's all. I parked it and started driving the old shop truck just to keep people from asking questions. It goes to Blake's body shop in a few days so that will be the end of it. But enough about me, tell me what happened in California. You know…about the last assignment. What did you do about your last project?"

"Jake, I'd like to hear more about this accident…"

"Hey, there ya' are stranger," said Millie as she placed a mug of draft beer in front of Alex. "We were just talkin' 'bout you. Here, honey, beer's on the house."

"Thanks, Millie. It's nice to see you too."

"Don't ask her what's good for lunch," said Jake as he leaned against the back of the booth.

Millie burst into a hardy laugh while pointing to Jake saying, "Ain't he a card? I got ya good today, didn't I, hon?"

"That you did," said Jake between sips of beer. "That you did."

"You fellers enjoy and if ya want anything just wave the good book."

Alex sprang to attention like a bird dog on point and actually startled Jake enough that he choked as he swallowed his beer.

"What was that, Millie?"

"What, honey?"

"What did you just say?"

Mille looked more confused than normal. "I said, if you need anythin' just wave."

"Millie," said Alex in a calm tone not wanting to frighten her, "Did you say wave the good book?"

"Oh, that." Millie placed both palms on the table and leaned forward as Jake and Alex also leaned into the huddle.

"Dangdest thing I ever seen. There's a fella over there readin' a bible." She started grinning as she continued. "Dangdest thing I ever seen. A bible reader in a pub."

Jake failed to see the humor in it but smiled along with Millie nonetheless. Alex, on the other hand, failed to see any humor in her comment at all.

"Millie, not too fast now, but take a look and tell me if he's still there."

Millie responded without question, turned slowly and looked to the booth.

"Nope," she said while straightening up. "He's gone." With that said, she made her way back toward the kitchen.

"What is it, Alex?"

"Humm…oh nothing. Listen Jake, I need to check the restroom. When I get back how about us adjourning to my patio? I have a cooler full of free Coronas iced down."

"Alex, what the hell is going on? What do you mean check the restroom?"

"Did I say that? I meant use the restroom. I'll be right back. Drink up and we'll go, okay?"

Jake watched Alex walk to the rear of the room, looking in every booth along his way, until he disappeared into the hall around the corner. He detected that something was bothering his friend, but attributed the uneasiness to his recent final assignment. Jake believed that undesirable events were most likely still fresh in Alex's mind and he had not yet put them to rest. He also surmised that perhaps an afternoon on the patio would be the best thing for both of them. Jake Kramer could not have been more correct.

Finding the restroom and storage room clear, Alex began to make his way back to gather Jake. Pausing at the corner booth that had been pointed out by Millie he found a half-full mug of beer and a crisp new ten dollar bill laying on a napkin with a note printed in black ink. Alex pulled the napkin free and read, "*Put up again thy sword into his place: for all they that take the sword shall perish with the sword…*Matthew 26:52."

"Ain't that the gospel?" said Alex.

# Fifteen

Jake parked his old shop truck in the driveway and made his way to Alex's patio by way of the side yard. He paused momentarily at the rose trellis and smiled as he remembered a photographer being shoved face first into the thorns by his protective neighbor, Alex Sanders. As he rounded the blue spruce that divided their properties he could see Alex uncharacteristically pacing across his patio like a caged tiger.

"Great idea coming here, Alex."

"Yeah, I thought so," he agreed, as he peeled the cap from a cold Corona before handing it off to Jake. "Pull up a chair and tell me about your defensive driving skills. Did the guy stop after he ran you off the road?"

"Oh he stopped alright. He stopped and gave me a smirk that I'm not likely to forget before he drove off. I think he was just having a bad day and wanted to have some fun at my expense. But hey…that's why we carry insurance. It's over…forget it. I want to hear about California. What did you do about your last assignment?"

Alex paused and looked away as he answered, "You know I could tell you, Jake, but then I'd have to shoot you."

Jake gave an understanding nod and answered, "You know, I'll always be curious."

“Nothing wrong with that, Jake,” said Alex as he stood and again moved slowly about the patio.

“I remember you pacing like that the day we decided to become treasure hunting partners. Do you remember that, Alex?”

“Remember, hell yes! I remember it was raining that day and I got so excited that I almost peed my pants.”

“So that’s why you walked off the porch and stood in the downpour.”

“That brought a smile to Alex’s face as he said, “God, that seems like a lifetime ago.”

“Want to go to Colorado? I know where thousands and thousands of dollars worth of gold bars are hidden. I’ve dubbed it the Chiseled P stash. Let’s go and get it. You and me…it’ll be good for the both of us.”

Alex grabbed two fresh brews and returned to his seat. He handed one to Jake and cupped the second as he said, “I really wish we could, old buddy. I really do. But there are things that I need to take care of…things that I’m afraid can’t wait while I go hunting for gold.”

Jake could see the troubled look in Alex’s eyes. He could tell that he was wrestling with deep problems and to this point Alex had not felt free to confide in him.

“What’s working on you, Alex? It’s me, Jake, you’re not talking to here. Maybe I can help.”

Alex stood once again and resumed his pacing, beer sipping and silence. Jake in turn leaned back in the lawn chair giving his friend some space. The quiet time was accepted by both and continued for several minutes.

"Something happened on your last assignment, Alex. Something that you didn't like. Something you couldn't do anything about…didn't it? How can I help you?"

Alex slowed his pace as he listened to Jake and marveled at how perceptive he had become. Retaking his chair he looked Jake directly in the eyes and said, "You're right, I could use your help, Jake."

"Good…what can I do for you?"

"I need to ask you to use your gift and search for someone. I'd like you to search for a Colonel John T. Wilkinson. I can't tell you how long he's been deceased, but I'll give you all the information I have. He was in the Army and served with the 5th group special detachment of the Green Berets in Nam. He was subsequently reassigned to the Pentagon before the close of the war. I believe it was he who befriended a Major W. Hudoff and was most likely instrumental in recruiting Hudoff into…"

Jake was surprised by this unusual request, but didn't openly show it as he listened attentively to Alex's every word while committing each detail to memory.

"…so, will you try to find him for me, Jake?"

"Of course I'll try, but just what is it you're looking for?"

"I believe Wilkinson was among the leading members of the club. I'd like for you to get the names of other players involved in the organization. Perhaps some of them are still active. See if you can uncover the crust of this fungus."

"And if I do?"

"If you do? Well, I'm not really sure. I feel these self-appointed vigilantes need to be curtailed. Maybe, just maybe, I'm the one to do it."

Jake leaned back in the patio lounger and shifted into a relaxed position as Alex watched him from the edge of the concrete. Looking back to the wooded acreage that adjoined their properties, Alex's sixth sense was again awakened. His intuition told him that someone, somewhere, was watching them and this was not unlike the awareness he experienced on Bivouac Mountain.

"I'll give you a little quiet time, Jake. I'm going to take a walk in the woods."

Jake didn't respond but heard him walk away.

From his vantage point 80 meters to the east he rotated the focus wheel on his camouflaged binoculars until the images on the patio became sharp.

"So, Sandman, I see you've befriended our mark. One should never allow this to happen. You of all people should know better, for such acts can only leave you with shadows that move. Perhaps this is why I was called to Washington when you were already there."

He continued to watch as Alex stepped from the concrete and moved through the lawn in his direction.

"Your senses stayed sharp my friend. It will be a dark day for us when you and I face off, Sandman. And

I fear that day is both inevitable and near." Then he whispered, "*Slay and utterly destroy after them, says the Lord, and do all that I have commanded you...* Jeremiah 50:21."

Jake was sitting behind the patio table with his fingers rolled around a cold bottle of Corona when Alex returned from the woods. Reaching into the cooler he removed a bottle for Alex and placed it on the table as the chair was pulled clear and Alex took his place next to Jake.

"Nature hike?"

"Nah, just giving you some space. Got any idea who owns the woods behind us, Jake?"

"The last I heard it was still in the McKinney family, but Connie mentioned she heard that Cooper Development was trying hard to buy it. Why?"

"No reason, just curious. Did you have any luck with Wilkinson?"

Jake leaned back in his chair and folded his hands on his lap.

"Your Colonel Wilkinson was an interesting individual indeed and he certainly had some unique ideas about loyalty, devotion and love of country. I believe he'd shoot his own grandfather if he caught him standing with a hat on during the playing of the National Anthem."

Alex without offering the slightest hint of a smile said, "So would I."

Jake turned to Alex with a stunned look and said, "You're serious?"

"You bet, but because he would be family I'd fire a warning shot first."

Both men hid their smiles before Jake continued. "I found your Colonel Wilkinson, Alex, and here's what I learned. You were right about Hudoff. Wilkinson recruited him into the club back in the late sixties and Hudoff took to it like chips to salsa. Eventually, under Wilkinson's direction and recommendations Hudoff moved up the organizational chart and became the Sergeant of Arms."

"What does that mean?"

"It means he was the one who disbursed troubleshooting assignments."

"Are you telling me that it was Hudoff's voice on my assignment calls?"

"Most likely. But you couldn't have known that because of the voice synthesizer that was used."

Jake watched Alex's expression as he tried to accept the fact that he had not been a fool. "Tell me about the club, Jake. Who recruited Wilkinson? Where do I find these people?"

"Wilkinson wasn't a difficult recruit…here's the way it went. Wilkinson left Viet Nam after being reassigned to the Pentagon as Special Advisory Assistant to the Office of the Deputy Undersecretary of the Army for International Affairs. Being a political officer he meshed well from the get-go. Now I won't cloud you with a lot of the colorful social particulars of his career, but I'll go directly to the crust of this fungus as you called it.

"Wilkinson was reunited with a Westpoint classmate at the Pentagon who had earned his way to the rank of Brigadier General. That would be one named Seth Crawford. Crawford was an intelligent, no-nonsense, hard-drinking administrator who loved to play poker. One evening Crawford invited Wilkinson to fill a void at the monthly poker game held at the downtown Washington Athletic Club, to which he readily accepted. As it turned out, he was not only playing poker, but was also being screened for an opening in an obscure, selective and very secretive club. He eventually accepted the opportunity and in time learned a great deal about its conception.

"Now, this gets better and a little complicated, so stop me if I get too far ahead of you. The original founders, although their names were withheld from Wilkinson, were also monthly poker players at the Athletic Club in D.C. Two were Circuit Judges for the Federal Court of Appeals and another happened to be Deputy Chief of Staff in the National Security Council. Also among this influential group was an Assistant Director of the Office of Military Affairs, a Vice Chairman of the Joint Chiefs of Staff, as well as a ranking member of the Office of the General Counsel. The final chair was filled by the commanding Brigadier General of the elite Special Forces Detachment."

"Names, Jake, I need names."

"That's just it, Alex. Wilkinson was never given names. Besides, this group was formed more than fifty years prior. They're all dead and buried. I'm just explaining how it came to pass."

Jake reached to his left and retrieved two cold bottles and passed them to Alex who promptly removed the caps and passed a single to Jake.

"Should I continue?"

"Hell yes! Go on please, this is getting good."

"One evening, well into the game and booze, the group listened as the Judges spoke about their disgust in overturning the conviction of a man who sold military secrets to the Soviets. This man was clearly guilty, but his civil rights had been violated by an inept attorney and they had no choice but to overturn his conviction and release him on a technicality. They went on to say that for a few dollars he sold out the very government that had provided for and protected him all his life. One judge who survived D-Day in Europe was reported to have said, 'If I had a weapon tucked under my robe I would have been proud to shoot him himself.' I believe that was the opening for the club as you know it, Alex."

"How's that, Jake?"

"The General of the Special Forces Detachment was believed to have said, 'Hell Judge, I have a whole detachment of men who would be happy to take care of that detail for you and still be back at the mess-hall in time for chow.' Do you see where this is going, Alex?"

"Yeah…a club is born."

"That's right. Of course no one at the table found the idea repulsive and everyone acknowledged that they couldn't be a party to it, but in theory they could fund money to support such a club from slush funds and channels in their own departments. In other words, they too had known scumbags that the world could live without and obtaining money to rid the world of those types would certainly be no problem. So the basic core of The Club was fashioned and confidentiality was the prime directive. Then during the poker games various troubleshooting projects were discussed in a casual, nonchalant atmosphere and generally agreed upon as to who was the month's foremost scumbag. Subsequently, without any acknowledgement from anyone, the next troubleshooting assignment was offered, accepted and completed by one such as yourself. As to the money distribution…I have no idea."

Alex leaned back in his chair, locked his finger behind his head and stretched as he gave out with a big sigh. "A very neat little package," he said softly.

"Very neat indeed," repeated Jake. "But I don't think we can consider it little if you keep in mind that this was over fifty years ago and factor in the evolution of technology and the dollars available to Government spending in today's world. No, I don't believe this is a fungus, Alex…it's a full-blown cancer."

Alex nodded in agreement as he said, "No one knows anyone other than his recruiter or possibly someone in the ranks below them. The core of this club gives a new meaning to the word anonymous."

"Have you been in touch with your recruiter, what's-his-name…Hudoff?

"I have, but he's not talking to me anymore."

Alex got up and moved about the patio once again in deep thought as Jake stood and followed him to the patio's edge. They both stood quietly looking at nothing in the woods and sipping beer.

"Thanks for doing that for me, Jake."

"You're welcome."

Again the silence prevailed until Jake, still looking at the woods spoke softly, "I must be the biggest scumbag the club has had in years."

He could sense Alex's head turn towards him, but he held his position and continued. "They won't hurt my family will they, Alex?"

Alex knew that the friendship between he and Jake had no place for pretense on this subject. Jake was very perceptive and deserved to know the truth.

"No, they won't hurt your family."

"Are you sure of that, Alex? I couldn't stand it if my family was hurt because of me."

"I'm sure. One of the prime rules in the troubleshooting indoctrinate was to only erase the mark. This was strictly instilled, monitored and enforced."

Jake nodded and gave an expression of relief.

"I should have been more discreet. You tried to tell me but I didn't listen." Looking back to the woods he asked, "How will they do it, Alex?"

Alex walked back to the patio table without answering and placed his empty among the collection.

"Alex…how will they do it?"

"Hell, I don't know, Jake. Why would you ask me that? Maybe I shouldn't have told you about this."

"NO NO! I'm sorry. I shouldn't have asked that and please don't feel bad about telling me. After all, I did ask and you were right to tell me. I forget that this has to be difficult for you too."

Alex retrieved the last two beers from the cooler more from habit than thirst. Handing one to Jake he said, "If done correctly it will appear to have been an accident, natural causes or a suicide."

"Thanks, Alex. That's why you were so interested in my truck?"

"That's why."

Jake took a small sip and said, "I'm not afraid to die, you know?"

"I know…but don't be in a hurry."

"No, I'm not in a hurry. I have a list of things I want to accomplish before I check out."

"And what do you have on that list, Jake?"

"I want to make sure that I put my treasure money to good use. Really, that's one of the big reasons I wanted to locate all the lost caches…not to mention that it was a lot of fun. But there are so many people in this world who need help and don't get any, mainly the kids. I was thinking of a camp for counseling, a park with nature walks, scholastic foundations, homeless shelters, and financial support for the hotline 800-missing because they do good things."

"I should have guessed that you would plan to do something like that, Jake. It's a wonderful idea and I want to be a part of it, so put me in for half of whatever.

"Knowing you would say that, I already have, Alex." Jake raised his bottle offering a toast, "Here's to my half."

Alex tapped the bottle creating a soft ring and responded, "Here's to my half."

"So, what are we going to call this little enterprise, Jake? Kramer Kamp, or Kramer Kids…what did you come up with?"

"I don't want my name attached at all. I'm not doing this for publicity anymore than you are, so I was thinking about Sandman Shelter."

"I don't deserve that, Jake."

"I think you do. Besides, who said it was named after you?"

Alex was moved by the tribute and wanted to express it, but only managed to say,

"It'll be good for the shadows."

"Let's sit, my legs are tired," said Jake as he reached out and put his hand on Alex's shoulder in an understanding gesture, "So what's our plan against the club, Mr. Sanders?" he asked, changing the subject. "I know you have one. What do we do?"

"I wish I did, old buddy, but unfortunately I don't. I've never felt so helpless. I was really counting on getting to the club members and buying our way out with the Gambaiani money, but I can see that's not going to happen. I also thought about asking your Inspector Pierson for access to their witness protection program, but I've learned there is little security in that as well. So right now I don't know what to think."

"Well let's think about this. I was obliviously your troubleshooting assignment. Now, if you don't complete your project, which I am counting on, then they will most likely send a backup. Am I on the right track?"

"It's called a piggyback. Yes, I would expect one," answered Alex.

"So let's flush him out."

"Flush him out? How?"

"Let's go to Colorado on a treasure hunt for the Chiseled P stash. We'll be in the mountains far away from harm to the family and we'll flush him out. It will be just like in the movies."

"Jake, this isn't a game, this is your life we're talking about here. There's a lot of open space in the Colorado mountains and it would not be hard for someone to hide from us, but it would be very easy for them to find us."

"That's the spirit…hide and seek with the piggyback for the Chiseled P stash."

Alex broke out laughing along with Jake at his suggestion. As serious as it was, it was good to laugh. "Maybe we can come up with a plan," said Alex, still laughing.

"Good. Then I can assume that I've been promoted from 00½ to 001?"

"Let's say, 00⅞."

# Sixteen

"Mrs. Kramer, Doctor Harrington will see you now. Go right in."

"Thank you," said Connie as she placed her magazine atop the others on the table. Moving toward the office door, as directed by the smiling receptionist, Connie entered the spacious office of Dr. Doreen Harrington.

"Come in, Connie. It's good to see you again," she said while greeting her at mid-room. "How have you been?"

"Fine, thank you, Doctor."

"Please call me, Doreen, Connie. Let's sit here on the sofa, shall we? It's more comfortable."

She followed Doctor Harrington across the office and although it was their third meeting, it was the first time she actually noticed how striking Doreen was. Her hair style was stunning, at a length that complemented her features while casting the slightest hint of auburn coloring. Connie estimated her age to be a few years younger than hers, but it was evident that the doctor allowed time from her schedule to include exercise. Something that she herself promised to do, but failed to accomplish. Connie noticed her walk was one of confidence, giving the impression that the doctor had at one time modeled, and if not, her eyes and smile should have demanded it. The doctor's suit was tailored but not pretentious and also complemented her lines. In a word, Connie would have to describe Doctor Harrington as classy.

Connie took her place and adjusted her position trying not to appear uneasy. "Thank you for seeing me again, Doreen, I know I must be complicating your schedule."

"Don't you worry about my schedule, Connie," she said offering a smile. "I always have time for you. So now, tell me what's been happening in your life."

Connie released a big sigh before saying, Doctor… Doreen, can I be open with you? What I mean is, if you ever get the chance to talk with Jake, you won't tell him what you and I have discussed, will you?"

"Let me reassure you, Connie, what we say here, stays here. I am bound as well as protected by law not to speak of my Doctor-Patient relationships. No, I won't tell Jake, or any other person, including the courts. You may and must speak freely, Connie, or I cannot be of any help to you."

She paused and watched Connie's eyes indicate that she was absorbing the sincerity of her comment. "Would you care for a soft drink, Connie?"

"Yes, diet please. Sometimes Jake frightens me," she said without prompting, and then fell silent.

Doreen stood and moved slowly to the office refrigerator while asking, "Frightens you…how?"

"I don't mean to imply that he would hurt me or anything like that, but last night he had a very bad experience. Doctor, if you could have seen his eyes."

"What about his eyes?" she asked, while taking her place and setting the drinks in front of them.

"They looked possessed. I've never seen such a deep red in a person's eyes…almost a purple."

"Tell me about last night, Connie."

Doctor Harrington listened closely to Connie as she recounted her husband's latest light experience. She watched Connie's gestures and expressions as she relived the incident of finding Jake trembling in the chair until he was reduced to tears. The doctor observed Connie as she too began to tremble as she spoke of finding Jake's nosebleed and haunting red eyes as he glared at her while she knelt at his side. She was happy with Connie's release yet couldn't help but feel troubled for she also knew that this was only the surface of her true sentiments.

"What do you think he meant by his statement, 'I can't stop them from hurting,' Doctor?"

"I'm not sure, Connie. What do you think?"

"Well, I thought it meant that by exposing those who caused the harm he could stop the hurting of the victims. But I don't know."

"Did you ask Jake what he meant by it?"

"I tried, but he refuses to talk about last night at all. I think he is embarrassed about breaking down."

"There's nothing shameful about crying."

"You and I know that, but trying to convince him is another trick. I believe he thinks he washed last night's encounter down the shower drain. That was the first night in our married life that we slept in separate rooms."

"How did that make you feel?"

"It hurt."

"Go on."

Connie reached for her diet Coke before continuing as did Doreen, not out of thirst, but rather not to rush Connie. She could see tears forming in the corners of Connie's eyes.

"Jake is all I have, Doreen. I don't have any friends. No close friends that is. Oh, I have acquaintances. The girls at work…we chat about things, but mostly they just want to gossip and I'm not into that, so there is no relationship. There's Cindy, our neighbor. She's very nice and we talk when we see each other outside, but that's occasionally and mostly on weekends or summer evenings. I have my sisters and brothers who live out of state and sadly, we really don't have much in common anymore other than childhood memories. Everyone is leading their own lives.

"Jake is really all I have. He's my life and I love him with all my heart. We have been blessed with two wonderful kids, whom I love and am very proud of, but still Jake is my life. One day soon our kids will be gone and he and I are going to find ourselves in full circle. Just he and I starting alone all over again. But now, Doreen, I'm so afraid that's not going to happen. I feel that I already lost him months ago and he's just here on temporary duty. God is going to recall him soon and I'll be alone once more. I don't know how I will stand it. But the part that hurts the most is…I feel he is slipping away from me while he's here and I don't know how to stop it."

The tears were free now and Doreen handed her a tissue while keeping one for herself as well. "All our lives we shared everything, Doreen," said Connie. "All our plans, dreams, our likes and dislikes, even our fantasies; but always…always, there was love and respect. However, that was before his accident. It's not that way anymore and I don't think Jake realizes it. I know it's not his fault, but that doesn't stop the hurt."

"Why do you think he was returned to us from the light, Connie?"

"I don't know and may God forgive me, but sometimes I wish he hadn't been because I can't stand being shut out this way. I don't know if I can go through the trauma of loosing him again."

Connie was crying now. Softly at first, but she continued until she yielded to her emotions. Doctor Harrington moved to her side and took her in her arms and although it went unnoticed, she cried along with Mrs. Jake Kramer. Her colleagues may have considered her actions unprofessional, but her heart told her it was good therapy…good for the both of them.

"I'm sorry, Doreen," she said while wiping her eyes and regaining her composure. "I really didn't intend to break down. I usually have better control of myself."

"Please, Connie, there's no need to apologize. I imagine you've been holding that in for quite some time."

Connie didn't immediately reply but Doctor Harrington could tell that she was correct. She stood and made her way to the refrigerator, then returned to refill their glasses.

"Connie, have you talked to Jake about the possibility of him talking with me?"

"Only once. He's won't have any part of it and he made that very clear. I don't want to create any wedges between us so I don't dare mention it again. But I do wish he would think about it. I believe you could help both of us."

"Well, you're right in not bringing it up again. He'll call when he thinks he needs me and I'll be here. Connie, I want you to take this card. It has my private number on it that will bypass any screening by the answering service. Just remember you can call me anytime, day or night. I'm here to help you."

Connie accepted the card and added, "I guess I can no longer say that I don't have anyone to talk to…can I?"

"No you can't, Connie…not anymore."

# Seventeen

"…so, Mother, if things continue to go well I should have some free time next month and will plan to come home for at least a long weekend. Give my best to the family and please stay well."
Sending my love,
Heinrich

When the letter was finished it was neatly folded and slid into the envelope. Once sealed, stamped and addressed he would drop it off at the front desk for mailing the first thing in the morning. Rich had selected this particular motel for its location. He was looking for a place that put a little distance between the Sandman and himself while avoiding a great deal of windshield time getting to his assignment. The I-70 exit at Cloverdale gave him the best of these two requirements.

Returning the stationery to his travel bag he rechecked the charge on his cell phone before placing it atop the grip and within easy reach. Rich moved to the unused queen bed that was doubling as a work surface. Opening the end flaps of the smaller of the two cardboard boxes that he had carried in from his SUV, he gently placed the contents on the table in order of their assembly. Rich considered the occasions of having these projects as his quality time. He would plan, create, check and double-check everything for no detail was too small or insignificant. While most people would try to surround themselves with friends, Rich avoided them, for friends would die and leave you. So he made it a practice to travel alone, eat alone and sleep alone. A practice that he had adhered to for years with no regrets. If he got lonely he went to visit his mother.

Raising a large box of Blue Tip matches, Rich examined it from all angles before placing it back on the table. He surveyed the Ziploc bags containing a modest amount of mercury fulminate, potassium chlorate, and smokeless power. He could feel a rush forming as he squirmed in his chair while thinking about creating a simple, yet effective detonator. With the chemicals blended to his specification he emptied the matchbox and filled the container with powder. Once this was done, he cut the blue tip heads from the match sticks and gently placed them in one corner of the box along side the powder. Rich then slid the box back into its jacket and placed the detonator aside.

He had located a spark igniter on a shelf next to the barbeque grill supplies at a local hardware store that would supply enough spark to ignite his detonator. Depressing the red button several times Rich checked and rechecked the quality control of the spark before moving ahead to the final step. Indeed this was the procedure that separated a beginner from an expert. While most demo men would have cut the hole for the igniter before filling the box, Rich thrived on the rush of cutting the hole with the box filled with explosives.

Using an X-Acto knife he carefully cut a small hole into the cardboard box, then inserted the ceramic tip of the igniter through the powder toward the match heads. The final step to his detonator was to add several layers of duct tape to seal the box and keep the igniter in place. The only thing remaining was to remember not to recheck the red button again.

Rich stood and arched his back in an exaggerated stretch while complimenting himself as he looked down at his homemade detonator. He moved to the cooler sitting on the floor next to the bath and removed a cold can of Pepsi while concentrating on his next task. This little project would be as dangerous and exciting as the first, but left zero room for error.

Moving to the larger cardboard box Rich removed one plastic jug of kerosene fuel and a box of generic soap without additives. The mixture was simple and there were only two safe ways to combine it: 50/50, or half and half. Either way was good. It was his practice to store this cocktail in glass bottles for obvious reasons, but today he was anxious to try a new method. Although unproven he hoped it would offer distinct advantages. He removed the box of Ziploc freezer bags from the cardboard box and pulled one large bag free and expanded the opening. Slowly he filled the pouch half full of his unique blend then sealed the opening. He then placed the mixture inside a second bag for the sake of safety. This container proved to be leak-proof when turned end to end and offered the ability to adapt to unusual shapes. The big plus of course was that, unlike a glass bottle, this package would disintegrate in the fire. Rich leaned back in his chair admiring his creation that would be worthy of special recognition, but then, no one would ever learn of this new incendiary pack, or as he called it…the Napalm baggie.

Every good project deserves a back-up plan and with Plan A in place Rich began to concentrate on Plan B. This plan was simple and as effective as plan A, but a little more sensitive. For this he would use the remainder of the kerosene fuel, a wireless security alarm kit, complete with a motion detector, which was also purchased at the hardware store and a few grams of C4 plastic explosives. The C4 was not available at the hardware store, but it was readily accessible to him when needed.

Rich rolled the C4 into a long pencil-shaped ribbon before looping it into a coil and setting it aside along with the other items. This done, his plan was now complete. He had two simple detonators that could be used to ignite his Napalm baggies. He would wait until dark to survey the Kramer and Associates building and spot the best location for the baggies before selecting the appropriate detonator. Having done that he would stand by for a go-call from the club. The waiting didn't bother him, but the concern that they might not reassign him this troubleshooting assignment did. Rich knew it was foolish of him to force Kramer off the road and equally foolish to have taken an open shot at Kramer in Manny's parking lot, but the rush of erasing a mark in front of a G-Man was too much to ignore, even though it was stupid and strictly against procedures. Rich didn't think the members had learned of this error, for if they had, he too could end up in someone's pick-up bag. The phone not ringing certainly didn't help to ease his uncertainties.

The drive east along I-70 was brief and relaxing for Rich in spite of the poor visibility due to rain, but then in his experience rain offered great cover. He exited the interstate at Six Points Road after electing to take the back roads to Kramer and Associates. His mission was clear as he reminded himself, "This tour will be strictly a reconnaissance and not, I repeat NOT, a search and destroy." He would go undetected, evaluate and ascertain the best placement for his devices to fulfill his assignment. That is all. Rich eased the pressure of his right foot atop the accelerator while simultaneously flipping the turn signal lever before pulling into the Kramer and Associates rear parking area. As he brought his vehicle to a stop he mentally began to review his mission for the night while repeating once again, "This mission is strictly a reconnaissance." Rich sat quietly in his SUV watching for any signs of movement in or around the area. Once satisfied that he was alone he stepped clear of his vehicle and moved across the graveled lot.

"Twenty-two minutes," he said to himself. "Twenty-two minutes was all that he needed to get in and out of the Kramer offices." He looked around the table for something to write on and removed the napkin that had wrapped his dinner utensils. With pen in hand he then printed: Time: 22 minutes max.

"Coffee?" she asked as she placed a menu on the table.

"Black please," he answered without looking up.

She paused for a moment before turning and walking away. Rich looked at the menu that was in dire need of a face-lift due to hundreds of handlings. The 70 West Auto/Truck Restaurant was barely visible through the yellowing plastic cover on the menu. He decided not to touch it.

"See anything you like tonight?" she asked while placing his coffee on the table.

"Not really," he replied, again without looking at the waitress. "Tell me about the specials."

"There's the Mac. That's a beef Manhattan with choice of two sides and the salad bar. The Peterbilt is fried chicken, two sides and the salad bar, and the Freightliner…that's white fish, sides and salad."

When Rich didn't immediately answer she added, "You can always have the buffet."

"Is the chicken any good?"

"We have a lot of truckers eating it," she answered. "But you don't look like a trucker."

"Thanks. I'll have the chicken."

"One Peterbilt coming up," she said as she finished writing on her pad. "Anything else I can get you?"

"Water, please."

This time Rich did look up as she turned and walked away. He continued watching until she disappeared behind the swinging kitchen doors. He then returned to his napkin and drew two rectangular boxes, one larger than the other. In the small one he penned the letter A and the larger one became B as he reviewed his plan.

Once he had confirmation for this assignment he would do one of two things. A, blow up Jake Kramer in his truck, or B, blow up Jake Kramer in his office. It was a simple, yet effective plan. Looking back at his napkin he wrote truck, seat and igniter. He sipped his coffee and reviewed Plan A. Open driver's door, slide the seat forward to the stop and place a baggie under driver's seat, set detonator between baggie, secure igniter to seat glide at the floor board.

Rich took another sip of coffee as he continued his thoughts of Plan A. Kramer opens the truck door and gets in. He finds the seat too close to the wheel to drive comfortably so he slides the seat back. The travel strikes the red button of the igniter the igniter triggers the detonator, the detonator sets off the napalm baggie and…Amen. This accident could be the result of an unnoticed gas leak that was caused by the mishap weeks ago.

He began to make the letter B but turned the napkin over as a glass of water was placed on his table. "Your chicken will be right out," she said with a nice smile. "I told him to add a couple of thighs to your order…no extra charge, my treat. Unless you like breasts better?" she added coyly.

He looked up and studied his middle-aged server for the first time, and said, "I like both…thank you."

She held the eye contact momentarily and then moved to another table. Rich went back to his napkin and printed Plan B. Office, desk, space heater. In review he mentally stepped through this procedure. Enter Kramer's office, press C4 in a circle on the back of the space heater located behind the desk. Place one baggie next to C4 charge and one inside desk drawer on top of the detonator. Attach wireless motion sensor inside the leg opening of the desk.

He paused for water then continued with this thought. Kramer enters the office. Kramer moves the chair at his desk and steps behind the desk, triggering the motion sensor. The sensor in turn triggers the detonators at the heater and the desk drawer. This unfortunate accident could be the result of a faulty oil heater.

"Dinner's ready. Better put your work aside," she said as she placed a huge plate of food in front of him. "I hope you're hungry."

"I'd better be," he replied as he looked at his dinner. "Thank you."

"Anything you need just ask for Meg. I'll be back to check on you."

"Are you Meg?"

With a wink and a smile she replied, "And don't you forget it."

Rich finished his meal as well as the strategy concerning his two campaigns. The Kramer and Meg campaigns. As of tonight there was nothing more he could accomplish with the Kramer mission for he hadn't officially been re-awarded the assignment. But the same wasn't true for Meg, for he had already received several go ahead signs from her.

"How was your dinner?" she asked while collecting his dinner plate and bowls.

"It was very good, but I couldn't eat it all."

"How about I put it in a to-go bag for you?"

"That would be nice, and speaking of to-go, I was just wondering what you were…" His question was interrupted by the cell phone ringing in his breast pocket. "Excuse me…incoming," he said.

Rich watched Meg carry the dishes away as he answered, "Yes?"

"Are you available?"

"Yes."

"Please enter your PIN number followed by the pound sign."

Looking at the phone unit he pressed 0108# and returned the set to his ear.

"We have one high profile troubleshooting assignment if you are available. Please press one for yes, or two for no, followed by the pound sign."

Rich was at a crossroad in accepting this project, for there was no assurance that it would be Kramer, as Kramer may have been reassigned during his Washington job. "May I ask the first initial of the last name in this assignment?"

"If you are interested press one for yes, or two for no, followed by the pound sign."

That answer was expected as he looked again at the key pad and pressed 1#.

"You have accepted our offer of a high profile assignment. Details will follow within hours. Stay available."

The dial tone then buzzed in his ear as he could only wonder if he had been reassigned or transferred. The idea of not fulfilling this Kramer project did not sit well with him as he contemplated a go-ahead without approval, but then that would not sit well with the club either.

Meg, noticing her customer had finished his call, approached Rich's table offering his carry-out and a smile saying, "I believe you were about to ask me something when your phone rang."

"Excuse me?" he said as he was startled back to reality.

"Just before your phone rang…you were going to ask me something," she repeated.

"Oh yeah, I was about to ask if you…" Once again they where interrupted by the cell.

"I'm sorry…this will only take a moment. Yes?"

Meg watched as her nameless customer began to smile as he listened to the conversation. She watched him press the key pad a couple of times then listen to the phone before placing it down on the table.

"Well, that didn't take long. Now, before we were so rudely interrupted, you were saying?"

Rich looked into her haunting deep blue eyes and said, "Check please."

The rain had picked up once again and the turn signal reflected off the wet pavement as he approached the Kramer and Associates building. Pulling slowly to the rear of the parking lot he backed up to the graveled area which was shadowed by the building and turned his lights and wipers off. Rich sat motionless inside his SUV listening to the rain pounding against the metal roof while watching for any signs of movement in the building as well as the immediate area. In due time he shut the engine off after assuring himself there would be no need to make a hasty exit.

With the aid of tinted windows Rich sat obscured in his black vehicle watching water roll down the windshield and listening to the thunder and the occasional crack from a lightning bolt that briefly lit his cover. He was not afraid to get wet, nor was he apprehensive about getting started. He simply was not in a hurry, for this time he was going to do things right. There would be no tolerated interference and no mistakes. This mark was his assignment and he was not to be denied. Once again he looked at Kramer's truck as it also sat obscure in the shadows of the building. He knew it was unlocked from his earlier visit and Plan A remained a distinct possibility. He also looked at the service door to the rear of the Kramer building that was lit by a single overhead fixture with no more than a hundred watt bulb. The back entrance was completely hidden from street traffic. He recalled the ease of entry and the helpful lighting inside that complemented a trusting owner, thus making his movement to Kramer's office quite simple. His Plan B was now becoming a favorite for several reasons. Primarily, Jake Kramer would most likely be the one to step behind his desk and two, entering the building undetected, setting the baggies, placing the detonators and leaving undetected for a second time was a challenge and offered a huge rush. Three, the blast would be bigger and he liked that idea.

The rain was now coming down in sheets, the thunder echoed and the lightening was sharp as he recounted the experience of setting in the bush along Hill-293 in Nam on just such a night. As his poncho shielded him and his weapons from the rain he sat motionless in a crouched position not more than twenty meters from a platoon of North Vietnamese Regulars. For two hours he sat stealthily until the rains eased and the Gooks picked up and moved out. His legs were numb and cramped to the point of being useless. If spotted he would have found it necessary to shoot until shot, but that didn't happen.

"I wonder if the renowned Sandman could have done that?" he asked himself. "I wonder if he's as good as I am. We were never squared-off during training but I've heard stories about his keen eye and senses. Still, I stayed active in service while he became a civilian and one day soon that will make the difference."

The rain eased to just a light sprinkle as Rich opened the door and stepped out into the crisp, misty air of a rainy night and moved once again across the graveled lot at the rear of the Kramer building with baggies in hand.

# Eighteen

Standing on the edge of his patio, shielded from the rain by the vinyl covering, Alex watched the reflection of lightning off in the distance dancing across the sky. He looked at the darkened woods to the rear of the property and couldn't help but believe that the Gospel was back there today. A thought that he didn't care for or couldn't prove, but it was one that he must accept nonetheless. He also had to accept the fact that if Ziegler was here then a piggyback assignment had been ordered and accepted on his friend, Jake Kramer. Alex knew that Jake was a hot item and a huge threat to so many people that, well, it was inevitable. He reassured himself that he would make every effort to protect Jake, but he was also aware that even if he would act as his bodyguard he couldn't guarantee his safety. No, Jake Kramer was vulnerable and that was that.

A double clap of thunder startled him into a slow pace across the concrete as it reminded him of a shotgun blast from the 12-gauge that he often carried into the bush in Nam. He sometimes preferred the shotgun in dense terrain, but tonight he could do without those memories.

While looking out toward the sky that reflected the lights from metropolitan Indianapolis he stuck his hands in the front pockets of his jeans and asked, "What are you up to tonight, Gospel?"

"What's who up to tonight, Mr. Sanders?"

Alex turned with a quick shift, "Cindy…I didn't hear you come out."

"I didn't mean to startle you, honey…you looked like you were having a private moment. Perhaps I should leave you to it."

"No, it's alright. Please, stay with me. I don't think I want to be alone anymore."

"I've made some fresh coffee; can I bring you a cup?"

"Please."

Cindy smiled and nodded before adding, "I'll be right back."

Alex watched her move about the kitchen collecting mugs and filling them with hot coffee. "I really don't deserve her," he spoke honestly. "I don't deserve to share her life or the right to help raise Becky. I am not worthy of any of this, but I am forever thankful."

"Talking to yourself again?" she asked while handing him the coffee.

Alex smiled while shaking his head no and pointed to the patio couch, "Let's sit."

"It's good to have you home again, Alex. It seemed like you were gone for a long time."

"It was a long time, but I think that's behind me now. I've turned in my papers."

"What do you mean turned in your papers?"

"I've done my time. I'm retiring."

Cindy sat up looking at Alex with surprised and excitement. "Alex, you didn't tell me that you were going to retire after this trip. You're not kidding are you? You really don't have to travel anymore? Really?"

"Really," he replied. "I really don't have to travel anymore without you…and Becky of course. However, I was considering taking a little trip out west with Jake, but we should only be gone a few days. He wants to try his hand at camping in the mountains, so I imagine a couple of days will satisfy his curiosity."

"Oh, Alex," she said as she settled back in the couch and rested her head on his shoulder. "You don't know how wonderful that sounds and how long I've waited to hear you say it. I never told you before but there were so many nights that I laid awake and worried about you. I was afraid that one of your reactors would explode and you would be killed by the radiation. I know that sounds silly, but I love you so much and we need you. I don't care if you take a camping trip with Jake. The fresh air and exercise will be good for both of you."

She leaned forward to offer him a kiss that he accepted without hesitation. As he held her tight in his arms he made a silent promise not to lie to Cindy from this day forward. She will never know of his past and will always believe that he is a retired nuclear reactor engineer. But in retirement they would have no secrets …other than little things like the real purpose for going to Colorado after the Chiseled P stash.

"What would you think of moving to New England and buying a quaint little bed and breakfast after Becky goes off to college next year?"

"You're full of surprises tonight, aren't you? Well, I'll help pull up stakes and follow you anywhere, Mr. Sanders. Just don't leave me behind."

Alex gently touched her cheek as he tilted her head upward and kissed her like it was the first and the last time.

"This is much better than being alone out here. I'm glad you came out."

"You were only alone because you chose to be, honey. I can tell when you have things on your mind. Just remember, I'm here if it's something you can talk about; I'm always here."

"I love you, Cindy, never forget that. No matter what, I love you."

"And I love you too, no matter what."

They were holding one another as they listened to the rain pinging against the vinyl covering above them and heard the echo of thunder that reported a clash somewhere miles away. Alex couldn't dare look into Cindy's eyes at this moment for fear that his weaker side might surface. Holding her in silence was best and she didn't object.

"Well now...don't you two look cozy?"

"Becky," said Cindy, "come on out. What have you been up to?"

"Nothing like you guys."

"Okay, Becky, you caught us. So what's up?"

"I was wondering it you guys would care if I asked Margaret to sleep over Saturday night?"

"Of course you can…anything special about tomorrow?"

"Just to hang out. We're going to watch the Elton John concert on Pay-For-View. They're doing it live because it's an AIDS fundraiser. If you guys give us a credit card we can pledge and watch it. It's almost as good as being there. Can we make a pledge?"

Cindy immediately shook her head yes as Alex shook his head no and said "absolutely not."

"Alex," they both said together. "Why not?"

"Because."

"Because why?" asked Becky feeling a little hurt.

"Because I just happen to have four tickets, third row center that are going to go to waste if you three girls don't go with me."

"What?" No way! No way, Alex!" screamed Becky.

"Yes way and if I were you I'd call Margaret and make plans before she accepts someone else's invitation. That is of course, assuming you would like to go and you won't mind your mother and me tagging along."

"Mind…mind…no we won't mind. Oh, Alex, thank you…thank you." Becky reached down and gave him a huge hug and a kiss on the cheek. "I'm gonna call Margaret."

Alex watched her dash through the door and jog past the kitchen. He was smiling as he turned to Cindy. "She's excited."

Cindy just sat quietly looking at him.

"What?"

"Oh, nothing," she answered.

"Come on, Cin…what is it?"

"Well, I was just wondering how you're going to come up with four tickets to a Elton John concert that sold out in five hours, four months ago."

"I have my ways."

"You better or you're going to have three very disappointed and angry women having their way with you."

Alex moved closer to Cindy and took her hand before saying, "Well, Mrs. Sanders, if you're going to have your way with me…perhaps you should know that I practically have the tickets in the bag at the will-call window."

"Practically?" she repeated. "Practically?"

"Yes, practically." Alex sat up to explain. "See Cin, it's an AIDS fundraiser and they held seats to be auctioned off to the highest pledge. Good seats that make them desirable, you know a few rows up front and center. Well, I've made a bid and as of my last check, my bid is golden."

Cindy nodded in understanding before saying, "I see. You know that's all well and good, honey, but if I were you I'd remember three things."

"What would that be?" he asked through a smile.

"One…I'd keep in mind the look in Becky's eyes when you told her about taking her to the concert. Two …I would keep a close eye on the latest bid. And three …You should never, never tell me how much Saturday night cost us."

Alex shook his head in agreement before asking, "Cindy…how much do you have in your life savings?"

Cindy kissed him on the cheek before standing to gather the empty coffee mugs then said, "Not enough to get you out of this and the four of us into Elton's concert. Coming?"

"Where are you going?"

"To get ready for bed."

"But it's only a little after nine."

"I know. You coming?"

"You bet."

# Nineteen

Connie had finished the dishes and the kitchen was once again in order. As she folded and placed the hand towel on the counter she turned off the overhead lights, leaving only a soft glow from the under-the-counter lights. Pausing at the glass sliding door to look outside at the rain-soaked patio she listened to the silence in her home. During dinner Jake had very little to say other than a few brief answers to questions about his day.

How was your day, Jake?…Fine. What did you do today, Jake?…Nothing much, had lunch with Alex. When did he get back, Jake?…Last night. I'm having a nervous breakdown, Jake…Fine.

Connie continued venting to the glass doors which somewhat relieved her hostilities before making her way to the den where she was sure to find Jake horizontal in his recliner.

"Mom…Mom…guess what? You'll never guess," shouted Margaret as she hurried down the hall.

"No, I most likely won't, honey, so why don't you tell me."

"Becky invited me to go to the Elton John concert Saturday night. Ain't that too wild?"

"Isn't that too wild?" corrected Connie.

"Yeah…it is," she said. "Alex got the tickets as a coming home present. I can go, can't I?"

"Of course. You go and have a good time."

Margaret was still bubbling with excitement as she turned to call Becky to accept her offer when she paused and turned back to her mother. “Mom, are you alright?”

“Sure, honey, I’m fine, why do you ask?”

“I don’t know. You just seem down, I guess.”

“Just a little tired, but thanks for asking. You better go and make your call, it’s getting late.”

Connie watched Margaret dash down the hall before she looked in on Jake. She wasn’t comfortable with her daughter picking up on her mood tonight, but some things couldn’t be helped and she really didn’t feel much like pretending. The den was lit only by the restrained glow of the lighting above the book shelf. Still she could see her husband in his chair looking out the window at whatever. She reminded herself that she planned to speak to Jake about joining her at her next appointment with Doreen. The plan was the easy part; the catch was having him listen and agreeing to it. Placing her plan on hold for the moment she made her way down the hall to remove her make-up, change into bed clothes and turn down the bedspread. Not that those things had priority, but she needed time to think.

Jake had overheard Connie and Maggie’s conversation from the hall and nodded with amazement at his neighbor’s resourcefulness. Alex did have a way of pulling off the impossible like finding those tickets, but Jake knew that his friend would fall short in his efforts to protect him. That would be the absolute definition of impossible and it should not be his responsibility anyhow. Jake reminded himself to make that clear to Alex the next time the subject came up.

The suggestion to go into the mountains of Colorado after the Chiseled P gold would only be a temporary fix and if they were successful in defeating his would-be assassin, the club would simply reassign another. "You have done this to yourself, Jake Kramer. No one's to blame but yourself and your bold disregard for discretion. Alex tried to tell you, Judge Ryan tried to tell you, but no, you had to go on live television and show the world how you can identify the bad guys." Jake stopped himself for this self-abuse was pointless. He had more important things to think about so he started to form a mental list: Contact accountant and lawyer about the sale and transfer of Kramer and Associates to Wesley; arrange for an administrator and update last will and testament; check on the legalities involving the Grand Cayman bank account; arrange a trust for JJ and Margaret; arrange details at Mortiman's Mortuary. Jake stopped himself and leaned forward in his chair.

"I though you might have fallen asleep, Jake. I'm going to fix a Coke…would you care for one?"

"No thanks, Connie. Can I help with the dishes?"

Connie shook her head in disbelief then answered, "Maybe tomorrow."

Moving past him she took her seat in the chair to his left. "Jake…honey, we really need to talk. I know this is probably not a good time, but I don't think there'll ever be a good time."

"I know I haven't been much company to you lately, Connie, but I have things I need to work out."

"There was a time we worked things out together."

Jake looked at her without responding, for she was right. They always shared the bad times as well as the good. But this was bad enough that she needed to be spared for her own good. She could not know nor be present when he…

"I've decided to retire completely from the business, Connie. I didn't know how you might react to that," he said without hesitation.

"Retire? That's what this is all about…retiring?"

"Well, yes. That and the fact that I'd like to turn the business over to Wesley."

"Jake Kramer, you should know that I don't care if you retire. Am I to understand that you have been moping around here for the last week because you want to retire?"

"Well, there is another small item. I'm meeting with Thompson, Cole and Padgett first thing Monday morning to arrange for a sales agreement between Kramer and Washington giving him full ownership of the company. I want to sell it to him, Connie…for one dollar."

Connie leaned back in her chair and repeated, "One dollar?"

"Too much?"

Connie leaned forward once again as she said, "Honey, when you let it out you really let it all out, don't you?"

"Not really, there's more. I would like for you to retire too. Let's travel. Let's go places and do things while we can."

"But, Jake…"

"No, no. No buts about it. Maggie will be at IU this fall and JJ is all but on his own. You and I can run away and hide from the rest of the world, wild and free."

"Is that all, Jake, or is there another bomb you want to drop?"

"That's pretty much enough for now. So are we going to retire together?"

Connie didn't immediately answer, but instead stood and walked to the window in silence watching the rain drops roll lazily down the glass.

"What is it, Con? Is it the business? I thought you would be happy for the Washingtons?"

"Oh, Jake," she said as she turned to look at him. "You know I'm happy for them and I'm glad you're not going back to work. That's fine with me. But we have to think about JJ finishing his schooling and the tuition expenses for Margaret to go to IU this fall. I realize that the title to the business is clear and you're going to walk away with a dollar, but is that enough to get us by? I don't think so, Jake! I think I should put my retirement on hold."

Jake smiled for he knew it was now time to share a hint about their financial future. He stood and walked to her and placed one hand on each of her shoulders. "Connie, honey, I think you had better sit down."

During the next five-minutes Connie sat motionless, speechless, and dumbfounded while listening to a mini-confession from her husband.

"You have how much, where?"

"Enough…you really don't need to know the details right now, just know that its legal, it's in a trust and in the event something should happen to me, just get in touch with our accountant, Lester Ledger, he'll know what to do."

"Jake, you can't just tell me that you have money, lots of money no less, hidden somewhere and just leave it like that."

"Yes I can. Please don't ask me things that I can't tell you right now, Connie. You'll just have to trust me on this. So, will you consider retirement?"

She didn't immediately answer, however, Connie eyes indicated that she was giving it plenty of thought, especially with the news that they may be well off financially.

"Daddy, did Mom tell you about Alex getting tickets to the Elton John concert tomorrow night?" said Margaret as she entered the den and interrupted their conversation. "Ain't that too cool?"

"Isn't that too wild," he corrected.

"Yeah I know, too wild. That's what Mom said too."

"Actually I overheard you two girls talking earlier. Maggie, good for you. I know you'll have a great time."

Margaret turned to leave the room saying, "I'm going to bed a little early. Tomorrow's a big day. Good night, Mom…night, Dad."

"That sounds like a good idea, Margaret," said Connie. "I'm tired too. What about you, Jake, are you ready for bed?"

"In a few minutes. You go on back, I'll be along shortly."

"Promise?"

"Promise," he repeated.

Connie rolled over and looked at the clock for the third time since taking her place in the bed and still saw no sign of her husband. She refused to get up and go to the den to check on him and also refused to get annoyed at him for putting her off again. However, at the moment she was losing the getting annoyed battle. She still had concerns to discuss with Jake but again he seemed to be avoiding her. "He's putting me off again," she sighed. "I wonder how Dr. Harrington would advise me to handle this situation. Would she suggest I go and get him or just go to sleep?"

# Twenty

In her spacious condominium located in the prestigious, gated community on the southwest side of Carmel, Dr. Doreen Harrington was ten minutes into her thirty-minute workout on the stair-climber. Directly in front of her was the attached bookshelf holding the notes from her meeting with Mrs. Jake Kramer. Reviewing the highlighted areas she read, "Sometimes Jake frightens me…such a deep red in a person's eyes …Jake trembling in the chair…he was reduced to tears …Jake's nosebleed…we slept in separate rooms…I feel he is slipping away from me…sometimes I wish he hadn't…I don't know if I can go through the trauma of losing him again."

Dr. Harrington looked away from her notes and caught the flash of lightning through the window as a thunderstorm made its way across Indiana. Speaking to no one she quoted Connie's remark from memory, "I can't stand being shut out this way and I don't know if I can go through the trauma of losing him again."

Picking up a yellow highlighter Doreen pulled the felt through the words "trauma of losing him again," then replaced the cap as the timer signaled that her thirty minutes were completed. Grabbing a towel she wiped the perspiration from her brow as she stood and watched the rain blowing across the third floor balcony.

"Connie, my dear, dear, Connie. I believe one of the first things we need to address is dealing with the reality of losing Jake. I feel there are many who would rest easier if they didn't have to concern themselves with Jake coming forward and exposing them." She tossed the towel across the bar of the stair-climber and added, "I know this to be true for I have one such person who has confessed this during his sessions. Yes, Connie, I fear there may be one or many who have secretly planned to take him away from you again."

## Twenty-One

"Good night, Meg. Be careful driving, it looks like it's still raining out there and the roads may be slick."

"Night, Harry. I'll be careful."

"Ya want me to drive ya home, sweetie? I'm shut down 'till six in the mornin'," said the pot-bellied, ball-capped, bearded trucker at the counter.

"Thanks, but no thanks," she answered.

Meg stepped through the double glass doors of the restaurant onto the wet pavement of the parking lot and hurried towards her aging Buick parked in the very last row. "Why couldn't you have been that cute chicken-lover asking to drive me home," she said to herself as she fought with her purse for the keys. Meg's old Buick started on the third try, reminding her that it was time to replace the battery before the car failed to start altogether and she would be forced to accept offers from the likes of Mr. Pudgy at the counter. That thought actually gave her cold chills.

Pulling away from her space she failed to notice the black SUV that followed about sixty meters to her rear as she made her way north on Highway 231 toward Greencastle. The rain had all but quit by the time she turned into her drive and came to a stop alongside the red pickup truck near the garage door. Again she failed to take notice of the slow-paced SUV trolling the street in front of her modular home.

"How were the kids tonight, Gladys?"

"They never give me any trouble, Meg. They're always just as sweet as can be. How was your night?"

"Slow. Tips were rotten, except for one guy who left me ten dollars."

"Ten! Hell, Meg, you should have brought him home. Never throw back a keeper."

Meg nodded in agreement as she removed a diet Pepsi from the shelf inside the refrigerator door. "I'm beginning to think you've hooked the last keeper, Gladys."

"Speaking of my keeper, I'd better get a move on… you know how Clyde gets when he thinks I'm late…but I guess that's not all bad," she added. "Are you scheduled this weekend?"

"Harry put me down for Sunday breakfast. I hate to ask, Gladys, but can you watch the kids?"

"Sure…Clyde and I'll come over and take them to church with us. Maybe after services we'll come by for breakfast at Mommy's work. The kids like that," she replied as she stepped toward the door.

"Thanks, Gladys, I don't know what I'd do without you. Be careful going home.

It looks like the rain is going to start up again."

From a hundred meters west of her home he watched the interior light come and go inside the parked pick-up truck, followed quickly by the headlights as the red Ford slowly rolled off the graveled drive. Sitting quietly behind the wheel he continued to watch until it safely disappeared around the curve and made its way to the main road ahead.

Sliding clear of the seat Rich stood and took a moment to allow the light mist to rinse his face as he inhaled the fresh country air that brought back memories of home. Stepping lively he made his way across the country road and became invisible among the shadows of the woods bordering Meg's lot. It was a short distance to the farm fence that he easily cleared and disappeared between the rows of corn before making his way to the back of her house.

Rich could see her clearly through the glass doors standing at the kitchen table, shuffling through the day's mail. He watched as she dropped the envelopes, arched her back to stretch and ran her fingers through her hair. Feeling the early signs of a rush, his heart rate increased while he examined the contour of Meg's lines.

As Meg disappeared into the hallway he turned to follow her to the rear of her home. He saw her reappear through the sheers that played in the breeze, thanks to the opened window in her room. The rain was beginning to pick up slightly as the light mist gave way to a sprinkle, but it was a small deterrent to this veteran of inclement weather.

Standing among the corn stalks this scarecrow of a figure continued to watch as she sat on the edge of the bed, removed and tossed her tennis-shoes into the corner and began massaging her feet one at a time. He saw her move out of his view before returning to the bedroom wearing the last two of her basic garments. Rich's heart accelerated as she turned her back to him then unhooked and removed her bra before again disappearing.

The weather began turning as the sprinkle became a hard rain by the time she returned to the bedroom wrapped in a blue-striped bath towel. The thunder rumbled as she brushed her hair and he gasped as it fell against her back like soft silk. Rich's knees grew weak as she removed and placed the bath towel aside before gathering her nightwear from the foot of the bed. The lightning flashed, then cracked through the adjoining hollow as he stood shaking with anticipation before she turned toward him and raised her arms to allow the red teddy to glide down across her body until it came to rest at the top of her thighs.

The wind had increased and was moving the rain in sheets keeping ahead of the thunder and lightning as nature's symphony surrounded Rich's fantasy in this sea of corn. By the time his waitress rolled back the bed covers and slid her legs between the sheets Rich was completely soaked with a combination of rain and perspiration.

The weather had been upgraded to a severe thunderstorm but he didn't care, for Rich was unthreatened by Mother Nature. He was now standing in a small pool of water and heavy mud gasping for breath as she leaned toward the night stand to switch off the lamp that turned the room dark.

Rich continued breathing deeply as his fantasy faded and he returned to reality. The rain sprayed across his face washing away his sin and giving him control of his body once again. He stood relaxed as he was at home here among the elements, for here he was alone and sensed neither fear nor commitment to anyone other than himself. He had experienced the rush and had satisfied his need to need. The heavy black clouds rolled as the thunder rumbled and echoed across the skies of central Indiana as fierce lightning continued to crack and flash showing its might. Rich raised his face to the rain and cried to the heavens, "*But I say unto you, that whosoever looketh on a woman to lust after her hath committed adultery with her already in his heart*…Matthew 5:28."

# Twenty-Two

Jake quietly made his way to their bedroom finding Connie sleeping on her side with the sheet drawn tightly across her shoulder. Standing at the footboard he never took his eyes off her as he removed his clothes and made himself ready for bed. How long he'd been standing silently watching her sleep he didn't know nor did he care, for she was stunning and he never grew tired of her beauty. There could never be a question of their love, devotion, or respect for one other and there had never been a time when they couldn't share their dreams, desires or secrets…until now.

Jake moved carefully around the bed and took his place beside his wife, taking special care not to awaken her. He preferred to have her sleeping at this hour rather than her wanting to talk about things he couldn't discuss. Perhaps that's why he delayed coming to bed this evening, for he sensed the need to be alone for awhile to think a few things out. However, the longer he sat, the more he thought and the more he realized there was no way out.

Locking his fingers between his head and the pillow Jake watched the blades of the ceiling fan rotating above him, for he was about as sleepy as a rabbit in a python pit. Oddly enough, that was most likely a fair description of his situation. A rabbit in a python pit attempting to evade the inevitable.

"Organize," he said to himself. "I must get organized and take care of things in order of their importance. I need to make a list. Create a trust for the kids and Connie. Sell the business. No, that doesn't need to be at the top of the list. Connie could always sell the business if worst came to worst."

Jake's mind was on a hunt now. Hunting for peace of mind, but instead he began arguing with himself. He wanted to start plans for the homeless shelter, arrange a trust for the folks at 800-missing and buy some land to bring it all together. "But maybe I should put together a board of directors like they do in corporations to take care of the details in the event of my…go ahead, say it …in the event of my death. MY Death," he repeated again and again to himself, trying to get used to it.

Jake continued monitoring the fan blades and retained his statue-like posture between the sheets. The only body part moving was his heart that had been pounding loudly enough to surely wake not only Connie, but also Maggie down the hall. His mind continued to juggle issues with and without his prompting. At one point he saw Walter Driscoll's body lying on the ground and for an instant Driscoll opened his eyes and smiled at him. Jake shook his head trying to clear that ugly thought. "I'm not afraid of Driscoll or any other Driscolls in the world. I'm not afraid to die, but like Alex said, 'Don't be in a hurry.' Still…I need to get my ducks in a row. I'll talk to Bernie, my legal eagle, first thing Monday morning and have him…no, no I'll call him tomorrow and make an appointment. I shouldn't put these things off because…because Connie and I should travel. Get away from here and do things together while there's still time. Maggie can stay with the Sanders. Alex won't care. Hold on a minute here. Maybe it's not such a good idea for Connie to be around me. I mean, what if something happened to me while she's around? What if she sees it? What if she sees who did it?"

Jake could feel his skin becoming clammy as the pounding of his heart echoed in his ears. He continued staring at the fan that appeared to have gained speed, but that wouldn't be possible. "It's not possible for that fan to go faster," he reminded himself trying to focus on a different subject. "That is unless someone got into the house and tampered with the controls. Maybe they loosened the screws in the connections. But it doesn't look like it wobbles, or does it?" Jake squeezed his eyes closed and looked again at the blades. "No it's not wobbling."

His mind was set on full alert and his body was set on freeze. "Everybody dies," he said as he continued talking to himself. "It's just not everyone knows when, except for those on death row. They know when. I don't know when. The terminally ill don't know when, but like me they don't know how long until…hey, I'm better off then they are, thank God, for I don't have to suffer from the pain they have every day. I can't wait to see Wesley's face when I tell him about the business. I wonder if he'll change the company's name? Washington and Son? Wesley and little Jake? I don't care. It'll be his do with whatever. I wonder if Connie will remarry? After all, she shouldn't spend the rest of her life alone. She's a beautiful young healthy woman who'll need companionship in the years ahead. Not that I've done such a good job at that lately. But I've got a lot of responsibility and commitments to take care of. She should understand that. She probably would if I'd just explain it to her. Still, I think she shouldn't live the rest of her life alone. I'll talk to her about that… stop it, Jake…change the subject. Think about something good. Think about…what? The future? I swear that fan is wobbling. Maybe someone did get in here and loosen the screws. Maybe they sharpened the blades too. The edges look shinier than the rest of the blade. No, maybe not. I'm not sure about that, but I do know they're spinning faster. If Connie remarries I hope she finds someone who will be good to her. She'll have to look a long time to find someone who'll be better to her than I am…I was…that is up until a few weeks ago. I guess she won't have to look very hard at all will she? That fan is definitely wobbling."

"She'll have to be careful too if the men learn that she has money. Maybe she could just go to the stable and rent a stallion when she wants to ride, but I don't like the idea of her playing in the hay like that. I probably shouldn't mention that to her though. NO! She'd get mad. But hey…the kids will look after her and she'll keep busy with the grandkids. Grandkids?"

Jake had the sheets wet with perspiration at this point; however, he hadn't moved a muscle other than his heart pounding against his chest. His mind was busy with sorting, planning, debating and being confused.

"I need to get away he thought. Me and Alex should take off and go locate the Chiseled P stash, and flush out the bad guy. I should buy a white cowboy hat when we go because I'm the good guy. I never owned a white cowboy hat. I never owned a cowboy hat of any color. That fan is really spinning now. I should get up and turn it off before it falls. It's shaking too. Hey, I can't move. What's going on? I'm numb all over. I can't move my arms. Those blades really are shiny. It looks like razor blades have been stuck along the edges. I gotta get up…It's gonna let go…Driscoll did this. Wait, I can't move…help me! Help me…it's falling! It's falling…falling! Can't let it fall on Connie. Move Connie…get out! Wake up! Move! Get out! It's going to hit us…get out!"

"Jake! Jake…what the hell are you doing? You just about pushed me out of bed. Stop it! Honey, look at you…you're wringing wet."

Jake opened his eyes and focused on the fan still firmly affixed to the ceiling and rotating at the low speed.

"Honey…you've had a bad dream. What was that all about?"

Jake managed to unlock his fingers that were still tucked under his head and slowly rubbed his hands across his face. "I don't know, just a dream I guess."

"Well whatever it was I must have made you mad because you just about had me on the floor."

"No, I don't remember that. In fact I can't remember anything about it now."

Jake was sitting on the edge of the bed checking the clock and learning that it was hours away from morning.

"You go rinse off," said Connie. "I'll warm some milk. It'll help you sleep."

Connie found Jake seated at the table as she turned away from the counter with a tray holding two mugs of warm milk, one white and the other chocolate.

"Honey, I was going to bring this to you, you didn't have to come after it."

"Thanks, but I needed to move around."

"Feeling better?"

"Yeah, sure. It was just a dream."

Pulling her chair free she sat the warm milk on the place mats in front of them. "Do you want to talk about it?"

"No. It was just a dream," he replied, while sipping the warm drink.

"Jake…"

"Connie, please. It's been a long day. Let's just enjoy our milk and get you back to bed. It looks like the rain has stopped."

"Good-night, Jake," she said as she slid her chair from the table, leaving her warm chocolate milk untouched as she left the room.

"Night."

# Twenty-Three

Jake had been up and moving quietly about the house for several hours. He had taken his coffee and newspaper out to the patio in order to enjoy the sweet smell of the fresh air that remained after last night's thunderstorm. But Jake's mind wouldn't stay focused on the newsprint. He found himself looking up toward the wooded area behind his home and visualized someone waiting amid the trees to complete their troubleshooting assignment. This made the entire visit to his back yard extremely uncomfortable as he reluctantly gave in to his fear by gathering his mug and paper and returning to the confines of his home. Jake found himself pacing around the kitchen once again while arguing with himself about his new paranoia. Obliviously he couldn't stay locked inside the house forever, but was it foolhardy of him to walk about so freely? Taking a sip from his coffee mug, Jake noticed how badly his hands were shaking as the black coffee swirled around the inside of his mug.

"How did all those men who charged the beaches at Iwo Jima find the courage to take the next step?" he asked himself while knowing he must come to grips with his anxiety if he was to expect any peace of mind. "Don't think about it, just do it…just do it," he said softly. Jake moved to refill his coffee, gathered his newspaper and then in a somewhat rebellious manner returned to the fresh air of his patio to catch up on the news.

Connie heard the patio door slide as she made her way down the hall, but was unable to tell if Jake had come in or gone out. In her current mood out would have been the best for both of them. She spotted him standing next to the patio chair looking directly overhead at something, or perhaps nothing at all, for he just stood motionless looking up. While standing at the counter Connie watched him for what had to be two full minutes before he took a seat and spread his newspaper across the table. With hot coffee in hand she started back down the hallway to sort laundry and occupy herself with whatever busy work she could find. Her mind was completely absorbed with unpleasant thoughts this morning that mainly revolved around her husband.

With just about everything in the back of the house washed, wiped, or changed, Connie grabbed her coffee mug and made her way back to the kitchen. Her next plan was to take the grocery list that she had created and spend the afternoon at the market. This, she had decided would accomplish two things. One, she really did need to restock the cabinets and two; she would continue to display her irritation with Jake. But admittedly, this would only be effective if he noticed.

Before leaving to do the grocery shopping Connie paused at the patio door to look out at Jake and noticed him frozen above the newspaper and scratching at the newsprint with his fingers. She watched his statue-like posture for a few moments before shaking her head and turning away determined not to be the first to prompt a conversation. Upon locating her purse and car keys she said to herself, “If he wants to be left alone…then I’ll leave him alone.”

Jake remained motionless at the patio table while staring at the City and State section of the *Indianapolis Star*. The index finger of his right hand was drawing circles around the lead article which read in part, “*Cooper Development’s Eel Valley project approved.*” He read on, “…has cleared the last hurdle with a majority vote for approval by the members of council. This is a step in the right direction for growth and job opportunity for our county,” said council president, Josh Shepard.

“…it’s disappointing and displays total disregard for mother nature and our heritage,” said lead historical activist, JoAnna Wilder, while announcing plans to “rally at Eel Valley today in hopes of creating public awareness for the need of legislature to further protect the virginity of our wetlands, as well as the historic dwellings of our nation.”

Wilder’s reference was directed at the planned demolition of the mid-19th century home of Doctor Horris Benjamin Stockton, who, according to Wilder, was reported to have been instrumental in aiding runaway slaves via the underground railroad during the eighteen-sixties. The Stockton home, in dire need of repair, had also served as a local hospital by caring for the well-being of the underprivileged as…

Jake continued to read, “…we offered the Stockton home, without charge, to any person or group who would assume the responsibility for relocating it to a site of their choosing, reported Ms. Dell, a Cooper spokesperson. But no reasonable or acceptable offer was presented by the close of business on Friday; therefore, the dwelling will be razored…"

Jake's index finger was drawing a large unintentional circle around the entire article at this point as he continued to reread Wilder's plea to protect this piece of history. His mind was creating an image of Eel Valley although he had never visited the area. He could see images of Canadian geese as they formed their glide formation before skirting across the water to complete their landing. The counterclockwise rotation of his finger around the newsprint remained constant as he became aware of a stinging sensation and numbness in his hand that slowly moved across his wrist and up his arm. "Oh, no." he whispered, "not again."

An obscure picture of the Stockton home began to develop between his eyes and the newspaper. Jake raised his head to look at the woods behind his house, but the image of Stockton plantation stayed centered between him and the trees. Eventually, the woods slowly faded as a portrait of the Doctor's home became dominate. He could see tall willow trees swaying in the breeze surrounding the white two-story structure. Directly to the left of the porch entrance there was a bay horse standing idly in front of a black covered buggy swatting flies with its tail. The lilac shrubbery was in full bloom and the flowering baskets hanging along the porch swayed lazily in the gentle wind.

By now the feeling in Jake's arms was gone as he realized once again that his body was being adsorbed by an unyielding numbing. He did not need to close his eyes to see this Stockman picture for it was clearly in command of his vision. He watched as three men, one white and two black, move cautiously from the rear of the house into the woods before disappearing among the trees.

Still seated at the patio table, Jake realized that he had not developed a headache nor were his ears ringing. This was another totally new experience for him. It was like watching a big screen silent movie. Jake made no attempt to move, for it would have been useless, because his body was numb from his feet to his neck. Knowing it would pass, he sat passively and absorbed the experience. As he concentrated on the Stockton home he saw another figure moving slowly to the house from the rear. He was also black and appeared to be very cautious, if not terrified. Jake noticed that his lack of confidence did not ease as he approached the home, but apparently he gave in to hunger and fatigue and made his move to the porch at the back of the house.

Jake could feel the numbing sensation moving gradually up across his throat, but he knew it was pointless to protest, so he concentrated on as much of the picture as he could see. The house was beginning to fade as it yielded to the colorful shower of lights flowing down from the heavens. "My lights," he said aloud, "they're back." As he watched in anticipation of the lights counterclockwise rotation he realized there was no rotation at all. Instead the lights grew in width, expanding left and right like a curtain across a stage. “This isn’t right,” he said, “They’re too wide. They’re not rotating. TOO wide!” But the lights continued to flicker and dance like a dangling stand of pearls.

The prickling needles he felt in his body prior to giving in to the numbness was now above his mouth, as again he sensed his tongue growing thick, dry and useless. Jake looked directly at the string of lights before him as there was little else he could do. His body had succumbed and his vision was controlled, but there was no headache or thunder in his ears. This in itself was a desirable experience regardless of what was to follow.

The first facial image to appear was small and somewhat blurred. Jake watched as it began sliding down the beads of colored lights while growing in size as it neared the center. He had no clue as to who this man with the evil eyes and devilish grin was, but he knew he would never forget him as long as he lived, for there was something sinister about this nameless face. His image held center stage in Jake’s show, but gave way to intruders when two male figures approached and separated the light as they walked forward. These two full figures struck a remarkable resemblance to the black men he had seen earlier leaving the rear of the Stockman home before disappearing into the woods at the rear of the property.

As Jake watched the central figure glance back and forth at the two black men before him, his attention was drawn to six more people strolling through the light and joining the first two. The central figure began to laugh at the sight of the others as additional figures surrounded him shouting and pointing in anger. Jake sat helplessly numbed by the needles and controlled by the vision as the screen became filled with men and women of all ages pointing and shouting at this man in the center of his string of colored lights.

Jake's movements were unintentional and uncontrollable for his body was numb but his mind was indeed coherent. He knew he was standing, but that is not to say that he asked his body to do so. He heard the deck chair fall over behind him; however, that is all he heard, for little, if anything around him made a sound. The lights were still clear and directly in front of Jake as were the images, but he could see through them to his own trees beyond. Jake was walking now, yet he didn't know why or to where. Nevertheless, there was no need to fight it for he knew he would certainly lose. Jake Kramer was going to wherever the lights wanted him to go and that was that.

Connie held the car keys in her hand and was making her way to the garage when the sound of the patio chair falling against the concrete caught her attention. As she walked to the patio door she saw Jake standing upright holding a crumbled section of the newspaper in his hand and staring at the sky. Now completely confused by what he was doing, Connie instinctively paused to watch him through the glass. Forgetting all the promises she made to herself about ignoring him today she reached for the door as Jake turned around to enter the house.

"Jake, are you alright?"

Jake heard her words but was unable to speak due to the numbness that had overtaken his body.

"Jake! JAKE, answer me!"

Any effort to answer Connie was hopeless as Jake simply continued to walk across the kitchen.

"Damn it, JAKE! Don't do this to me! I can't take much more of this!"

Again Jake heard her plea but couldn't respond as he walked silently past her and entered the garage making his way to the shop truck.

"Damn you, Jake Kramer. I don't need this," she repeated while rushing to him and beating on his back in anger. "I don't deserve this!"

Jake wanted desperately to turn to Connie but could only respond to the commands of the light before him. He opened the driver's door of the truck and raised the overhead garage door via the remote on the visor. Without hesitating, Connie released the passenger's door and climbed inside while pulling the door closed behind her with an aggressive slam.

Jake never acknowledged her presence in any manner. No eye contact, no verbal questions and no physical gestures. He simply pulled the truck gear lever into the 'R' position and backed out of the garage.

They rode along in silence for several miles as Connie also assumed a statue-like position, although unlike her husband's, hers was out of anger. She did take notice of his driving skills however, for they were textbook perfect. Always in the center of his lane, never failing to use his turn signals, not one mile per hour over the posted speed limit and most noted, there was no tailgating.

"Would you at least mind telling me where we're going?"

There was no answer from Jake as he held his firm posture behind the wheel.

Connie was fuming now and shifted her position as best she could, while confined to her seat restraints and turned towards Jake. It was then she allowed herself to notice his sedated appearance. His eyes never blinked. Not once.

"Jake…Jake, are you alright?"

Again no answer. He only responded with an occasional head movement when he checked the rear view mirror before changing lanes.

"Jake, damn it, you're scaring me," she said. "Where are we going?"

The Kramer and Son truck merged cautiously into the west bound traffic of I-70 at the SR 267 ramp then drove on in heavy traffic at exactly sixty-five miles per hour. Connie rode along concerned and confused, not only as to where they were headed, but mainly as to what had gotten into her unresponsive husband. Turning back in her seat she folded her arms across her chest and attempted to prepare herself for whatever was to come.

Jake still had no feeling in his body from the eyes down as he watched the road ahead through the faint vision of the strands of lights and the images they brought with them. They didn't obstruct his view, but they were disturbing. He had heard every word Connie had said but it was useless to attempt a response. He accepted this, but that didn't mean he liked it. Taking the exit ramp from the westbound lane, for reasons unknown to him, he moved north along the dual-lane highway for several miles before slowing to make a left turn past the Welcome to Eel Valley sign.

"I know where I'm going," he said to himself.

"Eel Valley?" said Connie aloud. "What in the hell brought you to Eel Valley?"

# Twenty-Four

To one less dedicated to their cause, one would have thought this was a dismal display of support. But for lead naturalist and historical activist JoAnna Wilder, today's protest rally was the first step in the long walk to success.

"People…people…quickly now…gather your signs and form a line. The press is coming. Form a line now …Quickly!" she shouted through the hand-held amplifier. The group responded immediately by selecting a makeshift sign from the stack and holding it with both hands above their heads before falling into place next to their fellow protesters. Ms. Wilder proudly led the group by chanting into the bullhorn. "Leave our land alone…leave this house alone…leave our land alone…leave this house alone."

"This is the big protest rally that we drove all the way out here from the city to tape?" asked Ken McGill, the assigned cameraman from WAXU news center. "Four women, one old man and two kids? We better take the pepper spray with us, Sheena; things could turn ugly pretty quickly."

"Well…we're here," said veteran news reporter Sheena Jawblondski. "Let's see what we can salvage. There's always a story in it somewhere, we just have to get lucky. Listen, Ken, when we start taping, let's try to get this mob directly behind the tree-hugger," she said while looking down at her notes. "That way the group will appear to look bigger."

"Good plan," replied Ken. "I'll keep the shots tight and we'll edit in some footage of the swamp and that fire trap they're trying to save," he added while pointing to the house.

"Save the sarcasm, Ken. Let's get-r-done."

"We are standing here in front of the soon-to-be demolished home of Doctor Horris Benjamin Stockton. Looking off to the west you can see the wetlands of the Eel River, located below this beautiful bluff, which is home to water fowl and other wildlife, as well as countless varieties of plant life. However, if Cooper Development has their way, this natural habitat and all its life-giving properties will be doomed, including this once proud and prestigious home in front of me built in the mid-eighteen-sixties. With me this afternoon is historian and naturalist JoAnna Wilder who organized this rally on behalf of the local chapter of the National Historical Society and the Wildlife Preservation Committee.

"Ms. Wilder, just what do you hope to accomplish here today?"

"May I first say thank you for joining us today, Ms. Jawblondski. It's always a pleasure to visit with the professional reporting staff of WAXU news."

"Oh brother," whispered Ken from behind the camera. "Lay it on, babe."

"We are here to draw the public's attention to big business and their dollar-driven atrocities in regard to nature and historic dwellings such as the one behind us. We believe that the planned flooding of the natural wetlands of the Eel River just to create scenic home sites for the well-to-do is…"

Ms. Jawblondski held the microphone and a poised head to give the appearance of deep concern and interest until she was distracted by her cameraman who was pointing toward the pick-up truck that came to a stop in the gravel drive at the Stockton house. The Kramer and Son logo painted on the cab's door sent an immediate thrill-chill throughout her body. Turning back to her interviewee, Ms. Wilder, who was in mid-sentence of an endless speech, Sheena squared up to the camera and said, "Thank you, Ms. Wilder, and good luck in your efforts. Reporting from Eel River Valley, this is Sheena Jawblondski of WAXU news. CUT! Lets go, Ken!"

Jake and Connie Kramer cleared the truck and were making their way past the hedge row along the side of the Stockton home. Jake continued on like a remote-controlled robot as Connie followed closely behind. Neither was aware of the small crowd of naturalists who were chasing the news reporter and her cameraman. As Sheena Jawblondski grew near she began to collect herself and mentally prepare for her would-be interview.

"That camera better have fully charged batteries, mister, or you're dead meat."

"You hold him, Sheena…I'll shoot him," replied Ken.

"Mr. Kramer…Mr. Kramer…Sheena Jawblondski, WAXU news, may I have a moment, sir?"

Jake and Connie both heard her calling out, but their pace never slowed as they walked alongside the overgrown shrubbery.

"Mr. Kramer, may we ask what you're doing here in Eel Valley?"

Connie was the only one to answer. "Go away… leave us alone."

They continued walking for about fifty meters into the woods behind the Stockton home before Jake suddenly stopped and stood perfectly still while looking around the area. The pursuing group of newscasters and protesters all paused behind Jake, with the exception of Connie who took her place along-side him. Only the faint rustling of the wind through the leaves could be heard as no one spoke. Ken held the camera fixed on his prime subject as Jake pointed to separate locations throughout the woods before kneeling down and picking up a handful of moist soil.

JoAnna Wilder turned and whispered to her assistant, "Jane…run back to the van and bring back a can of the spray paint we used on the signs. Hurry now!"

Jake could feel the numbness in his body easing as he stood and let the soil sift through his fingers. He looked through the strands of lights as the likeness of the figures gradually took their places in the woods. In one instance, two images remained side by side while motioning to the ground. Jake reached out for Connie's hand as they made their way in the direction of the couple who were motioning. He could now feel Connie squeezing his hand as the numbness was continuing to leave his body.

"I know what this is," he whispered through a dry mouth in a nearly muted voice.

"What is it, Jake?" asked Connie. "What's here?"

Sheena Jawblondski had moved directly behind the Kramer's and cautiously placed the microphone between them while turning to her cameraman who promptly gave a thumbs-up sign, signaling that he was receiving the audio.

"What is it, Jake?" asked Connie again.

"It's a graveyard."

As Jake moved carefully to the young black male and female, their figures began to fade as they rose up the strand of colored lights that had been surrounding them. They ascended until they eventually disappeared.

"Here," said Jake, while making a scuff mark with his right foot in the soil. "They're here."

Jake proceeded through the woods with Connie in hand and the WAXU news staff in tow, filming each step and every word of their sparse conversation. Behind the camera crew an ecstatic Ms. Wilder was spraying DayGlo orange paint on the marks made by Mr. Kramer's foot for she was confident that she was receiving justification to halt the destruction of this homestead.

He had rubbed a total of forty-three marks in the rich soil behind the Stockton home. Each mark had resulted in the image before him rising up the column of light towards the heavens then fading until only two remained. The numbness in his body was gone now, leaving Jake weak and exhausted. Nevertheless he moved to the last figures. Jake focused on a black male, wearing bib overalls and a dirty gray shirt standing next to a large red oak tree holding a shovel. He gave the impression that he was crying as he rapidly shook his head no…pleading to whoever would listen. The central face remained visible and never changed expressions. He continued to sneer and laugh as he was joined by the man in bibs. As only Jake could see, he watched the colored lights pulsate and flicker as the last two images were drawn down the light strands until they vanished into the lingering haze above the soil.

Connie could feel Jake's hand quiver as he said, "They're gone."

"Who's gone, Jake?" asked Connie softly.

"Mr. Kramer, Sheena Jawblondski…WAXU News …what did you see here, Mr. Kramer? Why were you making marks in the dirt?" she asked while offering the microphone to him.

Jake and Connie both ignored the news reporter's questions, as he led Connie away and strolled toward the bluff that offered a magnificent view of the wetlands and the Eel River below the Stockton property.

Sheena and Ken followed as closely as they dared trying desperately to eavesdrop on any conversation the Kramers had.

"Excuse me, Mr. Kramer, I'm JoAnna Wilder. We were holding a people-for-the-land rally here in hopes of drawing public attention and support for protecting the wetlands and Doctor Stockton's home. Mr. Kramer, you may not know that Doctor Stockton was a great humanitarian and devoted his life to healing the sick and aiding the needy. In peculiar, he was a beloved friend to hundreds of runaway slaves. In fact he…"

"In fact…Ms. Wilder," interrupted Jake. "In fact, your Doctor Stockton was a depraved man. He preyed on the helpless and desperate whenever the opportunity allowed and sadly, as you pointed out, that was all too often."

Wilder found herself gasping and stepping back as a result of Jake's remark. "I beg your pardon, Mr. Kramer. That can't possibly be true. Why, our research into the Doctor's history indicates that he prevented countless slaves from being captured by hiding them from bounty hunters…"

"He hid them there," said Jake as he turned and pointed to the area behind them. "He hid them there under your orange paint. Each one suffered and died while under the care of your Doctor Horris B. Stockton, Ms. Wilder."

Sheena Jawblondski again looked at her cameraman who offered her another thumbs-up sign assuring her that he was recording her news scoop. What he didn't share was his concern for the camera's battery life and his lack of a replacement. He knew telling her that the camera was not working would most likely mean that he wasn't either. He decided to keep his mouth shut and an eye on the battery charge indicator, and shut down when there was no conversation. He removed the handkerchief from his rear pocket and wiped the perspiration from his brow that was not the result of the heat.

"Mr. Kramer…can you shed some light on your accusations against Doctor Horris Stockton? What exactly happened here?" asked Jawblondski.

Sheena felt herself shudder and she looked into the deep red color of his eyes as Jake turned slowly and looked directly at her. She wasn't certain if she was going to receive an answer, but she was sure that Ken better have the lens focused on a close-up of Jake Kramer's eyes. If this man was not special, he certainly possessed something special. Sheena swallowed involuntarily and cleared her throat before speaking again.

"Are you to have us believe that Doctor Stockton murdered his patients rather than saving them?"

"Yes. Perhaps he would not have thought so in his state of mind, but yes, he let them die while in his care."

Connie had taken Jake's left arm and moved in close making her presence and support for her husband known. JoAnna Wilder also moved into camera view, as much as space would allow, knowing that any publicity for her cause was good publicity.

"Can you tell us what happened here, Mr. Kramer?" asked Jawblondski.

Jake looked at Sheena in silence, as once again she held her breath hoping that he would respond rather than retreat. She slowly exhaled as Jake began to speak softly.

"Stockton enlisted the aid of his stable boy Moyo to seek and befriend runaway slaves during the early eighteen-sixties. They took their guests in, fed them, offered them rest and shelter. They did, on occasion, let a few go on their way north. Some went to Wisconsin or Michigan and some made their way into Canada. But these select few were released simply because there were too many to detain and they were used to spread the word about the Stockton safe house."

"Please…go on Mr. Kramer. How and why did he take their lives?" asked Jawblondski.

"Basically, it was for research. He actually used his patients as we use mice and guinea pigs in today's laboratories. Stockton treated the wounds of black runaways, and also many locals by using primitive and crude variations of drugs, herbs, and potions."

"And what exactly was Doctor Stockton trying to develop in his makeshift laboratory?" asked Sheena as she pivoted the microphone between Jake and herself.

"He was attempting to find a cure for infection. By the time most of his patients sought his help their wounds were badly infected. He had little success with compresses while attempting to clean the puss from their wounds. In the majority of cases he was forced to send them on their way minus a leg or arm that had developed gangrene. This was years before antibiotics like penicillin and sulfa were developed."

Jake paused and looked to Connie, thus giving the impression to Sheena that he was finished and intended to leave.

"Just one more thing, Mr. Kramer. How did Doctor Stockton persuade the blacks to stay at his home? Weren't they suspicious and reluctant to trust the whites?" she asked while glancing quickly at her cameraman Ken, who again offered her a nod of the head and another thumbs-up signal. Ken's right eye however was alternating between keeping his subjects centered in the frame and the battery power indicator that was shrinking and had changed from green to yellow. He could see Jake turn back to Sheena as he quickly depressed the record button once again and the viewfinder came alive with Jake's face centered in the lens.

"As I mentioned, Sheena, he enlisted the help of his stable-boy Moyo. Moyo was taken from his homeland in Zimbabwe at a very early age and brought to America aboard the slave ship, Sea Dawg. It was Moyo's job to locate and befriend the runaways and they trusted him as one of their own. He would lead them into the basement of the Stockton house and once there, if they had no injuries, Moyo would inflict one. Usually it was a gunshot wound because the lead balls would develop infection rather quickly, and keep the Doctor happy. If the guest had scratches and scrapes from days spent on the run through the thickets, Moyo would render them unconscious and rub the open sores with unimaginable filth. So…the bottom line was, Moyo would create infections and the Doctor would try to cure them, even if it killed the patient. And that resolve brought about another responsibility for Moyo. He had to take care of burying the doctor's mistakes. Now most of these casualties were never expected to be heard from again by friends or family they left behind in the south, so they were never missed. As I said, the Doctor's intentions were good, but his methods were deranged."

Ken watched the camera's battery indicator change from yellow to red. As the charge faded so did his hope of recording the remainder of this interview between his reporter and Jake Kramer. He decided to play it cool and continue to shoot with a dead camera regardless of the results. He could always plead for mercy later by swearing that the camera never indicated low battery and that he must have brought a faulty unit. He knew that she wouldn't buy it, but she could never prove otherwise. Ken released a sight of relief as he listened to Mr. Kramer say, "Good day Ms. Jawblondski," before silently cursing his reporter as she spoke, "Why was Moyo so devoted to his employer, Mr. Kramer?"

Jake paused and turned back to Sheena while giving the impression that he was growing bored and she had intruded enough on his time, but he would oblige her with this one final answer.

"He was an addict," replied Jake, as he looked away from the camera toward the river bluff. Moyo was brought to Stockton after suffering a fractured hip at the hands of an impatient owner. Stockton treated him as best he knew, but the result was incredible pain with each step that Moyo took. Stockton eventually made a deal for ownership of Moyo's contract. As it turned out the only treatment Moyo received for pain was opium until there was no recourse but to do Doctor Horris B. Stockton's bidding."

"Then in summary, Mr. Kramer, what we were led to believe about Doctor Stockton was in reality untrue. This was not a house of hope."

"A house of hope, Miss Jawblondski?" replied Jake. "No…not at all. It was more so…a house of Horris. Good day."

Ken dropped his head in disbelief. The classic line to end an interview and he stood centered on his subject holding a dead camera.

# Twenty-Five

"Mr. Kramer, please…you must help us now more than ever. We can't let them desecrate this site. Please, Mr. Kramer…you simply must help," pleaded Ms. Wilder.

"Excuse me, Ms…"

"Wilder, JoAnna Wilder. Don't you remember? We're gathered here to bring attention to…

"Yes, of course you are, Ms. Wilder," interrupted Jake, "But I'm afraid you have confused me with someone who responds to the words, you must. Good day and good luck. Are you ready to go, Connie?" he asked as she remained tightly clinging to his arm. "I'm getting a headache."

"I'm ready whenever you are, honey."

Sheena Jawblondski was, at this point, no longer interested in JoAnna Wilder's plea for help from Jake Kramer and as far as she could tell neither was he. With microphone in hand, she made her way toward Ken McGill who was cradling his useless camera in his arms like a sick newborn.

"Did you get it all, Ken?

"I think I got most of it, Sheena," he replied without looking into her eyes.

"I'm expecting more than most of it, Ken. That was some great footage and I better not see a single sun-spot glaring across Kramer's face, or hear any wind noise whistling through the audio. I'm planning to argue with the brass for enough time to run it in its entirety."

Ken nodded in agreement but knew she wouldn't be needing as much airtime as she thought. He could hear Wilder's fast paced recruiting appeal to the Kramer's as they made their way back to the shop truck.

"But Mr. Kramer," persisted Wilder. "By your own words…this site is a sacred burial ground."

Jake stopped abruptly in his tracks causing Connie to bump into him and Ms. Wilder to stumble in the loose rocks. Raising his left hand to his forehead Jake squeezed his eyes tightly closed and remained standing still. Connie and JoAnna traded a confused glance before looking back at Jake who continued to cover his eyes with his hand.

"Honey…are you alright?" asked Connie.

Jake shook his head yes but failed to remove his hand or answer verbally.

At this point the WAXU news team was standing only a few feet away as Sheena turned to Ken and insisted, "Shoot this, Ken. I want all the footage we can get of this guy. Come on, fire it up."

"But, Sheena…I think maybe…

"I'll take care of the thinking; you take care of the camera. Shoot it!"

Ken went through the motions of filming as Sheena became the director.

"Close in on the Kramers…cut the tree-hugger," she whispered.

Jake removed his hand from his face but his eyes remained closed as he arched his head toward the sky and began shaking his head no.

"Honey, let's go," said Connie, knowing that she didn't want the world to watch her husband experience one of his personal moments in the lights if that was indeed happening now. "Please Jake, let's go home."

"No…no NO! I didn't call this a burial ground, Ms. Wilder…you did. I said it was a graveyard. It cannot be called a burial ground or cemetery. A cemetery identifies the deceased with headstones. Stockton's property has no headstones. It is also not a burial ground, for burial grounds are holy lands set aside as the final resting place for Native Americans. These were not Native Americans here, Ms. Wilder, so let's not confuse these sites shall we? This is a GRAVEYARD!" he shouted, as he pressed his right hand against his temple to ease the throbbing.

Ms. Wilder had taken a second step back, while Sheena moved closer to get within microphone range, but the stunned Mrs. Kramer never moved a muscle.

"I'm sorry if I've offended you, Mr. Kramer. I had not intended to do so. Please accept my apology."

Connie looked up at Jake who again was searching the sky, but this time without his eyes closed.

"Come with me, Ms. Wilder," he said while taking her by the upper arm and leading her and Connie toward the bluff that overlooked the river. Sheena hurried along a few steps to the rear while vividly describing the scene into a dead microphone.

"Follow me, Ken, and stay in close."

"Sheena," said Ken, "I think we should talk."

"Later, you just keep your mind on that camera."

"No problem there," he replied.

Connie, JoAnna and Jake stood quietly on the windswept bluff overlooking the wetlands in the valley below the Stockton property. Neither woman wanted to be the one to ask why they were brought here or exactly what they were expected to see, so neither woman did.

"There." Jake pointed toward the southwest with his right index finger extended at arms length. "See that large cluster of river birch?"

Neither lady answered.

"Right there…next to the bend in the river. There's a large clump of birch trees and just off to the right of them…see that large mound?"

"Yes…I do see the mound, Jake," said Connie almost excitedly. "About halfway between here and the river bend. Is that the place?"

"Yes, that's right. See it, Ms. Wilder?"

"Yes, I do, Mr. Kramer. I see it too," added Wilder in a nearly apologetic tone.

"Now, Ms. Wilder…that is a burial ground. Native American Indians have burial grounds and that mound you see along the bend in the Eel River is one of the sacred resting places for the tribal members of the Shawnee Nation. Although neither burial grounds nor graveyards have markers, they both have distinct differences. In the valley below, the dead were respected members of the great Shawnee tribe and were placed to rest with ceremonies in a holy burial ground.

Sadly, the same cannot be said for the less fortunate ones that were victimized, murdered and placed in shallow graves in the yard behind the Stockton house. Neither have markers as do cemeteries, but the burial grounds showed respect during entombment, where as only indifference was shown in the graveyard. Do you understand the difference now, Ms. Wilder?"

Connie could feel Jake trembling as he spoke of what must have been a terrifying vision to have experienced. Looking past Jake, she could see Ms. Wilder trying to grasp the magnitude and implications of the information she had just received.

"Mr. Kramer, am I to understand that there is a small Shawnee burial ground in that wetland, down there?" she asked while looking at the valley.

"No, Ms. Wilder. I'm telling you that it is a large Shawnee burial ground in that wetland down there and I'm also telling you that there is a large graveyard behind the Stockton home as well."

"Mr. Kramer, it's Sheena Jawblondski, WAXU news," she announced as she tried desperately to wedge herself between Jake and JoAnna. But Wilder held tightly to Jake's arm and would not allow anyone or anything to come between her and her new found historian.

"Mr. Kramer, how do you know that there's a Shawnee burial ground in this Eel River valley?" asked Jawblondski as she forced the useless microphone closer to Jake.

Jake didn't acknowledge Jawblondski, but answered her question to satisfy Connie and JoAnna's curiosity.

"Actually, I learned of this site from the Shawnee chief himself, Tecumseh."

"Get this, Ken," said Sheena as she whispered into the microphone. "Stay in tight."

Ken didn't reply because he couldn't hear her, but continued holding his powerless camera while staring at the dark rectangle in the viewfinder.

"Tecumseh?" repeated Connie.

"That's right," said Jake. "The Shawnee was one of the largest tribes in the Indian Nation's history. This massive tribe roamed freely across Ohio, Kentucky and Illinois, as well as all of Indiana. When the white man choked their hunting land Tecumseh fought back. He and his brother Prophet, a Shawnee medicine man, raged war against William Henry Harrison and the soldiers at Fort Vincennes, the capital of the Northwest Territory. Tecumseh and his braves would canoe down the Eel River from the north and camp in this switchback, or that bend in the river down there."

"So they came down here to hunt?" added JoAnna.

"Yes, to hunt wild game and the white man," said Jake. "The Shawnee were proud, brave and loyal, as well as being fierce and savage. They would torture captives in a horrid manner and adopted those who survived as tribe members. Some who died bravely during their torture were honored and buried with the Shawnee's own, many right below us."

"But Tecumseh's retaliations were mainly against William Henry Harrison and his soldiers at Fort

Vincennes, so they followed the Eel on south until it merged with the White River near present-day Worthington. Then they continued down the White River, short of the settlement called Bicknell, before making their way across land to attack Fort Vincennes. The Shawnee's dead were always brought back here to this Eel River switchback for burial."

Everyone stood silently looking down at the river bottom from the bluff once again. But on this occasion they were truly seeing it for the first time, as they were looking at the valley with a new found respect.

"How many?" asked JoAnna Wilder.

"Jake didn't give her a count, but said, "If this switchback is flooded, the Shawnees' great spirit will no longer be free to roam about the land."

"Mr. Kramer, if we're going to be successful in protecting these sites, you simply must help us," pleaded JoAnna Wilder. "Won't you help us, Mr. Kramer?"

As he looked across the valley, Jake replied, "I thought I just did, Ms. Wilder." He then turned to Connie who was still clinging to his arm and said. "Let's go home."

Jake and Connie turned and began making their way across the overgrown lawn of the Doctor Horris Benjamin Stockton estate toward their ride home. Today Connie had witnessed firsthand one of Jake's incredible cleansing experiences and felt the full ramification of its power. Jake on the other-hand, was quiet due to fatigue and a throbbing headache. They walked hand in hand until they neared Jake's trunk where Connie broke free and continued to the right side before saying, "I'll drive."

## Twenty-Six

As Connie lay in bed she counted the chimes from the clock down the hall striking six times on this Sunday morning. She hadn't intended to be awake at this hour, although still awake might be more like it. She could only attribute her restlessness to yesterday's experience, for she had relived the Eel River saga so many times that she was almost sorry she went along. Saturday evening hadn't quite turned out the way she had planned either. Jake was out like a light by the time she finished her bath. The thought had crossed her mind to awaken him, but she gave in to being considerate after recalling the kind of day he had. So he slept like a baby while she cycled through catnaps. Now torn between getting up at this ungodly hour on a Sunday morning or trying to force herself back to sleep, she rolled over and tucked her arm under the pillow and laid quietly watching Jake sleep.

Connie could feel her senses awaking as she freed her hand from under the pillow and gently slid towards Jake, closing the space between them on their king size mattress. She could feel her heart rate increase and short rapid breaths developing as she began to think of ways to arouse her sleeping husband. Pausing momentarily, she unbuttoned and slid out of her nightshirt before drawing herself closer to Jake, who still hadn't moved a muscle. Connie gently raised her hand above his chest and playfully drew her fingertips down across his skin. Jake however gave no response, so this only made Connie more determined.

"Jake, don't play hard to get," she whispered. Connie redrew her fingers down his chest and paused at his known ticklish spot trying to get a rise out of him. With each pass she added a little more pressure and moved down a little further.

"Mr. Kramer…it's time for you to rise and shine."

Connie meant business now. All consideration toward his need for rest had been replaced by needs of her own and hers at the moment were top priority. Placing her hand on the side of his face she leaned forward to kiss him while pressing her body tightly against his chest. Their lips never met as a startled Connie rose up quickly while pulling the sheet free from both of them in the process. Connie looked down at Jake who hadn't changed expression, position, or shown any signs of response to her sexual advances. What had startled Connie was her realizing that he was cold. As she lay against him, his body temperature was noticeably cold…too cold. She was trembling now.

"Jake," she whispered, "Honey can you hear me?"

She knew she had no recourse but to touch him again. She had to know. Fighting back her fear Connie laid her hand against his neck. His skin was certainty cold and given the fact that she didn't fully know how to check for a pulse, she didn't find one. Tears began rolling down her cheeks as she called…Jake!"

"You shouldn't start something you're not gonna finish, Mrs. Kramer."

"JAKE!"

"What did you stop for, Con? That was probably the most intimate thing you've done in years."

"JAKE!"

"Come on, get back under the covers before you catch cold," he said while reaching out and sliding his chilly hand under her waist and up along her back attempting to draw her to him.

"Jake, your hand is freezing…your whole body's cold."

"Hell, yes…you pulled the covers off."

"No, Jake, I mean it. Your body's cold. Feel yourself."

"I kinda got the impression you were about to do that for me."

Connie continued sitting upright for a few moments and managed to wipe away the tears that Jake hadn't notice until now. Trying anxiously to clear her mind of the unthinkable, she reached out once again and placed her hand gently on Jake's chest. He still felt cold. Maybe not as cold as before but perhaps that was only because she was expecting him to be…but he was still cold.

Jake watched as Connie's trembling hand reach out to touch him once again, but not with the same intent as earlier. This time she was troubled. She was giving him the impression that she was apprehensive. He could actually feel her hand shiver against his chest. "She's afraid of me," he said to himself. "She should never be afraid to touch me."

Pulling himself free of the sheet Jake stood and slid his feet into his slippers without comment.

"Where are you going?"

"To make some hot coffee, then take a hot shower …after that I'll put on some warm clothes."

Connie immediately felt her body quiver as she broke down and began crying while falling forward into her pillow.

"I'm sorry, Jake; I didn't mean to hurt you," she said between sobs.

"Yeah, I'm sorry too," he replied as he left the room for the kitchen.

A few steps into the hallway Jake paused as he listened to Connie's heart breaking. He placed his hand on his forehead but felt no noticeable temperature problem. "What in the hell was she talking about?" he asked himself. Stepping into the doorway he looked across the room as Connie reached for the tissue box on the stand. Jake slowly made his way to the bed and sat beside her while gently placing his hand on her shoulder.

"We shouldn't start our day off like this should we?"

"Leave me alone, Jake. Go and make your hot coffee."

"Look, I'm sorry…alright? One minute you're turning me on and the next you're telling me I'm acting cold. What am I supposed to think?"

Connie quickly rolled over and looked at him with her red tear soaked eyes, "I didn't say you were acting cold, Jake. I said that you felt cold. And you did. Your body was very cold and…and you didn't answer me when I called out. You…you never moved a muscle, Jake," as she started to cry again. "You scared me. I was afraid you'd…" Connie stopped to use her tissue.

"I thought that's what you wanted me to do! Hell, Connie, I was just playing my part."

"Well your part sure scared the hell out of me," she replied.

"Look, Connie, I said I was sorry. What do you want me to say?"

"Nothing, Jake, you don't have to say anything. Let's just forget it, okay?"

She felt the bed shake as Jake stood, "Okay…I'm gonna shower."

The alarm on the nightstand showed the time was now 10:07. Connie didn't know if she had cried herself back to sleep or just fell asleep, but whatever the reason for making the last three hours of this Sunday morning disappear was just fine with her. Standing next to the bed she looked back at the nightstand and noticed a long stemmed red rose in a bud vase sitting in the center of the stand. "I'm afraid it'll take more than a rose this morning, Mr. Kramer," she whispered. Once in the bathroom, Connie noticed yet another peace offering. Placed in the water glass on the counter were three yellow roses reflecting in the mirror. "Nice try, Jake," she thought. It was the roses that he had placed in the netting of the soap holder in their shower that began to make her mellow just a bit, but she refused to remove them as the overspray from the water made the petals sparkle beautifully.

Connie stepped from the shower while rubbing her hair dry with the bath towel and saw that her secret florist had struck once again. Sitting next to the three roses was a glass filled with orange juice and a cup of hot coffee with yet another rose laying across the saucer. Connie had to admit that his ploy was beginning to work.

While in no particular hurry Connie emerged from their bathroom dressed and feeling human once again. With an empty cup and glass in hand she made her way to the bedroom finding that the bed had been made and covered with what had to be the remaining roses.

"Now, I'll have to admit…that's a new one, even for Mr. Unpredictable," she said aloud.

On her walk down the hall Connie noticed fresh cut flowers in a make-shift vase, sitting in the center of her dining room table, as well as a large assorted bouquet in the center of the sofa table in the sitting room. Once in the kitchen it would have been hard to ignore the colorful flower grouping that was on the kitchen table. His creativity with substitutions for vases made her laugh aloud, for who but Jake would have used an iced tea pitcher?" After placing her cup and saucer down, Connie picked up an envelope that was placed at the base of the flowers and removed the card which simply said, "You married a Jake-Ass."

"Jake-Ass," she repeated aloud.

"You called," answered Jake from behind.

Connie turned finding Jake standing in the center of the kitchen holding yet another handful of fresh flowers.

"Can you forgive me, Con?"

Not knowing whether to laugh or cry she looked at his pathetic expression and answered, "I can only forgive you, if you can forgive me…Jake-Ass."

"Good and I love you too," he added while handing her the last of the flowers.

"Jake, I have to ask…where did you find all these flowers on a Sunday morning?"

"Kroger," he stated matter-of-factly. "Where else? Connie, let's try and salvage something positive out of this day…what do you say?"

"Oh yes, please," she replied.

"Good. I was thinking about calling Wesley and Stacie and asking them to join us on the patio. Maybe we can fire off the old grill and burn some steaks and wienies." Jake paused and looked at Connie's smile before going on. "Actually, I think it's a good day to turn the business over to him. I'd like you and Stacie to be around when the offer is made. You both should be a part of it."

"That would be nice, Jake, and it's a great idea…"

"But?" he added.

"But…why don't we just take them out to a nice place for dinner? We could take them to Little Italy. They'd like that."

"Jake hesitated as he rolled her suggestion over in his mind."

Connie continued, "I'd have to go to the store if we cook here. Let's go out."

Jake had started to pace around a bit and scratched his head in deep thought before saying, "I don't know if it's such a good idea to go out in public, Connie."

"Why, Jake Kramer…I never thought I'd ever hear you say that you didn't want to be seen out in public with the Washingtons. Shame on you!"

Jake looked rather shocked as he replied, "I never said that, Connie. You know I love that family and I don't give a damn what other people think. What I meant was…hold on, I'll show you." He paused and walked to the table bringing back the front page of the Sunday edition of the Indianapolis Star and held it up before Connie. "I just don't know if it's such a good idea to go out in public today."

Connie looked at the large font headline on the front page declaring, "Eel River Valley Sacred: Kramer decrees."

"Oh my God, Jake, look at that. Did you read it?"

"Oh yeah, I read it alright. Ms. Jawblondski should get a silver star for this one."

"Wow, this should bring out about every activist group imaginable."

"Still want to go out?"

"On second thought, why don't we have the Washington's over here for a change?"

"Good suggestion, dear. I'll give them a call."

Connie had just finished Jawblondski's commentary regarding Jake's experience Saturday at Eel River

Valley and had placed it atop the stack of colorful advertisements when Jake returned.

"Change of plans, Connie. We don't have to cook because we're going out."

"Going out? Are you sure about that?"

"We're invited to the Washington's for the afternoon. They sounded really excited, Connie. Stacie wants to show you little Jake's nursery and they have some new living room furniture that they're proud of. I couldn't say no."

"I'm glad you didn't. Would you mind if I share some of my flowers with Stacie?"

"Why not? Tell her they're from you and Jake-Ass."

# Twenty-Seven

It was a short distance between the Kramers and the Washingtons that seemed to take even less time due to the light Sunday traffic. Connie interrupted her humming of the Mamas' and Papas' *Monday, Monday* long enough to request a quick stop at the local Wal-Mart to pick up some toys for Tonya and little Jake. Jake agreed without a squabble, proving, once again, that their early morning fiasco was over and hopefully forgotten.

Pulling to a stop in the Washington's driveway Connie couldn't help but notice the face of a little girl looking out through the front window.

"They're here, Mommy, they're here," she shouted as the Kramers made their way along the sidewalk toward the front porch. "Uncle Jake…Uncle Jake," she continued as she pulled open the front door.

"I don't suppose you can tell she's very excited to see you two?" said Stacie who was following close behind and holding little Jake. Tonya ran with opened arms directly to Jake who immediately picked her up to receive a hug that only a child can give. "She's been looking out that window for the last half hour," said Stacie.

Before everyone made their way into the house Connie traded Stacie the flowers she was carrying for little Jake and both ladies were happy with the exchange.

"Jake, you'll find Wesley on the back porch trying to burn the house down with charcoal lighter."

"Hey, I bet I can help him do that," he said as he turned and started toward the rear of the house.

Shaking her head and smiling Stacie asked, "Do they ever grow up?"

"Well, I can't speak for all of them, but mine sure hasn't and I don't think we really want them to either, do we?"

"No, I don't believe we do. You have to admit that this way they're fun to watch."

"Hope you guys don't mind burgers, Jake."

"Are you kidding, Wes, we love them. Say, if you have plenty, you can roll another dog on there next to Tonya's for me."

Wesley nodded as he reached in the package for two more franks and placed them on the grill.

"We didn't expect you to feed us, Wes. Connie and I just wanted to see the kids and have a talk with you and Stacie.

"Well, it's not much of a feed, but you're welcome to all we have. What do you want to talk to us about? You sound serious."

"It'll keep. Hey…where's Granny Faye? I expected to see her here today too."

"She'll be sorry she missed you, Jake, but Granny doesn't live with us anymore."

Jake looked away from the flames on the grill that leaped from the juices of the burgers before responding, "She doesn't live with you anymore?"

"Nope. Actually she's been gone for over a week now. Gosh you wouldn't believe how much we missed her the first couple of days. You know, Jake…this is the first time in my life that me and her ain't livin' in the same house together. Like I said, the first couple of days I missed her more than the kids. She sure is special."

"You didn't throw her out did you, Wes?"

Wesley burst out laughing as he said, "Right on her butt. Caught her eating my Oreos."

They were still laughing as Jake watched Wesley's technique at flipping burgers, which reminded him of his own son who, not long ago, was headed for a career in a job like that. Thankfully he had turned his life around as well.

"Well, Wes…are you going to tell me where Granny is or not?"

"She's with Mother."

"Mother?" repeated Jake."

"Yeah, Mother. Mother's been asking Granny Fay to move in with her for sometime. I think I told you about that, didn't I?"

Jake smiled and nodded yes as Wesley went on.

"Well, I think Granny Faye thought that she was getting in our way here and maybe we needed to turn her room into a nursery for little Jake. But anyhow, she made up her mind to move in with Mother. I didn't try to talk her into or out of it. It was up to her. Just so she knows she's always welcome here if things don't work out. Jake…you're grinning at me. What is it?"

"Mother?" said Jake.

"Yeah, Mother. What about it?"

"Oh nothing, except mother is a far cry from referring to her as Granny Faye's daughter or simply Rosa. Ohhh…and this was my personal favorite. You once called her…'the one who's in the big house.' Now it's Mother?"

Jake had somehow managed to embarrass Wesley and was quick to add, "Wes, I didn't know black people could blush."

"Ahaaaa cut it out, Jake. You know, I'm probably as surprised as you are, but I'm learnin' that she's really not such a bad person. She just wasn't lucky enough to have a Jake Kramer looking out for her when she was young. Like I said, she don't make excuses for what she's done or what she's been, and I like that. She paid her dues and is really tryin' hard to make it up to Granny Faye. And if she's okay with Granny, well…I guess that makes her okay with me too."

"You've come a long way, Wes."

"Naaaaaah!

"You men have room out here for a couple of hungry women?"

Tonya directed the seating arrangements around the table making sure that she was sitting on the corner between Connie and Jake, with little Jake's highchair conveniently wedged between Connie and Stacie. This is how had she planned it and this was how it was done. With little prompting they listened to Tonya's version as to why Granny wasn't with them.

"Now she has to stay and help Grandma fix up her new place so Grandma won't have to live alone by herself."

Jake and Connie heard all about the plans to fix up Granny's old room for little Jake and how he was going to have curtains with basketball players on them and a cover on his bed with football players and how she was going to help Mommy and Daddy pick them out and…

After dinner Connie and Stacie put little Jake down for a much needed nap, then joined Jake and Wesley who had just finished loosening their belts and settled back in their chairs.

"Have you told him yet?" asked Connie as she looked to Jake.

"No. I was waiting for you girls to join us."

"What's going on?" asked Stacie while looking at Wesley.

Wesley shrugged his shoulders before answering, "Search me? Some kind of big secret I guess."

"Jake's going to retire," said Connie.

"Heck, I thought he already did," responded Wes with a big smile. "We ain't seen him around the job site in weeks."

"That just it, Wes, you guys don't need me anymore. It's time for me to move on. Get out of the business altogether."

Jake and Connie looked at each other as they sensed concern on the faces of Wesley and Stacie.

"Well, you know we're happy for you, Jake," said Stacie. "What are you going to do with yourself? Do you plan to travel?"

"Hey, Jake, that's great…congratulations," added Wes.

Jake knew it was forced enthusiasm coming from the Washington family and for good reason. They sensed that their livelihood was being threatened. No Kramer and Associates…no job…no work…no money.

"So what's next?" asked Wesley rather hesitantly.

"I'm planning to sell the business, Wes, lock, stock and barrel. Well, maybe not all the stock because some of the tools belonged to my dad and I'd like to keep at least one barrel."

Wesley tried to force a reassuring smile as he looked to Stacie but it was unconvincing.

"Have you found a buyer?" he asked turning back to Jake.

Connie could see that Stacy and Wesley were becoming very concerned as they changed seating positions several times. Sensing that Jake should get to the good part before these two kids had a stroke Connie interrupted, "Why don't you just tell…"

"…AS I WAS about to say, Wes, I'm looking for one now and I think I've found just the right person to handle the business."

"Who?" he asked immediately as he again looked at Stacie.

"Why you, Mr. Washington. You should know that I wouldn't sell the family business to anyone but family."

Connie's eyes began to water as she watched the expressions of this wonderful young family. Stacie pulled her hands up to cover her mouth as Wesley fell open mouthed back in his chair.

Connie looked at Jake as they smiled at each other and waited for a response.

"ME?" was all Wesley could manage to say.

"Yeah, Wes, you."

"But Jake, I don't know nothin' about running a business. Heck, I didn't even finish high school. And what about the money? Me and Stacie are doing alright, but…"

Wesley was standing and began pacing around the table while he continued to talk. "Shoot…no bank is gonna lend me that kind of money. And I don't know nothing about keeping books and records. Jake, this is really nice of you, but I don't think…"

"Wesley…Wes. Sit down…relax. Look, first of all remember that you've been running the day to day operations for months now. Hell, already you're doing a better job at it than I ever did. As for the books, I don't keep the books. There are people out there who do that kind of thing for a living. Give them the job. I'll put you in touch with Lester Ledger, my accountant. He'll take good care of you."

Jake could see Wesley's eyes rolling about as he was taking in every word.

Jake continued, "I'm also going to have a talk with J.B. Ashcroft and make sure he understands that continuing to deal with you would be in his best interest. I'm sure he'll keep offering you sub jobs. If he doesn't, just let me know because old J.B. and I go way back and we have an understanding about these things."

"I appreciate what you're saying, Jake, but…man! What do you think, Stacie?"

All eyes centered on Stacie as she brushed the tears away from her cheek before saying, "I think we have some very dear, wonderful and caring friends, Wesley. Two people who have stood by us, encouraged, guided and most importantly…believed in us. In some ways they've become more of a family to us than our own. I think we're very fortunate. And now…I think you should ask Jake how much money he's asking for the business because I know you can do it, Wesley. I know you can, because I believe in you too. We'll get the money somehow."

The attention turned to Wesley this time as it was his turn to volley. Clearing his throat and taking a sip of iced tea, Wesley looked at Jake and simply asked, "How…ahhh…how much are you asking, Jake?"

Jake glanced at Connie, who was smiling and bubbling with pride, before he looked back to Wesley and answered, "One dollar…American."

Two houses down the street a neighbor slammed their back door and the sound was deafening amidst the silence at the Washington's home.

"Jake, I thought you were serious, said Wesley. "You really had us going there."

"I am serious, Wesley. Very serious."

"A dollar?"

"American," repeated Jake.

"He's serious," reassured Connie while nodding yes at the same time.

"I don't get it, Jake," said Wes as he again looked to Stacie.

"Look Wes, I have things I want to do. Things I want to do with Connie. We want to travel and enjoy our time together while we still can. I want to create some foundations for abused kids and spend more time with our kids as well. I don't want to be burdened by the day to day business of Kramer and Associates anymore. I think it's time to pass the baton and move on. Wesley, I would be proud if I could pass Dad's business on to you. The idea of a dollar is for your benefit, because nobody can ever say that I gave the business to you. You earned it and you bought it.

Jake sat back and watched the Washington family soak in the news about their future.

"If it would make you two feel more comfortable I could raise the price to say…two hundred fifty thousand."

"No, no, that's not necessary, Jake. We feel pretty good about the current asking price."

"Why don't we leave it like this? I have a meeting tomorrow at ten with my attorney Gerald Bernstein who should have all the necessary paper-work for the transfer of ownership completed. Wes, you and Stacie talk it over tonight and let me know your decision in the morning."

"That won't be necessary, Jake. I would be honored to carry on the Kramer business, if it's okay with you. I just hope I don't let you down."

Jake looked at Stacie before he answered, "Wesley, you couldn't let anybody down."

"Jake?"

"Yeah, Wes?"

"Will you take my check?"

# Twenty-Eight

"Good Morning…Can I help you?"

"Jake Kramer to see Mr. Bernstein."

"Oh yes, Mr. Kramer," she said as she made a pencil note on her calendar. "Mr. Bernstein just called and asked me to tell you that he has been detained in court, but he should here in ten or fifteen minutes. If you would care to wait in his office you're most welcome to do so."

"No thanks, this will do nicely."

"Would you care for some coffee, or perhaps tea or water? We have bottled."

"Thank you, no, Miss…?"

"Fanning, please call me Lorrie."

"No thanks, Lorrie, I'm fine."

Jake moved around the reception area while scanning the countless magazines that were dispersed on the tables. He selected one with the lead headline, *Do You Need Counsel* and chose a chrome chair with black vinyl covering suitable for wasting time. As is the norm for any impatient person sitting in this environment, Jake could hear every sound in the room including each squeak of Miss Fanning's chair, not to mention the number to times she cracked her gum per minute.

Jake watched from above his magazine as Lorrie took the phone and dialed with the eraser end of her pencil before resuming her drumming against a book that was laying on her desk.

"Mom, it's me. Mom, I need a five letter word for a three-masted sailing ship."

Jake looked up at Lorrie as she hovered above her project while saying to himself, "xebec."

"I can't help it, besides you bought me the book. Come on, Mom, five letters for a three-masted ship. No …five letters," repeated Lorrie. "Okay…think about it. What about, footwear of canvas and twisted rope? Ten letters."

"Espadrille," said Jake just above a whisper.

Lorrie looked away from the phone while asking, "I'm sorry, Mr. Kramer, did you say something?"

"Espadrille," repeated Jake. "Ten letters for your shoe is Espadrille. And the other one you're looking for would be, X-E-B-E-C…the sailing ship question."

Lorrie looked down at her puzzle and filled in the missing letters before speaking into the phone and saying, "Mom…I'll call you back."

"Do you work crossword puzzles, Mr. Kramer?"

"Never…I hate them."

"But…just now you gave me…"

"I know," said Jake, "but let's say I couldn't help myself."

Lorrie ran her fingers across the page looking for a doozy before asking…"Igneous embedded rock fragment?"

"X-e-n-o-l-i-t-h," spelled Jake without hesitation.

Lorrie fired off another clue just to see if Jake was for real. “Alright, Mr. Kramer, since you’re on a roll how about buttercup plants…twelve-letters?”

“Funnelflower,” said Jake immediately. This little game, as amusing as it was, was bringing on an unwanted headache that Jake could do without. He knew the answers to these questions were coming directly from the puzzle’s author and not from his own knowledge. Jake tilted his head and rubbed his forehead trying to ease the pain as Ms Fanning submitted yet another clue to which he answered involuntary.

“Six-letters for a chubby, rosy-faced doll. Last letter is…”

“Kewpie,” interrupted Jake.

Neither Jake nor Lorrie saw Mr. Bernstein enter from his office and take a place behind Lorrie to watch the contest. Jake had slumped forward with his elbows resting on his knees and had placed his head in his hands. It was clear to him that the author was beginning to take control as a faint vision of the page slowly appeared before him. He could see the word kewpie printed in the boxes starting with 17 and going down.

Jake began quoting, “Thirty-seven down… orthogenesis. Thirty-seven across…Orsk, a Russian city, population 275,000.”

Lorrie could not keep up with Jake’s responses to her cross-word puzzle, but did manage to draw her finger across each space until Jake finished the entire page before saying, "Next page…twenty-four…one down…"

Mr. Bernstein deemed it best to end Jake's entrapment and moved quickly across the room while saying rather loudly, "Jake…good to see you. Sorry to keep you waiting."

Jake raised his head at hearing Bernstein's voice and attempted to focus on him as the crossword booklet began to withdraw.

"Oh, that's alright, Bernie," he said with a smile while attempting to stand on unstable legs. "I know how you lawyers like to give the impression that yours is the busiest practice in town."

"That's true, Jake. It helps keep the fees up. And speaking of fees, I have all your paperwork ready. If you'll step into my office we can go over them. Are you sure you want to go through with this sale, Jake?"

"Positive."

## Twenty-Nine

"You have reached the desk of Connie Kramer. I am either on the phone or away from my desk at the moment. Please leave your name, a brief message and a number where you can be reached and I will call you back."

"Connie, it's me, Jake. Where are you? You're supposed to be chained to your desk. I've just left Bernie's and have all the paperwork with me to complete the Kramer/Washington deal. By the way, Bernie thinks we're nuts. Anyway, I'm going to meet Wesley at the shop in about an hour and a half. If he has a dollar than this is a done deal and we're just days away from starting to live our lives to the fullest. Just you and me, babe. Connie, I know that I have been… let's say a little difficult lately, but not without good reason. I plan to make a lot of things clearer to you very soon. Perhaps as we stroll along the beaches of Maui…" Beep…you're message time has expired.

Jake looked at his phone long enough to press the end button before tossing it on the passenger's seat.

"I'll tell her later," he said to himself.

"Hello!"

"Stacie?"

"Yes."

"It's me…Connie. Have I caught you at a bad time?"

"No, not at all, Connie. I was just running after the kids. What can I do for you? Are you at work?"

"No. That's why I'm calling. I took the afternoon off so I could be at the shop when Jake and Wesley sign the papers. I want to take some pictures and maybe turn this day into something memorable. Then it occurred to me that you and the kids might like to be there too. I'll be happy to swing by and get you."

"Oh, Connie, that's a wonderful idea. We'd love to be there."

"I'll be by in about fifteen minutes. Can you be ready?"

"No problem."

"Good. I made arrangements for some food platters at the deli. We'll pick them up on the way."

"We'll be ready, Connie, thanks again. Oh Connie …We hope you realize how much this means to us. You have no idea how much we love the two of you."

Connie had to delay her response while she choked back the lump in her throat and finally managed to say, "We know, Stacie, and I…" then she lost her signal.

Looking at his watch Jake knew that he had over an hour before his meeting with Wesley. But should he happen to be a little late he was certain that Wesley would wait. He had two planned stops to make prior to heading down to the shop. One was to stop by the job site to ask the men to return to the office a couple of hours early for the news and a celebration. Second, he was planning to pick up some snacks at the deli and some cold beer and champagne from the Big Red Liquor Store.

"If Connie had been at her desk when I called, she could have joined this little blow out," he said aloud. "I wonder where she is?" he asked himself. "Probably called to some meeting. Oh, well, I'll try again later."

Wesley was the first to arrive at the Kramer and Associates building after lunch. He had made a special effort early in the morning to remove an old picture of Jake and his father standing in front of their shop truck which was parked under the sign at the rear of their building. Both Kramers were smiling as Jake pointed to the word Son, which had recently been added to the truck's door, while Dad pointed to the additional word on the overhead sign. Wesley knew that the photo had deep personal meaning so he had removed it in order to have it refurbished and reframed as a special gift to Jake.

He was about to enter the building to place it on Jake's credenza when Connie, Stacie and two smiling children pulled to a stop at the back lot and tapped the horn.

"Daddy! Daddy! It's me and little Jake," shouted Tonya from the rear window.

"Hey…what a nice surprise," said Wes as he approached the car. "What brings you guys down here?"

"Connie decided to turn this two man show into a family affair," replied Stacie. "Help us with the food, will you please?"

"Food! Say, this is great. Connie, take a look at this picture I had redone for Jake."

"Oh, Wesley. He's going to love it. That is the only known picture of Jake and his dad at the shop. Look how young he looks. Thank you, Wesley."

"Where do you want us to take the trays, Connie?" asked Stacie.

"Let's take them into Jake's office. Just put them down anywhere for now. The desk will be fine."

As Connie carried in the remaining sacks she managed to find Wesley giving Stacie a kiss while standing in front of the desk. "Don't go back there, Tonya," said Wesley. "That's Uncle Jake's desk and he doesn't like anyone back there."

"Oh, she can't hurt anything, Wesley," said Connie.

"No, no, that's still Jake's and she doesn't need to be back there."

"But I was only going to get little Jake's toy. It rolled under the desk."

"I'll get it," said Wes.

"Excuse me…Does anyone in here own that dark blue truck out there?"

All heads turned to the entry where a big bellied man wearing a Purdue ball cap was standing.

"Yes…it's my husband's," answered Connie. "Something wrong?"

"Oh no, ma'am, but if someone could move it, it would sure make my job of filling your propane tank a lot easier."

"Well, I'm not sure if there is a spare key here," said Connie. "Wes, do you know if Jake keeps extra keys anywhere?"

"No…I know there ain't none in the shop box."

"Maybe in his desk," she said "I'll look."

"Hold up a minute, Connie. I remember now. Jake told me once that he keeps a key above the visor in case I ever needed to use the truck. I'll go look."

"I'll come too, Daddy."

"I'll come too, Daddy," repeated the smiling delivery man.

Connie and Stacie watched from the window as Tonya walked between the two big people while holding one finger of each. On occasion she would skip, but mostly she tried to keep up with the guys.

"Daddy's girl," said Stacie with a shake of the head. "You can't separate them."

"I know what you mean…we have one too."

Wesley waved his hand with a victory motion while holding the key high in the air. They watched as he lifted Tonya into the bed of the truck and had her sit down and hold on while he moved it. It appeared that the delivery man wasn't going to let anything happen to Tonya as he also climbed into the bed of Jake's truck and sat next to the little girl. The puff of dark smoke from the exhaust reassured Connie that he had found the ignition key, but she was a little confused as to why he wasn't moving until she saw him reach down toward the bottom of the seat.

“His legs are too long,” said Connie, as she smiled and turned to Stacie, “but he’s found the seat adjuster. What do you think, Stacie…shall we put the food on the credenza?” she asked as she walked directly behind the desk and began to roll the chair away to create more walking space.

Pulling clear of the Big Red Liquor store’s parking lot, Jake looked back down at his cell phone lying on the seat and again thought of Connie. “I’ll call her from the office,” he mumbled.

# Thirty

The initial blast sent red, yellow and orange flames bellowing high into the air. Heavy black smoke followed the column as it soared into the sky before drifting east above the city. The sparse traffic stopped along the frontage road as one in every two persons frantically began dialing 911. Their descriptions placed an explosion and fire at the rear of 793 West Litton Street…the Kramer electrical building.

Within minutes of the first explosion a second blast erupted dwarfing the first by an unimaginable force. The shock waves alone shook the block building sending shattered glass, broken block, lumber sections and metal parts, in small jagged pieces, in every direction. Debris rained to the ground surrounding the building from every angle. Flames were beginning to appear from the single story structure and created an additional column of sickening black smoke that only roofing can produce.

Mitch Rinehart was sitting at the Fall Creek volunteer fire department's dinner/study table, re-familiarizing himself with the State of Indiana's EMT training brochures. Although not normally on duty at the station on weekdays, today Mitch excused himself from his day job at Quality Heating and Cooling in order to allow Clayton Miller to attend the scheduled birth of his first son. When the call to duty came in it triggered the audible pulsating sirens and the rotating red strobe lights while announcing the emergency via an indoor-outdoor speaker.

"Fire…explosion…casualties unknown…793 West Litton Street…all units, this is currently classified as a two alarm emergency. Repeating, fire…explosion… casualties unknown…793 West Litton Street. Cross-street Dugger Avenue. All units…all units…"

Mitch had all the station's doors opened and his safety gear on as he reached for the driver's door of the EMT emergency unit, only to find Debbie strapped in behind the driver's wheel.

"I'm drivin," she said, "Get in."

"Does that address sound familiar to you, Deb?" he asked while closing the shot-gun door and reaching for his lap belt.

"Not really…should it?"

"I'm not sure," he replied. "Maybe." Mitch picked up the unit's microphone and announced, "Fall Creek EMT unit enroute responding to West Linton Street. E.T.A. seven minutes."

"Fall Creek EMT…copy. It looks like a bad one, Mitch, glad to have you aboard."

Mitch replaced the hand-set in its holder as he looked up at the rising black cloud of smoke.

"There she blows," said Debbie. "My God look at the smoke. It looks like the whole damned block went up."

"Jake's," said Mitch aloud.

"Who?"

"That looks like Kramer's place. Come on, Debbie …hit it."

Jake could hear sirens approaching from every direction as he pulled to the side to let emergency vehicles of every description pass. Once he pulled back onto the black top he focused on the thick black smoke ahead.

"Hey…that looks like it's close to the shop," he said to himself.

Traffic began to snarl as he neared the 700 block as abandoned cars and trucks belonging to wannabe-helpers and rubberneckers littered the berm of the road. The horns, sirens and rotating lights could be seen and heard from this point, creating a sickening feeling in the pit of Jake's stomach. His heart raced as the realization that this was indeed his building. Jake tried to pull around the stopped pick-up truck directly in front of him only to be waved back by a county deputy guarding the access.

"Sorry, sir…you can't drive through here. You have to back up and leave the area. This area is not secure."

"That's my building!" shouted Jake.

"Sure it is…now back it up, buddy, before you get in a lot of trouble."

Jake leaped from his truck, leaving it running and abandoned in the center of the lane, determined not to be detained.

"Hey you…get back here. You can't go up there."

Jake was running between emergency units, past police officers and, of course, around reporters. He could see the building clearly now and he also felt the heat from the flames that leaped from the roof, windows and doors. The entire structure was completely engulfed in flames. He tired to make his way closer to the holocaust while praying that Wesley, or any of the crew, had not arrived before the fire.

"Please Lord; tell me they weren't here yet," he said aloud.

"Mr. Kramer, Mr. Kramer."

Jake turned to find a cameraman holding a video unit on his shoulder while lightly adjusting the lens.

"Get the damned thing out of my face."

"Mr. Kramer. Cameron Elliott, WAXU news. Can you tell us what caused the explosion, Mr. Kramer?"

"I said get that damned thing out of my face."

"Mr. Kramer, can you tell us who was killed in this accident? Were they Kramer employees?"

Jake's actions were instinctive as he was looking at the news crew with blurred vision. His left hand grabbed the lens of the camera and with one forceful jerk he pulled the unit free from the cameraman's shoulder and threw it to the ground. He could feel his foot crush the lens, but he didn't remember asking it to do so.

"Hey man, you can't do that."

Jake also didn't remember making a fist or swinging, but he did and the impact sent the cameraman directly to the ground where he laid motionless. Cameron Elliott didn't wait for Jake to share his hostilities with him and responded by running as fast as his legs could carry him. Turning again to his blazing building, Jake's vision began to return as he repeated Cameron's words, "killed…they?"

Firefighters were summoned from four surrounding areas as the explosion was upgraded from a two to a four alarm fire and additional stations were being placed on stand-by as the fight continued to extinguish and save the Kramer and Associates building. Jake was walking slowly as he stepped over fire hoses and debris in a dazed or sedated demeanor. No one noticed or attempted to stop him as he made his way to the rear of the building where the fire's origin became obvious to him. He could see the burnt shell of his truck smoldering next to a framed outline of another truck that he couldn't recognize due to the charred shell and missing pieces. All of the surrounding landscape was black and also smoldering. Turning to the back of the block building he looked into the shell of the window in his office that was omitting smoke from the smoldering timbers of the fallen roof joist above. Nothing was left. Along the burnt rear wall and across the gravel lot were countless pieces of debris from the roofing and numerous truck parts.

Mitch Rinehart caught sight of the comatose figure of his friend Jake Kramer walking through the rubble surrounding the back lot.

"Jake…Jake, over here," he shouted as he watched Jake walking about in circles.

"Jake, it's me…Mitch," he said while taking his arm. "Come with me. Come on…let's go over here."

Jake followed Mitch like a puppet, but he had not responded in any other way, nor did he know why or where he was going.

"Mitch, why? Why did this happen?"

"We don't know yet, Jake, but I think that a propane truck exploded."

"Propane trunk?"

"Jake, I have to tell you something. Do you hear me…are you listening?"

Jake nodded his head yes while looking at the burnt remains of the two trucks.

"That was my truck sitting over there Mitch," he said slowly while pointing in the general direction.

"I know. Jake…listen to me," he repeated. "Look at me."

Jake turned as Mitch looked into his red swollen eyes. We have transported two ladies and one young boy to County General. We think they're going to be alright though…"

"Two ladies and a baby?" repeated Jake.

"Jake, I'm sorry…but one of them was Connie. Can you tell us who was with her?"

"Connie?" repeated Jake.

"Yes, but Connie is going to be alright. We'll get you down there to be with her soon, but can you ID the other two? They were a black family. Jake, could she have been Wesley's wife?"

"Stacie?" said Jake. "They have a little boy named Jake and one daughter, Tonya. Mitch…they were here? Why? Why were they here?"

"We don't know. Did you say a little girl, Tonya?" asked Mitch rather excitedly.

"Yeah…Tonya. She's about eight or nine. Why?"

"DEBBIE!" shouted Mitch. "We could have a missing. Pass the word…one female child…black… eight years. Alert everyone…priority one…go…go."

Turning back to Jake, Mitch asked, "Jake I want you to sit right here. Do you understand? I'm going to get you something from my bag that I want you to take. It'll help you. Stay here, okay?"

Jake nodded as he sat completely numb and looked around the area. "Why?" he asked.

"We have the girl!" someone shouted from across the lot and down an embankment. "Hurry…

Jake attempted to stand but his legs wouldn't hold his weight as he fell once again to his makeshift seat. He watched a number of firefighters scramble to the rear of the lot and disappear down the slope.

"Over here, I've found her," he shouted. "She's alive! Bring a board. NO! Bring two boards. We've found another man down here too. We have two injured, one adult male and a young girl."

Jake sat helplessly as he watched the rescue squad's efficiency as they appeared above the embankment gently carrying a back board with one little girl strapped securely to the frame. Mitch ran directly to Jake.

"Jake, we think the little girl must be Tonya. Can you come with me and identify her for us?"

"Is she…?"

"She's alive, Jake. Come with me, quickly now. We'll have to move her out very soon."

"Is the other one Wesley?"

Mitch helped Jake to his feet as they hurriedly made their way to the EMT unit.

"Debbie is calling her vitals in right now, but it will help us if we have a positive identification."

"Mitch, was the other one Wesley?" he asked again.

"No."

Standing at the rear of the opened door of the ambulance, Jake watched as an oxygen mask was placed over the small mouth of Tonya Washington. She had air-bag casts around her right leg and left arm, and a snug brace around her tiny neck. An IV bag was hanging from a stainless steel hook above her delivering morphine in delayed droplets. The innocence of her young face was marred by burses and cuts above her eyes which Debbie was gently attending to with cotton swabs and antiseptic.

"Jake?" asked Mitch.

Nodding his head yes was all he could manage for he couldn't speak above his pain.

"She was barely breathing when they found her," said Mitch. "And she's lost a lot of blood. I hate to say this, Jake, but I know you want it straight. It's going to be touch and go, at best, for this little girl. I'm sorry."

Jake began walking in circles mumbling to himself, "I have to get to the hospital. I have to be with Connie. I have to go. I have to call Maggie and JJ and get them there. I have to tell Wes…Wes!" Jake stopped and looked at Mitch and asked, "Mitch, where's Wesley? I haven't seen him around. Did he go to the hospital with Stacie and little Jake? Where is he? WES!" he shouted. "Wesley! Hey Wesley…we're over here."

Mitch looked at Debbie as she quickly turned away shaking her head while hiding her tears.

"Jake, come with me," he said as he placed his arm around Jake's shoulder and lead him to an isolated spot away from all the activity.

"NO!…NO! Oh my God no. He can't be…oh God, why? Where is he, Mitch? I want to see him… take me to Wesley."

Debbie heard Jake's cries and although it may have appeared unprofessional, she lost her composure and began to cry while cradling the fatherless Tonya Washington as gently and lovingly as she dared.

"You can't see him, Jake. There's nothing to see, believe me."

"I want to see my friend, Mitch. Where is he?" asked Jake as he began to walk away.

Mitch reached for Jake's arm and said, "Jake, listen to me. He was in the truck when it exploded. The blast alone would have caused his death immediately, but the fire…Jake, he was trapped in a burning cab for an eternity. I'm sorry, but I can't let you see him. There's nothing to see."

"We're moving the little girl, Mitch," shouted Debbie as she reached for the handle of the door. "You guys coming?"

"Let's go to the hospital, Jake. That's where we're needed. There's nothing left here."

# Thirty-One

The ER staff had been alerted and was expecting Tonya Washington at County General Hospital as the ambulance approached. Dr. Donald Watkins stood behind the nurses' station reviewing the information that had been relayed ahead, while Nurse LaSalle rechecked exam room three to make sure it was ready.

"Incoming," shouted Jason, an orderly, before he rushed out to assist.

Tonya's trip from the ambulance to room three was completed with top efficiency and speed. Jake's offer to help was repeatedly refused as Debbie led and Mitch pushed with Jason taking control of the IV bags. Jake, in turn, followed as close as the rules allowed, stopping short of the double doors leading to the forbidden area beyond. Within moments Mitch Reinhart reappeared to find Jake standing motionless staring at the large STAFF ONLY sign on the doors.

"She's with the best, Jake. They'll take good care of her."

"Is she going to be alright, Mitch?"

"Yes, I think so. She's young and strong."

"I want her to have the best of everything… regardless of the…"

"She's getting that right now, Jake," interrupted Mitch.

Jake looked away from the doors and at Mitch for the first time and said, "I need to find Connie. Can you help me find her and Stacie?"

“Sure. Come with me.”

The elevator stopped on the second floor and the diagram on the wall indicated that room 277 was a short walk to their left. After he noticed Jake hesitating at the entry of the room to collect his composure, Mitch politely said, “I’ll be right out here, Jake…give Connie my best.”

Jake nodded then disappeared behind the white curtain.

“Are you Mr. Kramer?” asked the nurse who was busy trying to keep Connie comfortable while jotting down secrets gathered from the countless dials and printouts.

Jake nodded yes and asked, “How is she?” while walking around to the foot of the bed.

“I’m going to be fine, honey,” answered Connie as she opened her eyes and attempted a reassuring smile. “Don’t worry about me.”

Jake moved to the side of the bed opposite the attending nurse and gently took Connie’s hand.

“Connie, my God…you had me worried to death. Honey, what happened? What were you and Stacie doing down there?”

“I’ll be back in a little while to check on you, Mrs. Kramer,” said the nurse as she rounded the end of the bed.

“Nurse, if there’s a man out there in an EMT uniform will you send him in please?”

“Mitch?” asked Connie.

"Yeah, it's me," answered Mitch, while making his way around the bed and eventually to Connie's side. "We have a bad habit of meeting in the most undesirable places, Mrs. Kramer. Let's try to improve on that," he added while placing a kiss on her forehead and taking her hand. "How are you feeling?"

Connie's emotions couldn't be held in any longer as her tough side gave way to her heart. "Oh Jake, Wesley …he…he's…"

"I know, Connie. I know. Let's not think about that now. Let's concentrate on getting you well and then we'll deal with that."

"He didn't have a chance. The truck just exploded. Stacie and I saw it blow-up and burst into flames. Oh Jake…it was awful. Nobody will tell me anything about Tonya. Please tell me she's safe."

"She's downstairs in ER right now, Connie. Mitch thinks she's going to make it. She's a tough little girl."

"Thank God!"

"Connie, we found a man not far from Tonya. Do you know who he is?"

"A man with…oh yes, he was the man delivering fuel for the propane tank. Is he alright?"

"We don't know…we think so. He's in ER too."

"Connie, what happened down there?" asked Mitch.

"It was horrible," she answered while reaching for a tissue. Jake and Mitch stood silently at opposite sides of her bed to listen to her account of the nightmare on Litton Street. She explained Stacie's and her intentions of celebrating the business transaction with both families and the small crew. She spoke of the nice man from the gas supplier who asked to have Jake's truck moved during his delivery of propane gas to the holding tank. She described how excited Tonya was that she was allowed to go with the big guys and ride in the back of the truck while Daddy moved it. She added that she and Stacie were at the credenza setting up a serving area for the food trays when the accident happened.

"Oh Jake, poor Stacie. She was looking out the window at them when the explosion…why? What happened?" she asked.

"We don't know," answered Mitch, "but we're going to find out. You can bet on that."

"Excuse me, please…I need to speak with Mitch for a moment," interrupted Debbie as she gently pulled back the curtain. "Get well soon, Mrs. Kramer," she added as she turned to leave the room.

Mitch and Debbie moved away from earshot before she spoke just above a whisper.

"Mitch, I have to get back, but you are cleared to stay if you like. I've asked central dispatch to call in a sub for you."

"Thanks, Deb. Maybe I will hang around for awhile. I'm trying to get a handle on this."

"There's something else you should know."

Mitch held fast waiting for the second shoe to fall, but said nothing.

"That man we found with Tonya, has been I.D.'d as Otis Porter. I understand he's retired, but had been working part time just for something to do. His family's been notified.

"Good."

"No…bad, she said sadly. They're too late. Mitch. Mr. Porter died about ten minutes ago."

"HE WHAT?"

"Doctor Watkins did everything he could, Mitch, but…well, anyway I thought you might be the one to break the news to the Kramers. They'll have to know."

Mitch nodded in agreement, knowing that it should be his job, but he would have given anything for it to have been some good news. "What happened, Deb? He didn't give any fatal signs during the ride in."

"I know," she agreed. "It was his heart. Watkins said the scar on his chest suggested that he had open heart surgery recently. That combined with his age, weight and the trauma of the accident…well, it was just too much. No one saw it coming. He just died."

Mitch sighed and looked away toward the end of the hall. "I should have seen it. It's my job to see the signs."

"Stop it," she said. "Nobody could have seen it. We just lose some, you know that. It happens. Look, I have to go, are you going to be alright?"

"Yeah, sure. Thanks, Debbie."

"Call me later, Mitch. Let me know how things are going."

Mitch nodded yes and made his way back to room 277.

The news of Mr. Porter's death could not have struck Jake and Connie any harder if he had been one of their own. Two tragic deaths, two adults and two children were hurt, including one precious little girl in serious condition. All of which was the result of an accident due to an unknown cause of Kramer's equipment on Kramer property. The personal guilt and responsibility that Jake felt was becoming unbearable.

Mitch excused himself to attend to other duties but not without promising to check-in on Connie from time to time. Jake, on the other hand, reassured himself that Connie's injuries were only minor and her admittance to County General was primarily a precautionary measure, so he decided it was time to locate and check on Stacie, Tonya and little Jake's conditions.

"Hello, Connie, I hope I'm not intruding," she said while making her presence known. "Mr. Kramer, how good it is to see you again," she continued while offering her hand. "I'm…"

"Doctor Harrington," he replied, while taking her hand to continue the courtesy. "No, you're not intruding Doctor, I was about to leave. I'm sure Connie will welcome your company."

"Please, Jake, don't leave on my account."

"I wouldn't."

"Jake, give Stacie my love," said Connie trying to intervene and perhaps prevent something from being said by her husband that could be embarrassing to all.

"I'll do that, Con. Good-by, Doctor."

"Nice to have seen you again, Jake," she said with a smile.

Jake walked down the tiled hallway unsure of where he was going or how he might locate Stacie, but he wasn't in a huge rush. He knew that seeing Stacie without Wesley at her side would be heartbreaking and he was trying to prepare himself for how he would deal with the situation. He had relived today's events so often that he was now doing it unconsciously. How could such a thing happen? What was wrong with his truck? What made it blow-up like that? He didn't have the answers yet, but he made a personal promise to himself that one day he would know all the facts. If it took every dime he had, he would know exactly what happened.

"May I help you, sir?" she asked without prompting.

Jake was startled back to reality as he looked down at the pleasant smile of a retired volunteer with a perfect roller set in her blue tinted hair.

"Help me?" asked Jake.

"Yes sir. You look lost and not that I mind, but you've passed my desk four times in the last half hour. Do you need help finding something or someone?"

"Well yes, I suppose in some respects you could say I'm lost. Can you tell me what room I can find Stacie Washington?"

"Sure…let's see Washington…Washington…when was she admitted, sir?"

"Today…maybe a couple of hours ago."

"No…no, I don't see a Stacie Washington here. Let me call downstairs.

Jake paced in small circles while Lavern spoke ever so softly and politely into the phone. "Thanks Cheryl …I'll tell him. Sir, I understand that Stacie Washington was treated and released. That's always the kind of good news I love to report."

Jake continued to pace while looking both relieved and confused. "What about a little girl by the name of Tonya Washington?" he asked. "Do you have a room number for her?"

"I'll check," she replied.

"Jake, Jake…there you are. I've been looking for you," said Mitch.

"Looking for me…what for?"

"I was just talking with Doctor Watkins down in the ER and he said the little girl, Toni…Tina…?"

"You mean, Tonya?"

"Yes…Tonya."

"What about Tonya?" insisted Jake.

"Jake, she's taken a turn for the worse. They rushed her to the third floor about fifteen minutes ago."

"Mitch, damn it, I'm dying here. What happened to Tonya?" he asked while taking Mitch by the arm.

"They found some swelling around the brain."

"Swelling, what kind of swelling?"

"It most likely occurred when she was tossed over the embankment. She must have struck her head on a rock or something, Jake. They don't know what it was, but it has caused severe swelling and pressure under the cranium. They have called in a neurologist and his team to evaluate her condition."

Mitch watched Jake's expression change from concerned to numb, as he explained what little he knew about Tonya's situation.

"She can't die, Mitch. It's not fair. She's so young and helpless, she just can't die."

Mitch was savvy enough not to answer or agree with his statement, but wise enough to lead him away from thoughts of death.

"Let's go and find out what we can, Jake," he replied as he gripped Jake's bicep and led him toward the elevator.

# Thirty-Two

From the hallway Jake could see Stacie seated in the corner of the waiting room clutching little Jake tightly against her chest. Neither her position nor her expression changed as she stared blankly at the floor. Directly to her left sat a frail Granny Fay reading scripture from her worn leather-bound bible that was held closely to her face in order to see the words. It was the saddest scene anyone could happen upon.

"I'll be close by should you need me, Jake."

"What do I say to her, Mitch? What can I possibly say that will help her find comfort after losing her husband and having her little girl fighting for her life on an operating table?"

Mitch placed his hand on Jake's shoulder as he answered, "I expect you need to say nothing at all, Jake. Having you with her in her time of need will be her comfort. I won't be far."

After drawing a few deep breaths, Jake cornered his emotions and stepped through the waiting room door. The silence in the room was such that the soft hum from the overhead florescent lighting created a tranquil atmosphere that was interrupted by the echo of his footsteps. Granny Fay was the first to notice him as she peered over the top of her bible. Her eyes were magnified by the intensity of her eyeglasses and gave a clear view that they were red, swollen and tired. Jake's heart sank and broke into a thousand pieces as Granny Fay lowered her bible to her lap and reached out her trembling hands to Jake. His attempt to smile never surfaced as the tight-lipped Jake Kramer knelt before Granny Fay, and she rubbed her soft, wrinkled hands across his face to wipe his tears.

"He loved you so much, Mr. Kramer. You were the father he never had. Thank you for that…may God bless you," she said in a soft, cracking voice.

Jake couldn't answer Granny, but she knew what was in his heart. Taking her hands he placed a kiss on each palm before returning them to her bible. Jake looked toward Stacie who, to this point, had said nothing, but continued to hum the hymn, *Shall We Gather At The River*, while clinging to little Jake for dear life.

"Stacie, honey…it's me, Jake."

Unsure if she heard him, Jake began to stand but felt the tiny hand of Granny Fay pull against his arm. She was shaking her head no to Jake and her lips began to quiver once again.

"What is it, Granny?" he asked while leaning toward her.

"She ain't said nothin' all day, Mr. Kramer. She just holds on to her baby."

Jake nodded that he understood before standing to take a seat next to Stacie, but paused to take notice as another family member entered the waiting room. She was tall, slender, middle aged and carried a cardboard box filled with three cups of something that gave off a faint hint of steam. He watched quietly and returned her smile as she made her way past him.

"Here Mother," she said while handing a cup to Granny Fay. "You should drink this while it's still hot." She slowly stepped toward Stacie. "Stacie, dear, I've brought you something to drink. You should really try to drink something. Here, let me hold Jake for a little while, he may need changed."

"NO! I'll hold him. He's mine. He's mine!"

"Okay honey, okay. We all know he's yours and nobody is going to take him from you. But please try to drink some tea. It'll make you feel better."

Stacie shook her head no at least a dozen times before saying, "Give it to Wesley when he comes. He'll be here soon. Save it for Wesley.

Jake felt himself gasp for breath before bowing his head at Stacie's suggestion. He looked up at her as she resumed her position of rocking little Jake, humming the hymn and staring at the floor.

"You must be Mr. Kramer."

Jake nodded his head slowly but was unable to speak.

"I'm Rosa," she said while extending her hand. "Let's talk over here," she suggested while pointing across the room.

Jake followed Rosa without prompting or speaking, for he had not yet absorbed the full impact of Stacie's comment. Taking a seat at the opposite end of the waiting room Jake sat quietly next to Rosa as she took the first sip of her tea before speaking.

"I've heard so much about you and your wonderful family, Mr. Kramer. I'm glad we finally have a chance to meet."

Jake looked up at Rosa as she sat straight, poised and confident. Her eyes showed sadness, but refused to yield to tears. Her hand didn't show any sign of trembling as she raised her cup of tea for a second sip.

"I'm sorry it had to be under such conditions, Rosa. Wesley was…Wes, he…"

"Wesley loved and respected you, Mr. Kramer," she said. "No one could ask or expect more."

"It was mutual, Rosa."

"I'm sure of it. You see, Mr. Kramer, you got the greatest gift anyone could receive. Something I didn't earn and couldn't expect, for I was teaching him all the wrong things so early in his life. I let my son down, but you taught him how to stand-up like a man. I will always be grateful to you, sir, for being there for my Wesley."

"I wasn't there for him today."

Rosa paused for a moment while looking somewhat puzzled at Jake before saying, "No, no you weren't. But I would have thought you had taught my son by example, Mr. Kramer."

Jake raised his head to Rosa as she continued. "The most obvious thing that I have noticed about Wesley in the few short months that I've been around him is that he expected nothing that he didn't earn. No, you weren't around for him today because you taught him to stand on his own two feet. He was taking care of things on his own.

Jake nodded at Rosa in understanding before asking, "Did they teach you all that in the big house?" he asked with a meek smile.

"They gave me a lot of time to think."

"Well…you made good use of it, Rosa. You and Wes would have had a good life getting to know one another."

"I know, but I'm thankful for the time we had."

Little Jake's cry from across the room brought Jake and Rosa back to the more pressing issues.

"Jake needs fed and changed, Mr. Kramer and I'm afraid Stacie needs help."

"She's been through a lot today," he replied. "I have an idea. Will you excuse me?"

"Yes, of course. I'll see if I can talk Stacie into letting me have Jake."

Jake left the waiting room and immediately found Mitch poised like a guard in the hall.

"How are they doing, Jake?"

"Stacie's in bad shape…Granny is getting very tired but won't admit it and Rosa's hanging tough."

"Jake, I have to leave for awhile. I'm sorry, but there's something I need to attend to. You have my cell number. Will you call me if you need anything?"

"Of course, Mitch…I can't thank you enough for all you have done for us. You've been a good friend," replied Jake as he shook Mitch's hand with a bonding grip.

Jake made his way back to the second floor and went directly to Connie's room, finding it filled to the limit with visitors as Alex had brought Maggie to the hospital to be with her Mom. It became immediately clear to everyone who took notice of Jake's expression that all was not well with the Washington family. The room fell quiet as Jake explained Tonya's trauma and imminent surgery. He did, however, withhold the extent of Stacie's situation for the time being.

"Connie," said Doctor Harrington, "I'll check in on you sometime tomorrow. Don't hesitate to call if you want to talk." Looking about the room she added, "Nice to meet you, Margaret, and you, Mr. Sanders."

"I'll walk you out, Doctor," said Jake as he followed her to the door. Connie and Doreen were the only two to pick up on his suggestion, although neither commented.

Doctor Harrington and Jake walked slowly down the hall toward the stair exit before Jake broke his silence.

"Doctor Harrington, I need your help."

"Yes, Jake…what can I do for you?"

"It's Mrs. Washington…Stacie. If you can spare the time, I'll explain while we walk upstairs."

Jake had finished his explanation of Stacie's condition by the time he and Doreen reached the waiting room and found the Washington family where he had left them a short time ago. Rosa apparently had made no progress in relieving Stacie of holding rights to little Jake as she continued her rocking motion while clinging to the baby. Rosa rose to meet them in the center of the room as Jake exchanged introductions between the two.

"Will you try to talk to her, Doctor?"

"Of course, I'll try."

"See if you can take the baby from her," asked Rosa. "He needs fed and changed."

"Jake," said Doreen, "Why don't you take the ladies downstairs for some refreshments?"

From the hall, just a few steps from the waiting room, Jake looked back over his shoulder as Doctor Harrington took a seat next to Stacie. He watched Stacie shaking her head rapidly in a no statement before he turned and stepped between Granny Fay and Rosa, taking an arm of each.

Jake and Rosa had finished their coffee and Granny Fay had eaten all but a bite or two of her tuna salad sandwich when their table was approached by a young petite lady volunteer.

"Excuse me please, are you the Washington family?"

"Yes," answered Rosa, as Jake and Granny nodded in agreement.

"I'm Peggy. Doctor Harrington sent me to ask if you'll join her in her office."

"Yes, of course, Peggy, replied Rosa, as all three chairs began sliding away from the table.

"If you'll follow me I'll show you the way."

It was a short walk to Harrington's office, which Jake was grateful for as Granny Fay was beginning to show signs of fatigue. As they entered Doctor Harrington's office they found Stacie stretched out, resting on the couch and Doreen sitting in a chair next to her holding little Jake.

"Is she alright?" asked Rosa.

"Yes, she's resting. I gave her a light sedative to help her relax. This young man and I are becoming good friends. Peggy brought him diapers, some food and a bottle from the nursery, so he's happy. Please take a seat," she said as she stood to offer her chair to Granny and little Jake to Rosa.

"I'll tell Doctor Zorka you're here. He has new information about Tonya."

Harrington's office was library-quiet with the exception of a few whimpers from the baby as everyone prepared themselves, in their own way, for Doctor Zorka's report on Tonya's condition. The light tap on the door announced his arrival. He was tall, of medium build and had a combination of a bald and shaved head. He gave the impression of one who had little time for idle chit-chat and all the time in the world for his profession. Doctor Harrington handled the introductions before Doctor Zorka took the lead and spoke to each of the ladies in turn, then quickly got to the point of the meeting.

"Tonya is in recovery right now. The craniotomy or surgery went well. There were no surprises and I expect her to recover nicely. However, we must keep in mind that this was a serious injury, so her complete recovery could take some time and require therapeutic assistance. But she is young, healthy and strong, and children most often recover better than we adults," he added with a smile to Granny.

"What exactly happened to her, Doctor?" asked Jake.

"We don't know exactly, Mr. Kramer. I understand she was in an accident that resulted in her being tossed or thrown down an embankment of some sort. I can assume that she was either struck or hit by a blunt object against the skull that caused a concussion. The initial epidural hematoma was most likely the result. That means the brain banged against the inside of the skull and became bruised. In Tonya's case, her concussion resulted in blood inside the skull. We had to relieve the pressure."

"How did you find that, Doctor?" asked Rosa.

"Doctor Watkins became wise to her symptoms and called us in for an opinion. We found her breathing rate very slow and her blood pressure low. We also noted some fluid drainage in the ears. However, one of the leading factors was that she hadn't regained consciousness since the accident, and that wasn't good. We ran a CT scan that confirmed our suspicions."

The room became very quiet as Doctor Zorka waited for the next question or an opportunity to leave. Jake withheld his inquiry, thinking it was best not to ask, for the answer might discourage the family, but Rosa asked for him. "What is the worst we can expect Doctor? I mean if things don't turn out."

Doctor Zorka took a deep breath before answering and wished that he could have gotten away before anyone asked the 'worst' question. His answer was short, precise and indeed somewhat discouraging.

"There could be changes in her personality, emotions, or even mental abilities. She could have speech problems, loss of hearing, taste, or vision. She might experience seizures, or perhaps paralysis, and there's always some fear that she could regress into a coma. But as I said earlier, she's young and strong and we expect a full and complete recovery. Mrs. Washington," he said as he looked to Stacie, "We'll let you know when she's out of recovery and when you may see her. Will you be staying here?" he asked while turning to Doctor Harrington who in turn nodded yes.

Stacie spoke up for the first time and said, "I'm gonna wait here for Wesley. He'll be here soon and we'll go get Tonya and all go home together."

Doctor Zorka, who had obviously been briefed answered, "That will be fine, Mrs. Washington," as he turned to leave.

If his mind had been clear Jake may not have found himself wandering about the halls of County General Hospital lost and confused. But his mind wasn't clear and for good reason. His young friend and partner for so many years was dead. It was hard to accept that Wesley was killed in a tragic accident that also took the life of Otis Porter, the delivery man. And Tonya...the thought of that precious little girl lying in the recovery room fighting for her life at this very moment was unbearable. Jake's heart ached as his thoughts continued reviewing the day's events. Connie, Stacie and little Jake were spared serious physical injury, but Stacie would need a great deal of help in order to accept the reality of today's loss. Doctor Harrington would be the best influence in that area he thought, for she handled things very well today. In fact, he reminded himself to thank her the next time he ran into her. Jake's mind raced between incidents and results so many times that he was suffering a terrible headache, but he considered that the least of his problems.

"Sir, you look lost. Can we help you find your way?"

Looking up from the water fountain Jake responded, "Yes…I guess you could say I'm lost. Room 277," he said with a brief smile.

"Room 277. Well, you are lost alright, but the good news is you're still in the hospital. Follow me; I'll get you headed in the right direction."

Jake saw Maggie and Alex standing in the door entry of Connie's room talking with Cindy as he approached and ended his tour of the hospital.

"Cindy, nice of you to come down."

"Oh, Jake," she said as she reached out to give him a hug. "I got here as quickly as I could. I'm so sorry about Wesley."

Jake returned her hug while asking, "How's Connie?"

"She's sleeping, Dad. I think they gave her something. How's Stacie doing?"

Jake shook his head indicating to all three that things could be better. "Let's talk out here," he said as he moved away from Connie's room.

The small huddle at the end of corridor stood quietly as they listened to the latest on Stacie and Tonya. Jake saw his daughter reach for her Kleenex as the impact broke her heart as well. The good news was that little Jake was completely unharmed, but he was getting tired, so Rosa was taking him and Granny Fay home. Stacie, on the other hand, would probably be spending the night under Doctor Harrington's care.

"Alex," said Jake. "I could use a ride down to the shop while Connie's sleeping. I left my truck somewhere around there and rode here in the ambulance with Tonya."

"Sure, anything you need, Jake, anything."

"I'll stay with Margaret," added Cindy. "If we decide to leave, we'll call."

"Thanks, Cindy. Will you be alright, Maggie?"

"Sure, Daddy…we'll wait here for JJ," she said before giving her father a hug and a kiss on the cheek. "I love you, Daddy."

# Thirty-Three

"You alright?"

Jake nodded yes, but remained quiet as he continued looking out of the car's window.

"You want to stop somewhere for a drink first?"

"Thanks, Alex, it sounds good, but I don't want to run into people asking a lot of questions right now."

Alex drove on for a few blocks before turning left into an area strip mall and said, "You won't have to. I'll be right back."

In Jake's current state he hardly noticed that Alex had gone and certainly didn't realize where he went until he felt a cold bottle in his palm.

"Thanks, Alex."

Litton Street was still littered with slow-moving or stopped traffic as the city's rubberneckers and curiosity seekers waited for their turn to drive by the smoldering remains of the Kramer building. The charred steel of the propane truck and Jake's pickup could be seen from the road if one looked across the two fallen cement block walls. No one was permitted on the property as announced by the yellow ribbon drawn across the entire front easement and across the rear access as well. That is no one was permitted except Alex Sanders who stretched the ribbon in the back lot until it broke as he pulled to a stop behind the building. He turned off the engine and turned to Jake who sat quietly staring at the pile of black burnt debris surrounding his truck.

"Do you want to walk around Jake, or would you rather we just get the hell away from here?"

"Do you know where I was when this happened?" he asked without taking his eyes off his pickup.

"No."

"I had just left Bernie's and was on my way here to pass ownership of the business to Wesley. I had the papers in my hand, Alex. That's why his family and Connie were here. He was so proud…and now he's dead."

Alex listened with his head lowered but didn't comment.

"I should never have parked my truck there."

"Come on Jake, you know better than that. Shit happens."

"Yeah, shit happens," repeated Jake, "but it was my truck. It should have been me."

Again Alex withheld comment as he watched the slow-moving traffic occasionally pause and take pictures or point out their windows at something fascinating to them.

"Would you like to get out and walk around Jake?" he asked while turning away from the road.

Jake's eyes were as big as silver dollars and never blinked as he looked desperately at Alex.

"What is it, Jake?"

"It was my truck. It should have been me."

Alex said nothing. He neither confirmed nor rejected Jake's suggestion.

"You thought of it too…didn't you? Damn it, Alex. You thought of it too," he shouted as he jumped from the truck and moved toward the rubble.

Alex was quick to open his door and follow. "Hold on, Jake. There's no reason to think that this was anything but an accident. There is no indication otherwise."

"And there won't be, will there, Alex? Remember…you're the one who said, 'If it's done right it will look like an accident, suicide, or natural causes.'"

Jake was at the truck now and had both hands on the bed railing, pulling at the charred metal. He was deeply hurt and became furious at the thought that Wesley died for him.

"What about the mandate, Alex? What about the part that says only the mark is erased. What about THAT…DAMN IT!"

Alex didn't answer, for what could he say. Jake was right. And if it was indeed the Gospel's work, it would never be proven to be anything other than an accident. For that's the Gospel. Even so, Jake was convinced otherwise. Alex watched helplessly as Jake tore at the truck, shaking, beating and pounding at the metal until his hands were equally black and bleeding. Alex turned and walked back toward his car, leaving his friend alone to grieve and hate.

He made his way into Jake's office to the spot where Stacie and Connie were standing before the explosion. Looking at the broken glass, splintered metal and wood he was amazed that they survived at all. He could see Jake making his way toward the embankment and hoped that he would have an opportunity to check the truck himself before they left. If not, he would come back tomorrow because there were certain things he knew to look for. Alex watched Jake standing motionless at the top of the hill trying to locate the area where Tonya was found.

"Jake, my friend…this is doing you no good at all. I'm taking you away from here," he said to himself.

When Alex reached the back lot Jake had disappeared, presumably over the bank, so Alex seized the opportunity to make a quick search of the inside of the truck. A check under the dash revealed nothing but crusted wiring and warped braces. The seat was burnt until nothing but springs and frame remained. He was about to close the door when his eye caught sight of a small rectangular box next to the seat glide. Reaching down Alex removed the burnt remains of what his training, experience or instinct told him did not belong. While holding it in one hand and rubbing it clean with the other he tilted it to the sunlight until the stamping in the metal read, "Sure-Spark Igniter Co." "And that's the Gospel," Alex whispered.

"What's the Gospel? asked Jake, who had made his way back without Alex noticing.

"Oh nothing. You okay?"

"What's that?"

"I don't know. You tell me, it was in your truck."

"I don't want to be here anymore, Alex, take me home, please. We'll leave the shop truck. I don't want anything here."

They rode along quietly for the first half of the trip to Crest Street, when Jake muttered softly as he looked out his window, "It should have been me."

Alex didn't respond for he didn't want to go there, mainly because he knew he wouldn't lie to Jake, so silence was best.

"I really don't know how Stacie will handle the loss of Tonya if that happens too," said Jake. "It probably would be enough to take her over the edge."

"Tonya will make it okay, Jake. She's strong."

"This was so close to my family, Alex. If it had been Connie who went out to move my truck, she…"

"Jake…don't. That kind of thinking doesn't serve any purpose at all."

They rode on again for a few miles before Jake said, "They won't stop until they kill me or all of my family, will they? I don't care about me, that doesn't matter anymore, but I can't stand the thought of them destroying my friends and family. I've made up my mind that I'm gonna go down fighting. I'll start naming names, and…"

"Jake," interrupted Alex once again. "That will make them more determined than ever. Think about what you're saying here. You already have half of the bad guys in the world nervous, why tick off the rest of them?"

"I'm not just going to sit around on my patio and wait for the next funeral, Alex."

"I understand, Jake. I've been thinking about that side of it too. What I mean is, I know I would go crazy if someone hurt my Cindy or Becky because of me."

"Yeah…and what would Sandman do about it?" he asked sarcastically.

"Like I said…I've been thinking."

Alex wasn't sure if Jake was listening to him at all as they rode along, but still he did his best to try and plant something positive in Jake's mind. However, he had to admit to himself, at least, that Jake's situation had very little to be positive about.

"Uh oh, it looks like you have company, Jake…lots of it."

Jake turned his head toward the windshield saying, "Great. Just what I need…the press."

Crest Street was clogged once again with press wagons and Jake Kramer fans who wanted to offer their prayers and condolences for the Kramer and Washington families. There were no protesters or hecklers, only a silent group of people who had placed flowers and offerings along the front of 919 Crest Street.

"Slide down a little," said Alex. "I'll head for my garage."

"No…let me out in the drive. I'm not hiding."

Alex slowed for the bump at the curb as Jake watched one young lady and her two children approach his home and place a homemade wreath by the shrubbery next to the entry. As the car pulled to a stop he noticed she took three steps back then knelt in prayer. Everyone near the threesome stopped their conversations and bowed their heads in respect until the family stood and stepped away. Jake recognized

Cameron Elliott among the crowd and took note that Cameron actually pulled at his cameraman to stop shooting close-up footage of the family in prayer.

"Want to come in, Jake?"

"No thanks, Alex. I want to go home."

Jake took the direct route across the Sanders' and Kramer's front lawns and boldly walked directly into the center frame of the WAXU hand-held Sony camera. He let his eyes scan the crowd of twenty or so, while looking for a familiar face, but no one, other than Cameron Elliott, was recognized. Making a slight adjustment in his direction Jake continued on toward the news team. The cameraman, shifting from offense to defense, took one step back to counter Jake's movement.

"Cameron, nice to see you," said Jake as he approached and extended his hand.

Elliot was too stunned to immediately respond to Jake's gesture, but did manage to accept his handshake as caught on camera. Jake looked directly at Elliott's assistant who displayed a small white strip of athletic tape across the bridge of his nose and a purplish-black half-moon shaped blemish under his left eye. He tried to appear unaffected by Jake's presence but he was poised to take another step backwards at the first sign of trouble.

"I owe you an apology, sir," he said while again offering his hand. "And I also owe you for damages to your equipment."

"That's okay, Mr. Kramer. I know now that it was a bad time for you. Let's forget it."

"Mr. Elliott, what can I do for you?" he asked the stunned news reporter.

Alex was leaning back against the right front fender of his car watching Jake deal with his problems in his own way. There was little he could do to protect him other than watch his back when he could. But Jake Kramer's back was about as big as a billboard and growing every day. Alex moved into his garage and hit the close button on the overhead door as he turned to watch the group huddle around Jake. The long blast of a car horn from an impatient driver drew Alex's attention to the street. There, sitting dead still in front of 919 Crest Street was a black SUV and a red sports car that was in a big hurry. Again he tapped his horn, but the SUV sat undaunted as the driver lowered his tinted window and stuck his head out to wave the sports car around. Alex's overhead door continued its decent and the identity of the driver struck him as the door sealed closed at the concrete. He ran to the control panel reversing the door, finding the street to be clear and Jake standing among his flock.

"It was him, I know it," said Alex. "That was the Gospel."

# Thirty-Four

Rich couldn't tell you how long the drive back to the Cloverdale exit on I-70 took him, for his mind was completely absorbed with failure number three of his current troubleshooting assignment. However, this one was completely unacceptable to the Club's doctrine, and should they learn of it he could become as expendable as Major Hudoff. The key here was simply that the Club must never learn that it was his error that erased not one, but two nonessentials. "No one knows of my presence here…except Sandman," he said aloud.

Making the stop at the end of the exit ramp, Rich pulled into light traffic and made his way to the 70 West Auto/Truck Restaurant. "Sandman could cause me problems," he said aloud once again. He began to retrace his movements at Kramer's and reassured himself that he had made no errors. He left nothing behind that could be directed to him. No, it was just dumb luck that Kramer wasn't in his truck. It was just dumb luck that a propane delivery was made at that time. Of course this would have been just fine if Kramer was the one in the truck, but that didn't happen and so he lives for another day.

Rich was out of his SUV and at the double glass doors before realizing that he had parked his car and walked across the asphalt.

"Just one?" asked the hostess.

"Just one," he replied. "Is Meg working tonight?"

She sized him up from head to toe before giving a slow yes to his question.

"I'd like one of her tables please."

"One moment, I'll see if there is one available," she replied in a delayed response.

Rich looked around the dining room that was at about one-third capacity and said, "If not, I'll wait for one. I'm in no hurry."

This time she didn't respond at all, but turned and left him standing like someone with a contagious disease. Rich stepped away from the *Hostess Will Seat You* sign and stood at the glass looking out at the traffic speeding down I-70 a thousand meters away. The Sandman could become a problem he reminded himself. It became clear to him that Alex was not here to kill, but rather defend Kramer, and that was somewhat puzzling to Rich. He couldn't quite put the scenario together as to why that should be. It just didn't occur to him that Alex happened to live next door to Jake and they had become the best of friends. Friends to the point that Alex would lay his life on the line for him, which was a commitment Rich only understood and experienced in the forces.

"Your table is ready, sir."

The patron before him had left an evening paper on the seat for which Rich was grateful. He spread the front section before him and scanned the photographs of the burning building on Litton Street. He had no desire to read the reporter's print, for it would just be the opinions of several and most would be wrong. Page six had additional photos of the remains of the trucks and inserted pictures of Washington and Porter.

"I was told that someone asked for one of my tables and I couldn't imagine who."

"I assumed that happened all the time," said Rich.

"Right," she said with a forced smile. "My life is full of men wanting to sit at my tables."

Rich folded the paper and slid it aside. "I think I owe you an apology for last Friday. I was called away rather unexpectedly. It was rude of me to leave that way."

He could see her defense shield fall slightly before saying, "I thought you left town."

"No, just pressing business. I came in Sunday morning for breakfast."

"Really…I didn't see you."

"You were enjoying yourself with an older couple who looked like they brought their two grandchildren in for Sunday breakfast."

Meg's shields were indeed falling. "That was my aunt and uncle. The two kids are mine," she said looking for his response to her having two kids.

"You are very fortunate to be so blessed."

Shields down.

Rich ate from the largest seafood sampler platter that was allowed by law as Meg catered to his every need while other drivers, from across the country, who sat at the counter envied and hated him. For there was not one of them who hadn't tried and failed to win her favors. They may have won her smile, but she won their tips.

"Would you like some dessert? Abby makes a great apple pie."

"No thanks, just a little more coffee when it is convenient."

She began clearing his table, but Rich could tell her shields were beginning to rise once again.

"Maybe after your shift you could join me for coffee?" he asked.

Shields down.

"Only if you'll throw away your cell phone."

"What if I just turn it off?"

"I'll be about another hour, is that okay?"

"I'll be here."

*Dear Mother,*

*I hope this letter finds you and all our family in good health. I am sorry to find it necessary to write and tell you that my plans to come home have changed and I will be delayed here for an indefinite period. I will not bore you with the details, which you could never understand, but I should say that I am needed here.*

*I have some exciting news to share with you, Mother, as I know you worry about my growing old alone. I have met the most wonderful young lady here who reminds me so much of you and Grandmother. We have been seeing one another for some time now and if things go as God has planned, tonight will be the biggest night of my life. Yes, Mother, I plan to ask her to be my wife and live among our family back home.*

*I should tell you a little about her, but not everything because I want you to get to know her in your own way. She is widowed. Her husband was a missionary serving God and lost his life while trying to convert the savage heathens in New Guinea. God spared her and their babies. She has two wonderful children who are such a pleasure to be around and I have already started daily bible studies with them. Mother, you'll be amazed at how eager they are to learn God's word. My bride-to-be has a large farmhouse with hundreds of acres of corn fields and a huge dairy farm that tends to several hundred head of cattle. We plan to sell her farm and build one of our own on the ridge near the willow grove on the west forty if you and the family will agree. I have always dreamed of living out my life on that ridge. It's a special place for me and has a clear view of our cemetery. I'll be able to sit on the back porch and watch over it.*

"Am I interrupting?"

"No, no not at all, I was just dropping a note to mother. I can finish it later."

"It's a little late to go anywhere, Rich; would you like to come to my place for something to drink? It's not far."

"That would be nice, but I hate to disturb the children."

"You won't. They're spending the night with Aunt Gladys," she added with a reassuring smile. "Shall we?"

"You have a nice home here, Megan. It has a real home feeling,"

"Thanks you. It's not easy on a single income with two kids, but we do fine. Can I offer you a drink?"

"Water will be fine?"

"Water? Would you care for something a little stronger? I have a bottle or two of beer and some white wine if that sounds better."

"Beer sounds fine. Do you have ale?"

"Sorry, nothing that fancy on my wages."

"Anything's fine just so it's cold. Do you mind if I turn on the TV? The late news is about to start. I'd like to catch the local headlines."

"No, help yourself. The remote is on the end-table."

"…WAXU's own Cameron Elliot caught up with Mr. Jake Kramer at his home this evening. We'll have his comments and take you to the site of today's explosion that left two dead and three injured…one seriously…"

"I heard about that," she said as she handed Rich a glass of beer and took a place beside him on her couch. "That was a terrible accident."

"Yeah."

"I really feel sorry for him," she went on to say. "That poor guy has been through so much and still he's helped so many people. Now this accident happens to him."

"Yeah…it's back on."

The video footage started with Jake Kramer walking toward the camera from across the lawn. In the background, going unnoticed by the majority of the audience was a clear view of one Alex Sanders who turned away from the camera and made his way into the garage.

"Sandman," whispered Rich.

"Sandman," repeated Meg giving him a curious look. "What's sandman?"

"Shhhhhh…let's listen to this."

"…Mr. Kramer, may we all extend out heartfelt sympathies on the tragic loss of your employee and friend, Wesley Washington," said Elliott, as he shook hands on camera, giving the impression they were the best of friends.

"It's nice to see you again, Cameron, and thank you. But let's not forget to extend our condolences to the family of Otis Porter as well."

"Yes, of course. Mr. Kramer. WAXU has learned that the fire marshals have officially listed this incident as an accident. They have indicated that the probable cause was an electrical spark igniting fuel from a leak in your vehicle."

"Yes," said Rich under his breath.

"I believe the authorities do an outstanding job in evaluating the evidence in their investigations. However, in this particular case, it is my belief that they have dropped the ball. I believe this was not an accident, but rather a deliberate attempt on my life and unfortunately, I will be living the remainder of mine knowing that two innocent people have lost their lives as a result."

"Mr. Kramer…you realize, of course, the implications of such a statement."

"I do."

"And you have evidence to back up your allegations?"

"I do."

"Can we expect you to go to the authorities with your evidence, Mr. Kramer?"

"You cannot. I will be handling this matter in my own way. For example, I am making it public that I am personally offering a one hundred thousand dollar reward to anyone with information leading to the arrest and conviction of the person or persons responsible. I do intend to bring the guilty party or parties to justice."

The WAXU cameraman was all over this interview and managed to zoom in on Kramer's facial expression at the exact moment that Jake said, "I do intend to bring the guilty party or parties to justice."

"Mr. Kramer…Jake," added Cameron trying to develop a first name relationship in front of his audience, "I believe our viewers, your friends, feel your pain as well and would welcome an opportunity to tell you so. Would you accept my invitation to join me on another segment of, *Up Close and Personal*? Will you be my guest, Mr. Kramer?"

"I will. And Cameron, let me say this to anyone who plans to bring harm to me for telling the truth…I will not run…I will not hide. And to he who causes death or injury to my family, friends, or innocent people…I will not rest until justice is done…and that, Mr. Elliott, is the gospel."

# Thirty-Five

With the exception of a lone security light at the rear of her neighbor's property, all was dark and quiet along Putnam County Road 700-South, north of Cloverdale. Meg and her new friend sat quietly, side by side, on her blue floral couch listening to the closing statements of Jake Kramer on the late edition of the nightly news. Kramer's quest for justice had Rich smiling as he found the offer of a small ransom somewhat amusing, for no one could trace the ill-fated deed back to him. That was until Jake unwittingly finished his statement by saying…"and that, Mr. Elliott, is the gospel."

"Sandman," said Rich once again.

"Now that's twice you've mentioned the name Sandman, Rich. Is he someone special?" she asked.

Rich reached for his drink and collected his thoughts before answering, "No, not really. Let's just say he's work-related."

"Now that's interesting. You know you have never told me what line of work you're in."

"No, I haven't."

"Well? What is it you do?"

"You could say I'm with the government."

"That's pretty vague. Can I assume it's ours?"

"You can," he answered with a smile.

"Okay mister, I'll play your guessing game. Will you tell me if I get it?"

"Sure."

"Are you in the military?"

"Nope."

At first Rich was amused at her questions and played along with her silly little game. However, it didn't take long before her persistence began to annoy him and he had enough.

"I work for the United States Secret Service," he interrupted, "and if you tell anyone I'll have to come back and shoot you."

Meg fell back against the couch, wide-eyed and open-mouthed. "You don't?"

"Okay, I don't."

"You do? I mean, really? The secret service?"

"Yes…really," he answered while giving her a no-nonsense look.

"Well, I'll be. So what's the secret service doing hanging around Cloverdale, Indiana anyway?" she asked on a serious note.

"Can you keep a secret, Meg?" Although he knew with a question like that there was only one answer.

"Yes…of course. I won't tell anybody. Besides, if I did, you said you'd have to shoot me," she added with a giggle.

"That's true, I would. Okay, the truth is…I'm here to take care of Jake Kramer. That's why I was interested in the news tonight."

"No kidding? Who would have thought that I'd be sitting next to a secret service agent assigned to look after Jake Kramer?"

Meg was getting excited at the idea of having the closest thing to a celebrity in her home and moved a little closer minimizing the space between them. Rich, on the other hand was growing a little uncomfortable with her crowding him, for he wasn't accustomed to the type of attention he was receiving.

"It's no big deal…just a job."

"Why would the government be interested in Jake Kramer?" she continued. "He's not like an official or anything."

"I don't ask why," he answered. "I just do what I have to do."

"And how are you doing?" she continued.

"Well, you could say I've been doing a bang-up job so far. That is until this afternoon. Those two men shouldn't have gotten hurt. That was my fault. I must be getting careless and that's unacceptable in my line of work."

"Oh Rich, you shouldn't blame yourself for that," she said as she placed her hand on his thigh in a comforting gesture. "Things sometime happen that are out of our control. You can't be there for him all the time."

Rich felt her hand fall boldly on his leg which surprised and startled him, as he quickly gasped for breath and felt his chest heave. Megan could feel Rich's leg quiver at her touch and responded by sliding closer and pressing her breast firmly against his bicep. Rich was shaking like a school boy, and any effort by Megan to calm him only worked in reverse, for he was not in the habit of being touched. Rich's embarrassment grew as his face turned red and his body quivered. He tried to speak but his mouth was so dry that he only managed a humiliating mumble. His heart raced as she took her hand and rubbed it slowly along his leg.

He swallowed several times trying to find moisture in his mouth before attempting to speak. "I'm afraid…I mean, I'm sorry, but I have to go now. Thank you for…"

"You don't have to leave, Rich. It's alright. There's no need to be embarrassed."

"I'm not embarrassed," he answered unconvincingly. "I just need to get back to work."

Rich tried to stand on shaky legs but only managed to slide himself to the edge of the sofa allowing her hand to glide along his thigh.

"It's alright," she repeated. "I understand. But you don't have to go."

They were both standing now, each trembling for their own reasons.

Megan watched the black SUV disappear into the darkness before locking her door and turning off the post lamp that lit the front walk. As she moved toward the kitchen to place the two half-filled glasses in the sink, she couldn't help but feel some sense of rejection, but it was bearable because she knew he didn't reject her…he rejected himself. There was something about this secret service agent that had become very intriguing to her. There was no doubt about it, she was attracted to him and would be patient and supportive in order to help him gain his confidence. With the lights off throughout the house she made herself ready for bed while her mind stayed active on Rich the G-man. Meg stopped and stared blankly at her bed as she repeated G-man. Thinking to herself, I hope that doesn't stand for gay-man. She shook her head no several times in order to dismiss that thought, and convinced herself that, given enough time, she could cure him of that habit if it was true. With the last of her bedtime ceremonies finished she tossed her clothes into the hamper and raised the window to allow the fresh warm summer breeze to circulate in the room. She reached for her night shirt laying on the edge of the bed, then without hesitation she opted for her natural attire before peeling the sheets down and climbing into bed.

There were little differences between the night calls of the wild in the Appalachians and those in Central Indiana. However tonight, the Putnam County wild had a loneliness and sadness in its cry. Standing motionless Rich let the wind clear his senses as he listened to the sounds echoing through the hollow, for it again reminded him of home.

He estimated that the corn had grown another six inches, but then the rain had helped. He took his place once again between the first and second rows of corn while standing as still as his unsteady body would allow. He could feel his legs beginning to shake as he watched her place her clothes on something just out of his view. His heart raced and his chest heaved as she stood in front of the window to raise the lower half to allow the fresh night air to enter. His eyes followed her contour as she stepped toward the bed to rearrange her sleepwear before sliding between the blue sheets. Rich's entire body shivered until his shaky hand slowly rubbed the moisture from his face as he raised his head to the heavens and spoke softly, "*Watch and pray, that ye enter not into temptation: the spirit indeed is willing, but the flesh is weak*...Matthew 26:41."

# Thirty-Six

Tuesday morning in the greater Indianapolis area was warm and clear and promised to remain that way for the next few days. Jake had been up for a couple of hours and was standing next to the counter patiently waiting for his second pot of coffee when a light tap on the patio door caught his attention. Without moving he motioned for Alex to come in.

"Coffee's about done, Alex. Grab your cup."

"Thanks, don't mind if I do," he replied as he reached for his designated cup from the hook under the cabinet.

Alex pulled a chair from the kitchen table and took a seat while looking over the morning paper spread out in front of him. The headlines boldly stated, "Two Die in Southside Explosion." Another section had accompanying pictures showing the destruction of the Kramer building along with two inserted photographs of the deceased, namely Wesley and Otis. These reminders were things Jake didn't need to see nor dwell upon, but Alex was sure he had. He turned and took a long look at his friend who still held his stare at the dripping coffee, but Alex knew Jake's mind was on something other than coffee. He also realized that this was the first time, in all the years he had known Jake, that he was seeing him unshaven. Not only unshaven, but actually scruffy looking, for his hair was unruly and his clothes looked like he had slept in them. This was the guy who showered and shaved before taking out the trash. Indeed, this was the most uncharacteristic image of Jake Kramer he could recall.

"Did you sleep alright?"

"Yeah," said Jake inconvincibly. "I'm was hoping for a call telling me that Connie would be released today. I'll rest better knowing she's well and coming home."

Noticing that his Mr. Coffee had stopped dripping, Jake picked up the glass pot and moved toward the table to fill the two empty cups.

"Any news on Stacie or Tonya?"

Jake shook his head no before he turned to return the pot to the burner. "Nothing yet. It's hard to believe that it was only yesterday that all this happened."

Alex, in a thoughtful gesture, reached to gather the newspaper from the table top.

"LEAVE THEM!" shouted Jake as he moved quickly across the kitchen. "Leave them right there."

"Sorry, Jake, I just thought it might be better…"

"Well you thought wrong."

Alex let the issue drop and sipped his coffee. Although surprised by Jake's temperament he knew there was just cause for it.

"I caught your interview on the late news, Jake. You're not seriously thinking about going on live television again are you?"

"Sure…why not?"

"Well, I think you should take a little time and get yourself together again for one thing. Elliott will have you for lunch if he interviews you in your current state.

Exposing yourself now with the wolves on your heels, well…"

"There's nothing wrong with my current state. I'm just mad. I'm mad because two people are dead because of me. I'm mad because you and I know it'll likely be tried again and the next time it could be my wife and kids. To hell with the wolves, Alex. Bring them on because I'm going to take as many of them with me as I can. I'm going to point the finger at as many as my time will allow and maybe, just maybe, I'll get lucky and hit one of them."

Alex resisted the temptation to debate this destructive issue with Jake, for it was clear Jake's mind was set on revenge. He instead sipped his coffee and hoped for a subject change, which came with the ring of the phone.

"Hello. Oh good morning, Con, how are you feeling? I'm fine thanks, don't worry about me. Has the doctor been in? Great, what time can I come and get you? Okay, I'll be there…Any word on Stacie or Tonya? I see. Does Doctor Harrington think she'll be able to help her? Good. What about Tonya, any news? No! Tell me now. Look, Connie, I don't want to wait until I come down there. If you have news about Tonya, tell me.

Alex was standing and looking out at the backyard when the conversation turned to Tonya and the tone of Jake's voice didn't ease his concern for the little girl.

"Oh my God, no. That sweet, precious little girl. When? Okay, Connie, thanks. I'll see you in a little while…No, I'll be okay. No, I'm not alone. Alex is here having coffee, I'm okay. Bye, honey."

Jake returned the phone to its cradle and paused with his back to Alex and his head lowered. Alex could feel his heart pounding as he waited in silence for the report.

"She slipped into a coma, Alex. Sometime last night; Connie's not sure when. Doctor Harrington is checking with Doctor Zorka for information."

"Jake…I'm so sorry."

"Yeah…me too," he said as he started across the kitchen. "Me too."

Jake was about to sit down at the table when he paused to look at his watch and said, "He should be up by now," and again made his way to the phone.

"Hello?"

"Inspector Pierson, this is Jake Kramer."

"Jake, good to hear your voice. I have been thinking about you. Please accept my sympathy on the loss of young Wesley. I know how close you two were."

"Thanks, Bob. Actually that's why I'm calling. I need a favor."

"Sure, Jake, you know I'll do anything I can."

"Bob, I'll get right to the point. I'd like you to look into Wesley and Porter's murders."

"Murders?" repeated the Inspector.

"That's right…murders," repeated Jake.

"Jake, do you have some information to indicate that this was something other than an accident?

Because from what I've read and heard on the news, the fire Marshall has labeled it an accident."

"I have my reasons, Inspector. No proof, only suspicions."

"Jake, really…I think…"

"Inspector," interrupted Jake, "you owe me big time. I'm calling in my markers."

"Okay, Jake, slow down a minute. I never said I wouldn't help you. And you don't have to challenge my appreciation either. I'm just asking for some sort of justification for your suspicions, that's all."

"Sorry, Bob. I've been a little out of it lately, please don't take it personally."

"Let's start over shall we, Jake? Why do you think this was more than an accident?"

"Nothing specific that I can give you now, Bob… nothing you can use. I'm just asking if you'll check it out for me."

"Have you been threatened, Jake?"

"Threatened? Hell Bob, I've got a whole box of hate mail in the den. Come on over and pick out one you like."

Jake waited through a short pause on the phone before Pierson spoke. "I imagine this was originally a local jurisdiction matter that most likely has been handled by the State Police due to the magnitude of the explosion and the resulting deaths. Jake, officially speaking, there doesn't seem to be a Federal crime here. That is to say, nothing that the FBI typically investigates. But if the State asks for help we can assist. I have a contact in the State Police whom I can confide in and I also have a friend in the A.F.T. I'll make some calls, okay?"

"Thank you, Inspector, I will be returning the favor."

"Oh Jake, I also have the information you asked for concerning 800-MISSING. Do you want to pick it up or should I mail it?"

"Just mail it, Inspector. Thank you very much. I'll be in touch."

"Good-bye, Jake."

Jake returned the phone to its hook and ran his fingers through his unruly hair until his hand reached the back of his neck where he paused to massage away the tense muscles. He turned back to the table to explain the reasoning behind his call to Alex.

"The Inspector is going to look…" Jake stopped as he noticed that Alex was no longer seated at the kitchen table. He had left sometime during Jake's conversation with Pierson, leaving his cup and saucer sitting directly on the newspaper covering the headlines.

"Coulda least said good-by," he said aloud.

"Who are you talking to, Daddy?"

"Hey…good morning sleepy-head."

"Morning, Daddy. Have you heard from mom?" she asked as she opened the refrigerator and removed the orange juice.

"Yes, just a little while ago. She's been released and I'm on my way to pick her up."

"When?"

"Right now…you want to go along?"

"No, I'll stay and pick up a little while you're gone. Daddy…you're not going looking like that are you?"

"Like what?"

"Like that. Daddy, go clean up first. Mom will die if you go in looking like that."

There was a brief hush before Margaret said, "Sorry, Daddy, I didn't mean to say…"

"It's okay, honey, I know what you mean. I guess I could shower first."

"No…I guess you better shower first, Daddy."

Alex made his way home and stood quietly on his patio trying to develop a plan that would end Jake's troubles. But the problem was, there was no end, and subsequently, no plan. His concentration was interrupted as he quickly reached for his cell phone that vibrated against his waist.

"Yes."

"Please enter your pin number followed by the pound sign…now."

"Now they call," he said as he entered 147021# and waited for a response.

"Sandman?"

Alex had no difficulty in recognizing the unmistakable sound of the voice.

"Yes."

"We've been monitoring your inactivity concerning your final assignment. You realize that you have exceeded the standard timetable?"

"Yes."

"You also realize that this assignment has been awarded a piggyback?"

"I am aware."

"Sandman…there have been questions raised concerning your judgment. Why didn't you call home and inform us of your relationship with the mark?"

"I tried, but no one accepted my calls. Sir…may I respectfully request an option to buy my assignment and have it placed on the endangered species list?"

"Regrettably, that's not an option. However, be advised, you are hereby relieved of your assignment. I repeat…you are relieved of your current assignment. Do you understand?"

"I understand."

"Sandman, your current commitment rests one short of final evaporation. Do you still wish to pursue that end?"

Alex didn't answer immediately and prompted the caller to add. "We have been monitoring with great disappointment the number of substandard actions in your area. These are intolerable, and regrettably the last dishonor resulted in multiple civilian casualties. This event was not only unacceptable, but has also magnified public awareness and compassion toward our objective. We assumed, however, that these inferior efforts were not of your doing, Sandman."

"They were not."

"Sandman, we will cut to the prime. It has been deemed by the family that your piggyback shall be reclassified as a virus. We feel you can satisfy your obligation to this organization by eliminating this virus. Do you accept this as an option, Sandman?"

"I accept, if you agree not to attach a piggyback to this option."

"It is agreed, Sandman. Have a nice day."

Cindy saw Alex slide his phone on its clip and stand quietly on the patio looking out over the woods behind them. Silently, she made her way to him, wrapping her arms around his waist and placing her head against his shoulder. "How's he doing?"

"He's not," he answered while placing his hands atop hers. "Connie is going to be released and Jake's going down in a little while to get her."

"That good news," said Cindy. "I've been worried about her."

"Yeah, but the bad news is Tonya's in a coma."

Alex felt Cindy shudder and squeeze his waist before moving to his side.

"Oh, Alex, she's so young."

"I know."

"Is there any hope?"

"I don't think they know yet. This happened sometime through the night so the details are vague. Maybe we'll find out more when they get back. To tell you the truth, I'm a little worried about Jake. He's taking this very personally."

"What do you mean? He can't blame himself. It was an accident."

"He doesn't see it that way."

Alex turned and faced Cindy, taking her hands and kissing each once. "Cindy, there are some things I need to do. I would rather you not ask questions, because I can't tell you. I only need for you to trust me and know that I love you."

"You're going away again?"

"No, my work shouldn't take me very far, but I may be keeping some long hours."

"You're going back to work aren't you, Alex?"

"Yes…but when this is done we're going away, Cindy. We're going to New England and find that bed and breakfast we promised ourselves and buy it. It will be our time together."

Cindy's eyes watered as she softly replied, "I better start packing."

Alex's heart ached as he looked into Cindy's eyes. Withholding the truth from her hurt him more than she could know, but once again, it was necessary…once again it would be the last time. He was going back to work. He had accepted another trouble shooting assignment, but unlike the others, this one he wanted and that was the gospel.

## Thirty-Seven

"But I don't want to ride. I'm perfectly able to walk, thank you very much just the same."

"I'm sorry, Mrs. Kramer, it's hospital policy and no one is exempt."

"But we're not leaving the hospital. We're going to visit another patient, so…"

"Mrs. Kramer, if you expect to be released from County General sometime in your lifetime you are going to have to sit down in this chair and let me wheel you out."

"Forget it, Connie," said Jake who's patience was beginning to wear thin, "sit."

Connie had mellowed by the time they entered the front lobby and was smiling as she was escorted outside into the fresh air and warm sun. She was even pleasant enough to thank the aide for the nice ride and immediately followed her back through the automatic doors on foot.

Doctor Harrington was expecting them and gave both a warm and sincere welcome. Jake had left his sarcasm for psychologists somewhere along the way and actually acted human toward Doreen.

"I know you two are extremely concerned for Tonya's welfare and let me assure you that she is receiving the best of care."

"I want all the expenses sent directly to me," insisted Jake. "Make sure that everyone knows that money is no object. I want her to have the best…"

"JAKE!" interrupted Connie. That's not necessary. Doreen is well aware that we want the best for Tonya so there's no need to insist."

"Mr. Kramer, let me assure you once again, Tonya is being well cared for."

"Sorry, Doctor, I didn't mean to imply she wasn't."

"I've asked Doctor Zorka to stop by and brief us on what to expect with Tonya's current condition. He should be here shortly. Would anyone care for coffee, tea or perhaps a soft drink?"

Drinks were accepted and as Doreen passed the cokes around Jake said, "Tell us about Stacie, Doctor. Did she rest well last night?"

"Stacie rested well last night because we saw to it. We have ways to make it so. This morning I checked on her and I'm afraid she still suffers from delusions. Mr. and Mrs. Kramer, I think Stacie is going to require help for some time. Mine or someone of her choosing, but nonetheless, she will need a great deal of help in getting back to reality."

The quick tap on the door and the light squeak from the hinges once again announced Doctor Zorka's arrival. His mannerisms today were even more of one on a tight schedule as compared to their last consultation. He was dressed in green scrubs and still wore his white hairnet that would have made him look ridiculous if it had not been for the respected reason for it.

"Doctor Zorka, thank you for stopping by," said Doreen. "Can I offer you something to drink?"

"Thank you…no. How is Mrs. Washington doing this morning, Doreen?"

"As well as can be expected, George. It will take time."

The room became quiet as it was Zorka's turn to make his report on Tonya. Connie was the only one who watched him move slowly into position to allow a clear view of all seated parties.

"I'm afraid Tonya suffered a second swelling in the brain sometime last evening. As a result we felt it in her best interest to induce a coma with Phenobarbital."

"You put her in a coma on purpose?" asked Connie.

"Yes, ma'am, it's a common practice under these circumstances. Actually, you should consider this as our putting Tonya to sleep while her body heals itself."

"Doctor Zorka," said Jake. Yesterday during the craniotomy, did you install an ICP?"

"Yes," answered an astonished doctor. "It's customary."

"And today before you introduced Phenobarbital, what was the intracranial pressure reading?"

"Mr. Kramer, are you trying to lead me to believe that you've studied the field of neurosurgery?"

"No sir, but I have been checking the notes of some distinguished surgeons and teachers who have. I'm still curious as to her ICP reading before you introduced Phenobarbital?"

Doctor George Zorka couldn't have taken a deeper breath or his face turned any more red without bursting as he said in no uncertain terms, "Mr. Kramer, sir…I'll have you know that I have devoted my life to the study of neurosurgery science and I do not intend to have my qualifications questioned by anyone…especially one who has no formal education in my field. DO I MAKE MYSELF CLEAR, SIR?"

Jake immediately stood and faced Zorka before speaking. "Doctor Zorka, I am NOT questioning your talents or qualifications. I am merely asking the ICP reading prior to the decision to induce Phenobarbital." With that said, Jake quickly raised his hands and pressed them firmly over his ears trying to relieve the spontaneous pressure and ringing. Connie, Doreen and George watched as Jake staggered about the room trying to retain his balance and ease the throbbing in his ears.

Jake…Jake are you alright?" asked Connie. "Honey, what's wrong?"

Jake continued applying pressure to his head as he continued moving slowly across the carpet toward the window. "I…I just was asking…you don't understand. I was concerned about deep intracerebral hemorrhaging. It could be very dangerous. Tonya's ICP reading…it…" Jake quickly ran his hands across his eyes rubbing hard against the sockets then returned them to his ears. "Wesley's dead...don't you get it? Wesley is dead because of ME. I just wanted to help Tonya…I didn't mean to…"

Everyone was standing trying to grasp Jake's current outburst of emotions. Connie moved toward him but her attempt to calm him was rigorously pushed away.

"Mr. Kramer, you have actually suggested a possibility that we have yet to explore," said Doctor Zorka as he looked to Doreen who was giving a nod of approval. "Please accept my apology for becoming short with you. I had no idea that you were so well informed, Mr. Kramer."

Jake paused for a moment and turned to the group while lowering his hands. He appeared to be mellowing some, but the tension in the room remained intense and confused.

"Perhaps you wouldn't mind sharing some of you views with my staff, Mr. Kramer, we most certainly would…"

"You most certainly would like to see me put away in some rubber room, that's what you most certainly would like to see, isn't it doctor?" asked Jake. "Then you and your shrink friend here…"

"Jake!" shouted Connie. That will most certainly do. Now you apologize to them right now. There's no need for you to say things like that."

Jake stopped in place as Connie's tone caught his attention. Everyone stood silently watching him lower his hands to his waist and bow his head. Momentary his body began to shake as he spoke so softly that on one heard.

"Mr. Kramer," said Harrington. "Please sit down, won't you?" I'll freshen your drink and we can talk for a while."

Jake's body continued shaking when Connie reached his side. She knew now that he was crying. With his head still lowered he was saying over and over

…"I can't make them stop hurting. I can't. Wesley is dead because of me. I can't make them stop hurting. I can't."

"Here, Jake," said Doreen as she walked slowly in his direction, "drink this…it will make you feel better. Come on, drink it and let's sit for a while."

"HELL NO!" I don't need any of your witchcraft potions," he screamed. "Take it away," as he backhanded her offer, knocking the glass across the office until it rolled to a stop against her desk.

"Jake!" cried Connie.

"Now see here, Mr. Kramer," said Doctor Zorka who had been quietly taking it all in. "There's no need for that kind of outburst."

"Leave me alone," Jake shouted as he again pressed his hands against his ears while rapidly shaking his head. "Why can't they just leave me alone," he shouted again as he hurried past the three speechless people staring in awe as he made his way to the door and disappeared in the hall. Connie was the first to reach the door to look for him as the two doctors followed closely. They located Jake in the hall leaning with one hand against the wall to steady himself.

"Jake!" shouted Connie. "Honey, come back, please."

Jake looked in the direction of her call, but ignored the plea as he moved toward the opening elevator doors. The volunteers' gift and magazine cart was almost clear of the door when Jake stumbled into it, sending the metal cart to its side with a thundering crash that echoed for an eternity in the hall. The contents were still sliding in every direction as Jake stepped over and on them to enter the empty elevator before it left without him.

He found himself standing outside in the warm sun at the pick-up area of the drive. The very area that he would be helping Connie into their car about now if things hadn't gone south. His head had not stopped its relentless pounding and the bright sun didn't help the situation. Cupping his hand above his eyes as a visor, Jake stepped off the curb directly into the path of a yellow cab.

"If you plan to get run over, Mac, I guess doing it in front of a hospital is the best place," said the driver.

"Sorry."

"You okay, buddy?"

"Yeah."

"You need a lift?"

"I don't know…I don't think so."

"Come on, jump in, buddy. I'll give you a lift to wherever it is you need to go. You aren't walking so well, maybe you should ride."

"Maybe so," said Jake as he opened the rear door and took a seat opposite the driver.

"Where to?" he asked while resetting the flag.

"I don't care."

"Is that north or south?" he asked with a smile while pulling away from the curb.

The cabbie adjusted his rearview mirror to check on his passenger for Jake hadn't offered any response to his destination question.

"You okay, buddy?"

Jake nodded yes.

I'm headed back uptown, is that alright?"

Jake again nodded while answering, "Yes."

"Do I know you from somewhere? Are you on television or something? You look familiar."

"No, I'm not on television or nothing."

Okay buddy, I'll let you rest. You look like you've had a bad time of it."

Jake rested his head against the seat, closed his eyes and listened to the street noise as the yellow cab took him away from County General Hospital.

"Hey Mac, my garage is on the next block and my shift is over. If you have somewhere you want to go you better speak up."

"Right here. This is good," Jake responded.

"You sure? There are better streets in town."

"I'm sure. How much do I own you?"

"No charge, I was coming up here anyway. Besides, I just figured out who you are. Your, Mr. Kramer ain't you. See, Wesley was my cousin, Mr. Kramer. No sir, no charge and if you ever need a cab …just call yellow and ask for Bubba."

Jake shook Bubba's hand that was offered over the seat and directly stepped from the cab that left him standing alone among the flashing neon lights of downtown Indianapolis.

"Thank you for the ride home, Doreen. I really hated to take you away from your schedule."

"Think nothing of it, Connie. Actually, I was hoping we might find Jake here. To be perfectly frank, I'm becoming more than a little concerned about him."

"So am I Doctor, but his truck is not in the drive. I don't think he's here.

"Who's not here, Mom?" asked Maggie."

"Oh, hi honey…has your father made it home yet?"

"No, I thought he was with you. Hello, Doctor Harrington…what's going on guys?"

Connie paused looking for a soft explanation, but Doctor Harrington spoke in an effort to help.

"Your father suffered a huge loss Monday, Margaret. You all have of course, but your dad worked closely with Wesley and, as can be expected, he is having a difficult time accepting his loss. But I can almost guarantee you, that in time, he will be fine."

"Where is he, Mom?"

"We don't know, honey, but don't worry, he'll work things out. He's probably with Alex somewhere talking guy talk. Everything is going to be okay."

"I thought he was acting a little strange this morning, said Margaret."

"How so, Margaret?" asked Doreen.

"I don't know…he just wasn't Daddy…you know? I mean, he was ready to leave for the hospital to get you, Mom, but he hadn't showered or cleaned up any. He was just acting odd."

"Well, it's like Doctor Harrington mentioned, Margaret, your father has been through a difficult time."

"Yeah, you're right.

As the evening wore on at 919 Crest Street, so did Connie's concern for her husband. She managed to downplay his absence at dinner with Maggie, by suggesting that Dad needed time to deal with the situation at hand. Not to worry. There had been no calls from Jake, and any attempt by her to contact his cell was useless because her first try located his phone on their kitchen counter. She was becoming very worried considering his frame of mind when he ran from the hospital. Connie knew that Doctor Harrington was correct in suggesting that Jake get some professional help. He had been slipping before Wesley's death, and now as a result of it, he was sliding.

Connie reached for the phone and pressed the speed dial button that remembered the Sanders' number for her.

"Hello?"

"Hi Cindy, it's Connie, am I interrupting anything?"

"You bet…I was standing over an ironing board with a hot iron. Thanks for calling. I have been thinking about you, Connie, how are you feeling?"

"I'm fine thanks, just a little sore. Cindy, I was calling to talk to Alex. Is he free?"

"He's not home, Connie. He mentioned to me this morning that he would be working for the next few days…sorry. Can I give him a message when he calls in?"

"No…that's alright, thanks anyway."

"Connie…is everything alright? Is Jake okay?"

Connie paused, creating a noticeable delay in her answer to Cindy who then asked, "Connie would you like me to come over for a little while?"

"Thanks, Cindy, but I'm just a little tired, that's all. I think I'll take a warm bath and make an early bed time."

"Promise you'll call me if you need anything, Connie?"

"I will…good night, Cindy."

Connie hadn't left the room when the phone rang again, "Hello Jake?" she answered.

"Hello…Mrs. Kramer? This is Rosa Washington."

"Oh hello, Rosa. I'm sorry, I must have been thinking out loud."

"That's quite alright; actually I was calling for Mr. Kramer. Is he in?"

"No Rosa, I'm afraid you've missed him. May I take a message?"

"Yes please. I've made arrangements for a memorial service for Wesley at Mortiman's Family Mortuary for one p.m. Thursday. I knew you would want to know the arrangements."

"Why, yes of course, Rosa. One p.m. Thursday," she repeated.

"That's right, Connie. We're asking that donations be made to the 'Save the Children' Foundation, instead of flowers. You'll see that Jake gets the message?"

"Yes, of course."

"We don't have much family around, so I was hoping that he might say a few words, if it wouldn't be an imposition. Wesley admired him so."

"I'll be certain and mention it to him, Rosa. I'm sure he won't mind."

"Thank you, Mrs. Kramer…good night."

Connie returned the phone to its cradle while asking, "Oh Jake…where are you?"

# Thirty-Eight

The clock in *Miller's Pawn and Loans* indicated that it was ten thirty-five, considering of course that the batteries were good. However, that mattered little to Jake as he stood motionless in front of the glass watching the pendulum swing. The air was on the cool side for this time of year and he shook occasionally due to the chill or his nerves. Jake hadn't eaten anything since his bowl of cereal in the morning, but hunger never occurred to him as he stood stationary looking into the store.

"Hey Buddy, you got a match?"

Jake shook his head no without answering or turning.

"You got a cigarette?"

Again he shook his head no.

"You got any money? You look like you got money."

This time Jake didn't respond at all.

"You too good to speak to us, man?

There were three of them; two were standing about a step and a half behind the talker and grinning at one another like kids. Jake knew this because he could see their reflections in the glass. He could also see a fourth man approaching in the shadows to his right, but he felt no fear. He just continued to watch the pendulum swing back and forth on the clock in front of him.

"Turn around and look at me when I'm talking to you, old man," said the talker as he reached out and grabbed Jake by the shoulder. "Hand me your wallet. I want to borrow some money."

"Why don't you leave the man alone, boys? He's not bothering you."

Jake could feel the boy's grip release from his shoulder with the suggestion from the man in the shadows.

"Well now, look at what we have here guys. The old man's got a guardian angel, or maybe he's his keeper from the home. Are you his keeper mister, or are you just looking for trouble?"

"Just leave him alone and move along, sonny."

"Sonny! Hey bro's, this dude's real brave for someone who's alone."

"I'm not alone, sonny," he said while pulling his jacket open revealing the holster at his waist. "I have my friend Mr. Beretta at my side."

Jake could see that the two boys had stopped grinning and closed the gap between them and the talker.

"Are you just a carrier, Mr. Keeper? You better be man enough use that piece, because I'm gonna take it and pull the trigger to see if it's loaded."

There were now five people on the street anxiously waiting for someone to start something, but it didn't happen. The boy on the right, wearing a blue muscle shirt, noticed that his leader was in a bad spot and spoke up, "Hey Dude, he ain't worth it man…let 'em live."

"Yeah, Guzzler's right, Dude…let's roll man," said the other.

The talker then pointed his finger at the man in the shadows, "You may not be so lucky next time, Mr. Keeper. Take the old man and get off our turf."

"Are you alright?" he asked Jake, who responded with a head movement.

"You look like you could use some food. Come with me and we'll get you off the street."

Jake continued staring at the motion of the pendulum, but a gentle hand on his arm broke him away.

"Come with me. It's alright."

They walked two blocks along East Raymond Street before turning the corner and moving under the red and green awning that stretched between the block building and the curb. The storefront windows had been frosted to give the guests anonymity from the street traffic. Jake slowed as they approached the entry, but was given friendly encouragement by his guide.

"It's alright; no one will hurt you here. Listen… they're singing inside, do you hear it?"

Jake nodded that he did as they paused and listened to the makeshift choir singing, *Shall We Gather At The River* in a variety of keys.

"Stacie," whispered Jake, as he moved to the door of the Lasting Light Mission.

"Welcome Brothers. Please come in from the night's chill. I'm Sister Marie."

"Thank you, Sister. My friend here seems to have lost his way. I was hoping you may have lodging for him tonight?"

"We somehow always find room for one more in God's house, my son. Will you be staying with us also?"

"No, Sister, thank you. I have work to do. We just need space for one."

Sister Marie turned to Jake who was listening to the collected group of singers seated in folding chairs that circled an old upright player-piano.

"Does your friend have a name?" she asked.

"I didn't ask, Sister. Does it make a difference?"

"No, of course not." She then turned and motioned to the one who was wiping the table next to them. "Ernie…Ernie, will you please warm-up some of your potato soup for our late arrival?"

"Yes, Sister. And I'll make him a sandwich too, okay?"

"Thank you, Ernie, that would be nice."

Ernie gave her a smile and walked away favoring his left leg that had been injured when he miscalculated the speed of a westbound boxcar twelve years ago.

"Sister," said Jake's guide, "I know you don't charge for your services, but please accept this donation for the mission."

"Thank you, brother, these are trying times indeed," she said as she received the stack of folded cash. "This is certainly generous, my son, are you…"

"No more generous than your mission, Sister. Please look after our friend."

"God looks after them, my son, we only help."

"Good night, Sister."

Sister Marie watched him leave the building while clasping the roll of money between her fists and crucifix. She gave thanks in prayer before turning to make good on her promise to take care of the lost one, who hadn't moved from his vantage point while listening to the choir.

Ernie returned carrying a tray filled with Jake's evening meal and found him sitting quietly listening to the Lasting Light Mission choir's second struggle at getting the words right to *Shall We Gather At The River*. Moving to the opposite side of the table he slid the tray in front of Jake and waited for a response of gratitude.

"Thank you, Ernie," said Sister Marie. "We're not sure our friend here can talk. You understand don't you, Ernie?"

"Yes, Sister, I didn't know. You want me to give thanks for him?"

"That would be nice, Ernie…please."

Ernie stood in front of Jake, then lowered his head, clasped his hands at his tarnished belt buckle and spoke softly while being accompanied by an out-of-tune piano playing *Mine Eyes Have Seen The Glory.*

"Father, we have another lost lamb from your flock with us tonight who found his way home to your house. And Father we stand here before you again to give thanks for this food he's receive'n. May it fill his body and ease his hunger and fill his heart with the love you share with all us sinners. This we ask in Jesus' name… Amen."

"Amen," said the Sister.

"Amen," repeated Jake.

"Thank you Ernie," said the Sister. "That was lovely."

"Thank you Ernie," repeated Jake. "That was lovely."

Sister Marie and Ernie moved away from the table in hopes that their guest would eat his meal while it was warm.

"Sister, do you know who that is?"

"No, he hasn't shared his name, Ernie."

"That's Kramer. I didn't recognize him until I got in front of him. Kramer…what's-his-name…"

"He's still welcome here, Brother Ernie."

"No, Sister. That's not what I meant. He's the guy who talks to dead people. Remember when he was on the television and people asked him questions about dead people and he would know all the answers."

"Only God, talks to the deceased and has all the answers, Ernie," she added as she began growing tired of his suggestions.

"Wait, Sister," he said as he grabbed a stack of newspapers and frantically searched for the front page. "Here…look…the explosion on Monday. See…that was his building. It says right here…two dead at Kramer building."

Sister Marie paused and took the paper from the outstretched hand of her loyal aide, Ernie, and read the headline. The inserted photo confirmed his tale. As she lowered the paper and looked back at her latest lost lamb she agreed with Ernie that the exhausted man eating at their table was indeed Jake Kramer.

## Thirty-Nine

"Morning, Mom, did you sleep alright?"

"Good morning, Margaret. Would you like some breakfast?"

"I'll get something later. Have you heard from Daddy?"

"Not yet, but don't worry, I'm sure he's okay."

Margaret moved toward her mother and placed her hands on her shoulders in a massaging motion before bending down to kiss her on top of the head. "Mom… you know we should check with the hospitals and police to see if…"

"Your father is fine, Margaret. There's no need to worry."

"Okay, Mom."

The phone rang interrupting their debate about Jake which allowed Margaret to move in its direction.

"I'll get it…maybe it's Daddy. Hello? Oh hi, Mrs. Sanders. No, she's right here. One moment please," she said before handing the cordless receiver to her mother.

"Good morning, Cindy."

"I was checking in before I left for work, Connie. Did Jake make it home alright?"

"No, he didn't, Cindy…but we're sure he's fine."

"Of course he is. He just needs a little time alone to sort things out, that's all. Men are like that."

"Have you heard from Alex, Cindy?"

"I found him sleeping on the couch this morning. He must have come in late and didn't want to disturb anyone. His note said to wake him when I got up, but I haven't yet."

"Ask him to call me, will you, Cindy?"

"Sure. Don't worry, Connie. Jake will be fine. I'll call you later."

"Thanks, Cindy. Bye."

"More coffee, Mom?"

"Please."

Margaret moved slowly across the kitchen with the glass pot in hand as the phone rang once again.

"I'll get it, Mom…maybe it's Daddy."

"Margaret…if you say that one more time, I'll…"

"Hello. Oh good morning, Doctor Harrington. No, she's right here. One moment please. Mom, it's for you…Doctor Harrington," she said while passing the receiver to Connie.

"Good morning, Doreen…nice of you to call."

Margaret saw her mother wave and took the cue that she would like a little privacy for her talk with the doctor, so Margaret hurriedly scratched a yellow Post-It note saying she would be next door at Becky's.

The sunlight was muted in the male dorm at the Lasting Light Mission and in keeping with the rules of stay, there was no talking permitted in the sleeping quarters. Respect for another's need to rest was mandatory. Jake Kramer rolled to his back while listening to the snoring of the tenant sleeping four cots to his right. Having no idea as to the time of day he pulled himself upright and studied the unfamiliar surroundings. He sat for awhile rubbing his eyes trying to bring some clarity to his sight before standing. Feeling a light tap on his shoulder he turned slowly and focused on a thin, balding man wearing a tan pullover, who gave a friendly smile with teeth that matched the graying stubbles of his beard. He was motioning for Jake to follow.

"I'm Ernie," he whispered, "The washroom is down here."

Jake's body ached from the firmness of the cot and as a result he was slow getting to his feet, giving the impression that he was closing in on his ninetieth birthday. Ernie led him to the washroom and catered to the latest celebrity at the mission by offering a dry faded green towel and a used bar of Ivory soap.

"Sorry, we ain't got no spare tooth brushes, sir. Supplies don't come until Friday. But you can use mine if your want. You can use my razor too, I don't mind. The blade ain't too bad. On Friday I'll get you one of your own. I do the passin' out."

Jake shook his head no and offered a quick smile to his benefactor. "Thanks anyway."

"Come downstairs when you get done, Mister. You slept through breakfast and lunch, but I can fix it with Cookie, the cook, to git you some soup if you're hungry."

Jake again smiled and nodded in appreciation, as an excited Ernie turned to leave the washroom.

"You're him, ain't you, Mister? You're Mr. Jake Kramer. I seen you on the television and your picture is in the paper. You talk to dead people don't you?"

The thin green towel that Jake was using to rub his face dry froze in motion at Ernie's suggestion. As he lowered the towel his face reflected in the mirror above the wash basin. "Jake Kramer?" he repeated softly to the man reflecting back at him.

"I knew it," said Ernie. "I just knew it. Now you take your time, Mr. Kramer, no hurry. When you come down you ask for me if you don't see me right away, 'cause I'm gonna take good care or you. I'll be in the kitchen at the bottom of the stairs checkin' with Cookie about getting you somethin' to eat. Just take your time, Mr. Kramer, sir. Okay if I call you Jake now that we're best friends?"

Jake didn't respond but continued looking at the stranger in the mirror while softly repeating the name …"Jake Kramer."

"Okay, Jake…I'll be in the kitchen."

The stairs leading down from the male dorm were dimly lit and in dire need of paint, but that was a low priority for the volunteers at the Lasting Light Mission. They had their hands full just managing the basic needs of the less fortunate who sought their help. Jake's slow descent from the stairs was greeted by Sister Marie who stood at the bottom.

"Good afternoon, Brother. I hope you slept well in God's house. Ernie has taken a special interest in seeing that you're well cared for, so he's preparing something hot for you now. You should feel honored. Ernie doesn't normally give such personal service."

Jake nodded in understanding and softly said, "Thank you, Sister."

"I understand from Brother Ernie that your name is Jake Kramer. Is that so?"

Jake didn't give her an answer but instead asked, "Where's the kitchen?"

"Behind you and to the left…just follow your nose, it'll take you there. Now I'm on my way to bible study so you're welcome to go find Ernie…unless, of course, you would rather accompany me to bible study."

Jake lowered his head and said, "Another time. Thank you, Sister."

"Indeed, Brother Kramer," she replied, "There's always another time."

Connie heard the phone ringing for the umpteenth time, but didn't have any desire to talk to anyone, so she decided to let it go to the answering machine. She did, however, listen in on the recording just in case it was Jake calling.

"Mrs. Kramer…this is Sister Marie calling from the Lasting Light Mission in Indianapolis. Are you there, Mrs. Kramer?"

Connie lifted the receiver and answered, "This is Mrs. Kramer, Sister. What can I do for you?"

"Mrs. Kramer, I realize I'm breaking one of our most trusted rules by calling, but I do believe it is in the best interest of Mr. Kramer."

"Jake…do you know where Jake is, Sister?"

"I believe your Mr. Kramer is one of our guests. He's safe and has been well cared for, Mrs. Kramer."

"Oh thank God, Sister," said Connie.

"Indeed," replied Sister Marie. "But for reasons I can't explain, I do fear for his well-being, Mrs. Kramer."

"I'll come right away, Sister. Can you keep him there?"

"If it's God's will, Mrs. Kramer, if it's God's will."

Connie moved about the house frantically gathering her purse, cell phone and car keys as the phone again rang. The machine in turn announced to whoever was calling that they had reached the Kramer's and were asked to leave a message.

"Connie, it's Alex. Have you heard from Jake?"

Connie reached for the phone to take Alex's call and explained Sister Marie's call from the mission.

"That's not a place for you to go alone, Connie. Let me go and bring him home."

Alex learned immediately and in no uncertain terms, that Connie had made up her mind to go to the mission to find her husband. After some friendly persuasion, she did agree however, to let Alex drive. They were on their way downtown in less than seven minutes.

Jake moved through the narrow passage unsure of exactly where he might find the kitchen, but it would have been difficult to get lost in the mission. Jake stopped short of the adjoining hall as the voice he heard sounded like that of his newly acquired friend, Ernie.

"You're the guy that wanted to know if Kramer ever showed up here?"

Jake stood quietly listening to Ernie on the hall pay phone around the corner.

"That's right, he come in last night. Oh yeah, it's him alright. I seen his picture in the paper. It's him. How much is the reward? I don't know, but he oughta to be worth a lot…say, fifty dollars. No, no wait… seventy-five. Yeah, I want seventy-five dollars. Sure, I can keep him here, we're best friends now. I'll meet ya at the delivery door behind the kitchen. You can park in the alley and come in that way so no one will see ya," said Ernie. "You won't forget my money, will ya. Sure I trust ya, we're best friends."

Ernie hung up the pay phone and with all the excitement of becoming one of the richest men at the Lasting Light Mission he hurried off to the men's room before he wet his pants.

Jake had heard Ernie's conversation with his unknown benefactor at the remote end of the line and as Ernie's footsteps faded down the hall, so did Jake Kramer's.

Sister Marie noticed Mr. Kramer leaving through the front entry and abruptly interrupted her bible study class to check on her straying lamb. Perhaps he was just getting some air she suggested to herself, but she feared that he was on the run again. Standing on the sidewalk in front of the Mission her fears were confirmed, for Mr. Kramer was nowhere in sight. She paused for a moment and gave silent prayer for another one she'd lost.

As he pressed the end button on his cell phone a rare smile broke across his face. He estimated that he should be at the Mission in no less than thirty minutes considering his location and traffic on I-70. Nonetheless his prey was cornered once again, and this time cornered by a sinner in a house of God…how ironic. As he hurried to his SUV he spoke to himself in a soft tone, "*For they love to pray standing in the corners of the streets, that they may be seen of men. Verily, I say unto you, they have their reward...* Matthew 6:5."

Pulling to a stop in the alley behind the mission, Rich could see his informant's head peeking through the small opening between the metal door and the casing. He stepped away from his SUV that was parked dead-center in the alley and made his way toward the delivery door.

"You him?" asked Ernie. "The one I talked to on the phone?"

"I'm him."

"You got the reward on you?"

"I have."

"Got something to tell ya," said Ernie, as he pushed opened the door. "Don't get mad, cause it ain't my fault," he said in a nervous voice.

"Where is he, little man?"

“He was here…right out there. I…I came in to get him some food…and…and…you want some food?”

“I asked…where is he?”

Ernie turned to scamper away but Rich caught him by the arm and gave it a modest squeeze that made Ernie cringe with pain.

“You didn’t lie to me, did you, little man? I don’t like being lied to.”

“No…no, I left him right out there. He was here alright…we was best friends. Look, he gave me his key ring. See…it’s got his name on it and he said I could have it for watchin’ him while he slept.”

Rich pulled Ernie’s hand towards him to get a better look at the treasure that Ernie had stolen while Jake was sleeping.

“Alright, you have his keychain and he was here, so where is he now?”

“I don’t know. After I called like ya told me, I went to find him, but he was gone. Mister, are ya still gonna pay me? I did everything like you told me.”

“Where did you leave him?”

“Over there…here, I’ll show ya.”

Ernie started to open the kitchen door, but was pushed aside by Rich who gently eased a small opening in the door.

“Sandman,” he whispered as he allowed the door to ease closed as he turned to Ernie.

“Who else did you call, little man…who else?” he asked in a deep frightening tone.

“Nobody…nobody. I ain’t called nobody else. Just you.”

"That's Kramer's wife out there, little man. Did you call her too?"

Ernie had back-stepped to the butcher block trying to stay clear of Rich's anger, but the anger moved closer as Rich continued his questioning.

"Who else did you call? Tell me."

Ernie was now cornered like a rat and if he didn't die in the next minute from a heart attack he surely would from Rich's attack. In desperation he reached for a carving knife laying on the stainless steel table and pointed it at Rich in a pathetic gesture of defense as the blade's tip weaved like a candle's flame.

"I don't like you anymore, and I don't want your money," he said. "You go away…I'm not your friend."

Rich turned to the rear door easing Ernie's heart rate by about one-half beat before he quickly turned and grabbed Ernie's hand and began squeezing his finger tightly against the knife's wooden handle. Ernie whimpered in pain and his eyes welted with fear as his powerless, crimped little hand turned and pointed the blade that no longer shook towards his own chest.

"Please. No. Don't hurt me."

Rich exited the rear of the Lasting Light Mission's kitchen making his way to his waiting SUV escape vehicle while calmly saying, "*But Ama'sa did not observe the sword which was in Jo'ab's hand, so Jo'ab struck him with it in the body…*Samuel 20:10."

Alex stood quietly by Connie as they waited in the olive green lobby of the Mission.

"This place needs help," remarked Connie.

Alex nodded in agreement knowing that it was in Jake's master plan to give the Mission some much deserving help one day. Moving to the adjacent dining hall, Alex paused as he again sensed the awareness of danger. This sensation was becoming more frequent, beginning weeks ago at Bivouac Mountain, then the woods behind his home and now here at the Mission. Alex went on full alert, which was unnoticed by Connie.

"You must be Mrs. Kramer. I'm Sister Marie," she said while extending her hand. "It's nice to meet you and welcome to the Lasting Light Mission."

"Thank you for calling, Sister. We've been terribly worried about Jake. Can you take us to him?"

The Sister clasped her hands around her rosary as she took a deep breath before responding, "Mrs. Kramer, would you care to sit for a moment."

"No thank you, Sister. Please take us to my husband."

"I afraid I can't do that, Mrs. Kramer. You see… Mr. Kramer left our Mission shortly after my call. Of course I hoped to detain him, but I'm afraid he's gone."

"Did anyone happen to see which way he went, Sister?" asked Alex.

"Yes, he appeared to have gone uptown along Hope Street. Perhaps we should check with Ernie. He seemed to have befriended Mr. Kramer. Follow me, please."

Connie and Alex moved along behind Sister Marie as she made her way down the hall toward the kitchen.

“Dear me, look at that.  Ernie knows better than to leave the back door open and unattended,” said the Sister.  “Ernie…Ernie, we need you,” she shouted as she made her way to close the rear door.

“I think I’ve found Ernie, Sister,” said Alex.  “You need to call 911.”

Connie and Sister Marie turned toward Alex and saw him rise from the opposite side of the butcher block table.  “Ask them to send homicide and a coroner.  I’m sorry, Sister, but your Mr. Ernie has been murdered.”

# Forty

"I just can't stop thinking about that poor man being killed that way. It could have been Jake lying there too if he had been in the kitchen. Oh Alex, who could do such a thing to someone so helpless. I'll never understand what kind of sick mind could knowingly take the life of another human being."

Alex remained quiet as he drove slowly along Hope Street on the unlikely chance that they might spot Jake along the way. Connie's comment about a sick mind stung a little, but he knew it was not aimed at him personally.

"Alex, I think it's time to ask for some help in finding Jake."

"Let's drive around for awhile before we bring in the police, okay?" he asked as he scanned each store entry and alley opening along the way."

"I don't know. I just can't help but think Jake's in danger, Alex. Who knows, Mr. Ernie's death may have been intended for him. If you could have seen the way he acted yesterday in Doctor Harrington's office, you… SLOW DOWN! That looks like…no, sorry, it's not Jake."

"Connie would you like to stop and get some lunch before we go on? Or better yet, why don't you let me take you home to rest for awhile and I'll continue looking for Jake?"

"No, but thanks anyway. I don't want to go home and I'm not hungry. Besides, four eyes are better than two. You need me to watch this side for you."

"Fair enough, but let me know if you need anything."

"You're a good man, Alex Sanders. Jake is lucky to have you as a friend."

"Yeah, a good man with a sick mind," he thought to himself.

"I have an idea, Connie. It's a long shot, but we just may find him there."

Connie's eyes showed a glimmer of hope as she nodded in approval without asking where he was taking them.

The sun felt warm on his face as Jake sat quietly sharing his attention between a young couple tossing a frisbee to their collie as it ran to catch the disk, and a little red headed girl as she fed her popcorn to a small flock of pigeons. Something had drawn him here and he was unsure as why he came or what he was expecting to find, but never had he experienced greater déjà vu. Sitting alone on his half of the park bench he tried to remember just what was so special about this White River State Park.

"Want some popcorn, mister?"

Jake looked down at the freckled faced little girl who was looking at him through big brown eyes while holding out a half-filed bag of popcorn to him.

"You look like you're hungry, mister," she said as she continued holding the bag for him.

"Thank you, I don't mind if I do."

She watched as Jake reached out and carefully picked a single white kernel from her bag and popped it into his mouth.

"You can have another one if you're not full."

"Thank you, but I think the birds need it more than I do."

"Okay…bye."

"Wait," he said, "what's your name?"

"Amber."

"Amber, now who gave you a beautiful name like Amber?"

"My mommy and daddy. But Daddy doesn't live with us any more. Mom said he's not nice."

"I see," said Jake. "Why isn't your daddy nice, Amber?"

Amber looked back to her mother who was talking to someone in a jogging suit, before she answered, "He stoled my brother."

Jake felt a shiver that went unnoticed by his new little friend. "Why did your daddy take your brother?"

"Mommy said it was 'cause he hated me and her. He only liked boys, he don't like girls. Men are pigs… Mommy says all men are pigs."

Jake smiled at her before asking, "What is your brother's name, honey?"

"His name is Adam."

"Does your Mommy know where Adam is?"

"No, but Mommy thinks Grandmother O'Shea knew where Daddy took him 'cept she's dead and…"

"Amber…Amber, come here this minute young lady."

Jake looked up at one angry mother as she approached their bench and shocked Amber into dropping her bag of popcorn. The pigeons flocked to their feet bobbing their heads at the white kernels that scattered erratically across the ground.

"How many times do I have to tell you about talking to strangers, young lady? How many times? Come with me this instant," she said while looking suspiciously at Jake.

"Good bye, Amber. Thank you for the popcorn."

"Bye mister."

"Amber…how many times do I have to tell you," repeated her mother as she pulled the little girl away by the wrist making her scurry along on the tips of her toes.

Jake's heart ached for young Amber who was too young to understand the grounds for her punishment. Nonetheless, he understood that a mother's love knows no boundaries, for if she did indeed lose a son, she would be overly protective of her daughter for the remainder of eternity. He watched as they approached the on-duty park ranger who listened as Amber's mother pointed at Jake as he sat calmly on the public bench.

"That man right over there," she said. "He was questioning my daughter. You shouldn't allow that type of person in a park where children are present."

"Are you pointing to Mr. Kramer, Ma'am?"

"I don't know who he is. I just know I saw him taking popcorn from my daughter."

Jake watched as the ranger began shaking her head no as the mother became more insistent and jabbed her finger toward Jake. She appeared to become less ruffled as the ranger talked, then slowly knelt to her daughter's level and gave her a hug and a kiss on the forehead. Within moments the threesome began moving toward Jake with Amber walking between them flat-footed.

"Mr. Kramer, my name is Debra O'Shea. I'm Amber's mother and I believe I owe you an apology. I'm afraid I acted rather irrationally. Please accept my apolo…"

"What was your mother-in law's name, Debra?" interrupted Jake. "Was her name Erma, or Ellen?"

"Why, her name was Ellen, Mr. Kramer…Ellen O'Shea, she was."

"Her husband was Richard, or was he Patrick?"

"Patrick…a finer man you could never have met."

"And Ellen and Patrick had two sons…Michael and Charles?"

"Yes, but…"

"But Charles was killed in a car accident in the late fall of his twenty-seventh year."

"Yes…I believe that's right, Mr. Kramer, but how did…"

Little Amber was growing bored with this conversation between her new friend and her mother so she crawled up on Jake's lap with no protest from her mother.

"Your mother-in-law didn't like you very much did she?"

"Well, I don't know. I always thought we got along."

"She was very instrumental in convincing your husband to take young Adam with him when you separated."

"What? Ellen was behind Michael's taking Adam?"

"She convinced him that since the courts mandated a fifty-fifty decree of all assets, then why should you keep both children."

"But why would she encourage Michael to take my son and run? The reason had to be pure vindictiveness toward me."

"She was concerned about the O'Shea name. Her fear was that you may one day remarry and your new husband would adopt Adam and want to change his name to something other than O'Shea. Adam, as you know, is the last of the males in the family to carry on the O'Shea name."

"That's a sick reason," said Debra.

"I agree," said Jake.

"Mommy, I'm hungry," cried Amber.

"Okay honey, we'll go. Mr. Kramer, I can't thank you enough for shedding some light on this nightmare. You look like you could use some food too. Would you care to join us for a bite somewhere?"

"15868 Bay View Drive, San Francisco, California," he said without prompting.

"I beg your pardon. What's at Bay Drive, California?"

"Your ex-husband Michael and your son Adam are at 15868 Bay View Drive, San Francisco, California."

Debra threw her hands over her mouth and whimpered, "Oh my God…how could you possibly know that?"

"Your mother-in-law knew. But you should go soon and get him out of his current environment, Mrs. O'Shea."

"Why, Mr. Kramer?" she asked frantically, "Is he in danger?"

"No, not at present, but they are living in a gay house."

"Alex, look over there at that man sitting on the park bench. Doesn't he look like Jake from the back?"

"It sure does, Connie."

"This is White River Park, isn't it?

"Yes."

"Why would Jake wander all the way up here?"

"I don't know, but this is where the Moving Wall was displayed a few months back. Remember, you and the girls were down at Gulf Shores and Jake was caught on camera talking to the wall?"

"Oh yeah, I remember learning about that when we got back."

Alex hit the remote to lock his car and it responded with the double chirps, as he and Connie walked toward the park bench that was surrounded by people and pigeons.

"Mr. Kramer, are you implying that I was married to a homosexual?"

"I'm not implying anything, Debra. I'm only telling you that your mother-in-law was aware that her son and your son were sharing quarters with three other men who declared themselves as gay. And I'm just suggesting that you go and bring your son home and leave her son there."

"Mommy, what's a home sextool?" asked Amber.

"Never mind, Amber. Get your things, we…"

"Jake…Jake Kramer, what are you doing here?" shouted Connie as she made her way past the ranger and Debra before centering herself in front of him.

"Hello, Connie, what are you doing here?" he asked calmly.

"That's what I asked you, mister, and it better be good. We've been worried sick. What in the hell are you doing here?"

"This is my friend, Amber. We're feeding popcorn to the pigeons."

Alex could see Connie's face turning red with anger as she drew a deep breath.

"Jake, you can't do this to me. First you insult Doctor Harrington before running out of her office yesterday; then you disappear and end up staying in some fleabag halfway house; and now that we've found you, all you have to say is, 'we're feeding the pigeons.' What in the hell is that supposed to mean?"

Jake quickly looked down at the few remaining birds like a young child who had just received a scolding and had his feelings hurt.

"I'm sorry."

"Excuse me, Mrs. Kramer, I'm Debra O'Shea. If you don't mind my intervening, I should tell you that Mr. Kramer may have saved my son's life. He just gave me the address of my ex-husband who took our son and fled the state. I've been searching for him over the last two years, but now, thanks to Mr. Kramer, I can go and bring Adam home."

"Well I'm very happy for you, Mrs. O'Shea. But if you don't mind, this is a private matter between my husband and me."

"Yes, of course, Mrs. Kramer, I understand. Come along, Amber, we should be going."

"Good bye, Jake. I love you."

"Bye, Amber," said Jake. "I love you too."

"Jake…get in the car," demanded Connie.

"Okay…which one?"

"Thanks for going with me, Alex. I hope you know that I do appreciate it."

"No problem, Connie. Anytime, you know that. How's he doing?"

"He's sitting quietly in his recliner. I'll be honest with you, Alex; I don't believe he remembers much of anything about the last twenty-four hours."

"He certainly didn't have much to say on the ride home," said Alex. "Did you notice the way he stared out the window, Connie? It was as if he were riding into new surroundings."

"He acted the same way when I walked him back to his den. It's like he'd been sedated. No questions, no comments. He just sat where I told him to. I'll tell you, Alex, I don't think I can handle much more of this."

"Have you thought about asking Doctor Harrington for help?" he asked.

"Oh yes, and she is very willing, but Jake isn't."

"I see. Well maybe he won't be so strong-willed now. I better be going, Connie. Don't hesitate to call if you need anything."

"Thanks, Alex," she said as she walked him to the back door. "Thanks for being so understanding."

"Cindy and I will be going to Wesley's services tomorrow. We'll stop by around ten-thirty and you two can ride with us."

"Oh my God…I almost forgot about that. I think my mind is about numb."

"You should try to get some rest too, Connie. Good night."

"Night, Alex. Thanks again."

Connie approached the den quietly, but found Jake's recliner empty and Jake nowhere about. This immediately alarmed her that perhaps he had left the house again. Knowing he hadn't made his way to the kitchen, Connie hurried down the hall checking all the rooms until eventually she located him in their bedroom. He was lying on top of the spread, sleeping in the fetal position on the wrong side of their bed. Connie pulled a pink quilt from the linen closet and gently draped it across Jake's body before she leaned forward and placed a kiss on his forehead.

"I'll be back in a little while. I love you."

# Forty-One

Connie's first habit each morning when she awoke was to roll over and check the time. However, today she found the clock was missing as well as her nightstand and the lamp. It took her a few moments to clear her mind before she realized that, after choosing not to disturb her husband who had taken her place earlier, she had slept on Jake's side of their bed last night. This in itself was no big deal, but it did present an interesting start to the day. "I hope this doesn't add some meaning to the old myth of getting up on the wrong side of the bed," she said to herself.

Rubbing the sleep from her eyes, Connie completed a mental checklist of the things she needed to do on this Thursday. Sadly, number one on her list was to get ready for Wesley Washington's funeral service. Easing herself out of bed so as not to disturb Jake, Connie turned toward him only to find that he was no longer lying there.

"Okay," she said to herself, "let's go and find out what surprises Mr. Kramer has in store for me today."

Wrapped in her favorite green terrycloth bathrobe, Connie slid on her house slippers and once again made her way through the house as the smell of coffee led her to the kitchen and ultimately to Jake who sat at the table blowing into his coffee cup.

"Good morning, honey. I'm glad you had a chance to sleep in a little. How about some coffee?"

"Morning, Jake…how are you feeling today?"

“Great, thanks. I must have really been tired if I fell asleep on your side of the bed last night. Maybe I should do that more often. I slept like a baby. Please, sit down…I’ll pour you a cup of coffee.”

“Thanks, but I can get it. How long have you been up?”

“Not long. Listen, Connie, I’ve been thinking that maybe we should go down to the hospital first thing this morning and see how Stacie and Tonya are doing. What do you think?”

“I would imagine Stacie went home yesterday, Jake. But we can ask her about Tonya when we see her this morning. If you’re up to it we can stop by the hospital after the service.”

“Jake smiled at Connie as he said, “You’re a day early here, dear. The service isn’t until tomorrow, remember, Thursday? I was going over the morning paper and there are more pictures of the building and a picture of Wesley in the obituaries,” he said as he slid the paper across the table towards Connie. “You can look at it while I get your coffee. It says right here,” he said while pointing at the paper, “that services will be at Mortiman’s Family Mortuary on Thursday at eleven o’clock.”

“Yes, I know…I’ve seen it.”

“You’ve already seen it? So that’s how the paper got in here. You must have gotten up pretty early. What’s the matter…couldn’t you sleep?”

Connie waited for Jake to set her coffee cup down and retake his seat before answering.

"Jake, this is yesterday's news," she said while holding up the paper. "Today's Thursday, believe me. I'm not joking about this."

She watched as the impact of her statement began to sink in as he leaned back in the chair and stared at the paper.

"This isn't funny, Connie. I know we've been through our share of crises, but now is not the time to lighten up with practical jokes."

Connie stood and started toward the patio door, "I'll be back."

"Where're you going?"

"I'm going out to get the morning paper for you."

She heard his chair slide away from the table as he said, "Drink your coffee, I'll go. And when I get back you can have your little laugh on me. I don't know why you're carrying this so far, but I probably deserve it."

Connie was still seated at the table when Jake returned with the Thursday morning edition of the *Indianapolis Star* clenched in his hand. He truly looked like one totally confused male. Her heart ached for him as he stood by the table staring at the paper while trying to accept the truth.

"What happened?" he asked softly.

"I don't know, Jake. But don't lose sight of the fact that you've been through a lot these past few days." Connie leaned forward and continued, "You got angry with Doctor Harrington as she and Doctor Zorka were briefing us on Tonya and Stacie on Tuesday. Do you remember that?"

Jake nodded that he did.

"Then you ran out of her office and disappeared from the hospital. We tried to find you, but you were gone. Alex spent most of Tuesday night looking for you too. It wasn't until Sister Marie called yesterday afternoon to tell me that you had stayed at her mission Tuesday evening that we learned of your whereabouts. Do you remember the mission, Jake?"

Jake shook his head while softly saying, "No."

"Well, you did, and I would sure love to know why. Alex drove me down there for you; however, by the time we got there you had disappeared again. Jake, did you know there was a murder at the mission house?"

"Murder?"

"That's right. Some man named Ernie was killed at the Lasting Light Mission Tuesday night. Did you know that?"

"I don't remember, Connie. I don't understand what's happening to me. How did I get home?"

"We found you at the White River State Park feeding the pigeons with a little girl."

"Pigeons?"

"Yes, feeding pigeons. You were feeding pigeons with a little girl. I've forgotten her name, but her mother said you helped locate her son who had been kidnapped by his father."

"Pigeons?" he repeated as he took his seat for the first time. "Murdered?"

"You really don't remember do you, Jake?"

Jake didn't have to answer, for as he looked up from the paper that had been laying on the table his eyes answered her question.

"No you don't. My God, Jake, I'm so sorry."

Jake leaned forward placing his elbows on the table and resting his head in his hands. He could feel a throbbing beginning in his temples and expanding to the back of his head. Squeezing his eyes closed he tried to suppress the growing pain, but words like pigeons and murder kept repeating in his mind and added fuel to his discomfort.

"Can I get you anything, honey?"

"I could use three Acetylsalicylic acid tablets."

"Well, I should be grateful that you can still manage a little humor at a time like this. Three aspirins coming up. I'll be right back. Will you be alright?"

"Yeah…I think I could use some air too. I'll be outside."

On her way to the medicine cabinet Connie passed the front door as the bell rang.

"Great, just what we need…company."

Opening the door Connie found two neatly dressed men standing at the entrance.

"Can I help you?"

"Mrs. Kramer?"

"Yes."

"I'm Detective Martin and this is Officer Lewis. We're from the Indianapolis police department, Mrs. Kramer. We'd like to speak to your husband. Is Mr. Kramer in?"

"Yes, he's in, but he's not feeling well at the moment. May I ask what this is about?"

"We'd like to ask him a few questions, Mrs. Kramer …strictly routine. May we come in please?"

"A few strictly routine questions about what?" asked Connie.

"Perhaps it would be best if we didn't discuss this on your front porch. May we come in, Mrs. Kramer?" he repeated.

"Yes…of course. Please, won't you?"

Connie stepped back making way for the two officers to clear the door before she closed it behind them.

"Jake's on the patio gentlemen, please follow me."

They found Jake standing on the edge of the concrete patio facing the sun and looking out at the woods that enclosed the rear of their property. He stood fixed as they approached.

"Jake, these police officers need your help."

Standing with his back to his uninvited guests he responded, "Tell them I have a headache."

Detective Martin and Officer Lewis gave each other a puzzled look before turning to Connie who simply shrugged her shoulders and said, "I told you he wasn't feeling well."

Martin took the lead and began speaking to Jake's back. "Mr. Kramer, we would like to ask you a few questions about your stay at the Lasting Light Mission on Tuesday night."

Jake raised his hands to the side of his head trying to relieve the pain that throbbed in his temples, but gave the impression that he was muting their questions.

"How well did you know Ernie Dingle, Mr. Kramer?" asked Martin.

Jake remained frozen.

Detective Martin took three or four steps closer to Jake. "Do you recognize this key chain, Mr. Kramer?" asked Martin while holding out a plastic bag about chest high. "It has your name and address embossed in the metal."

Jake turned while lowering his hands and looked at the bag containing his property. "That's mine…I didn't realize that I had lost it. Where did you find it?"

"We found it clutched tightly in Ernie Dingle's hand, Mr. Kramer."

"Oh, I see. Well, please thank Mr. Dingle for me, won't you?"

"Alright, Mr. Kramer," said Martin showing signs that his patience was wearing thin. "We know that you and Dingle had conversations at the mission. We also know that you were most likely among the last to have seen Mr. Dingle alive. We know that, Mr. Kramer, because we have several witnesses who can substantiate that fact, and among that list of individuals is one, Sister Marie. Now I believe it would be very fool hardy to call Sister Marie a liar, Mr. Kramer. So tell us about your stay at the Lasting Light Mission."

Jake turned and retook his position of watching the tree tops sway in the breeze at the property line.

Detective Martin turned and looked at his partner who only gave him a non-understanding shrug. He then looked to Connie, who was noticeably embarrassed to be seen before her morning make-up by anyone other than her husband, as she grasped the top of her robe with her right hand and pulled the flaps tightly together.

"Mr. Kramer," said Martin, while again talking to Jake's back. "I think you should know, sir, that I…we have the utmost respect for you. We are fully aware of your history in helping law enforcement solve some of their most difficult cases. Again, I respect you, sir, but we have a job to do. We have a murder on our hands that we will solve with or without your cooperation. Now, you can answer my questions discreetly here in the privacy of your patio, or we can go public and do this downtown. How do you want it?"

"Detective," said Connie. "May I have a word with you and the officer?"

"Of course, Mrs. Kramer," said Martin as he and Lewis moved closer.

"As you can see, my husband is clearly not himself today. I don't believe he is intentionally ignoring your questions. I actually had to convince him, not more than an hour ago, that today is Thursday. He honestly believed it was Wednesday. I also learned as I talked to him that he has no recall of anything beyond Tuesday around noon."

Connie paused and looked at the officers who were showing signs of disbelief.

"I know this sounds fictitious, but you must understand that he has been through a difficult time.

The explosion last Monday at his office took the life of a very dear and close friend. Jake blames himself for that and we've been unable to convince him otherwise."

"You have our sympathy, Mrs. Kramer, but we still have questions. We would like to know how the deceased managed to be clenching Mr. Kramer's property while lying with a kitchen knife parked in his chest."

Connie shuddered at the thought as she recalled the scene but continued. "Did you know that I was at the mission shortly after Mr. Dingle was killed?"

"Yes, but we were hoping you would mention it before we asked."

"Jake was gone before we arrived."

"We?"

"Yes, Alex was with me."

"Does Alex have a last name?"

"Sanders…Alex Sanders. He's our next-door neighbor," she said while pointing at the house to her left.

"What were you and Mr. Sanders doing at the mission, Mrs. Kramer?" asked Officer Lewis with his first question of the interview.

Connie turned her head slowly towards him and said sarcastically, "We went there for lunch. They have a great prime rib sandwich and a clam chowder that's to die for." Connie released her grip on her robe to place her hand across her eyes as she shook her head and regretted her answer, "I'm sorry, Officer, it's been a bad morning. The truth is I received a call from Sister

Marie telling me that Jake was at the mission, so we went down there to bring him home. That's all."

"We? That would be you and your neighbor Alex Sanders."

"Yes, Officer Lewis. We being Alex and me."

A pause between questions gave Martin time to imply to Officer Lewis through eye contact that he would handle the remaining inquiry. Then, without prompting, all three looked in Jake's direction simultaneously and found his position hadn't changed.

"Gentlemen," said Connie. "As I said…Jake is not himself at the moment. We have a funeral service at eleven o'clock this morning to bury a dear friend. If I may offer a suggestion? Give us today to grieve our loss and tomorrow I will bring Jake down to your office where you can ask questions to your hearts' content. He's not going anywhere."

Detective Martin offered his hand to Connie as he said, "Please accept our condolences, Mrs. Kramer… until tomorrow."

# Forty-Two

The ride to Mortiman's Family Mortuary was a noticeably quiet one, with the exception of an occasional question and answer between Connie and Cindy concerning the Elton John concert.

"I don't care if he does like men, I think he's chubby and cute," said Cindy matter-of-factly.

"And rich!" added Connie.

"That's right...see Alex. If only you could sing and play the piano we could be rich too."

"How do you know I can't, Cindy?"

"Can't what?"

"Sing and play the piano...you've never asked me."

"Well, that's true, I haven't. Can you sing and play the piano, Alex Sanders?"

"No, I can't do that, but the good news is, I'm not chubby, I don't like men, but I am cute and rich."

That broke the somber atmosphere in the car as the girls laughed in the back seat and Jake gave Alex an understanding smile that was worth Alex's fortune just to see.

Parking was not a problem for Alex at Mortiman's as he pulled to a stop in the third space behind the black hearse and equally black limousine. Again the mood in the Sanders' car turned serious as they looked through their respective windows at the inactivity in the lot that made it painfully clear that this was indeed a small family.

"Do you think you could drive around and find something closer, Alex?" asked Jake.

"Jake…that's terrible," said Connie as she reached across the seat to slap him on the shoulder as they all broke out laughing.

"I'm sorry, but Wes would have understood."

"Yes, I believe he would and he would have expected you to say something like that, Jake," she agreed through her laughter.

They were greeted at the door by Mr. Mortiman himself, dressed in his traditional single-breasted black suit, over starched white shirt and deep burgundy tie. His sympathetic smile was fixed from years of experience as he pointed the way to the podium in the corner of the entry that held the visitors' register.

"Have the Washingtons arrived yet?" Jake asked.

"Yes, sir, we sent the car. You'll find them in the viewing room to your left," he said as he extended his arm and continued his smile.

Jake, Connie, Alex and Cindy stood still in a tight cluster looking around the room while listening to the canned music that played the familiar songs that everyone dreads to hear and no one can identify.

"I hate these places," said Cindy as she took Alex's hand. "They give me the willies."

"Let go," responded Connie as she took Jake's arm to lead him toward the room on the left.

Jake paused at the entrance, bringing their small party to an abrupt halt as he looked around the room.

The flowers were few but still very beautiful. The dark brown folding chairs outnumbered the need, but weren't overly obvious. He looked toward the family section and fought back tears as he focused on frail Granny Faye dressed in black and holding her worn bible between her wrinkled fingers. She wore a matching veil that failed to hide her pain.

Seated next to Granny was her daughter Rosa, also in black, but smartly suited and sitting straight and proud. She held little Jake on her lap with such possession that no one would dare to challenge her. This strong-willed woman managed to restrain her sorrow and clearly was the pillar on which the family would lean.

Jake's heart cracked a little wider as he looked to Granny's right and saw Stacie. She sat somewhat limp with her head resting against Granny Fay's left shoulder. Her eyes focused squarely on the modest brown casket a few feet in front of her. She never blinked nor moved a muscle, but only stared at the closed casket as if believing that Wesley wasn't inside.

"Jake, let's go," said Connie as she tugged at his arm.

Rosa stood to acknowledge them as they approached. Little Jake reached for Jake and was released by Rosa as he wrapped his little arms around Jake's neck and hugged him.

"He doesn't understand," said Rosa.

"Neither do I," responded Jake. "How's Stacie holding up?"

Rosa answered by shaking her head and answering, "In time."

Jake looked at Connie and passed little Jake to her. He then moved to Granny Faye and knelt and bowed his head before taking her tiny soft hands in his. Slowly he raised his head and gazed into her red eyes as a tear broke free and rolled down across the lines of wisdom on her face.

"My Wesley," she whispered. "My Wesley's gone, Mr. Kramer."

Jake lowered his head in her hands and began to cry. "It should have been me, Granny. I'm so sorry, I wasn't there for him. I loved him like my own...It should have been me."

He was crying hard now and Granny could feel the moisture from his tears in her hands.

"No, Mr. Kramer. It wasn't your fault, she whispered. Please don't blame yourself. It was God's will, I know that. Look at me, Mr. Kramer. Wesley's in a better place. It was just his time."

"I know, Granny," he replied. "I know."

Jake released Granny's hands long enough to brush the tears from his face and looked at Stacie who hadn't changed expressions since they arrived.

"Stacie...Stacie, honey, are you alright?"

"She's not alright, Mr. Kramer," said Granny.

"We'll see that she gets the best of care, Granny. I owe that much to Wesley."

"When Wesley comes, we're gonna go get Tonya and go home," said Stacie without moving.

"That's right honey, everything is going to be fine," reassured Granny.

On shaking legs, Jake slowly rose to his feet and stood looking at Stacie. His trembling was noticeable to anyone who watched as he turned and walked toward Wesley. Standing directly in the center of the casket he reached out and gently placed his hand on the casket lid, lowered his head and began to cry once again.

"I'm sorry, Wes. It should have been me. I let you down," he said above a whisper.

The muffled voices throughout the room ceased and the canned music continued as all eyes tried not to stare at Wesley's grieving friend. Alex found himself turning away and choking back the lump that was rising in his throat. Cindy shared a tissue with Connie and even the strong-willed Rosa accepted a tissue as well.

"Rosa, will you take little Jake? I'd better go to my husband."

"Give him a moment, Connie," said Alex. "If confessing to Wesley helps him ease his guilty conscience…then this is the place to do it."

Connie stood fast, knowing Alex was right, but she would rather have been at Jake's side. Passing little Jake to Rosa she said, "You're right of course, Alex."

Connie looked at the entrance and located JJ, Karen, Margaret and Becky who had just arrived.

"The kids are here, Cindy. They look lost, let's go to them."

On their short walk Connie noticed Doctor Doreen Harrington sitting alone in the last row. Connie stopped to acknowledge her and offered thanks for her compassion.

"How is Stacie doing, Connie? I've been concerned as to how she's accepting this."

"I'm afraid she's not accepting it at all, Doreen. She's going to need a great deal of your help."

"That's what I'm here for, Connie…and of course, for you and Jake too."

"He hasn't fully released yet either, Doreen. I'm becoming very concerned about him. We need to talk soon."

"Anytime…just call."

"Thank you, Doreen, if you'll excuse me?"

Connie joined Cindy with the girls and noticed JJ talking to two men in the lobby. She recognized them as Chuck Rummer and Malcolm Tyler, the last of the now unemployed Kramer and Associate's workforce.

Mr. Mortiman began moving about the guests advising them that the service was about to begin and asking each to find seating of their choosing. Connie looked to Jake who hadn't strayed very far from the casket. Placing her purse on the seat she turned to get him, but saw that their son had taken it upon himself to lead Jake back to his seat. Connie took a chair in the row in front of Margaret and Karen and watched JJ standing with his arm across Jake's back trying to console his father.

“Excuse me…is this seat taken?” he asked.

“No…please have a seat,” she whispered.

“Thank you. I had a little trouble finding this address,” he added. “I was becoming concerned that I might miss the service.”

“No, you’re not late. Are you a friend of the family?”

“No, not really…actually, I have a contract with Mr. Kramer.”

“I see…I’m Doreen Harrington,” she said, as she offered her hand and studied his eyes.

“Warren Bible…nice to meet you, Ms. Harrington.”

“Mr. Bible,” she nodded.”

They sat quietly and listened to the muffled coughs and whispers throughout the room as Mr. Mortiman and the Reverend exchanged conversation. Doreen found herself stealing glances at Mr. Bible, who in turn sat quietly with his legs crossed, hands on his knees and appearing to be in deep thought.

The very Reverend Barry White, assistant Pastor of the First Baptist Church spoke to the captive audience for thirty-three minutes trying desperately to explain God’s reasoning for taking our loved ones to join him in his kingdom. As he offered a closing prayer he was satisfied that he had done his job, but couldn’t help but wonder who among them, if any, heard his words.

“It was nice to meet you, Ms. Harrington and thank you for sharing your row.”

"You're welcome, Mr. Bible. Will you be going to the cemetery?"

"I'm afraid not…I have another obligation. Have a nice day."

The brown folding chair slid back against the hardwood flooring as Mr. Bible stood and hurried toward the exit.

Alex quickly turned and looked over his shoulder, catching only a brief glimpse of the guest and somewhat startling Cindy in the process.

"What is it, Alex?"

"Oh…nothing. I thought I saw someone I knew," he answered as he rubbed the tingle in the back of his neck.

During the ride to the Eternal Rest Cemetery, there couldn't have been less conversation in the hearse than in the Sanders' vehicle. Jake reassumed his position of looking out his window at everything or nothing, while Connie and Cindy rode quietly in the rear seat, each giving personal thanks that it wasn't her husband they were about to bury. All three of them could hear Jake mumbling as he looked out the window. He was speaking softly and slow and no one was sure what he was saying or to whom he was speaking, so each, for their own good reason ignored him. Alex caught Jake fidgeting with his hands as they rode along. Nothing dramatic, only rubbing at his fingers…just enough to be annoying.

Alex remained alert to the distance between him and the black limo, taking care to trail by two car lengths as the motorcade moved slowly, but steadily through the light traffic. He looked at his rear-view mirror and noted that JJ was doing a first-rate job of keeping his distance as well. However, it did appear that the foursome in JJ's car was having a more enjoyable time. He counted five vehicles behind him in the procession, but failed to include the one following last in line…a black SUV.

The midday sun was warm and the gentle breeze made it a perfect day to be anywhere other than a cemetery, but then again life isn't always perfect. Connie stood silently while holding Karen's and Margaret's hands as Cindy held Margaret's and Becky's. They lined the path for the pallbearers and gazed upon the somber faces of their husbands, fathers, brother or boyfriend as they made the slow parade to Wesley's final resting place. The ladies moved hand-in-hand along behind them before taking a place under the temporary tent that provided shade and seating for the family. They watched as the casket slid easily across the rollers of the camouflaged elevator before the pallbearers were released by Mr. Mortiman. Jake was reluctant to break his grip on the bar knowing that it was the very last thing he could do for Wesley L. Washington.

"Come on, Jake, it's time to let go," said Alex, while trying to be casual about prying Jake's fingers free. "There's nothing more you can do here," he whispered.

"It should have been me," he said. "It was supposed to be me, wasn't it, Alex?"

"Jake…let go of the damn bar and come with me," he said in no uncertain terms.

Jake's released his grip immediately and moved away from the casket much to everyone's relief; especially Connie's, for she didn't want a scene from her husband before final prayer was offered.

Alex directed Jake under the tent as they took their places standing next to JJ and behind the seated women. Reverend White took his cue from Mr. Mortiman and placed himself between the family, friends and Wesley.

"Dearly beloved…we are gathered here today to commit the body of Wesley Washington to…yadda… yadda…yadda," he said to the wind as he stood alone on a grassy knoll to watch the ceremony at The Eternal Rest Cemetery below him.

"Well, Mr. Kramer, I say you have more lives than a cat, but your numbers are beginning to shrink although not as quickly as my patience. So now I'm taking the gloves off and it becomes do or die for one of us."

Moving away from his vantage point, he sat in the passenger's seat of his SUV and turned to look out the rear window. The grouping was tight but he could see Kramer from here without difficulty. Reaching into the travel case laying on the rear seat, he once again removed his valued PSG-1 rifle and attached the scope, thus completing the set. This attempt would have been called foolhardy at one time in his mission, but the

SUV's blacked-out windows concealed him and as he said, the gloves were off. His rush began to develop as the group of mourners around plot 717 began to take their leave and he positioned his rifle.

# Forty-Three

Jake moved away from the crowd under the tent trying to find some unshared air that was lacking under the canopy. Milling around the headstones he became aware that his need to cry was gone, but the need to get even was growing stronger. No one could convince him that Wesley's death was an accident. Wesley was murdered, as was Otis. Brutally and senselessly murdered in what was intended for him. Jake vowed silently as he looked to the sky that he would dedicate his remaining time on earth to bringing villains to justice.

"So help me God," he said softly.

"I'll be happy to help too if you'll tell me what you need," said Connie as she took his arm.

"Connie…I didn't know you were behind me."

"I'm always behind you Jake…you should know that."

"I do know that and you should know I love you very much," he said as he pulled her close and put his arm around her waist.

"Jake…"

"Un-huh…"

"This isn't the most romantic place that you told me you loved me, but I'm not complaining."

"Do you think you could stand one of my Rhett Butler embraces, Scarlet?"

"Oh please, Rhett, hold me.

He estimated the distance to be 600 meters. A gimme for Rich or a chip shot for anyone with basic skills. The crowd had completely dispersed from under the tent and most were making their way to their respective cars. Using the aid of his telescope he saw the shiny head of Mr. Mortiman as he helped Granny Faye make her way to the limo as Rosa stood by with little Jake in hand. He located the Sandman talking to the same lady who sat next to him at Mortiman's. The trees and headstones scrolled past the small round glass of the telescope as he moved the rifle until he located Jake holding his wife in his arms. Without hesitation he centered the crosshairs directly at the base of Jake's neck just above the first vertebra. Curling his index finger through the guard and around the trigger he began his deliberate and controlled squeeze sensing its gentle restrain while whispering, "*When the godly are in authority, the people rejoice. But when the wicked are in power, they groan…*Proverbs 29:2*.*"

The rifle shot echoed throughout the peaceful valley like thunder in a hollow building. Most people didn't recognize its origin and assumed it was backfire from a passing truck.

"My…what in the world was that?" asked Doreen.

"Jake…" said Alex. "JAKE!" he screamed as he immediately set-out running in his general direction.

"What is it?" shouted Doreen who hurried along behind while losing pace.

Alex hurdled the first row of headstones before he spotted Jake slumped on the ground.

"Jake!" he shouted again while changing directions. Drawing closer he could see blood on the side of Jake's face before he lowered his head and disappeared behind the large block of white granite.

"Call 911," shouted Alex back to Doreen causing her to stop her pursuit and reach in her purse for the cell phone buried inside.

"What happened?" she shouted. "What happened?"

"Call them damn it…just call them."

Alex slowed as he approached the Kramer's position and for the first time in his life he was afraid… afraid that all his fears for Jake had finally surfaced.

"Jake," he repeated as he moved around the stone and saw Jake holding Connie in his arms. Alex moved quickly to his side. "My God…Connie."

Jake looked up at Alex and with tears streaming down his face he spoke in broken words, "That bastard…shot my Connie."

Alex felt his body trembling as he slowly dropped to one knee.

"Jake…we should lay her flat," he said while slowly reaching out to help.

"Don't you touch her," screamed Jake. "Don't even touch her."

Doctor Harrington was the second to arrive and found the result of the thunder that caught the attention of everyone at the cemetery.

"Oh my God no…Connie. Jake, please let me help you until the paramedics get here. I've had training."

Jake didn't respond to Doctor Harrington's suggestion, but allowed her to reach out and together they gently lowered Connie's head to the grass.

"MOM! DAD!" shouted Margaret as she ran across the cemetery lawn while darting between headstones with JJ, Karen and Becky following close behind. "What's happening?" she screamed.

"Alex, keep the kids back," said Doreen. "They don't need to see this."

This time it was Alex who responded to her command as he immediately jumped up and moved quickly toward the four pursuing kids.

"Margaret…whoa, slow down, honey," he said as he held out his arms. "Let's give the doctor some room."

"Alex, what happened?" cried Margaret.

"Honey…we're not really sure, but it appears that your mother has been shot."

"Mom…shot?" she repeated as her legs turned weak and she fell to her knees, placing her directly above Albert Henry Kingston's abdomen. JJ and Karen quickly knelt beside her as Becky asked, "She's going to…Connie…she's going to be alright, isn't she, Dad?"

Alex gestured with his head that he was unsure and added, "Becky, please keep them here. Where's Cindy?"

"She was calling 911…she'll be here in a moment."

"Find her for me will you, Becky? Bring her here with you and then make sure you guys stay together. Don't let anyone stray. I'll be back."

As Alex turned to hurry back he paused and looked to the small knoll to the southwest and saw a reflection of the afternoon's sun from the car on the hill. "There," he said to himself, "about 600 meters in the pines… that's the Gospel."

Alex moved to Doreen's right and opposite Jake as he slowly knelt on one knee. He drew a long sight of relief as he noticed Connie's eyes were opened and she was looking at her husband. Doctor Harrington was pressing a blood soaked cotton cloth firmly against the right side of Connie's head.

"Hold this, Alex," she said, "and keep applying pressure while I make a fresh dressing."

Alex responded without word and smiled at Connie who rolled her eyes to him and made contact. He looked at Jake who, in turn, never took his eyes off Connie as she rested with her head on his jacket. Doreen pulled the edge of her dress up to her thigh, exposing the slip that was quickly torn into a long three-inch strip for a makeshift bandage.

From off in the distance they could hear the sirens of the emergency vehicles as they approached the access road and made their way to The Eternal Rest Cemetery.

"Under the circumstances, Connie, I'd say that's a very welcome sound," said Doreen as she relieved Alex's hand with the fresh cloth. "It looks as though the bullet grazed the side of your head from above the ear forward," she added. "You can expect some serious headaches, but you're going to be just fine. You are a very lucky lady."

Connie smiled through the pain while squeezing Jake's hand, "I know," she managed to say.

"I'll go and lead the paramedics here," said Alex as he stood and Doreen nodded in agreement.

Alex recognized the lead paramedic as Mitch Rinehart and his partner Debbie weaving their way in their direction. Alex also noticed that they were accompanied by two sheriff deputies and one member of the Indiana State police.

"What do we have this time, Alex?" asked Mitch as he drew near.

"Gunshot wound, Mitch…grazed between the right ear and eyebrow. It's deep but not life-threatening," answered Alex.

"You guys were here to bury Wesley, weren't you?"

"Yeah. Mitch, there's something you should know?"

"What's that?" he asked as they approached the crime scene.

"It was Connie who got hit."

Mitch took a quick look toward Alex and immediately picked up his pace, "Damn."

# Forty-Four

Alex found Jake sitting alone in the corner of County General Hospital's Emergency waiting room watching an artificial potted fern growing from across the room. He approached slowly as not to startle Jake from his deep thought and took a seat beside him.

"Any word on how she's doing?"

"No," said Jake after a long pause.

"We convinced JJ to head back to Terre Haute. They didn't want to leave but Karen has an early class tomorrow. Margaret is with Cindy and Becky. She's going to spend the night. I figured it would be best and you would want it that way."

Jake nodded and managed a soft, "Thanks."

"Jake…"

"Save it, Alex," he interrupted while making eye contact that showed the intensity of his anger. "I don't want to hear it."

"I know how you must feel, Jake, but w…"

"How in the hell could you know how I must feel? I would really like to hear that, Sandman. Your friends are trying their damnedest to kill me and my family one by one."

"Jake, that's not fair. You can't blame…"

"Not fair! NOT FAIR!" he said while turning in his chair. "I'll tell you what in the hell's not fair. Wesley dead, is not fair. Otis Porter dead, is not fair. Tonya lying in a coma and Stacie's loss of reality, is not fair. And…AND my dear sweet Connie coming within inches of being killed by a bullet intended for me, is not fair. As a matter of fact, all of my friends are causalities because of me. That's what's not fair. So don't tell me what's not fair, Sandman…tell them."

Jake turned and dropped his head into his hands and began shaking.

"Maybe I should go, Jake…Can you get home alright?"

Jake held his position while waving go with his hand.

"I'll check on you tomorrow, okay? Please give Connie my love and tell her we're thinking about her."

Alex stood and took a half step before Jake spoke.

"Who is he, Alex? I have a right to know who he is."

Alex stopped and without looking back replied, "I'm not certain."

"Yes you are…who's the bastard that's killing my family?"

Alex made a slow turn and looked down at Jake. "He's called the Gospel."

Jake looked up at Alex and asked, "Does this Gospel have a real name?"

"I've only heard him referred to as the Gospel."

Jake looked deep into Alex's eyes before saying, "You're the best, Alex. I know you're the best and may God forgive me, but I'm asking you to find this Gospel person and kill him. Kill him before he hurts anymore of my family."

Alex watched quietly as Jake lowered his head and looked back at the tiled floor. He could see Jake's body quivering as he rested his head in his hands once again. Unsure if Jake had just laid partial blame on him, or if he was just searching for a place to lay blame, Alex knew that there was nothing more to be said tonight. They both needed to be left alone.

"Kramer…is the Kramer family present?" asked the doctor in green scrubs standing in the entry of the waiting room.

"I'm, Jake Kramer."

"If you'll follow me, sir. We have a young lady who would very much like for you to take her home.

"You're releasing her?" asked Jake as he and Alex moved toward the doctor.

"She can expect to have headaches and perhaps some slight blurred vision, but that will clear in time. I have some prescriptions for pain and infection that you should start her on before bedtime. But we see no need to keep her here any longer. I don't have to tell you that she is one very lucky lady."

"Yeah," said Jake. "How lucky can she get?"

"Yes…well, if you'll follow me, I'll take you to Mrs. Kramer."

"Alex…" said Jake as he turned in his direction.

"I'll be out front, Jake. Let's take Connie home."

Alex pulled to the curb after turning the north corner at Crest Street and noticed the WAXU mobile news unit parked directly in front of the house at 919. The lawn was littered with the media and well wishers, including a few who held burning candles. From their vantage point in Alex's car they noticed the lawn was once again laden with flowers, teddy bears and makeshift get well signs.

"Why don't they leave us alone?" asked Connie. "I don't feel up to this."

"Do you want me to pull into my garage, Jake? We can get Connie home across the back yard, or you guys can stay with us."

Connie and Alex waited silently for Jake's response, but he just sat and watched the crowd mingling in his yard.

"Jake?" said Connie.

"No. We're going home and we're going in the front. Just pull up to the garage door, Alex, and I'll use the keyless pad to let you inside. Connie, you stay in the car and away from the cameras until Alex lowers the door. I'll deal with the maggots."

"You sure, Jake?"

"I'm sure. Like you said, Alex, 'Let's take Connie home.'"

Jake's plan was effective, if not deceptive, for the video cameras recorded and the flash from countless cameras flashed, but the best shot of the lot could only have been the reflection from Alex's darkened windows. Jake saw Alex move from the car and lower the overhead door as he made his way to the street taking a small group with him. The shouts were filled with questions and comments from everyone in the cluster, but none were immediately addressed by Jake.

"Mr. Kramer…Mr. Kramer, Cameron Elliott, WAXU news. Was that Mrs. Kramer in that vehicle? Is she home, sir?"

Jake stood silently and looked hard into the faces of the crowd as their shouts began to quiet one voice at a time until nothing was said.

"I don't see Sheena Jawblondski? I know you're here, Ms. Jawblondski."

"Right here, Mr. Kramer…My cameraman is checking his equipment."

"We'll wait for you, Ms. Jawblondski…I don't want to leave anyone out. I also should tell you that I will cancel this little impromptu if that man over there doesn't get his camera out of my window."

"I'll take care of that for you, Mr. Kramer," shouted a burly black man holding a burning candle. "Leave him to me," he said as he passed his candle and took off running toward the house.

"Hey you…get away from there."

The would-be picture-taker outdistanced the big man and most likely did so because he knew that he was in a race to prevent a broken nose…his. The laughter from the crowd subsided and the big man made his way back while drawing deep breaths and retook his candle.

"Thank you," said Jake.

"Anything for you, Mr. Kramer. I'll stick around if you want."

"Thanks again, but that won't be necessary, Mr…?"

"Washington, Tyrell Washington, but you can call me your friend."

Jake was lost for words and stood looking intently at the man's face that bared a slight resemblance to his lost buddy.

"Wesley was my cousin, Mr. Kramer. He told me all about you and how you took care of him. So if you don't mind I may hang around a bit…you know, just in case. I figure Wesley would've done the same for me."

Jake managed to say thank you after choking down the lump that gathered in his throat.

"Mr. Kramer, Sheena Jawblondski, World Guardian reporter…May I first express my outrage at these unprovoked attacks against you and your family, and secondly, was that Ms. Kramer in the car, sir?"

"Yes."

"What is her condition?"

"She was treated and released. She will recover, thank you."

"Was she struck by a bullet intended for you, Mr. Kramer?" asked Elliott.

"I should like to think so, Mr. Idiot."

"That's Elliott, sir…Cameron Elliott."

"Oh yes, of course…my error."

"So, in your opinion someone has been making threats on your life and today, while at the cemetery, he or she deliberately shot at you and struck your wife instead."

"Well let's see, Mr. Elliott. If you take into account the events over the past four days I'd say yes…in my opinion someone deliberately shot at us today."

"Do you have any idea as to who would do such a thing, Mr. Kramer?"

"Yeah, I know who it is."

The crowd immediately fell quiet as only the occasional sound from street traffic could be heard above the anticipation of his answer. Cameron moved in a half step closer and placed the microphone dangerously close to Jake's mouth before realizing so and pulled it away.

"Would you care to tell us who has been threatening you, Jake?"

"He's a coward…a low-life who preys on innocent victims by lying in the dark or striking when they're not looking or able to fight back. He has no sense of morals or values. He's nothing more than a terrorist. One who would blow up a bus full of children rather than challenge a single soldier. He was born without the compassion of a mother's love. He's godless…and that's the gospel."

The circle of people around him nodded their heads in agreement as Elliot asked, "Do you have a name for him, Mr. Kramer?"

"I believe we all have a name for him Cameron, but none of us can say it on your newscast, can we?"

Laughter broke throughout the huddle, with Tyrell Washington responding above the others…"Right on, brother, right on."

"But if I may add, Cameron" said Jake. "I believe it was said best by Matthew, Chapter 3 verses 23-24 when he wrote… *'Whoever he is, he will be found and justice will be served, the Lord hates those who love violence.'"*

"Mr. Kramer," said Sheena, "I for one agree with your theory of the threats against your life. But what can you tell us about your involvement with Ernie Dingle?"

"Ernie Dingle? I don't know any Ernie Dingle."

This raised the brow above Sheena's eyes as she reloaded and pursued.

"Sir, I'm speaking of the late Ernie Dingle that you were seen talking to the day he was killed at the Lasting Light Mission on Hope Street. Ernie Dingle."

"And I'm telling you that I don't know, never met, or ever talked to anyone called Ernie Dingle, nor have I been to the Lasting Light Mission on Hope Street."

"But, Mr. Kramer," she persisted. "The police records show that…"

"Then the police records are wrong, Ms. Something-ski," he replied showing signs of nervousness and disorientation. "They're wrong," he insisted. "Wrong."

Jake was now pacing back and forth in small three step circles while repeating, "Wrong…wrong…wrong."

"JAKE! Connie needs you right away," said Alex as he grabbed his arm, "Come-on."

They hurried to the front porch before Alex answered Jake's repeated questions as to what was wrong with Connie.

"Nothing," he answered. "She just sent me out to get you away from the maggots."

"Good, they were starting to get infuriating. Oh, I forgot. There's one more thing I have to do, Alex, hold up."

Jake turned back to the small crowd and shouted, "Mr. Elliott…have your producer, what's-his-name… Silverman, give me a call. I'll do your show on Saturday."

"That only gives us tomorrow to get ready. How about the following week?"

"This Saturday and live, Mr. Elliott, or I'll give Larry King a call."

"Like I said, Mr. Kramer…Saturday's perfect. We'll be in touch."

# Forty-Five

Rich turned his black SUV east on County Road 700 and made his way unhurried down the narrow road toward Meg's house. Although unsure that she would be home, nonetheless he felt the need to see her one more time before he pulled up stakes and left the area for another assignment. Ninety-nine percent confident that he had completed his Kramer assignment that afternoon, Rich packed up and checked out of his temporary dwelling at the I-70 junction.

He caught the news as often as his time allowed, but he heard no mention of the killing of Jake Kramer. As past practices instilled, he would stay in the area until the news broadcasts or newspapers confirmed his expertise. He had Kramer in his sight and he saw Kramer fall, but still that sudden movement…that unexpected movement Kramer made before the kill still plagued him. He would have stayed and watched the results from the hill, but the Sandman had stepped within his comfort zone and he never challenged his comfort zone for it had kept him alive all these years. As he continued along the country road the smell of fresh air served as his masseuse as he became relaxed, confident and content in having done his duty.

"Rich…what are you doing here?"

"Hi, Meg. Am I intruding?"

"Well…no. But I must look a mess. I wasn't expecting company, especially you. But it's a nice surprise, please come in."

Rich stepped onto the small tiled entry and stood at relaxed parade rest. "I brought you some flowers. The lady said you would like them…I don't know much about flowers, except they smell good."

"They're beautiful, Rich, thank you, I'll put them in water. Would you like something to drink? I have some cola and a few beers."

"I'll have a beer, thank you."

He watched as Meg placed the flowers on the kitchen counter, then moved to the refrigerator and pulled open the door.

"It's pale ale if that's alright?"

"Great…I like pale ale."

"I know."

Rich stood quietly next to the table and sipped the cold ale as he watched Meg place the flowers in the vase before adding water.

"They're beautiful," she said once again as she looked to her guest who appeared a little embarrassed.

"Are the kids here, Meg?"

"No, Gladys has them. There going to a weenie roast tonight at the church and then doing a sleepover."

"A church weenie roast. Boy, that brings back memories," he said softly.

"Really? Well, I just got home and was going to take a shower and then meet them there, would you like to come along?"

"ME?"

"Yeah, you. You said it brought back memories, so, if you would like to go, you're more than welcome. You can meet my kids and Clyde and Gladys. All that and an old fashion campfire weenie."

Rich began to shiver enough for her to notice as the thought of going out with a girl on a real date overcame him. It would be a first. Meg noticed his discomfort and added, "of course if you'd rather not…"

"Oh, no. It sounds like fun," he said actually surprising himself.

"Great. I've been telling Gladys all about you and the kids are real excited about meeting a real secret service man."

"Yeah…good. I'm looking forward to meeting them too," he lied as he began to wonder what he was doing there and why he had accepted the invitation to join her group of family and friends.

Meg stood at the kitchen table looking at the first hopeful in her life since her bitter divorce from who turned out to be a drug-polluted, wife-beating alcoholic. But this guy was different. He was decent, clean, God-fearing and very possibly the last middle-aged male virgin.

"I thought you would be working tonight, Rich."

"Why's that?" he asked.

"Well, with Kramer being shot today at the cemetery…do you know who did it?"

"I have a pretty good idea."

"Well, I know you'll catch him. Help yourself to the beer and I'm going to grab a quick shower…you can watch TV if you'd like."

"Okay, thanks."

Meg started down the hall as he sat on the couch and visualized her every movement.

"By the way, how's she doing?" she asked from her room.

"Who?"

"Mrs. Kramer, silly. How bad was she hurt?"

Mrs. Kramer he repeated to himself. MRS. KRAMER!

"Well, Rich, how's Mrs. Kramer doing? The radio said she was released from the hospital."

"Ah…she's going to be fine…why don't you take your shower and I'll try to catch it on the news."

The television came to life with…"can be yours with no money down, no interest and no payments for seventy-two months. And if at anytime during your seventy-two month, risk free, no obligation trial you decide you're unhappy in any way, just return it with no questions asked. You cannot be turned down, guaranteed…call today 1-800-its free. Call now!"

Rich stood and made his was to the kitchen to locate the trash receptacle. The yellow swivel lid accepted his empty bottle and rocked to a slow stop as he returned to the sofa. The running water in the rear of the house stopped as any preconceived notion of easing down the hall to sneak a peak at Meg was lost to his new interest in the news.

"We're back and WAXU News at six now takes you to our Cameron Elliott with excerpts of an interview earlier this afternoon with Jake Kramer...Cameron."

Rich sat at the edge of the couch with the remote in his right hand and the fingers of the other rubbing at his chin. Both hands were shaking as he became obsessed with the results of his deplorable mission. Engrossed in the news, he failed to notice Meg as she moved down the hall wrapped in a bright yellow bath towel that complemented her bronze tan rather nicely.

"Thank you, Roger. Today, I caught up with Jake Kramer at his home after a day of mourning, followed by tragedy while attending the entombment of his long-time friend and business partner, Wesley L. Washington. As already reported, shortly after the burial of his partner, a rifle shot rang out from a hill above the cemetery as yet another attempt was made on the life of Jake Kramer from a would-be assassin. As fate dealt another devious hand in Mr. Kramer's life, the bullet missed its target and instead struck his wife of many years...Connie Kramer. Mrs. Kramer was rushed by paramedics to County General Hospital, where after many hours of treatment and observation she was released and reported to be in fair to good condition.

"State Police Lieutenant Cyrus Connell talked with us about the incident earlier..."

"Damn," muttered Rich.

Meg stepped forward to the back of the flowered print couch and softly placed her hands at the base of Rich's neck, then gently began massaging his stiff muscles with her fingers, using the thumbs to slide up and down the nape of his neck.

"It wasn't your fault, Rich."

"Yes it was."

"You can't blame yourself for things you can't control."

"You don't understand. I'm trained to do better. Some have said that I'm the best…I don't know, but I've never bungled an assignment like this before. Maybe I'm getting careless."

Meg released her hands from around his neck and moved around the sofa taking a seat next to Rich. She placed her arm across the back of the sofa and continued rubbing his neck. Rich looked into her eyes and saw compassion and a tenderness that he had only seen before in the eyes of his mother. Meg noticed Rich's eyes were occasionally drawn to an opening in the towel that exposed her left thigh when she took her seat. His modesty was apparent and encouraged her to inconspicuously shift her position to widen the towel's opening until his embarrassment triumphed and he looked away. Meg reached out and placed her hand against his cheek, pulling his face gently to hers. She could sense his uneasiness as she cautiously moved closer until the kiss transferred the quiver from his lips to hers. As Meg opened her eyes she looked directly into his brown eyes that she knew had never closed. Surely this couldn't have been his first kiss too.

"Let's listen to this," he said as he pulled free from her snare.

"…have any idea as to who would do such a thing, Mr. Kramer?"

"Yeah, I know who it is."

"My God…he knows who's doing it, Rich."

"Shhhhhhh!"

"He's a coward…"

Rich gave an involuntary shudder at the insult of being called a coward, but let it pass.

"…preys on innocent victims by…"

"He's right," said Meg.

"Please, Meg…let's listen."

"…without the compassion of a mother's love. He's Godless…"

Rich jumped directly to his feet and took a half step toward the television.

"…that's the gospel," said Jake finishing his impression of his would-be assassin.

"Sandman!" Rich said as he began to pace in the small space between the set and the sofa table.

"Who's Sandman?" asked Meg as she stood and re-tucked her cotton towel covering the center of her chest. "I'm afraid I don't understand."

"Didn't you hear him? He said, 'Without the compassion of a mother's love.' Well…no women ever gave her children more love and devotion. Without a mother's love and compassion, indeed."

"But he wasn't talking about you, Rich. He was referring to the…" Meg's eyes grew wide as she stopped in mid-sentence and watched her guest pace in front of her.

"He actually had the audacity to stand there and say, 'He's Godless.' There's not another home on earth that lived under God's word more than…Hold on, he's back," said Rich as he slowed his pace and was recaptured by the newscast.

Meg's heart was racing as the impact of Rich's outrage against Jake became clear. She started to move to the kitchen, thinking that with any luck, she could run out the back door to a neighbor for help. Rich took her by the wrist without taking his eyes from the television, more so to share his interest than to keep her from running.

"Listen to this, Meg. This Kramer doesn't know what he's talking about," he said as he pointed to the set and sat on the edge of the seat cushion.

"…it was said best by Matthew, Chapter 3 verses 23-24 when he wrote… *'Whoever he is, he will be found and justice will be served the Lord hates those who love violence.'*"

"Did you hear that, Meg? Did you?"

Meg shook her head yes as she was unable to answer for fear of crying.

"Did you hear that? He called me Godless. ME… and he's the one who can't get the scripture right. Did you hear that?" he asked as he turned to her. That verse wasn't from Matthew's book…it was Psalms. Psalms 11:5… *'The Lord tests the righteous and the wicked, and his soul hates him that loves violence.'* Psalms not

Matthew. He had it all wrong. And he calls ME Godless," he repeated as he turned and caught himself confessing to Megan.

She in turn saw Rich's expression change as he lost his smile and confirmed her fear that he realized he had just admitted to being a killer.

"Well, I better go and finish dressing or we'll never get to the church on time," she said in a voice that was noticeably nervous. Her plan to run out the back door was now useless as her next best hope of escape was through the bedroom window. Rich hadn't spoken a word, but his eyes told her that he was thinking... damage control.

"Come on, Rich, let go of my wrist so I can get dressed. Help yourself to the beer in the fridge if you like," she added while trying to pull away. She could feel his grip tighten and her wrist began to ache as he refused to release her.

"God is punishing me for having impure thoughts, Meg. I didn't mean for you to learn of my work. I am truly sorry."

"You told me that you're with the secret service, remember?" That's all I know, Rich," she said unconvincingly. "Let go, please...you're hurting me, Rich."

She was unsure if he released her or if it was her desperate tug to free herself from his grip, but she lost her footing in the effort and fell awkwardly to the floor, striking her head on the sofa table. Rich stood tranquil above her feeling neither relief nor sorrow, as he looked down at his hostess lying at his feet. He moved slowly to the far end of the table and knelt down at her head where he spotted a small amount of blood coating her hair. He noticed the corner of the table also had traces of her blood. Rich checked her pulse and found it to be strong and released her wrist while noticing the skin was red from his grip. She was out, but he allowed himself one final check. With his left thumb he slid her eyelid back and looked at the small pupil that remained unmoving. Then, without notice, he jabbed his left index finger at her eye, but she remained frozen. "She's out," he said to himself.

Rich stood in place surveying the small room. He reached down, picked up the television's remote control from the table and wiped it free of his prints while he examined her home and retraced his presence there for identifying evidence. Once satisfied, he stepped over Meg's body and moved to the front door.

"Without the compassion of a mother's love, indeed," he said as he stepped from the porch and made his way to his SUV. "Godless, he called me…ME!" he repeated as he raised the rear deck lid and reached inside. Slamming the glass lid closed he immediately turned and looked about the area, confirming that there was no movement on this section of the county road.

Returning to the front porch with a small cardboard box in his left hand, Rich pulled the front door closed behind him as he stepped inside. Meg hadn't moved during his brief exit and he felt no need to recheck her at this time. With box in hand, he made his way down the hall to the laundry room that tightly housed the washer, dryer, hot water heater and oil furnace. Rich raised his right leg and forced the heel of his shoe against the furnace's flexible tubing that connected the burner to the oil tank outside. The tubing tore without any additional effort as small, but steady, droplets of oil became a pool and slowly spread across the linoleum floor. Rich sat his cardboard box on the top of the washer and removed one leftover baggie from Plan B at Kramer and Associates. He placed the mixture in the center of the hall just outside the laundry room, giving it ample room to expand. Once done, he placed the custom detonator under the Ziploc plastic and cradled the generic garage door transmitter before he moved to the front room. The cardboard box was ignored for it would self-dispose.

Rich stood above Meg taking a moment to look at her as she remained lifeless on the carpet. "Sorry, Meg," he said. "I didn't intend for you to get hurt. You should know that I feel sorrow for your children, but they should fair well with Gladys."

Rich forced the table clear and knelt down next to Meg.

"I should have been stronger. I should have never come into this evil house."

He looked across her wrap that had exposed portions of her tanned body and placed his hand on her right shoulder rolling her from her side onto her back. His heart began pounding deep from within his chest as he shook from desire and shame.

"Lead me not into temptation," he said softly, "though you continue to do so." Reaching out with his shaking hand, he pulled the yellow towel free and he drew it to his face to cover his eyes.

"I am a sinner, but you are wicked and it is written… *'I myself will lift up your skirts over your face and your shame will be seen*…Jeremiah 13:26,"' he quoted as he dropped the towel letting it fall across her face. With his mouth dry, his skin moist and his body shaking wildly he gazed at Megan's unconcealed beauty.

Rich felt the impact and the instant pain that followed, but couldn't have guessed its source as his vision quickly began to blur and fade. He fought to maintain consciousness, but it was futile as he slumped forward across Meg's legs.

"NO! I am not wicked…but YOU are a sick man," said Megan, as she rolled Rich off her legs and watched him fall to his back and lay lifeless. Meg stood over him, but before dropping the large glass ash-tray that she clutched in her hand, she kicked him one time in the groin just to be sure.

"Out cold as a creek rock," she said.

Her head hurt like hell as she looked down at Rich, but she knew the next thing to do was to get away…fast. She ran down the hall jumping over the pool of oil lying on the floor in her hallway and quickly pulled on her cut-off jeans and sweat shirt that she found in a pile on the bed. Her next decision was how to escape. Should she dare go back to the front where he might be waiting, or crawl out the bedroom window? It was a no-brainer for Meg as she jumped from the window and landed in her neglected flower bed at the base. Easing her way to the front, she paused behind the evergreen as she saw Rich's SUV backing away from her home. He stopped at the foot of the drive and with his left arm extended, pointed to the house.

"God…he saw me," she said aloud.

The explosion inside her home was deafening, as large red and orange fireballs broke free from windows in several directions. Meg was stunned by the blast and cradled herself tightly in a squatted position next to the block foundation. She could feel the heat around her, but held her place until the SUV began rolling away. Heavy black smoke emerged from the openings and rolled skyward in separate columns. As Rich's vehicle disappeared around the curve, Meg began the run for her life across the wooded lot.

## Forty-Six

"Thank you, Bob, I do appreciate your calling. Yes, I remember her. That will be fine…just have her let us know she's here. Good-bye, Inspector."

Jake turned back to Connie who had been listening to his half of the conversation."

"That was Inspector Pierson."

"So I gathered."

"He has it on good authority that the police may have a break in the identity of our shooter. I understand he tried to kill a single mother yesterday somewhere near Greencastle. She was fortunate to get away, but lost her home and all her worldly possessions."

"That's one of those good news, bad news things, Jake."

"Yeah, and the worst news is he's still at large. However, the police have a good description and they're looking…they'll find him. Say, Connie, do you remember Linda Stern, the bailiff who took care of us during the Reverend Divine trial?"

"Sure…I remember Linda."

"She's coming here tonight. She's going to hang around while I'm gone."

"No, Jake, I told you…"

"Now, Connie, we've been all through this and you're not going with me. You can watch the show on television. There's no way you're up to it and besides, you don't want to be seen out in public with a bandage wrapped around your head like a turban, do you?"

"But, Jake, I want to be there with you, to show my support. And, I really want to be there to watch Bruce put your makeup on again. He thinks you're…what was that he called you?"

She could see that Jake was trying to ignore her, but this was too good to let drop.

"Dashing…that was it. He said you were dashing."

"I'm going to get some air before I have to go," he said trying to change the subject. "You can come out too if you'll promise to play nice."

"I'll be out in a moment. I need to take my medication first."

Jake took a seat at the patio table facing the woods to get the midday sun out of his eyes. This older neighborhood allowed for another quiet afternoon with the exception of the lawn care service mowing across the street at the Sutterfields.

"This is nice," he said aloud, "Nice and peaceful. That was good news from the inspector about the police having the name of the suspect, even if it's only a first name. I wonder why the police didn't mention that to me yesterday when I was downtown trying to convince them that I never heard of their Ernie Dingle. They really should have been asking me for details on people like, Thomas Fernoglio and Steve Howell, or even Eunice Combs…now she was a real dandy. But, instead they kept asking me over and over about someone I never heard of…Ernie Dingle. Oh well, it doesn't matter. It shouldn't matter if they believed me or not, but I guess it does trouble me a little. I'm just not accustomed to having my word questioned, but that's their job. Tonight, I'm going to…"

Connie watched Jake talking to himself from the kitchen. She shook her head as she saw him gesturing with his hands while shaking his head in agreement with himself. She also noticed that he continued his latest practice of rubbing his fingers, one digit at a time, while alternating between hands. "Oh Jake," she said to herself as the door slid open. "Starting without me, Jake?"

"Oh, there you are…started what without you?"

"You were sure having a big conversation with yourself out here."

"Sure I was. Come on out, the sun feels good."

Connie sat down but never moved her eyes from him.

"No, I'm serious, Jake. You were having a big talk out here with someone. I heard you."

"That bullet must have passed closer to your brain than the x-ray showed, Connie. I've just been quietly sitting here waiting for you," he said while again rubbing at his fingers.

Connie paused and drew a deep breath, as lately she was becoming aware of his talking to himself and his absentmindedness, but for now she decided it really didn't matter and just let it pass.

"I wish you wouldn't go tonight, Jake. It's only been five days since…Well, what I mean is, you look tired. Maybe you should take a couple of days to rest and get things sorted out. What about that trip you and

Alex were planning to the mountains? GO! Get away and when you get back, if you still want to go on Elliott's program…fine. I just think you should give it some time."

"Time," he repeated as he looked up. You should know the best part of mine has been shared with you, Connie, and that makes me the luckiest man alive. But, I'm painfully aware that my time is limited and there's so much I want to accomplish that I'm starting tonight. This is something I have to do, babe, and I have to do it alone."

Connie felt her body quiver from the sincerity in his voice and his choice of words.

"Jake, what are you trying to tell me?"

"I'm trying to tell you that I love you and that you've made me the happiest man on earth. And, I'm telling you that tonight I'm going to go on television and try to help some people find the answers to questions about their lost loved ones. I'm going to try to give a little hope to some and a little peace of mind to others. That's all."

Jake looked up at Connie who had the combined look of fear and sorrow in her eyes.

"You know, Connie, I've never told you this before and I mean it from the bottom of my heart when I tell you this now…that turban you're wearing does absolutely nothing for you."

"Thanks," she said while half-laughing and half-crying.

The ring of the doorbell was a welcome intrusion bringing an end to round one.

"I'll get it," said Jake.

"Good. I don't feel like talking to company," she added as he left the patio.

Connie sat and listened to children's voices from the woods that took her back to JJ and Margaret playing in their yard, before recalling Jake's comments about his time. She thought about his plan on how to use his time, but more so, his concern for the lack of it. Connie was beginning to read things into Jake's comments that she didn't care for.

"Connie, we have company."

"Oh…good," she replied.

"You remember, Officer Stern?"

"Of course," answered Connie while standing and offering her hand. "Nice to see you again, Linda."

"Nice to see you too, Mrs. Kramer. I'm happy to see that you're doing well."

"Thank you, Linda."

"If you ladies will excuse me, I'll go and freshen up while the two of you get reacquainted. My ride will be here shortly."

They both watched Jake walk inside and pull the door closed behind him before either spoke.

"Connie…Linda," they said simultaneously causing them both to smile and insist the other go first. Then Linda spoke, "Connie, I can understand how you may feel about my need to be here, but under the circumstances, it's not a bad idea."

"Linda, it's not that I don't want you here, it's just that I don't feel like I'm in any danger. That guy must be long gone by now."

"Hopefully he is, but if not…he best not try anything on my watch."

Connie smiled at her and asked, "Would you like something to drink…coffee?"

"Not at the moment, thank you. I think I'd like to take a walk around the house and get familiar with the area."

"Glad to have you here, Linda."

"Glad to be here for you, Mrs. Kramer," she said as she turned to leave.

"Oh Linda, if you don't mind my asking…any word from your daughter?"

"No, ma'am, nothing yet, but I pray a lot."

Connie nodded in understanding. "I believe one day she'll realize that she needs her mother and she'll want to come home."

"Yes, Ma'am…that's part of my prayer."

Connie waved from the front porch at the long black limo pulling from the drive as WAXU's *Up Close and Personal* producer, Mr. Silverman, in keeping with tradition, had sent his staff car for Jake. Taking one last look before the car disappeared she saw Ms. Stern standing quietly with her thumbs tucked under her utility belt watching the street from the edge of the drive.

"I'll let you know when the show starts, Linda."

"Thank you, Mrs. Kramer. I would appreciate that," she said without turning.

Connie started to step inside when her attention was drawn to movement in the Sanders' yard that Linda had already noticed and had started toward.

"It's ok, Linda, that's my neighbor Cindy," shouted Connie.

Linda waved to acknowledge and moved back to her position.

"It's looks like you're under house arrest tonight, Connie."

"Jake's idea, Cindy, but she's nice. I like her. What's up?"

"Alex's idea. He said there's an old army buddy in town that he's determined to find. He thought you might want someone to be here with you during Jake's show. I hope you don't mind."

"You're always welcome, Cindy," she said while placing her arm around Cindy's shoulder. "Let's go in and fix some snacks, shall we?"

# Forty-Seven

"Mr. Kramer, how good it is to see you again," she said while offering her hand.

"Nice to see you too, Terri."

"Wow, I'm flattered…you remembered my name. May I say how sorry I am to hear of your loss and I hope Mrs. Kramer is doing well."

"She is, thank you. I'll be sure to tell her that you asked about her."

"Good…now if you'll follow me, sir, I'll show you the way to our stand-by room."

"Fine, but please call me, Jake."

The walk through the hall was a short one as tonight's show was going to be aired in WAXU's own studio due to the short notice Jake provided. Once inside the modest stand-by room, Terri explained the show's format and reminded him that due to the limited seating, the majority of questions and requests would be by phone.

"Please make yourself comfortable, Jake, and if there's anything you need just pick up the studio phone," suggested Terri while pointing to the beige set on the wall.

"I'll be fine, thanks. Don't worry about…"

"My…my…my. Looky, looky who we have with us again," he said as he began his stroll across the room.

"I was just about to leave, he's all yours," said Terri while glancing up and smiling at Jake.

"Hello, Bruce."

"Mr. Kramer, I can't tell you how excited I was when I learned that I was going to get to do you again," he said while offering Jake the back of his hand. "You're one of my favorites you know."

"Thanks, Bruce…And you should know that I don't let anyone do my face but you."

"Oh, Mr. Kramer, how you do go on."

Terri did her best to conceal her smile as she pulled open the door and stepped into the hall.

"You have about thirty minutes, Bruce. Any problem with that?"

"Go, go, go," he said waving at the door without looking.

Bruce finished with Jake, taking a little longer than necessary because he enjoyed Jake and he enjoyed his work. Bruce also knew that after doing a retouch on Mr. Elliott, he would have little to do until the ten o'clock newscasters required his services.

"I'm so proud of you, Mr. Kramer…You did a good job not squiggling in your seat this time. You know, I usually give a sucker to all my good boys."

"Thank you, Bruce…I'll pass just the same."

"Well…" he said while snapping closed his make-up case. "You know best."

Jake took a seat on the sofa which proved to be surprisingly comfortable. The cloth protector left between the collar and the neck to prevent makeup from staining his shirt was distracting, but not uncomfortable. However, he knew Bruce would have a hissy-fit if he removed it without permission. Jake looked around the room and noticed that the television hanging to his left was silently showing WAXU real-time programming with closed-captions scrolling through the black box at the bottom. He ignored the programming once he realized it was a commercial.

Leaning his head against the back of the sofa he closed his eyes and tried to relax. Jake had rehearsed his intentions for this evening to the point that he was becoming bored with the plan. He intended to bring to the surface as many of society's villains as time would allow on tonight's broadcast. With that done, he would then devote the remainder of his life to that end. To this, Jake Kramer was committed.

After the show Jake planned to have his driver take him uptown to the Easton Hotel on West Washington Street where he had pre-registered and moved in. His plan was extensive, including changing hotels if necessary depending upon Alex's ability to find him. If Alex did indeed locate him, he would then be firm in saying, "You found the wrong guy, Sandman." Jake knew Alex was good, but he preferred that he devote his time to finding the Gospel. The decision was made; he would not, under any circumstances, endanger his family and friends any longer.

"Mr. Kramer…we're getting close to air. Please follow me," said the young intern wearing a wrinkled white shirt and Nike sneakers. He led Jake down the narrow hall to Terri as she stood in place behind the dark green curtains and looked intently at her clipboard.

"Jake…good, Cameron is making your intro now."

"Where's Bruce?" asked Jake while smiling at Terri.

"I'm here, Mr. Kramer…right here, lover. Quickly now, let's have a look see."

"No shiny forehead, Bruce. I have a reputation you know."

"Not to worry, lover…Brucie's here."

"Okay…in five," said Terri into her head set, again hiding her smile behind the clipboard. She then looked at Jake and said, "You're on, lover."

"Ladies and Gentlemen, won't you please give a warm *UP Close and Personal* welcome to our very special guest, Mr. Jake Kramer."

The show's theme music began immediately as Terri nodded to Jake and pulled open the separation between the curtains making way for him to pass. Jake felt the heat of house lights as he made his way across center stage in the direction indicated by the stage hand as he pointed toward Cameron. The applause light was illuminated and the sound volume was raised as Jake walked toward the desk of Cameron Elliott who was standing behind it while smiling in Jake's direction and clapping enthusiastically. As Jake approached, Elliott offered a warm handshake before he again resumed his applause.

Jake acknowledged his reception to the audience several times before taking his seat, as did Cameron, who immediately began adjusting his cup, pencils and notepad.

"Jake, welcome once again to *Up Close and Personal* and may I add how good it is to have you with us."

"Thank you, Cameron. It's nice to be here."

"Jake, before we begin, I…and I'm sure that I am speaking for all of our listening audience, both here and at home, when I offer our deepest heartfelt sympathy on the loss of your friend during the tragic events last Monday. And to also say that we are appalled that such a horrendous act could happen in the Indianapolis area and we demand a quick resolve to justice."

A spontaneous round of applause erupted in the small studio that was aided by the engineer in the control booth as the camera focused in tightly on Elliot's expression of compassion.

"Thank you, Cameron."

"Jake," said Elliott. "If I may ask…how is Mrs. Kramer's recovery progressing?"

"She's recovering nicely, thank you, Cameron…and I'm sure she's watching right now at home."

"May we all wish her God's speed in her convalescence…isn't that right folks?" he added while looking to the audience as the applause light lit and the clapping began on cue.

"Thank you again, Cameron."

"You know, Jake" said Cameron while adjusting himself in his chair. "I may be speaking out of turn here, but I just have to say it. I think these people who commit such acts are not only sick, but cowards as well."

Another light round of applause echoed in the small room as Cameron continued. "I'd say he's not only a coward, but he's one who preys on victims by lying in the dark or striking when they can't fight back." The applause again rang out as Elliott was on a roll. "He has no sense of morals or values and I'd say he's nothing more than a terrorist. He's Godless."

Many in the audience were standing as the camera scanned the room during an impromptu playing of *God Bless America.*

"Ladies and gentlemen, we'll be right back with our special guest, Mr. Jake Kramer after these brief messages…please stay tuned."

"Back in ten."

Jake looked at Cameron and with a straight face he said, "I couldn't have said that better myself, Mr. Elliott."

"Thanks, Jake. Sometimes you just have to say what's in your heart."

Jake looked around the tiny studio and estimated seventy to seventy-five people in the audience, which was a respectable size for the camera that occasionally spanned the group during the applause light. Jake sat quietly as Cameron looked over his notes and talked with Terri, giving the impression that they were having a dispute over the schedule on her clipboard.

"In…5…4…3…2…" said the stagehand, as his fingers counted down before pointing directly at the host.

"We're back…I am your host, Cameron Elliott and this is *Up Close and Personal* with our special guest, Mr. Jake Kramer. We're here tonight attempting to bring some relief to those of you who feel hopeless in finding answers regarding a loved one. We'll welcome your calls at 800-UPCLOSE and please, please be patient, for we have many calls coming in from those wishing to speak with Jake.

"Now, for our first guest this evening, let's go to the audience shall we and see who we have at the podium. May we have your name please and tell us where you're from Miss…"

"I'm Mrs. Eleanor Summers from Bloomington, Indiana."

"Welcome, Eleanor. What would you like to ask Jake Kramer?"

"First I'd like to say, Mr. Kramer, that I think you're wonderful for the way you help people."

"Thank you, Mrs. Summers, that's nice of you to say," said Jake as he looked over her background card. "I read here that you have a question concerning your son, Robbie."

"Yes sir, that's right," she answered while looking back to her husband before continuing. "Robbie has been gone for eight years next month and we still miss him terribly."

"Yes, ma'am, I'm sure you do," replied Jake as he finished with her card and looked at Mrs. Summers."

"Well sir, this is very difficult because my husband thinks I'm foolish for being here and that I should just let Robbie rest, but I need to know. I need to know for sure."

"You need to know what?" asked Elliott while looking at the camera.

"I need to know if he heard me."

"I'm afraid we're not following you, Mrs. Summers."

"I believe I am," said Jake as he took the lead from Cameron. "Eleanor, I think this will become clear to everyone if you'll tell us why you're unsure if Robbie heard you."

Courtesy of the cameraman, the entire viewing audience watched a close-up of Mrs. Summers squeezing her nose with her tissue and again glancing at her husband. Then after taking a deep breath, she looked back at the stage and spoke.

"Robbie was a good boy, bright, talented and so young. Two weeks after his seventeenth birthday, his car was struck by a drunk driver. Our Robbie lay in the hospital on life support for ten weeks as the doctors exhausted every hope that he could survive without it. Ross and I made the difficult decision to place Robbie in God's hands and requested the life giving machine be turned off. To say that Robbie lived would be a matter of opinion, as we eventually brought him home where we cared for him for the next eight years, three months and six days. Some doctors said he was in a coma, while others thought he was brain dead, but I know he was aware of my presence. I know he heard me talking to him about our family, or telling him the news, weather and things that were going on around him. I just know in my heart that he heard me, but you're the only one on this earth that can confirm it, Mr. Kramer."

Once again she raised her Kleenex to her nose before continuing. "My Ross thinks I'm foolish to be here, but I don't think so. I have to know. I'm asking you, sir, did we make a difference? Was he comfortable? Was he in pain? I have to know…did my Robbie hear me?"

All eyes turned to Jake as silence filled the small studio. Connie, Cindy and Linda sat without speaking as were the thousands of viewers glued to their sets throughout the televised area. Jake looked down at his hands that he was rubbing, before he squeezed his eyes closed. Elliott ignored the producer's plea to make a comment and eliminate the dead air time, because he knew this was what ratings were made of…suspense, drama and anticipation. No, this was too good, nothing he would say could be better.

"Oh my God," said Connie softly while watching from thirty-three miles away. "He's rubbing his hands."

Linda and Cindy exchanged glances to see if the other understood her comment, but recognized that neither did nor asked.

Jake slowly raised his head toward Mrs. Summers as she stood with the audience at her back, bringing a sigh of relief to the show's producer.

“You made a difference, Ms. Summers.”

Jake paused while the audience acknowledged their approval of his answer. The producer quickly switched to Camera 2, which focused on Mrs. Summers who immediately began crying, along with a few others seated near her.

“I might add, Eleanor, that Robbie was never in pain because…” Another light round of clapping erupted causing Jake to pause momentarily. “…because,” he continued, “Robbie had no sense of feeling in his body. I should make it clear, Mrs. Summers that Robbie’s awareness was sparse and brief, but he knew that you were with him and this he found to be very comforting. He was not afraid.”

Again the audience broke out in loud applause with a few chants of, “Good for you Eleanor.” Elliott spoke into his microphone adding his two cents by saying, “Only a mother’s love. Never underestimate a mother’s love,” as he began a light clapping also. Mrs. Summers turned to her husband and said, “See…I told you so, Ross,” loud enough to be heard by the audio and much to the delight of the viewers.

“Are you a non-believer, Mr. Summers?” asked Cameron Elliott. “Stand up, sir…please.”

As the camera focused on Ross Summers, everyone could see his embarrassment and reluctance to go public, but still he yielded to the challenge and took his place beside his wife.

Cameron repeated his question, “Sir, are you skeptical of Mr. Kramer’s comments.”

Ross Summers cleared his throat directly into the microphone, giving the show's producer yet a new reason to chew another *Tums* antacid tablet.

"I wanna believe him, sure, but you know…if it brings comfort to Eleanor, then it's okay with me."

"But you don't share her confidence in Mr. Kramer's comments? Is that right?"

"I'm not gonna call him a liar, but anyone could say 'he heard you.'"

"Jake…" said Cameron as he spun in his chair toward his guest."

Camera 1 focused on Jake as he continued rubbing at his fingers and appeared to shift in his chair several times before speaking. The cool, calm and collected Jake Kramer that emerged on the first show was noticeably not here tonight as everyone waited for his response.

"Well…I'm not going to sit here and try to convince you, sir. If you don't want to believe me that's most certainly your prerogative, but I do know Robbie heard his mother tell him about President Reagan being shot and men walking on the moon, as well as the devastation caused by Hurricane Camille."

The audience withheld any sign of support for either man as they waited for Ross to accept or reject Jake's evidence.

"See Ross," said Eleanor. "I told him about those things. He did hear me."

"Okay, Eleanor, if you say so."

"Still skeptical, Mr. Summers?" asked Cameron.

"Look…those were some of the biggest news events of the century and certainly the ones I'd pick if I were guessing."

There was some soft conversation surfacing in the background as the producer increased the audio volume to complement the effect while he brought Camera 1 in and centered it tightly on Jake.

Cameron again turned toward Jake and began drumming his pencil as he said, "He makes a good point, Jake. Are you grabbing at the news?"

Jake looked at the monitor that gave a sharp image of him wringing his hands while shifting about in his chair. He put an immediately stop to his nervous appearance by crossing his legs and placing his hands on his knee.

"Well, Jake?" added Elliott who was grinning at his guest while watching him squirm. Jake made a fist and covered his mouth as he cleared his throat, then moved his hand to the side of his head.

"He's getting a headache," said Connie to Linda and Cindy. "Look, he's rubbing his head. This is not a good thing." She watched as the camera again caught him wringing his hands.

"Mr. Summers does make a good point. I won't argue that," said Jake as he looked at Elliott and fell silent.

The producer again reached for his antacid tablets as only a mumble from the studio audience could be heard.

"Commercial…break for commercial," he shouted while toggling the controls.

Cameron Elliott caught the commercial light flashing, but chose to ignore it and not let Jake off the hook that easy.

"Well, Jake? Mr. Summers appears to have you cornered."

"Well, Cameron…as I said, he's right about the news stories, but Mr. Summers' occasional night visits to Robbie's room after his exhausted wife was asleep wasn't in the news, nor were his trips to his bedside when she was out of the house doing her marketing."

The camera quickly shifted to Mr. and Mrs. Summers standing at the podium. "Ross…is that true?" she asked.

Ross's face immediately turned beet red suggesting it was without his answering.

"Ross?" she said again causing him to shake his head yes in confirmation.

"But why, Ross? You rarely went into Robbie's room."

Ross didn't answer, but the camera managed to pick up the tears that formed in his eyes while he reached into his hip pocket for his handkerchief.

"I'm sorry, Mr. Summers. I know this must be painful, for it's a private matter that perhaps you may wish to explain to Mrs. Summers later."

"I didn't want anyone to know," he said in a broken voice. I can't…"

"May I?" asked Jake.

Ross shook his bowed head yes, but again didn't answer.

"As I have said, Robbie was void of any feeling in his body which was a blessing in disguise because there was no pain during his moments of awareness. But he heard his father say many times, “Robbie, we’re alone …just us guys.”

The camera centered on Mr. and Mrs. Summers as Jake continued.

“Your husband would kneel at the bed, take Robbie’s hand and pray for his son. He prayed…he cried…and he prayed and cried some more. I imagine he was too proud to have confessed that to you, Eleanor, as he must have some ridiculous notion that male crying is a weakness. If it’s of any comfort to you sir, Robbie’s favorite prayer went something like, ‘Lord, we’re alone and I’m back at Robbie’s side asking that you continue looking after my boy. I know you had your reasons to do this to him, although I’ll never understand…maybe one day you’ll explain it to me. But I am asking again, Lord…if my son is lying in pain, please take him home.’ See, Mr. Summers… Robbie heard you and you too, made a difference.”

A warm, thunderous round of applause erupted without prompting as the camera alternated between the Summers, the seated audience and center stage. Cameron was trying to add his comments, but the applause for Mr. Summers took preference as the couple hugged each other tightly and both cried. Cameron gave in to the moment and leaned back in his chair, clapping also. Then on cue and surrounded by applause, he looked at the camera and said, “We’ll be back with more from our very special guest, Mr. Jake Kramer, after these messages. Stay tuned.”

# Forty-Eight

"It's going great, Jake. You had me worried there for a minute, but you handled Mr. Summers beautifully. Terri said the phone lines are jammed with people trying to talk to you."

"Do you think you could rustle-up a couple of aspirins, Cameron?"

"Sure, Jake, sure…no problem," he answered while motioning to the script girl.

Jake leaned forward in his chair trying to rub away his headache, perhaps due to the harsh lighting, but nonetheless it was going from bad to worse.

"When we come back, Cameron, I have a list of some people who are responsible for…"

"Sure, Jake, sure. We'll get to that, but we're hot and need to keep the show on a roll. Here's a card from a woman whose parents were deceased when she was very young and she was raised in foster homes. Now she's been told that she married her own brother two years ago without knowing it. She wants you to check it out. Yeah…we should do this one next."

"NO! Cameron," said Jake while accepting the aspirin and water. "I want to go through my list. That's why I'm here. These people think they got away with murder and…"

"Sure, Jake, like I said, we'll get to it. Hold on we're coming back."

"In…5…4…3…2…" and again the finger pointed at Elliott.

"Thank you…and if you're just joining us, this is *Up Close and Personal* with my special guest, Mr. Jake Kramer. We're taking your requests, as time allows, to speak with Mr. Kramer by phone at 800-UPCLOSE, or if you're among the select few here in our studio audience."

"Cameron," interrupted Jake. "I have a rather long list of names, dates and locations, regarding victims of homicides during the last several years that I'd like to bring to light and…"

"Good, Jake, that sounds very interesting and we certainly want to get to that, but first let's go to our studio audience once again and hear from Mrs. Dorothy…"

"No," said Jake interrupting once again without apologizing. "I have created a list of names of some people who were responsible for taking the lives of helpless, innocent human beings. These people need to be brought to justice, Cameron, and I am pledging to make these names and details available to the proper authorities immediately after this program."

Jake's pause was long enough for Cameron to seize the lead. "That's a wonderful gesture on your part, Jake, and we here and at home support you in your campaign…don't we folks?" added Elliot as a round of applause quickly followed. "So now, let's go to the phones and see who wants to get, *Up Close and Personal,* with Jake Kramer."

As the camera drifted from the close-up shot, Connie watched as Jake held his crumbled list in a tight fist while rubbing his arm with the other hand in a nervous behavior. She wanted desperately to run to the studio and bring him home, or at least have this show end early, though neither of the two was going to happen and all she could do was sit helplessly and watch.

"Is he alright?" asked Cindy.

"I don't know…I hope so," she replied as she saw Jake begin to straighten his paper and attempted to press out the wrinkles against Elliott's desk with the palm of his hand. He then pointed to the list with his index finger and continued, "See Cameron, right here it says that Lester Holverson was shot by Joe Burrell on June 18, in a parking lot, over a heated discussion concerning Burrell's wife. And Mary Prange was murdered by her husband, Jeremy, in a jealous rage on…"

"Jake that is some very fascinating information," said Cameron, "and we will get back to that right after we take a call from a viewer. Who are you sir, and tell us why you would like to get, *UP Close and Personal* with Jake Kramer."

"Oh, I'd like to get up close and personal alright. Up close enough to personally punch his lights out."

"Easy sir, we won't allow threats to be made against our guests. If you have a question for Mr. Kramer, please state it."

"Hell yes, I have a questions…about fifty-thousand of them. What did you do with the money, Kramer? You better cough it up or I'm gonna take it out of your hide."

The camera quickly centered on Jake while leaving Elliott to ask, "Money…sir, are you implying that Mr. Kramer owes you money?"

"I ain't implying nothing. I'm saying that he took it right off our farm. Money that my old man buried and he found it and then he stole it. Now I want it back. It's mine…me and my sisters. He done gave our brother his share, but took ours with him. He's a damn thief, that's what he is. Admit it, Kramer…it's true, ain't it"

The studio fell very quiet waiting for Jake to respond, but he didn't. He sat quietly squirming in his chair and looking at his wrinkled paper.

"Jake…Jake, would you care to respond to this gentleman's…I'm sorry, sir, you didn't give your name."

"Gillespie, Henry Gillespie from…ah, he knows where I'm from. He was there. Damn thief."

"That will do, Mr. Gillespie. We cannot allow profanity on the air." Cameron again turned to Jake and finished his question. "Jake, would you care to elaborate on Mr. Gillespie's allegations? Did you remove money from his property without proper authorization?"

The studio again fell quiet as the show's producer took the last of his antacid tablets while waiting for Jake to reply.

"Jake?" repeated Elliott.

Jake raised his head to look at Cameron and in a weak tone said, "I have this list of names of people who were responsible for…"

"We know that, Jake, but we need to know if you are responsible for taking money from Mr. Gillespie. Money he claims didn't belong to you and was rightfully his. Do you care to respond to Mr. Gillespie's allegations, Mr. Kramer? Did you visit…"

"Hey, he don't have to respond…can't you tell he's guilty as hell?" shouted the caller over the phone. "How much money have you taken from other people who asked for your help, Kramer? It's time you people out there wake up to this con artist. I'll bet if the truth was known, somewhere he's got a bank account full of other people's money…mine included and I want mine back."

The seed was planted and the harvest was growing in the minds of everyone in the audience and at home, including the Kramer's house. Connie sensed Cindy's and Linda's heads turning toward her as Cindy commented, "That's the most absurd thing I've ever heard." Linda however remained quiet as they again looked to the set and saw the pitiful image of Connie's husband sitting hunched over with his head bowed staring at the crumbled paper in his hands.

"For the love of God…go to a commercial and get him off the stage," said Connie.

The producer of *Up Close and Personal* held Camera 1 tightly centered on their guest, Jake Kramer, as host Cameron Elliott continued his questioning.

"…but this shouldn't be a difficult question for you, Jake. Simply deny or confirm Mr. Gillespie's claim. Did you, or did you not, locate and withhold monies from his property?"

Jake stood so quickly that the camera only showed a close up of his belt buckle that spread havoc in the control room as they scrambled for another shot. While stepping off the stage platform, Jake began to wave the wrinkled list in front of Cameron and said in a firm and harsh tone, "Doesn't anyone care anymore? I have a list of names and places."

He began a slow pace in front of Elliott's desk as he continued. "Doesn't anyone want to know what happened to Emily Marshall or Patrick McElroy? Don't you people care about Bess Boswell?" He was standing directly in front of Elliott's desk again looking down at his crumbled paper, as Cameron slid his chair to the edge in order to stay on camera.

Jake slowly looked up from the list in his hand and while visibly shaking he turned to Elliott and asked, "Why aren't you listening to me?" He then turned to the audience and repeated, "Why aren't you listening to me? Why does everyone want to listen to that other man? I'M JAKE KRAMER!" he shouted. "He's nobody. I help people all the time. I helped that lady, what's-her-name up there, find out about her son, didn't I?" he asked while waving his paper at the audience.

"Go to a commercial," shouted an unknown from the studio audience.

"Jake, please take a seat," said Elliott who was now trying to show some sign of compassion to his guest. "Come…sit down, please."

Jake responded to Cameron's suggestion by gradually moving away from the desk toward his chair as the viewers watched with doubt that he would make it without some help. Once seated, Jake remained quiet with his feet squarely on the floor, knees pressed together, arms folded and shaking like a school boy waiting for the principle.

"See what a guilty conscience will do for ya," said the caller breaking the silence.

"Hang up on that guy," shouted someone in the audience bringing a few claps and chants of agreement.

"Sir," said Elliott, "I believe you've made your point…good day."

"Hey, I was just telling it like it is. That guy's a thief…a money hungry thief. I wouldn't be surprised if he burnt down his own building just to get the insurance money."

Jake was rapidly shaking his head no to that suggestion, as shouts of anger erupted throughout the studio with one male voice volunteering to rearrange the caller's face. Cameron knew he had permitted latitude to the caller well beyond the station's guidelines. But the producer hadn't severed the line, so as far as he was concerned he was getting a little payback for Kramer telling the world on his previous show about his little fling with young Ashley Sutherland. Elliott watched Jake pull a handkerchief from his pocket and wipe his brow before he asked his guest, "Any comment, Jake?"

The entire viewing audience watched the depressing image of Jake Kramer on live television while waiting for a response that might support their love and admiration for him.

"Hell…he's not gonna' answer. I believe I hit the nail on the head with that one. He took my money and blew up his own building for the insurance…killed two people doin' it, too. That make's him a thief and a murderer. Hey, Kramer, is your name on that list?"

"NO! NO! NO! NO!" shouted Jake as he shook his lowered head and rubbed at his face with the handkerchief. "Wesley…he was not…he was like my own. It should have been me. Don't you understand …it should have been me," he shouted while hiding behind his handkerchief.

"I understand alright. Hey, Kramer…you can keep my money. You're going to need it for a lawyer." With that said the caller hung up and the dial tone emerged.

A hush immediately filled the studio as each person strained to hear what Jake was saying so softly. There were a few who looked away and one couple who exited the studio.

The commercial light caught Elliott's eye, but he ignored it to ask, "Jake…before we take a break, do you have anything you wish to say to your family, friends and the thousands of loyal fans who have followed you, and in many cases worshiped you?"

Camera 1 zoomed in on the bowed head of Jake Kramer as he sat noticeably shaking and slowly raising his head. If the gasp from the studio audience wasn't loud enough to startle everyone…the appearance of Jake Kramer's face was. His skin was sunburn red and his eyes were wide open and as large and round as quarters. The whites of his eyes had turned to a deep burgundy color.

As Jake continued to raise his head, screams could be heard from a few in the studio as he took the blood soaked handkerchief away from the lower half of his face, exposing the blood that ran from his nose, across his lips and down his chin.

He then stood and looked around the studio at no one in particular and said in a soft tone, “It should have been me…I should have died, not them. I’m sorry… I’m so very very sorry.”

Jake Kramer then calmly turned and walked off stage.

# Forty-Nine

No one said a word at the Kramer's house. They just sat and stared in disbelief at what they had just witnessed on television. Cindy turned to Connie just as she broke down and began to cry.

"Oh Connie…I'm so sorry," she said.

"That man's crazy," added Linda. "The caller, I mean."

The phone rang bringing Linda to her feet. "I'll get it, Mrs. Kramer…you just take it easy."

"Kramer's…no she can't come to the phone right now, can I take a message?"

Connie took the tissue that was offered by Cindy while listening to Linda's conversation.

"Is that so…well, I'll tell you what, buster. Why don't you just do that? I'll be out by the street waiting for you…that is, if you're man enough to show up." With that said she replaced the handset. "Another crazy. Do you get a lot of that, Mrs. Kramer?"

Connie nodded her head yes as the phone rang again.

"Leave it off the hook, Linda, please. They'll be at the door next."

"Not on my watch…no way," she said as she laid the handset on the counter. "I'll be right outside if you ladies need me."

"Do you need anything, Connie?"

"No thanks, Cindy. I don't think so."

“We’ll, I do. I’m going to help myself to a drink if you don’t care.”

“Make me one too. Is that my cell phone ringing or yours?”

“Doesn’t sound like mine…I’ll get it,” she added as she moved across the room. “Connie…It’s Doctor Harrington for you. Can you take the call?”

“Sure…thank you.”

“I’ll make the drinks,” said Cindy as she handed Connie the phone.

In the rear lot of the WAXU television station Jake’s driver, Becky Schmidt, paced slowly along the side of her shiny black limo while glancing between her next step and the exit door of the building. Becky had watched most of the program on the monitor in the hall then hurried to the car when she saw Jake walk off the stage. She heard all of the accusations and saw Jake’s lack of refutation, but nothing or anyone could change her opinion of him. For if it wasn’t for Jake Kramer, her sister, June Grodey, would not have her son Jimmy with her today. She smiled as she recalled watching little Jimmy sitting on a stool next to Jim taking his first cow milking lesson, with June’s supervision. No, sir, as far as Becky was concerned, Jake Kramer could find all the gold in the world and it still wouldn’t outweigh the good he’d done. She stopped her pacing and moved to the rear car door as she saw Jake appear at the exit.

The alleyway that cut through the WAXU property ran parallel to the back of the building’s parking lot and the fenced area of Jones Mowing Service to the south. In the darkened section of the alley, the Gospel stood motionless in the shadows next to the brown trash dumpster that supported his rifle. He was looking at a one-hundred percent unobstructed view of the exit door, the twelve steps leading down to the lot and the awaiting car, not to mention one female driver with her hand on the door handle. He had failed miserably on this assignment and he knew it. He was confident that another club member must have been piggybacked by now to fulfill his failed responsibility. As he watched the WAXU's rear exit he revisited the number of times his prey had escaped his snare and never had he felt so incompetent, for troubleshooting was his life; it was all he knew. He also was sure that the Club would recognize the Kramer building fiasco as his blunder, meaning he would need to go underground after this kill if he wanted to live. Someone's pick-up bag most certainly would have the Gospel in it.

His attention was alerted to movement at the rear door and the appearance of Jake Kramer standing on the landing. While making less noise than the flies around him, he took his rifle and pointed it toward the stationary Jake Kramer standing eighty meters away and centered the rifle's sights between the eyebrows. Sensing the metal of the trigger, the Gospel curled his index finger and began the slow steady draw toward his nose.

Rich never saw him coming, but he did hear, "Not today, Gospel," as the rifle rang out sending the bullet against the concrete block three feet above Jake's head. The origin of the sound was unmistakably that of a rifle. Nevertheless, Becky selflessly ran up the stairs and hurried a confused Jake Kramer to her car while hearing a scuffle from across the lot.

Alex held a death grip around the wood of the fore-end as Rich held tightly to the buttstock with both determined to have the other's share.

"Sandman, I should have known."

"Give it up, Gospel…it's over."

Alex felt two quick blows to his ribs from Rich's free hand that hurt more than they should. He quickly countered with his free hand to Rich's abdomen and compared it to striking a sandbag with bare knuckles. The struggle for the weapon continued as they pulled each other away from the dumpster in a circular motion while bouncing on and off the chain link fence. Alex's only comfort zone at this point was catching a glimpse of Jake's car speeding away as he continued taking blow after blow to the ribs by the Gospel's sledgehammer-like fist. It was an empty wine bottle that Alex stepped on while backpedaling in the dark alley that caused him to lose his footing and fall to the ground. He broke his grip on the weapon as he felt a corner of the dumpster strike his head, leaving him dazed and with blurred vision as the pavement rose to greet him. Alex knew instinctively that he needed to stay conscious and regain his footing, but at that moment nothing cooperated.

"Well…well. Look who's down," said Rich as he knelt on one knee in front of Alex. "The legendary

Sandman," he added while placing the rifle barrel against Alex's Adam's apple. "You're out of shape old man."

Alex's vision was beginning to return and he began to focus on the grinning Gospel.

"Let it go, Hinny," he said. "Let it go."

"Let it go? I can't Sandman…you know that," he replied while rubbing the rifle's sight against Alex's chin. "It's my assignment. Just like the Major. Just like all of them. Nothing personal."

"You botched this one, Gospel…you know it. They'll be after you next," said Alex while stalling for time as his vision returned."

"That man does have nine lives, I'll give him that, but they're running out."

Alex, in desperation, reached out for the rifle's barrel, but was much too slow as Rich pulled back and turned the weapon one hundred eighty degrees. Alex's sight became clear enough to see the butt-end close in on his forehead just before he lost consciousness altogether.

As Rich stood quietly and stared at the rear of the WAXU building, he had to wonder if God wasn't really looking after Alex's friend, Mr. Kramer…for no one gets pardoned that often. Turning around to look down at his comrade who lay motionless amid the trash he spoke to deaf ears. "You saved my butt near Dau Tieng during the Attleboro campaign, when my back was against the wall, Sandman, and I owed you one. We're square now. If there's a next time…I'll kill you." Rich then added as he turned away, "*And if ye do good to* *them which do good to you, what thank have ye? for sinners also do even the same…*Luke 6:33

The WAXU's limo made its getaway around the first corner at Chestnut Street with the tires squealing and Jake bouncing in the back seat.

"That was a gun shot, sure enough, Mr. Kramer. Do you think we should pull over now and call the police or something?" asked Ms. Schmidt from behind the wheel.

Jake's non-response prompted her to look up at the rearview mirror to find him sitting ridged while looking directly ahead.

"Look sir, I know that I'm only the driver here, but your itinerary says you want to go downtown. I'll be happy to take you home, or do you want to stay on your schedule?"

As she waited for an answer, Becky sped across the double tracks on Kentucky Avenue and again rechecked the mirror noticing Jake's head bobbing forward.

"Okay, Mr. Kramer, you're the boss, downtown it is. If you'll look in that armrest, sir, you'll find some *Wet Ones* to use on your face. Help yourself. Let me know if you need anything at all, Mr. Kramer, I'm here for you."

They completed the short seven-minute ride to the Easton Hotel in complete silence with Ms. Schmidt pulling under the well lit canopy. The darkened windows prevented anyone from seeing the passenger with the exception of the driver who immediately became aware that Jake hadn't taken advantage of her moist towelette offer. Her respect and compassion again surfaced for her passenger as she drove away and circled the block before pulling to a stop at the high security and very private V.I.P. entrance. After personally attending to Jake, she helped him from the car and held his arm until his legs became solid.

"I would feel better about this if you would let me drive you home, Mr. Kramer."

Jake slowly turned his head to her without answering, but as she gazed into his eyes she felt a sense of warmth and kindness unlike anything she had ever known.

"It should have been me," he whispered, while reaching out for her hand.

"God bless you, Mr. Kramer," said Becky as she gently squeezed his hand.

While pulling away from the V.I.P. entrance onto West Washington Street she focused on her rearview mirror and noted that Jake Kramer was nowhere to been seen.

# Fifty

"There's a Doctor Harrington out here to see you, Mrs. Kramer, may I send her in?"

"Oh yes, Linda…please let her in and thank you."

Connie and Cindy had to smile at Linda Stern's efficiency, but they did find comfort in the fact that she was watching out for them.

"How are you feeling, Connie?" asked Doreen as she joined them in the den.

"Physically I'm fine. Mentally…I'm a wreck. I assume you watched the show and that's why you're here."

Doreen nodded yes then said, "Officer Stern told me that Jake hasn't made it home yet."

"No and I'm worried sick about him. Oh Doreen, did you see his eyes, they…"

"Yes, I saw, Connie, that's why I wanted to be here when he came home."

"What's happening to him, Doctor?" asked Cindy.

"Any number of things, most of which could be grouped by simply saying he's experiencing a nervous breakdown. I believe he should to be placed in care before he gets hurt."

"That's my cell, excuse me," said Cindy as she reached for her purse. "Hello?"

"Cindy…it's me."

"Oh, Alex, thank God you called. Where are you?"

"I'm still downtown. Listen, Cindy, did Jake make it home?"

"No. He's not home yet. We were hoping that he might be with you. What's going on, Alex?"

"I don't want to go into that now, Cindy, and please don't let Connie sense that anything is wrong. That poor lady has been through enough already."

"Okay, honey, I understand. You have a good time," she said while smiling into the phone.

"Good girl," said Alex. "Now, if Jake does come home you call me right away, okay?"

"Sure I will, don't worry about us."

"I'm going to continue looking for him, but I'll be checking in…and Cindy…"

"Yes?"

"If you don't hear from me, or if Jake doesn't make it home by morning…"

"Yes?"

"I want you to call Inspector Pierson, he's Jake's FBI friend. Connie will have the number. Tell him that I asked you to call and report Jake missing."

There was a short pause on the phone as Alex began thinking that he may have shared too much information.

"I understand, Alex, but promise me you'll be careful. I've heard stories about old army buddies coming to town. And remember, if you have too much to drink, take a cab."

Alex smiled into the phone and cleared his throat before adding, "That little bed and breakfast is sounding better all the time, sweetheart…bye."

Cindy heard the dial tone in her cell phone, but still said, "I love you too…bye."

"Everything alright, Cindy?" asked Connie curiously.

"Oh yeah. Alex ran into an old army buddy tonight and you know how that goes."

Linda Stern returned from the outdoors to find Connie, Cindy and Doreen making small talk in the den. "It's becoming a zoo out there, Mrs. Kramer. There are four, bald-headed jokers in orange jumpsuits kneeling at the house."

Connie nodded at Linda, "They've been here before. Jake calls them our grub inspectors or something like that. They're harmless. Actually we've had some real dandies over the past months, but I guess it goes with the territory," added Connie. "Well ladies, I think it's about time I show a little hospitality and fix some snacks before the evening news starts. I imagine this is going to be a long night."

"You sit right where you are, Connie," insisted Cindy. "Have you forgotten that you have been in the hospital twice in less than a week? I know my way around your kitchen well enough to make do. You have a seat too, Linda," she added while handing her a glass of red wine. "You've been on your feet ever since you got here."

"Well, I hate to argue with a lady holding me at bay with a glass of wine. Thank you, Mrs. Sanders…I don't mind if I do."

"You're welcome and please…call me, Cindy."

"Thank you again, Cindy."

Flipping his cell phone closed, Alex Sanders sat quietly in the Walgreen's parking lot at the corner of East 38th Street and Sherman Drive gently rubbing the bottom three ribs on the right side of his chest. Thankfully, this drug store was a twenty-four hour operation because the Sandman was in dire need of some pain relievers. He rolled the three extra-strength Excedrin tablets around in the palm of his hand before removing the cap from the warm bottle of water and downing the medication.

His ribs definitely hurt, and he assumed they were badly bruised if not cracked, but there was little he could do about that at this point. Besides, the ribs were a small matter when compared to the pain in his head. Alex leaned back against the headrest and closed his eyes waiting impatiently for the miracle drugs to kick in. Rolling his head slightly to the right he caught the first look at the swelling above his eyes and the black that surrounded them. *Good Lord…no wonder the cashier looked at me so funny.* His eyes were all but swollen closed, however, his vision remained clear and for that he was thankful. Alex's first hope was that the worst of the damage would be gone before Cindy caught sight of it.

"Back to business," he told himself. "Where did the driver take Jake? It wasn't home, so where did he ask to go?"

Alex reached for his cell phone and with the help of directory assistance he was in touch with WAXU station and was speaking to the operator.

"I'm sorry sir, but I have no idea as to where she took, Mr. Kramer."

"Would you please try to call his driver and ask?" he pleaded "It's extremely important."

Alex could hear her taking a monotony sigh in the phone as she said, "One moment please," before the elevator music began.

"Yeah…this is Becky, who's this?"

"Becky…I'm Jake Kramer's neighbor, Alex Sanders."

"Yeah?"

"Listen, Becky, you were Jake's driver tonight… Right?"

"If you say so."

"Becky, I certainly respect you're protecting his privacy, but I do need to catch up with him."

"Good luck."

"Becky, please…it's very important that I locate Jake. We both know that his life is in danger. You were there tonight. You heard the gunshot and drove him away. Now it's my turn to protect him, but I need your help to find him."

There was a short pause on the phone before she spoke. "You know about the shot tonight?"

"Yes. I was there trying to protect him just like you."

"And how do I know it wasn't you that took that shot, butthead?"

The next short pause was from Alex as he realized she had a very valid point and he didn't have a convincing answer.

"Becky…what can I say to convince you?" he asked.

"Two things: One…you have a million dollars in small bills for me, and two…you have proof that there's ice skating in hell."

"Nice talking to you, Becky."

"Yeah."

Alex closed the cover on his phone and again rested his head against the seat as the lightning streaked across the sky seconds ahead of the trailing thunder.

"Great…just what I wanted tonight…rain."

Alex got his wish, for the light rain began within minutes as the thunder announced its intentions to continue for awhile. This also promised to complicate his visibility while driving and checking the foot traffic for someone resembling Jake. At this point his only plan was to check the Lasting Light Mission in the event Jake headed there, and also take a drive to the ruins of the Kramer building in the unlikely event something was drawing him there. Neither choice seemed promising, but he couldn't think of alternatives at this late hour. With the help of the security lighting in the lot Alex looked at his watch before starting out.

"Good news," he said softly. "Only three hours and forty-five minutes until my next aspirins."

"Checking out, are we, sir?"

"Yes…duty calls…time to move on."

“Your balance is zero. I hope you enjoyed your stay and you’ll keep us in mind if your work brings you back this way, Mr. Jones.”

“Thanks.”

Rich Ziegler pulled the door closed and slapped the lap belt across his body. It was time to move on, but not away, for his work here was not yet done. He would be making his way south of the city to Martinsville this time to unpack at the Lee’s Inn. The new location connected two state roads and offered excellent access back to his assignment. Either route would provide enough traffic for him to blend and become a routine daily commuter. As he made his way south past the Centerbrook Drive-In, he checked his watch noting that he had ample time to check in before the late newscast to catch up on the latest information on Jake Kramer.

“It’s uncanny the number of times that man should have died, but didn’t,” he said aloud. “Sandman… where did you come from? I never heard a sound… nothing. If that had been Nam, I’d be a dead man,” he said as he continued talking to himself. “I may live to regret using the butt of my rifle instead of the business end, but I did owe him. He’s probably counting aspirins through a couple of black eyes and nursing his ribs about now. Yeah…I may live to regret it, but I took the Sandman once…I can take him again.”

Rich slowed at the access lane leading to the Junction 39 bypass and continued across the fading green and rusting bridge spanning the White River towards his new sanctuary.

"It's time for the late news, Mrs. Kramer. Do you mind if we turn it on or would you rather we didn't?" asked Linda.

"No, please turn it on. I already have the show burned in my memory."

Doctor Harrington was the closest to the controls and brought the television to life.

"...lose up to twenty pounds a week with just one capsule daily, when taken with a 700-calorie diet and exercising just sixty minutes twice a day, five days a week. Results may vary and always consult your doctor before beginning any form of..."

All heads turned to Doctor Harrington who smiled and said, "It should work without the pill, but what do I know, I'm just a psychologist."

"Repeating our lead story...tonight during WAXU'S own *Up Close and Personal*, Cameron Elliott's guest, Mr. Jake Kramer, was confronted by a caller claming that he, Mr. Kramer, located and stole money that was buried on his property. Mr. Kramer neither confirmed nor denied the allegations much to the disappointment of his devoted followers. We take you now to Cameron Elliott with his evaluation and some footage of Mr. Kramer's actions...Cameron?"

"Thank you, Roger...Yes, it was an accusation without refutation as Jake Kramer refused to acknowledge our caller's claim. As the show progressed and the charges mounted, Mr. Kramer succumbed to what some suggest was a mental breakdown. We have some footage of Mr. Jake Kramer before he ran off the stage during tonight's broadcast of *Up Close and Personal*. But before we start the footage I should caution you that some of the images are graphic and may not be suitable for young viewers. Parents…viewer discretion is advised."

"Thanks, Cameron," said Connie. "Why didn't you just call him a freak and get it over with?"

The first scene was of Jake addressing the audience. "Why aren't you listening to me? Why does everyone want to listen to that other man? I'M JAKE KRAMER! I help people all the time," he said as he pointed his paper at the audience.

Then the camera zoomed in on Jake as he sat shaking and slowly raising his head. The gasp from the studio audience was replayed with the appearance of Jake's face as everyone revisited his large burgundy eyes. The screams followed as he lowered his hands showing the blood that ran from his nose, to his chin.

Everyone heard Connie's sobs as Jake stood and said, "It should have been me…I should have died, not them. I'm sorry."

The final footage showed Jake Kramer walking off stage with Elliot commenting, "What can one add that hasn't been said by what we've just witnessed? For WAXU…I am Cameron Elliott."

The television was muted and the only sound in the room was that of Connie softly crying.

“Connie, you should try and get some rest,” suggested Doreen Harrington. “Why don’t I check your dressing before you lie down?

“I don’t want to lie down, Doreen. I can’t rest until I know that Jake is alright.”

“We’ll let you know if he calls. Besides, you won’t be much good to him if you’re dead on your feet.”

“She right, Connie,” agreed Cindy. “I’ll get some fresh bandages.”

“And I’ll check on our guests outside, although I imagine the rain has dampened their spirits.” said Linda.

“See Connie, everyone is looking out for you. So let’s get you back to your room where you can stretch out comfortably.”

“Well maybe you’re right,” agreed Connie, thinking that she would like to be alone for a while.

“You go on back, said Doreen. “I’ll be along after I check my pager.”

Doreen found Connie sitting on the edge of her bed with Cindy removing the gauze from around her head in a slow gentle motion.

“Can you two stand some good news?”

“They found Jake?” asked Connie excitedly.

“Sorry…but it’s still good news. That page was from the hospital. It’s reported that Tonya Washington has come out of her coma. Isn’t that great news?”

“Oh thank God, said Connie. “Did they say how she’s doing?”

“She was eating ice cream when they called. Stacie is on her way to the hospital and they asked me to be there when she arrives. I think it’s a good idea. Will you be alright?”

“Yes go…go. Cindy will take good care of me. GO! And give them our love.”

# Fifty-One

The wind was picking up slightly on the streets of Indianapolis and bringing with it a much-needed light rain to the city. Reflections from the street lighting gave the pavement a fresh waxed appearance as Jake Kramer walked along the sidewalk indifferent to Mother Nature's endeavor. Standing at the intersection of Maryland and West Streets, he listened to the sudden cheer that erupted from a baseball game at Victory Field before he continued on his way through the puddles filling in the walk. Jake's pace was slow and his direction was unclear as he sauntered along the city sidewalks in the light mist.

Out of the shadows in the deserted parking lot of the Hoosier Dome, the threesome stepped into Jake's path and spread out as the talker asked, "Got a cigarette, buddy?"

Jake attempted to continue walking past them, but he was grabbed by his rain-soaked shirt and pulled into the shadows.

"Well, well…look who we have here, dudes. The old man broke out of the home again. Did you break out of the home old man? I don't see your keeper around this time," he said as he shoved Jake's unresisting body against the chain-link fence. "Okay old man…now let's see how much money you're gonna give us."

He jerked Jake forward and spun him around before pushing firmly against his back and driving him face first into the rusting fence. Then, without hesitation, he promptly relieved Jake of his wallet.

"Hey, Guzzler, check it out…we've hit the big time, man." said the talker. "A hundred and forty big ones. I knew this old bastard had cash, man. I knew it."

The talker then turned back to Jake and with his right fist struck him in the kidney with enough force to drop Jake to his knees.

"That's for holding out on us, old man."

"C'mon, dude…there's a lot of traffic. Let's split before someone calls us in."

The talker continued dissecting Jake's wallet by removing the credit cards and then with a flick of the wrist he tossed the remainder over the fence into the darkness. He looked down at Jake who was leaning against the fence with his fingers gripping to the diamond shaped holes and said, "You can pass this along to your keeper too, old man," as he kicked Jake in the small of the back and once directly in the hip forcing him to spring back and forth against the fence.

"That was for your keeper and this one's for you," he said before striking Jake again with the heel of his boot. "That's for walkin' on our turf without payin' toll, man."

A blaring car horn from the street stopped Jake's next punishment as the three boys broke out in a dead run up Maryland Street before disappearing into a dark, deserted alley leaving Jake clinging to the chain link fence and quivering in pain.

"Sit tight, mister," said a voice from the car. "I called 911…they should be here right away. I gotta go …sorry, but I don't want to get involved…you understand. Just stay still and help will be right here. Good luck, buddy." And with that said the good Samaritan's car faded down the rain soaked street.

The sirens in the distance encouraged Jake to pull himself to his knees and with the aid of the fence, he winched himself upright. While nursing a painfully bruised body, he shuffled diagonally across the asphalt separating the east and west sidewalks before making his way along the bridge toward White River State Park.

With the rainfall continuing to rinse everything it touched, Jake Kramer was no exception as the rainwater washed the grime from his body, but not the pain. The storm wasn't considered severe but the thunder brought a rumble as well as an occasional lightning bolt streaking across the skyline of Indianapolis. The park was void of visitors at this hour with the exception of one lone jogger striding across the trail as Jake sat alone in profound pain on an open park bench massaging his bruises. He raised his head to the sky sensing the cool rainwater on his skin as a lone lightning bolt raced across the heavens before abruptly changing course and dipping directly towards him. In an instant the lightning darted in a straight line and struck the soil thirty meters in front of him. Jake shuddered at the brilliance of the lightning bolt that never faded, but only continued to intensify and pulsate before him. While staring directly into the light he watched as it began to widen while dripping colored particles from above. The colored particles began to collect themselves then rotated in a counterclockwise motion much to the satisfaction and comfort of the trembling Jake Kramer. He watched with contentment as it had been much too long since the circling rainbow of lights had visited him. He leaned back against the bench gently rubbing his wounds as the pain increased with each movement. The rotation of lights continued as a quick burst of bright white ripped through the center allowing an image of one soldier, with rifle in hand, to step free of the light shower and give the signal, okay to follow. As he moved to Jake's left another soldier hurried from the lights giving a similar signal. Jake watched as a procession of Armed Forces veterans followed their point guard from the light shaft and formed a tight parameter around him. Some were kneeling with their weapons at point while others were standing, as each constantly scanned for hostiles and none yielded their allegiance.

Jake looked back at the light as one US Army medic rushed from the light particles directly to him and knelt at his feet. Jake could see clearly the intensity in this young man's eyes as he rummaged though his aid pack desperately searching for and removing a bottle that turned his white sterile gauze to red before he reached out to the open wound above Jake's left eyebrow.

Jake couldn't feel the medic's touch, but he was aware that the burning and stinging sensation ceased immediately. The medic then placed his hands on Jake's ribs and put an end to the intense pain, thus allowing him to take a full breath for the first time since his attack. As Jake looked around the area he saw that he was completely surrounded by numerous soldiers and marines who were, in no uncertain terms, defending someone they respected. No one would do harm to this man on their watch…no way.

He looked back to his medic and watched him policing his area by returning the unused supplies to his pack before securing the flap. Jake noticed a sadness in his eyes as he stood and promptly offered a quick salute followed by a brief warm smile before turning and fading into the rotating lights.

Jake sat completely without pain as he watched some of the bravest of America's military being relieved of their post and returning to the light one by one. A number of them turned and waved, a few snapped a salute, some nodded while others simply considered it another job and walked away.

The light particles slowed their rotation as the last of his defense force entered and withdrew up the light shaft into the heavens, leaving only a brilliant pulsating glow from the original lightning bolt. With a quick flash and a tremendous rumble of thunder, the white light was gone as quickly as it came, leaving Jake sitting in White River State Park in compete darkness and without pain. Not until now had he realized that this phenomenon took place at the same site he had visited months ago when the Veterans of Foreign Wars presented The Traveling Wall.

"Hey buddy…are you alright?"

Jake didn't answer because he really didn't hear him.

"Hey buddy. You can't stay here. Do you have any place you can go to get out of the rain?"

Again no answer from Jake.

The two police officers moved around to the front of the park bench as one called into the station and the other knelt down to Jake's level.

"Hey…old man…you okay?"

"They're asking what we got, Percy."

"Tell em' a homeless…soakin' wet and bombed."

Percy then looked closely at Jake, who never offered the first sign of acknowledgement, before calling back to his partner, "Hey, Mo…tell em' he looks like he's been through a mugging. I think he's hurt. Better send a wagon."

Alex Sanders had completed his search for Jake at the Lasting Light Mission only to learn from Sister Marie that she hadn't seen any sign of his Mr. Kramer tonight or any night since the killing of God's devoted servant Ernie Dingle. Alex's next stop was around and through the carcass of the Kramer and Associates building, but it gave no sign of recent activity, prompting him to grab at the next straw which was checking the White River State Park as it seemed to have an uncanny magnet that drew Jake to the grounds.

As Alex arrived he gave way to the red strobe lights from an EMT vehicle that pulled out onto Washington Street from the park before he continued on to the general parking area. The drizzle had eased as Alex stepped from his vehicle and began his search of the rain-drenched park for his friend Jake Kramer.

# Fifty-Two

The early morning brought a fresh smell to the air in the surrounding Indianapolis area and the warm sun was quickly drying everything it reached. Cindy had left the patio door open after returning with the morning paper allowing the kitchen to be serenaded by the chirping birds singing in the back yard.

"Can I warm your coffee, Cindy?" asked Linda.

"Please. Which section of the paper would you like?"

"Sports, if you don't want it," she answered while adding coffee to Cindy's cup.

"You must be tired, Linda. I didn't sleep well, but I don't think you slept at all."

"No problem. I have a friend from work named Lacy who is going to relieve me in a little while. She's a good person and she'll take care of you until I get back."

"Thank you," said Cindy. "We feel better having you around until things settle down. It's unimaginable just what all has taken place in this family over the past weeks. I don't even like to think about it."

Linda Stern nodded in agreement as she pulled the sports section to her and laid it open against the kitchen table.

"Were you two going to let me sleep all day?" asked Connie as she entered the kitchen. "I certainly am a poor hostess. You two must be starved; how about I start some breakfast?"

"How about you having a seat and let me check your dressing first? I think we can probably leave it exposed for awhile today and let some air get to it. Come on, sit down…breakfast can wait."

"I'll get you some coffee," said Linda offering her chair. "A touch of creamer, right?"

"Yes, thank you. My Gosh, you two are treating me like I'm an invalid," she said as she took a seat. "Anything in the paper about last night's show?"

Cindy didn't immediately answer, but instead started to remove Connie's dressing to check her wound that was healing nicely.

"I take it that you not answering me means yes," she added as she reached for the front page and scanned the print.

"Don't read it now, Connie. It'll only upset you. You know how insensitive reporters can be when they want to sell papers."

It wasn't the lead story, but nonetheless the fonts were bold enough. "Kramer loses touch with reality." Connie read on…"Jake Kramer, while appearing on last night's *Up Close and Personal* program experienced what some have called a mental breakdown in front of the viewing audience, creating mayhem and concern for his vast beloved supporters…"

Connie tossed the paper to the floor while trying to conceal her heartache and making room for the coffee that was offered by Linda Stern.

"They shouldn't be allowed to print stuff like that."

"Oh, I don't know, Linda…none of it is a lie. It's just that news like this hurts when it hits home."

"Well, you're taking it better than I would," added Linda. "They should be writing more public interest stories about people who are down and out and need help. I read in there a little piece, probably just a filler, about some poor, homeless man who was mugged at White River Park last night, then left to die in the rain. Who knows what would have happened to him if the cops didn't stumble onto him. I tell you it's a shame that this goes on in our city."

Connie and Cindy nodded in agreement, although neither commented.

"Connie…I hate to bring this up," said Cindy, "But I was wondering if we shouldn't call the authorities and report Jake missing?"

"They won't take the call, Cindy. Not until the individual has been absent for twenty-four hours," said Linda.

"I understand, but Alex suggested we call Jake's friend at the FBI and tell him that Jake's missing. Do you know who he's talking about, Connie?"

Connie shook her head yes as she answered. "That would be Inspector Pierson. He and Jake have worked closely on many missing cases. I'm sure I could find the number, in fact, I think Jake also has the Inspector's personal cell number. I can look if you think it would help?"

"Couldn't hurt," answered Cindy with Linda shrugging in agreement.

Connie stood to find Jake's address book as the phone rang.

"Want me to get it, Mrs. Kramer?"

"No thanks, Linda. I can't hide forever."

"Hello," she said softly into the phone.

"Connie…Connie, it's me, Stacie. I didn't wake you did I?"

"Stacie…no you didn't wake me. I've been thinking about you. So, tell me how is Tonya doing this morning?"

"All the doctors and nurses are calling her the miracle girl. She just came down from having an MRI a little while ago and the initial finding was no permanent damage. We're so thrilled, Connie…she's going to be just fine. Oh Connie, if you could just see her big smile. I just thank God for giving her back to me. I don't think I could have made it if she…"

"Please give her a big hug from all of us, will you, Stacie?"

"Oh, of course I will. She's already asked when Uncle Jake and Aunt Connie are going to come and visit."

Stacie sensed the pause in the phone and softly added, "Oh Connie, I'm sorry. I wasn't thinking. I watched some of the show last night with Rosa and Granny. But that man got Granny so upset when he kept calling Jake a thief that Rosa turned the set off. I know it must be painful for you. Is Jake alright?"

"We don't know, Stacie. Jake hasn't come home yet, but I'm sure everything is going to turn out fine. Don't you worry about him. You just concentrate on getting that little girl home where she belongs. Is Doctor Harrington with you now, Stacie? I'd like to talk with her."

"No, not at the moment. She was here when we got to the hospital last night and for some reason she stayed with us for a long time. I think she's lonely and just wanted to talk to someone. She's nice, but she asks a lot of questions. She was called away on an emergency here in the hospital. Something about a homeless man getting mugged, but I'll give her your message if she stops back in."

"Thanks, Stacie. And I have to tell you again that it's such a relief to hear you sounding so well. Our prayers have been with you, dear. Thanks again for calling."

"Don't you guys worry about us, Connie, we're going to make it now. Little Jake and I are going to take Tonya home and we can all wait together for Wesley to get back. Bye, Connie."

The activity around the Kramer house over the next few hours was mixed between phone calls requesting interviews, people offering support and of course, some sharing insensitive comments as well as a few threats. All of which were promptly handled by Linda who seemed to enjoy responding to the heartless remarks and the threats in particular. Connie got dressed as Cindy took a break and ran home to freshen up as well. It was lunch time when they gathered around the kitchen table once more to map out a plan for their day. Linda Stern's fellow bailiff, Lacy, was now seated at the table as she volunteered to relieve Linda for some much needed rest.

"I think we should call Jake's FBI friend," said Cindy. "It couldn't hurt."

The phone ran once again interrupting the suggestion as Lacy responded, "I'll get it."

"Kramer's. No, this is Officer Lacy. One moment please."

"Mrs. Kramer, will you take a call from a Doctor Harrington?"

"Yes…of course," replied Connie as she reached for the phone.

"Doreen…" said Connie. "I was hoping you'd call. We heard the good news about Tonya."

"Sorry it took me so long to get back to you, Connie, but something came up…something I dread to tell you."

"Jake?"

"Yes, Jake, he's…"

"Is he alright, Doreen? Where is he? I want to go to him."

The kitchen fell library quiet as each tried to imagine what was being said on the other end of the conversation.

"Connie…slow down. I'm here with Jake at the hospital."

"At the hospital? What's wrong? Is he hurt?"

"We think he was involved in a mugging, Connie. He has some bruises and a couple of cracked ribs, but his physical wounds are not life-threatening. The police found him in White River Park and had him brought here."

"Mugging, last night?" repeated Connie. "But why didn't they call me last night? Nobody called here to tell us. Why?"

"He didn't have any identification, Connie. The muggers took his wallet and…"

"But they could have asked him, Doreen. I'm coming right down."

"Connie, wait! Listen to me. They couldn't ask him because Jake's unresponsive."

"Unresponsive? What do you mean he's unresponsive?"

"I want you to know this and be prepared before you see him, Connie. Jake is what we term… traumatic."

"Traumatic? What in the hell does that mean?

"It means Jake's in shock. He doesn't speak and hasn't responded to anything we've tried."

"Oh my God."

"Maybe seeing you will trigger something, we don't know. But you should be prepared before you see him. I'm terribly sorry to be the one to tell you this, Connie especially over the phone."

"Thank you, Doctor. We'll be right down."

# Fifty-Three

Cindy drove Connie to County General Hospital, leaving Lacy to keep the house secure while Linda took the remainder of the day off. They made their way directly to Doctor Harrington's office before being directed to room 466 on the fourth floor, east wing, to locate the doctor and Jake. As the elevator doors opened Connie rushed into the center of the lobby, but stopped at the secured doors to either side of the nurse's station. The bold print on the sign clearly stated the area beyond was restricted…Authorized Personnel Only.

"Can I help you, ladies?"

"We're trying to get to room 466," said Connie. Can you let us through the doors?"

"Yes, I can," she answered without raising her head from her work.

Cindy caught the sarcasm of the duty nurse's answer and quickly added, "Mrs. Kramer to see Doctor Harrington and her husband, Jake Kramer, in room 466."

"One moment," she said before crunching away at the computer keyboard. "Yes, we have a Mr. Kramer with us in 466. I'll summon Doctor Harrington for you. Please take a seat in the waiting room."

"But…"

"Connie, let's have a seat," said Cindy while leading her away.

Connie never sat down during her impatient wait for the doctor, but paced and retraced her steps around the small waiting room until her attention gave way to Doreen as she entered from the hall.

"Doreen…they won't let us in. What's wrong? How is he?"

"No change I'm sorry to say. Hi Cindy…I'm glad you came along."

"Doctor Harrington," said Cindy as she nodded.

Doreen looked around the empty room before deciding it was private enough to use for consultation.

"Connie, Jake is suffering from what we'll call, for now, a mental breakdown. He is unresponsive to anything we say or do. No reactions to light, sound, scent or touch whatsoever. I'm sorry to say that Jake has completely withdrawn."

Connie sat quietly listening to the Doctor while watching the Kleenex that she toyed with in her hands.

Doctor Harrington continued, "If we think back, he's been acting irrationally for several weeks now. You've commented on that yourself."

Connie shook her head yes in agreement without looking up, but again said nothing.

"We witnessed a textbook example of this behavior just a few days ago in my office with Doctor Zorka. Do you remember Jake's conduct? Not so much that he questioned the doctor, but he became emotional and exigent before rushing out of the room and disappearing. Let's remember that Jake has been though some very distressing experiences since his accident. I believe he has appointed himself the protector and prosecutor to so many that it's overwhelmed him."

Doctor Harrington took a seat next to Connie before continuing, "I understand that this is difficult to accept, but Jake has been diagnosed as traumatic. Classic traumatic cases such as Jake's have produced lasting psychic effects and in some cases have evolved into neurosis. Our job is to prevent that from developing and that is exactly what we are going to do. But, Connie, you have to be aware that it's going to take a long time for us to get Jake well enough for you to take him home again. He's a very troubled man."

The silence yielded to the muffled cries from Connie and Cindy as the impact of Doreen's analysis took affect.

"Something was said about Jake being mugged last night, Doreen," said Connie as she looked into her eyes. Is that true?"

"It's true. He was assaulted and found in the park by two police officers before being brought here."

"Was he hurt?"

"Jake has some swelling and discoloration on the hip and several large contusions across the back. He has a small laceration along his cheek as well as one above the eyebrow and the x-rays show two cracked ribs on his left side."

Connie's body began to tremble as she tried to suppress her crying while listening to the report on Jake's physical condition, giving Doreen a reason to pause.

"I'm sorry, Connie, but you need to know these things before you see him. If it's any comfort…Jake doesn't feel any pain."

"How can that be?" asked Connie. "He surely must feel the pain from the broken ribs."

"You would certainly think so, but for reasons I can't explain none of his wounds appear to bother him. I've personally pressed against his fractured ribs to the point that it should have brought him upright, but he never so much as flinched. It was like there was no accompanying pain at all. I don't understand it and certainly can't explain it."

"Can I see him now?"

"Sure…follow me. Cindy you're welcome to come along too. The more to awaken Jake, the better."

"Maybe it would be best if I just waited here."

Connie reached for Cindy's hand as she stood and said, "Please come with me, Cindy, I need your strength."

It was a short walk from the secured entrance to room 466 where Doctor Harrington held open the door allowing Connie and Cindy to enter. Jake's bed was raised slightly at the shoulders and other than a small bandage to protect the wound on his cheek; he looked to be well and only resting in bed. There were no life giving IVs and the only sign of monitoring was a single attachment to the wrist and fingertip that supervised pulse and blood pressure.

"Jake…Jake, how are you feeling, honey?" asked Connie while praying for an answer. She moved to the side of his bed and sandwiched his hand between hers, but felt no response from him. His eyes were open and he appeared to be staring directly at some point in the ceiling tile. Connie also noticed that he seldom blinked as she leaned forward and placed a kiss on his forehead.

"Cindy and I came down as quickly as we heard that you were here, honey. She and Linda stayed with me last night because they didn't want me to be alone. Wasn't that nice of them? Linda didn't sleep a wink all night, Jake…she kept us safe. Doctor Harrington was called down here because Tonya came out of her coma last night. Jake? Did you hear me? I said Tonya is going to be just fine. Oh Jake, please answer me… please."

Connie began crying as her emotions increased, but Doctor Harrington let her continue hoping that Jake would sense her heart breaking and respond in some manner.

"Connie," said Cindy as she made her way to her side and placed a hand on her shoulder. "I'm going down to the main lobby to see if Alex is here yet. I told him we didn't know where we would be and I'd just meet him down there after we found Jake."

Connie nodded that she understood but never took her eyes off Jake as he lay motionless.

"I'll walk down with you, Cindy," said Doreen. "I need to check my messages."

As they waited for the elevator to take them to street level, Cindy asked, "How long will he be like that, Doctor?"

"I wish I could answer that, Cindy, but it's impossible to tell. All cases differ. Some only a matter of days, but others have lasted years and a few for the remainder of their lives. I hope to find Jake back with us every time I enter his room."

The soft chime announced the elevator's arrival moments before the doors withdrew and they stepped inside the stainless cubical.

"We must keep a close eye on Connie," continued Doreen. "She's been on an emotional rollercoaster for a long time. as well. We need to be alert to any signs of abnormal behavior on her part also. Please let me know if you see any evidence of this, won't you, Cindy? I'll give you my card and I'm available at these numbers twenty-four seven. Oh, and you'll need this too; it's a family pass allowing access through the security doors on the fourth floor. I'm sure Connie would want you to have one.

Cindy accepted the Doctor's cards as the elevator opened on the ground floor allowing them to step clear and move into the lobby.

"Thank you, Doctor Harrington."

"Please call me, Doreen, and thank you for being there for this troubled family," she added with a smile. "Now if you'll excuse me, I have a few things that I need to attend to. I'll catch up with you later."

Neither Cindy nor Doctor Harrington had noticed Alex as he approached asking, "How's Jake doing?"

"Alex…Alex, what in the world happened to you?"

"Oh, I had a little run in with a door header last night. I was looking for Jake down at his office…it was dark and oh, you get the picture. It looks worse than it is."

Alex knew there would be the inevitable twenty questions concerning his bruised and swollen forehead, not to mention the two black eyes that hadn't been seen yet, thanks to the sunglasses. He had dedicated a lot of time to preparing answers, or more so, lies for each of the most obvious questions and so far Cindy's first question hit number one.

"That does look bad, Alex," said Doctor Harrington. Did you have a doctor look at it?"

"You're the first, but I'm pretty hard-headed. I've been popping aspirins…they help a little."

"Well, follow me to my office and maybe I can help a little too, but I'd feel better if you'd let me arrange for an x-ray."

"Thanks anyway, Doc."

"Okay, but I wouldn't miss hearing the story behind this for anything," said Doreen. "Lead him along, Cindy. We won't ask him to remove his glasses in the lobby for fear of scaring the children," she added with a smile.

The day's following Jake's hospitalization blended together like clones. Connie spent most of her time at Jake's bedside during the first several days then tapered off to before and after work. Going back to work proved to be good therapy, for it gave her emotions a break and her mind other things to concentrate on.

The phone was being ignored at the Kramer house, allowing the answering machine to earn its keep. Most of the calls were from unknowns wishing Jake a speedy recovery, but the prank and heartless calls were to be expected and were received as well. Connie had countless requests for interviews as television and newspaper reporters from all over the country sought information and comments on Jake's condition. She had avoided all televised news and stacked the daily papers in a limited attempt to avoid their commentaries. She did, however, get a sample of the insensitivity of the tabloids while waiting her turn in a check-out line during a brief stop at the market where she read:

"**JAKE KRAMER CRACKS**"
"Kramer, A Human Vegetable"
"Doctors agree…Jake's Brain Dead"

Leaving her groceries in the cart, Connie quickly ran from this type of cruelty in tears.

At the close of the second full week of Jake's stay at County General, no one saw any changes in his demeanor even at the slightest level. He still wasn't speaking and to everyone's knowledge, he wasn't hearing their conversations either. He merely lay in bed and stared at the ceiling tile. The calls to the Kramer house diminished and the get well and sympathy mail slowed, as everyone reluctantly accepted the circumstance as, "give it time" and attempted to resume some direction in their lives.

By the time Jake Kramer ended his third week in room 466, the swelling in Alex's forehead had receded to the point that only a hint of dead blood remained under the eyes, making him fit for public view. This was only his third trip to visit his friend which was something he was not proud of, but he assumed Jake didn't know one way or the other. Using his family pass to gain access, he tapped lightly on the door before he entered and found Jake sitting in a chair facing the window. His nurse had taken advantage of Jake's absence by changing the bed linens and giving his lair some sprucing up. She nodded and smiled at Alex as he entered the room.

"How's he doing?" asked Alex.

"He hasn't given me anything but trouble all day. I can't get him to shut up…jabber…jabber…jabber. He's about to drive me bonkers."

They kept their eyes on Jake watching for a reaction that neither of them saw.

"Nice try," said Alex as he walked toward Jake. "How you doing, buddy? I need you to snap out of this pretty soon, Jake. Just between you, me and the nurse here, I'm having a hard time taking care of Millie all by myself."

Alex actually thought he caught a hint of a reaction from Jake, but of course it was just wishful thinking as he continued to sit rigid and look ahead at the window.

"Nice try," she said while walking around the bed. "If you're going to be here for a few minutes, I'll go find some help to get him back in bed."

"Can I help?"

"Are you sure you don't mind?"

"Mind…I've been carrying this guy around for years. I don't see why today should be any different."

"Well that's strike three," said the nurse. "You can't say we didn't try."

"I'll get him for you, Miss. If you'll just pull the chair out of the way after I pick him up."

Alex squatted and placed one arm under Jake's legs and the other behind his back before gently standing and raising him free of the chair. As the nurse quickly pulled the chair free, Alex turned and moved toward the bed while carrying Jake like a sleeping child before gently placing him on the fresh sheets. The nurse watched as Alex released Jake by slowly pulling his arms free and standing upright. Alex then looked down at Jake for a moment or two before turning to the smiling nurse.

"You made that look very easy…if you ever want a job…"

"No thanks. I have to go now, nice to meet you."

"Nice to meet you too. Give my best to Millie."

Cindy found Alex sitting at the back porch table with his hands folded across a map looking out across the lawn in a hypnotic gaze. Sliding the screen door closed behind her captured his attention.

"You were in deep thought out here, honey. Am I disturbing you?"

"Never," he said as he pulled her to his side.

"Planning a trip?"

"How did you know that?"

"Alex…you're resting on a map."

"Oh, yeah. I was thinking about a trip to Cape Cod."

Cindy pulled away and took a chair next to him as she looked down at the map of Massachusetts before them. "When are you leaving?"

"I'm not…we are. I think I'd like to leave as quickly as I can get it arranged if that's alright with you."

Cindy looked at him with her all knowing eyes and asked, "How did your visit go with Jake, Alex. What happened?"

Alex slid away from the table and began to pace along the edge of the concrete.

"You don't have to answer if you don't want to. I don't mean to pry?"

"No, it's alright. It just bothers me to see him that way. I guess today it hit me especially hard."

"And that's the reason to rush away on a trip? Because of Jake?"

"I guess you could say that. It made me realize how quickly things are taken away from us. I took a long look at Jake this morning as he lay in bed like a rag doll. One day he's on top of the world and the next day he's under it."

Alex walked back and retook his seat across from Cindy as he continued, "I realized how short our lives are, Cindy, and I don't want to miss any of ours. I want to get away from all the killing. I want to go to New England and look around to see if we like it and if we can make a new start there…what do you think?"

Cindy gave Alex a smile as she stood and took a place behind his chair. While running her hands down across his chest she leaned forward and kissed the top of his head and answered, "I think I've told you before, Mr. Sanders…I will follow you anywhere. Now, if you'll excuse me, I had better go and start packing."

At 7:15 a.m. Saturday morning Alex and Cindy Sanders left Indianapolis International with their final destination being Cape Cod, Massachusetts, for a much needed mini-vacation. It had been suggested that they were combining their getaway with a bid for a hundred-plus-year-old inn located on a bluff near Barnstable, Massachusetts. Alex was hopeful that this property would fulfill their plans of retiring and owning a Bed and Breakfast. However, Becky had informed them, in no uncertain terms, that she would not go with the deal. She would just die if she had to tell her friends in Indianapolis that she was going to be living in a barn stable. Alex believed she would eventually come around, but Cindy realized that her daughter would be off to college in a few months and doubted that she would need to put much effort in her room on the Cape.

The flight attendant offered the couple seated in 2A and 2B drinks as Bloody Marys were accepted and they settled in for a relaxing ride to New England.

A clear view from room 17 at the Lee's Inn in Martinsville, Indiana gave the guest an unlimited opportunity to see nothing much at all. Rich Ziegler had hibernated in this room for the past several weeks while going out for only the very basic of necessities.

His room was littered with newspapers and magazines, each having a page folded to the subject of his obsession…Jake Kramer.

Rich had clear knowledge that Jake was housed at County General Hospital and was rumored incoherent, but that was unacceptable to him for he didn't want Kramer nuts…he wanted Kramer dead. And dead was exactly what Jake Kramer would be before he went underground and removed Heinrich Zeigler from the world.

He had learned through news reports of the arrangement for Mr. Kramer to be relocated to an exclusive private institution in Southern California early next week for comprehensive psychoanalysis and therapeutic attention. Rich's experience had taught him that private establishments were often very secure and access was extremely difficult when compared to public facilities. Therefore, he would act now while the opportunity was simplified. He had a plan. Simple and risky…but simple was good and risky was acceptable under the circumstances. He would put his plan into motion tomorrow assuming his reconnaissance went well and his needed wardrobe was obtainable. These things he would know before noon tomorrow, leaving plenty of opportunity for his dastardly deed. Rich was now content and actually relaxed enough to smile as he accepted his plan. Then for the first time since his exile to Martinsville he allowed himself to think of Meg.

# Fifty-Four

The nurses' station at County General was typically busy and today was no exception as head nurse Susan Solomon labored over the endless routine of monotonous forms. The elevator door on the fourth floor opened and allowed one lone passenger to emerge pushing a gurney toward the nurses' station. Ms. Solomon was sitting at the center counter of the station, but never so much as looked up when he approached. Standing quietly he waited patiently for her attention while shuffling the papers in his hands.

"Yes…what can I do for you?" she asked before making eye contact.

"EverCare Transport…here for one Mr. Jake Kramer."

He anticipated her not expecting him and added, "Looks like he's getting a ride to sunny California."

"I didn't think that was scheduled until tomorrow," she said as she looked him over for the first time. His blue uniform jacket, with an embroidered patch on the left side, clearly identified him as Walter and a clip-on badge displaying EverCare Transport was hanging from his right breast pocket. Above his thick glasses he wore a company cap that also depicted their logo.

"I don't have a release for Mr. Kramer," she added matter-of-factly.

"I don't know about that. All I know is that they gave me these papers and said to pickup Mr. Kramer and take him to the airport. His family must have big money because they booked the EverCare Transport plane and that baby don't come cheap. I get to ride out there with them. Never been to California before… have you?"

She didn't answer his question about her travel history, but commented, "Well, I don't have a release for Mr. Kramer and I've never heard of EverCare."

"EverCare Transport," he corrected. "You will…we're new in this area. Home office is in North Carolina."

"Hang on a minute while I do some checking," she said.

"Lady, a minute is about all the time I have. It costs a lot of money to keep that plane idle and I don't want any of that coming out of my next raise. You know what I mean?"

She looked at him with an I could care less expression before asking, "Doctor Samuel, do you know anything about Mr. Kramer being released tonight?" while spinning her chair in the doctor's direction.

"Well…I knew it was either going to be today or tomorrow. Why?"

"Transportation is here for him, but I don't have any paperwork."

"Now, does that surprise you any, Susan?" asked Samuel. "Doctor Harrington must have been expecting them either tonight or early tomorrow because she signed his release before she left today."

Doctor Samuel walked up to the front desk and handed her Harrington's release packet. "Take his papers and sign him in, Susan. Everything appears to be in order."

Nurse Solomon mumbled to herself something about always being the last to know as she took his envelope and offered Walter a clipboard to sign himself in.

"You tell your management to come in and register as a carrier with this hospital. And next time call ahead and let us know you're coming."

"No problem, Susan…and you tell your management to have the paperwork together when we get here because it costs a lot of money to keep our plane sitting idle on the ground." He looked up and caught a suppressed smile from Doctor Samuel as he stood behind the station nurse.

It took him less than two minutes to clear the secure doors, then collect and roll the non-protesting Jake Kramer to the service elevator. The moment the doors opened he eased his gurney inside opposite a smiling little nurse who was attending to a wheelchair and its occupant. Standing with his back to Nurse Solomon he adjusted the sheet covering Jake as he waited calmly for the doors to close while listening for sounds of discovery.

Through the round reflective mirror in the corner of the elevator he saw public elevator number two open and one male walk to the nurses' station with a flower arrangement in one hand and a long narrow white box in the other. As the service elevator doors were closing he overheard the deliveryman say, "Flowers for a Mr. Jake Kramer."

"Well this is a busy night for Mr. Kramer, I'll say that," said Susan.

"I don't understand?"

"You just missed him. He just went down on that service elevator headed for the airport. You'll have to take those flowers to California if you want Mr. Kramer to have them."

"Thanks," he said as he immediately turned leaving the vase of flowers on the counter. He then darted toward the elevator call keys and frantically punched at the down button several times before moving to the stairwell exit and disappearing behind the gray door.

The four flights of stairs seemed endless as Rich cleared two steps at a time before hitting a landing and continuing downward again. As he rushed through the steel doors bearing a large painted P, he paused long enough to locate a white van with the rear doors open receiving a gurney by a lone attendant. Slowing his pace, he reached to his waist holster to recheck the presence of his 9mm Beretta as he walked confidently along the elevated dock. He didn't notice any visible staff traffic on foot or driving within the garage during his quick reconnaissance. He watched as the EverCare Transport driver closed the rear doors then took his place behind the wheel and pulled the lap belt across his body. With the flower box still in hand, Rich made his way leisurely toward the transport so as not to create suspicion to the driver before moving to the driver's blind spot directly behind the van. The engine started, giving him his cue to open the rear door and climb inside while moving quickly past the gurney to the driver.

"Just freeze," said Rich as he placed the barrel of the hand gun against the driver's neck. "Up until now I have no reason to hurt you, so don't give me one. Now…I want you to slowly pull away from the garage and I'll direct you from there. I don't want you…I only want your passenger. So just stay calm and drive. Do you understand?"

Rich felt the van moving as the driver nodded his head that the instructions were clear.

"Make a left at the light and don't exceed the speed limit," he commanded. "What's your name?"

"Walter."

"Okay, Walter, just keep your eyes on the road. Your chances of living are better if you don't see me. Make a right on Harding at the next light."

Rich watched through the windshield as Walter made the course change and then turned and spoke to the top of Jake's head.

"So Kramer, we finally get to meet one other. They say you can't hear me but I think you can. I think you can understand everything I'm saying. I think you're faking, Mr. Kramer, but it doesn't matter; you're a dead man anyhow."

He looked back at Walter and said, "Make a left on Troy and slow down and remember…you don't want to give me a reason to kill you."

Rich looked back to the gurney and said, "Now where were we, Mr. Kramer? Oh yeah…I don't mind telling you, sir, that you have been one big pain in my ass and if it's any comfort to you…you have cost me, not only my job, but my respect as well. But that's alright, for it is written, '*I will pour out my terrible fury. Its people, animals, trees, and crops will be consumed by the unquenchable fire of my anger*…Jeremiah 7:20.'"

Rich looked ahead through the windshield watching the driving and direction. The street traffic was light and offered few causes for concern, especially while the driver had a gun to his head.

"Alright, Walter, slow down and make a right through the gate."

"Into Calvary Cemetery?"

"That's right. Nobody will bother us in here," said Rich. "Pull to a stop over by that limestone crypt and don't turn around."

He could feel the impression of the barrel from the Beretta pressing against the nape of his neck as he heard his intruder shifting about behind him. Suddenly the barrel was lifted away from his neck and in a matter of seconds he heard the muffled pops from the silencer as the 9mm released four rounds from its clip and then quickly returned to his neck.

"Mr. Kramer, if you live through that you are indeed immortal," said Rich as he slid forward between the two front seats while resting his back against the divider.

"Alright Walter, in this box I have one of my homemade napalm baggies. Do you have any idea what that is?"

Rich looked up to see his driver shaking his head no.

"I didn't think so…so I'll tell you. It's a fire bomb. Just that simple…a fire bomb. You see, the late Mr. Kramer here was supposed to have experienced one of my creations in his truck, but he failed to show up in time and made a mockery out of me with my superiors. Now, thanks to him, I'm out of work and I feel it's only fitting that he gets the rest of what's coming to him. So Walter, I'm setting the timer right now for two minutes and when I say go you can open your door and try to escape the wrath of hell."

He could feel the gun barrel moving erratically across his neck as Rich adjusted positions to set the timer in such a cramped dark space. With a desperate life or death move, Walter quickly turned and reached for the gun, forcing it toward the headliner of the van as one round fired and exited through the thin metal. Caught by the unexpected aggression, Rich dropped the bomb and devoted his total attention to saving the gun. With his back to the seat, Rich was at a disadvantage as they struggled for the weapon. He tried to raise himself while attempting to turn around but fell flat on his back between the seats as the weapon came dangerously close to his head. His position was impossible for it left no room for leverage against his opponent who, at this point, had the upper hand. Rich could see the barrel inching its way past his nose until he felt the steel resting under his chin. Freeing his right hand in a desperate attempt to save his life he swung at the driver's head, knocking off his cap and glasses.

"YOU!" shouted Rich. "Why?"

"He was my friend," and those were the last four words Heinrich, the Gospel, Zeigler ever heard as the 9mm Beretta again discharged and gave off another muffled sound from the silencer.

Without delay the door of the van opened as the driver sprinted across the grass lawn of the Calvary Cemetery knowing there could only be seconds remaining on the timer. He spotted a large granite marker that looked large enough to give protection and dove behind it before rolling tightly to the base of the stone. The explosion was huge and loud giving off a blinding red, yellow and orange fireball that flashed quickly around him. He stayed to the ground until the parts and pieces of the vehicle stopped falling, then he slowly stood and looked around the granite at the burning rubble. The black smoke rolled into the sky and across the city as the heat from the flames could be felt from his position. While standing in the shadow of the large rock he offered a snap salute then took the position of parade rest and spoke, "This was not of my choosing. You both deserved better. I am sorry that it had to end this way, but it had to end…and that's the Gospel."

# Fifty-Five

The reports that Jake Kramer had been kidnapped and rumored to have been killed quickly became international news. The FBI had stepped in to handle the investigation, with Inspector Bob Pierson being the team lead. The Calvary Cemetery became the alleged crime scene and was immediately sealed off, as all evidence was thoroughly collected and sent directly to the laboratory for analysis. The Inspector made several visits to the Kramer residence with confidential updates for Connie and her family, out of courtesy to her and respect and gratitude for his friend Jake. Connie was informed that the EverCare Transport Company was a shadow. Their alleged office site proved to be a vacant lot on the city's near eastside. The van that was used had been traced to a leasing firm who had contracted it to the EverCare Transport Company for a period of thirty days. All information obtained on the lease was fictitious as well. The address and phone numbers on the lease located police stations, churches and daycares. The names that were used happened to be replicas of the *Indianapolis Star's* obituary notifications days prior. Connie also learned that the papers collected at the hospital giving authorization to EverCare, though genuine in appearance, were instead forgeries. Inspector Pierson commented that the felony did indeed have the mark of professionalism. Until now, Inspector Pierson had refused to speculate that one of the bodies found in the van was that of Jake Kramer. He firmly insisted on waiting for forensics to complete their investigation.

It was on Bob Pierson's third trip to 919 Crest Street that he would confirm Jake's death to the Kramer family. The Inspector paused in his vehicle outside the home to review the facts of the report, deeming it unnecessary to divulge all the details to the family. The pathologist had completed his postmortem autopsy and the report was finalized. Pierson read in part…"The remains had been seventy percent incinerated however with the aid of dental records and technology the evidence was conclusive. The victim died as a result of one of four 9mm gunshot wounds to the cranium at close range. The bullets were retrieved and ballistics tests matched them to the weapon found in the hand of the second victim, considered to have been the alleged assassin. The report went on to state that the identification of the second victim was non-conclusive, but death was the result of a single 9mm gunshot entry introduced beneath the chin. It was officially filed as kidnapping/murder/suicide. The Inspector folded the report and tossed it into his open briefcase on the passenger's seat then pulled the lid closed. He always hated making these types of calls, but this one struck him particularly hard because the victim was his friend and his friend had a wonderful family. Neither deserved this.

With her children at her side and surrounded by her close friends, Connie sat quietly listening to Bob

Pierson's report confirming her husband's death. He was impressed with her strength in dealing with the facts, but she had been dealing with them everyday since Jake's accident at The Meadows Industrial Park months ago. Inspector Pierson handed Connie a gold wedding band that was removed from the deceased's finger and she immediately confirmed it to be her husbands. It was now official and the public would be informed through a new conference held by FBI's Inspector Bob Pierson.

Doctor Harrington was in the house during the Inspector's visit in the event someone needed someone to talk to, when indeed, it was she who needed to come to grips with her self-imposed guilt. For she had placed squarely on her shoulders the responsibility for Jake's kidnapping and indirectly his death. All of which were clearly not her doing, for pre-signed releases are not uncommon and certainly in this case, would not have prevented his death. However, Doreen had let herself become closely involved with the Kramer family and felt the pain as deeply as they.

Connie rarely moved from the den after the Inspector's visit, preferring to sit in her recliner opposite her husband's chair and reflect. She was numb from mourning for already she missed him terribly and the desire to go on was only motivated by her children. However, during this time, her mind never stopped unfolding memories of their life together. Margaret stood quietly in the doorway as she heard her Mother whisper, "…for better or worse, for richer or poorer, in sickness and in health…until death do us part."

Margaret gave her mother a few minutes before intruding. "Mom, I brought you some tea," she said as she eased into the den. "You should drink it while it's hot. And I see that you haven't touched your soup either. Would you like for me to heat it up?"

"No thanks, dear. I guess I'm not ready for soup yet. But your tea sounds good. Thank you. What are you kids up to?"

"Becky has Cindy on the phone. She finally got through to them. I think they were on Cape Cod or something, but I'm sure they'll be on their way home as quickly as they can get a flight. It's JJ and Karen's turn to be in charge of the phone."

"Is Doctor Harrington still here?"

"Yes. She's sitting out on the patio by herself. I think she wants to be alone too."

"Tell her I'll be out in a little while."

"Okay mom. Everything is going to be alright, you'll see. JJ and I will take care of you. We love you, Mom."

"I know you will and I love you too," replied Connie as she looked up at Jake's little Maggie, who was becoming a woman faster than either had cared to admit.

JJ and Karen continued taking turns fielding the countless calls that shared condolences and generous offers ranging from donations to food catering, with one woman volunteering her assistance with their domestic needs. The offers of cash donations were directed to the worthy foundations of, Abused Children, Battered Women, or 800-MISSING.

On the outside of the house, both Linda Stern and Lacy Meeks handled the foot traffic at 919 Crest Street allowing no one to disturb the Kramer family without their consent. The front lawn was blanketed with silk wreaths, fresh flowers, teddy bears, balloons and cards to include store bought as well as hand crafted. Each item was carefully placed as not to disrupt the reverence of the one preceding it. The street traffic became so snarled on Crest Street that patrolmen had volunteered their time to manage the flow. Many of the sympathetic visitors parked blocks away and walked to deliver their offerings, while others quietly passed them through the car's window before driving on. The flow appeared endless.

Northwest flight 771 arrived at 7:45 P.M. at Indianapolis International Airport allowing Alex and Cindy Sanders to exit gate B15 and make their way down the concourse to the escalator and ultimately the lower level baggage claim. Cindy joined the group of impatient travelers at the carousel and waited for their baggage as Alex shuttled to Premier's long-term parking, a move that was intended to expedite their fast paced itinerary.

As the Sanders approached Crest Street they encountered the string of slow moving traffic and opted for Bittersweet Lane as a bypass to take them home around the congestion. The officer standing in the center of Crest Street ignored Alex's turn signal until confirming his address on his license and then motioned him into his drive. Cindy and Alex were completely awestruck as they sat in their car looking across the lawn at the Kramer's property. There were hundreds of people of all races, religions, vocations and ethnic background standing united, holding hands or burning candles while singing hymns. It was more than anyone could bear. Alex Sanders, who had seen and done it all in his lifetime, took Cindy in his arms and they cried until the need was gone. Once their composure returned they made their way to be with their family …all of whom were right next door.

Linda Stern was the first to greet the Sanders as they slowly walked through the singing mass and approached the front door of the Kramer house.

"Cindy, I'm glad to see you back. We missed you around here."

"Oh, Linda, if I give you a hug will you promise not to hurt me?"

"I promise," she replied. "Hello, Mr. Sanders… how's your head?"

"Fine thanks…can I have a hug too?"

"Sure, but I won't promise not to hurt you."

The Sanders were greeted at the front door by Karen, who in turn led them to the den where they found Connie going through old photos and talking to her children. The image of Alex standing in the doorway caused an outpour of her suppressed emotions as Connie softly called his name and began to cry while reaching for him. Alex stepped quickly to her side as they hugged one another and cried. The entire population of the den quickly caught the contagious heartbreak as Becky ran to Cindy saying, “Mom, Mom I love you…I’m so glad you’re here.”

In time everyone collected themselves and the light conversation that was intended to change the focus and eventually the atmosphere had begun. JJ came in carrying gin and tonics for the Sanders which Alex accepted and drank so quickly that JJ offered him Cindy’s as well. In time, Connie began to tell tales of finding Alex and Jake on their patio after finishing a cooler full of Coronas. She told Alex how Jake would look forward to his coming home from his trips, just so they could meet down at Manny’s. Alex shared his favorite yarn about how Jake and he only ordered draft beer at Manny’s so they could watch Millie draw the beer from the tap. He described how she filled each mug until the foam rolled over the top, down the side and across her hand. Doreen Harrington sat quietly on the floor smiling at the stories while watching this wonderful family come to grips with their loss and considered it to be the most priceless therapy she could hope for.

The stories went on as everyone shared his or her favorite until it became apparent that it was getting late and everyone needed to get some rest. They had two days forthcoming that would be filled with many unpleasant tasks that needed to be addressed before Jake Kramer’s memorial services on Thursday.

# Fifty-Six

"…as WAXU takes you live now to our own Cameron Elliott who has been on the scene at White River State Park…the site of today's memorial service for the late Jake Kramer. Cameron, what is the mood there?"

"Thank you, Randy. The mood here is certainly one of sorrow and sadness as family, friends and Jake Kramer's devoted disciples gather here at the site he held dear to him…White River State Park. You can see behind me the crowd is immense and growing as the mourners continue to collect on the lawn where the Vietnam Traveling Wall once visited. Mrs. Kramer's wishes have been honored here as she requested only a modest setting for the Reverend Neil Downs to offer benediction and those wishing to pay homage to her late husband, Jake Kramer. The singing you hear behind me, Randy, is the choir from the Lasting Light Mission located in Indianapolis and led by Sister Marie."

"Cameron, do you have any information as to whom we may expect to speak and give tribute to Mr. Kramer?"

"Yes, Randy, I have been informed that we can expect to hear from Governor Vernon Rodenbeck, and Mayor Cecil Pruitt. Other notables will include words from Indiana Senator Seymour Gaskin and Congresswoman Beulah Wells. There will be, of course, time offered to an open microphone to anyone else who wishes to speak.

"Randy, I'm being advised that the Kramer family has arrived and is now being seated…Yes, that's Mrs. Kramer there in the black dress, being escorted by her son, Jake Jackson and daughter, Margaret Ann. Immediately following are close friends and neighbors, Mr. and Mrs. Alex Sanders."

The camera closely followed each step of the Kramer's foot procession until they were seated and began adjusting their clothing. Cameron continued softly…"Seated directly behind the Kramers is the family of the late Wesley Washington. As you recall, Mr. Washington lost his life in a fierce explosion at the Kramer building just weeks ago, and his daughter, Tonya, also incurred life threatening injuries. Now taking a seat between Mrs. Washington and Wesley's grandmother is the distinguished Reverend Jackson, while seated to Mrs. Washington's right is the Reverend's son, Michael, who is playing with young Jake Washington. It appears that the services are about to begin so let's go now to the proceedings."

"…May we all stand and bow our heads as we ask our heavenly father to bless this family during their hour…"

The services began with Governor Rodenbeck's touching tribute to Jake, then continued with each official adding warm comments describing Mr. Kramer's friendship, morals, leadership and family values, all of which were sincere observations made by politicians who had never met him. The WAXU camera focused on Connie and the kids often as the memorial service continued into the afternoon, breaking occasionally for a hymn from the mission's choir. With the scheduled list of eulogies completed, the open microphone was offered. Connie smiled as she recognized the young lady in the print dress as she approached the podium hand in hand with a man carrying a young boy.

"Mom isn't that…?"

Connie smiled and nodded to Margaret as she held her eyes on the speaker.

"My name is June Grodey and this is my husband Jim and our little boy, Jimmy," she said as she pulled the men in her life close to her. "We're from Benton, Illinois and you should know that we would not be standing here today with our son if it wasn't for your husband, Mrs. Kramer. For those of you who don't know, our son had been taken from the hospital nursery when he was only three days old. Nobody believed us …nobody would help. Nobody, but Jake Kramer. With his help, the FBI located Jimmy and brought him home to us." June began crying as she hugged the little boy in Jim's arms. Moving a tissue to her nose she again spoke while looking directly at the Kramer family. "The last time I cried in front of you, Mrs. Kramer, your lovely daughter, Margaret, handed me a whole box of tissues," she said through a smile. "I only want to say to you and your wonderful family, Connie …you weren't the only ones who loved Jake, and I want you to know that we all feel the loss. May God bless you." With that said the Grodey family turned and walked away leaving few among them with dry eyes.

Stepping to the microphone, the young lady waited as the stand was lowered to her level before speaking directly to the Kramer family. "My name is Diane Driscoll and with me is my son, Josh. I understand the terror and relief that Mrs. Grodey experienced, because I too lost my son to a kidnapper. Josh's kidnapper happened to be his father…my ex-husband who fled with our son. It was Mr. Kramer who reunited us, and Mr. Kramer's impact on our lives will never be forgotten. Josh…did you want to say something?" she asked as she lowered the microphone to him. Josh raised his small hand to grip the mic and said in a soft voice, "Good bye, Mr. Kramer, thank you and I love you."

"I'm Mrs. Farnsworth and I'm sad to say that this is only my second trip to your state from my home on Long Island, New York, with both visits being submerged in sorrow. You see, I was here on my first trip to take home the body of my daughter, Debbie, whose life was shortened by a very sick man… Reverend Hector E. Divine, who will be paying his debt to society for the remainder of his life, and one day soon, will answer to the Almighty for eternity. It was Mr. Kramer who directed the authorities to my Debbie and her friend Billy Prescott as they were left abandoned and lost to the world. He made it possible for me to take my daughter home. Now, I have returned to your city once again in order to pay my respects and eternal gratitude to your husband, Mrs. Kramer. For thanks to him, my Debbie, is no longer missing. Debbie is no longer discarded, for she is home. God bless you and your wonderful family."

As Mrs. Farnsworth turned from the dais the Lasting Light Mission choir broke out in song, *Shall We Gather At The River*, while slowing the pace for the next speaker, Inspector Bob Pierson of the Federal Bureau of Investigation. Farnsworth and Pierson exchanged smiles and handshakes as she recalled him from her first Indiana visit. He stood patiently at the microphone adjusting his notes as the choir sang, "…that flows by the gates of our Lord."

"Thank you, Sister. That was beautiful," he said as he acknowledged Sister Marie. Inspector Pierson made acknowledgements to Connie Kramer and her children before he went on to describe his first encounter with her husband and the ensuing relationship that followed. He shared a few examples of Jake Kramer's immeasurable assistance by referring to Tina Myers, who likely would never have been found at the bottom of Studdard Lake in Kentucky, if not for Jake. He spoke of Jennifer Sutton, who was located along an isolated road in Pennsylvania, and Lilly Garner, the woman who may have saved the life of young Josh Driscoll in Arkansas. The Inspector commented that it was Mr. Kramer who directed them to Ms. Garner's remains in a shallow grave behind a dilapidated woodshed.

He took a moment to tell of the recovery of the remains of three Georgia Fraternity pledges from a cavern identified as Sumter Cave. The investigation that followed failed to make arrests; however, it succeeded in closing two fraternity houses and placing three on probation, bringing an end to needless overzealous hazing of vulnerable young students. This brought a soft applause of approval from guests.

In closing Inspector Pierson presented the Federal Bureau of Investigation's distinguished and coveted *Merit of Allegiance* award posthumously to Mr. Jake Kramer which was humbly accepted by his widow, Connie.

The flow of speakers narrowed until it became apparent that those who came to speak had done so, with the exception of Alex Sanders. Alex stood from his wooden chair and placed a kiss on Cindy's forehead before pausing and taking JJ's hand. He then moved to Margaret and placed a kiss on her cheek before kneeling in front of Connie. No one ever learned what he said to her; however, everyone saw that it made her smile and also cry. Alex then stood and adjusted his tie in his closed jacket before walking directly to the dais, then turned and addressed the congregation.

"It's clear to see by the number of people here that Jake Kramer touched a great number of lives…some personally, many respectfully and regrettably a few fearfully. But the fear was yours, whoever you are, for he was a man who knew no fear. He only knew compassion and he was passionate to anyone and everyone who needed his help, regardless of the danger." Alex paused during the soft applause. "There were rare occasions when Jake and I talked about the threats he received…and sadly, there were many of them. I once suggested that he should go away. Take the family and ask for protection, but Jake just looked at me and asked…'You mean hide?' Clearly that was not the way Jake Kramer intended to live his life. He explained that he intended to live his life as God presented it…as a gift to be used to the fullest everyday that he woke and found that he was blessed to have another…as a gift not to be taken lightly. Jake Kramer couldn't hide and never took his gift lightly. He used it as it was intended and ultimately defended his beliefs with his life."

"I learned many things from my friend. By observation, I learned that he received more from helping the oppressed than receiving their gratitude. He was often embarrassed by his fame. He rarely wanted to talk about what he had done, but would talk forever about what he wanted to do…and that was always for someone in need."

Again Alex paused, giving way to the soft clapping.

"I was with Jake Kramer the day he learned and reported the location of young Josh Driscoll to the authorities. It was raining when Jake walked away from making that call and I watched as he simply stood out on the sidewalk smiling in the rain. He was so gratified…so fulfilled to know that in some way he had helped a desperate little boy that he failed to notice the rain. You see…Jake lived his life by looking through the rain…and seeing the sun. That was the Jake Kramer I knew. The Jake Kramer I loved and respected. And the Jake Kramer I'll miss."

"Reporting live from Jake Kramer's memorial service here at White River State Park in Indianapolis, Indiana, this is Cameron Elliott, WAXU, saying…today we laid an old friend to rest."

# Fifty Seven

*One Year Later*

The breeze from the Atlantic was cool today, but not sweater-cool, as the afternoon sun kept the temperature at bay. Alex had devoted most of the morning to readying the guest room for today's late arrival and as a result had parked himself at the lawn table taking in his prized view of the ocean. Negotiations for this Barnstable, Massachusetts, century-old bed and breakfast were swift inasmuch as Mr. and Mrs. Sanders fell in love with the property and had cash for the purchase. Although the deal was sealed in a matter of days, this cash acquisition was not a new experience for their Cape Cod realtor.

Alex looked to the sky as the gulls circled without wing movement high over the head of Raymond, the inn's handyman, as he snipped at the hydrangeas along the far wall, one leaf at a time. Alex smiled at Raymond's speed before turning and revisiting the three-day-old newspaper from Indiana's state capital.

"I believe you should have that article about memorized by now, honey," said Cindy as she sat a tall glass of iced tea on the table in front of him. "Do you regret not going to the groundbreaking?"

"Nah, I'm not much for ceremonies. Besides, she'll be here in a little while and she'll tell us all about it.

I'm just glad the construction is finally getting underway."

"You should be proud, Alex. If it wasn't for you, the Washington Center would…"

"Cindy…remember, I don't want anyone to know that I was involved with the funding of that project. You promised me that you'd never reveal our part in this. We are to be anonymous…invisible…"

"I know, Alex. I'm not telling anyone, but I can tell you how proud I am of you, can't I?"

"Let's change the subject, okay. What time is it?"

"Why Alex Sanders…you're nervous aren't you?"

"Me! No, I'm not nervous."

"Alex…"

"Well, maybe just a little. It's been over a year since we've seen Connie."

"She's still the same old Connie we left on Crest Street, sweetheart. After all, we trusted her to look after our daughter until she moved into her dorm at Butler, didn't we?"

"Oh I know, but we've all changed a little since…Well, I'm just a little anxious for her to get here, that's all. Did Elena put fresh flowers in her room?"

"Yes dear. One vase from you and one from me."

"Mrs. Sanders…Mrs. Sanders," came the call from the back terrace.

"Yes, Elena. What is it?"

Standing next to the railing was Elena Niederhauser, the inn's day housekeeper and the Cape's historian. This proud third-generation, born, raised and never left the Cape lady, was actually part of the inn's purchase package, as insisted upon, by the former owners. It took only a week until Alex and Cindy realized that they received the best part of the deal. Elena was a gem.

"Mrs. Sanders…the Smalls are leaving."

"Thank you, Elena. Ask them to wait, please. I'll be right up."

"Yes, ma'am."

"Would you like to say good bye to the Smalls, dear?"

"Give them my thanks will you, Cindy?"

"Alex, is that your Raymond out there leaning against the tree…sleeping?"

"No, my Raymond is out there trimming the shrubs."

"Well I don't know how many Raymonds you have, but that one is sleeping. Maybe you're working him too hard."

"I'll try to let up on him."

Cindy went on her way to attend to their guests and extend an invitation to return to the Sandman Inn on their next vacation to the Cape. Alex continued to review his paper as it told of plans for the Washington Center that would be erected on the site of the former Kramer and Associates building. The land was donated by Mrs. Jake Kramer and the project was one hundred percent privately funded by charities, supportive foundations and civic minded individuals.

The Washington Center would be the headquarters for 800-MISSING and was intended to be available for abused and battered women, homeless citizens and runaway youths. There would be counseling available to those who would accept it as reported by Doctor Doreen Harrington who was earmarked to head the guidance committee. "We have such a long list of professionals, skilled laborers and volunteers who want to help, that it is overwhelming and gratifying," said Mrs. Kramer. "I know that Jake and Wesley would be proud."

"Alex, we have a new guest checking in."

"Thanks, Cindy. That would be the Netherys," he said as he folded the paper and set it aside. "I'll get their luggage."

"No…it's not the Netherys."

"Well, we aren't expecting anyone other than Connie and she's not due…"

"Hello Alex."

"CONNIE!"

"I caught an earlier flight. I hope that was alright?"

"Connie?" he said again as he turned and found Cindy and Connie smiling at him from the step.

"Connie," he repeated again as he rushed to the steps and accepted her hug.

"He's been like a kid waiting for Christmas morning," said Cindy. "Actually, we both have."

Connie and Alex hugged until the tears of joy began to creep from the corners of their eyes, and kisses on the cheeks were exchanged.

"Connie, you look wonderful," said Alex, as he took a step back. "You've cut your hair. It makes you look ten years younger."

"Cindy, I must say this Cape Cod business has done wonders for your husband. He's turned into a real charmer."

"It's been a good thing for everyone, Connie. Come…sit down, we have a lifetime to catch up on."

Taking a seat on the veranda, Alex, Cindy and Connie sat quietly at first, taking in the moment that each, for their own reasons, had anticipated for over a year. Today they were once again reunited to relive, or put to bed, the past.

"Mrs. Sanders, I thought you might enjoy some tea," said Elena, as she sat the pitcher near the center of the table.

"Thank you, Elena. That was thoughtful."

"Mrs. Kramer, I took the liberty of unpacking for you. You should find your belongings in order, with the exception of the navy dress. I found it in need of pressing and I have it in my quarters attending to that. You'll find it on your door in the morning, but if you should need it this evening, I will be happy to get right on it."

Connie was so taken by Elena's efficiency and attention to detail that she didn't immediately answer, but rather just sat looking astounded.

"Tomorrow will be fine, Elena. Thank you," answered Cindy as Elena returned to the house.

"Cindy…my word, where did you find her?"

"She was forced on us when we bought the inn," said Alex. "We're going to fire her if she doesn't start taking an interest in our guests."

"She's wonderful," said Connie. "This inn is wonderful. I can see how you two fell in love with it. Do you have other help?"

"We have a chef who oddly enough insists on being referred to as the cook. And that would be, Selma. However, as you will learn, she is, without question, a master in the art of fine cuisine. Tonight, she's preparing a lobster thermidor in your honor that is to die for. She's modest and loves to cook, but doesn't crave fame. You're in for a real treat, Connie."

"That sounds wonderful," said Connie.

"We also have a gardener," said Alex. "That's him working out there by the tree."

"It looks like he's sleeping," said Connie.

Alex looked a little embarrassed, but answered, "No, he's gets a break now and then. You'll have to meet him too."

"Maybe later. You should let him rest," she said laughing.

"Let's walk," said Alex. "You need to see our ocean."

Alex walked between Connie and Cindy to the ocean bluff at the rear of the Sandman Inn property that offered a striking view of the waters of the eastern seaboard as seen from Barnstable, Massachusetts.

"This is absolutely beautiful," said Connie, as she looked out across the rolling water and the breaking waves.

"We have a nice little setting over here in the shade, Connie, with a bench and swing. Let's sit for awhile shall we?" suggested Alex. "We're glad you accepted our invitation," he continued. "Cindy and I have been wondering how you're doing. I mean with Margaret away at Purdue this year and…well, it's…"

"I know what you mean, Alex, and thank you. I'm adjusting a little everyday. Some days are harder than others and honestly there were times I didn't think I could get through another day without Jake. I really miss him, but life goes on. And now I try to stay busy, especially with the Washington Center getting started. That's really exciting."

"We're sorry that we couldn't make the groundbreaking ceremonies, Connie, but you know how it is? I'm just not into all that public stuff. I just thought we could show our support in other ways."

"I understand, Alex, you don't need to explain. You two have been very supportive. I always knew that you were only a phone call away. I hope you know how much we appreciated your charitable gift to the foundation. Your check was very generous and…" Connie paused as she moved slightly while looking past Alex.

"Something wrong, Connie?"

"What?…Oh, no. It's just your gardener. He keeps looking over here."

"Raymond? I just think he's anxious for me to introduce him to you," said Alex as he looked over his shoulder. "Connie," continued Alex, "Cindy and I have a few apologies and confessions to get off our chests that we feel are long overdue."

Connie exchanged a confused glance between the Sanders, but then smiled and asked, "What in the world could you two owe me an apology for, Alex?"

"Well, one thing in particular…we feel that we should apologize for moving so quickly away from Indiana during a time when you needed friends the most. We'd like to explain."

"You two don't need to explain to me why you wanted to move to such a lovely place, and you certainly don't owe me any apologies for doing so. I'm really happy for you." Connie paused before she changed the subject, "He's coming over here."

"Who? Raymond?"

Connie nodded yes as she stood and looked directly at Raymond as he made his way slowly toward them. His white full-faced beard was meticulously trimmed and gave an air of distinction to this aging gentleman. He was wearing a red ball cap that covered his white hair as the bill of the cap rested against the rim of his sunglasses that concealed his eyes. Alex and Cindy watched as Connie stood quietly watching their gardener approach from the bluff in slow deliberate steps that appeared to hold her captive.

"I guess our apologies will have to wait, Connie. It appears that Raymond can't."

They were all three standing now as Raymond closed the short distance between them. Cindy had moved to Alex's side and held tightly to his arm as Connie stood motionless watching each step Raymond took. Alex noticed her hands as they began to tremble as she raised her fingers to her lips, but she did not shiver alone on this windswept bluff.

Raymond paused at arms length in front of Connie Kramer who was visibly shaking, as he offered her a comforting smile.

"Oh my God," whispered Connie. Tears began to roll down her cheek as she swallowed hard and raised her trembling hand to Raymond's cap and gently pulled it from his head allowing his white hair to toss in the breeze. Raymond held steadfast as Connie stared deeply at his face before again raising her hand to his sunglasses. Without his objection, she pulled his glasses free until they fell from her hand to the lawn."

"Oh my God…it's you," she whispered.

"I'm so sorry, Connie. You'll never know how much."

"Jake…Jake, it's really you?" she said as her hands ran gently across his face."

"It's really me, Connie. My God, did I never truly realize how beautiful you are?"

"JAKE! She said once again as she fell into his arms surrendering to her emotions. She then began to cry as she repeated his name again and again. While releasing a year's worth of heartache, neither had noticed that Alex and Cindy were slowly making their way across the lawn toward the Sandman Inn.

# Fifty-Eight

Alex stood looking out the double-glass doors of the sunroom at Raymond and Connie as they sat on the bench watching the ocean below. Her head rested against Raymond's shoulder as his arm held her close to him. It was a heartwarming picture-perfect scene that only existed in storybooks, until today.

"They've been out there a long time," said Alex.

"They've been separated a long time," replied Cindy. "Come…sit down. They'll be in when they're ready."

"I wonder how she is taking it?"

"How would you take it if it were you?"

"I'd be too happy to be too mad."

"Come on, sit down. Tell me about that sizeable donation you contributed to the Washington Center."

"I told you about that."

"But you never told me how much. You must have been very generous."

"Do you mind?"

"No…only curious, but I shouldn't have asked… sorry."

Alex took a seat next to Cindy and put his arm around her before placing a kiss on her cheek. "You have every right to ask. The truth is I gave them my severance check."

"Really? Well that was nice of you."

"Actually, I hadn't been expecting one because I was one project short of my contract, but when I was asked to go back to work…all obligations were fulfilled."

"And now you'll never be called out again?"

"Never. You want to know the funny thing about that check?"

"What?"

"They must have thought I did the work of two men and they paid me double."

"You're kidding?"

"Nope. I didn't want any of it and I felt that the Washington Center could use it, so I sent it to the foundation. Besides, the company has an endless supply. That was what Connie was referring to. It was a lot of money that you and I didn't want any part of. We didn't need it. I have everything I need right here in this room."

The light tap at the door broke their embrace as Cindy acknowledged, "Yes?"

"Mrs. Sanders, Selma and I took the liberty of preparing a light snack for you and Mrs. Kramer. We couldn't help but notice that she has taken a fancy to our gardener," she added with a smile, "So we made a little extra assuming that Raymond would be joining you."

"Why thank you, Elena," said Cindy through a suppressed smile. "That was very thoughtful. It looks delicious."

"Mr. Sanders," she continued. "I also took liberty in selecting wine for your reunion. I hope it's satisfactory," she said as she handed him a bottle of port. "I have additional selections chilling."

"You make a fine wine steward, Elena."

"Thank you, sir; I'll take that as a complement. I notice your guest is returning. I'll see that you're not disturbed." With that said, Elena pulled closed the pocket doors that adjoined the inn's vestibule.

Cindy and Alex watched as Raymond opened and held the glass door leading to the sunroom for Connie allowing her to quickly step in and across the carpet until she stood face to face with Alex.

"Alex Sanders…I don't know if I should slap you or kiss you for what you helped Jake put me through," said Connie as she looked deep into his eyes.

Alex had often wondered about Connie's reaction when she learned the truth about her husband, but this comment he hadn't considered. He stood quietly for a moment as his face turned a nice shade of red, before saying, "I'll have whatever Raymond's having."

Connie shook her head and laughed before placing an embarrassing kiss on Alex's lips, then said, "Well part of it anyway. Alex, I'll never be able to repay you and…well…I just hope my telling you that I love you is enough," she said with a cracking voice, as she hugged him once again.

"Paid in full, Connie. Paid in full."

The wine was shared as the first bottle was emptied and quickly replaced before the conversation turned to a more serious note. With each couple seated on sofas separated by a turn-of-the-century table that bore the weight of the hors d'oeuvres and wine, Connie began to ask her countless questions.

"I know you've been waiting for the second shoe to fall," said Connie. "I think it's time someone here tells me what the hell happened and why in the hell was I the last to know?"

The room fell noticeably quiet as Cindy, Alex and Jake looked at each other expecting the other to take the lead. Alex spoke first, but only after he took a sip of wine to moisten his tongue.

"Connie, I know that you must feel that you were part of a conspiracy, and the truth is, you were…a very large part. However, you should know that no one here wanted to put you in such a position. But you were the key. You made it successful to the end result. That being, we still have Jake…who shall be from here forward known as, Raymond Baker. It's critical that you adjust and refer to Jake as Raymond. That will become clear before the evening ends. Do you understand?"

"Not yet, but I hope to," said Connie. "Please go on."

"Well, I think you should hear first from Raymond. He can start from the beginning as his explanation should have deeper meaning."

Connie looked to Raymond with probing eyes, but without saying a word.

"Connie," he stated. "Believe me when I say that I absolutely did not want to deceive you or hurt you in any way. But it became painfully evident that there were many people who felt threatened by my gift. In fact, they felt so threatened that they wanted to kill me in order to prevent the possibility of my exposing them to the authorities.

"Like Walter Driscoll?" said Connie.

"Yes…Walter Driscoll…an excellent example. Don't you see, Driscoll crossed the line? He attacked me in our home. He could have hurt you or Margaret if he wasn't stopped by…by shooting himself."

Raymond picked up his wine glass, looked over the rim at Alex before taking another small sip and setting the glass down.

"When I finally accepted the fact that I would never be able to right all the wrongs in the world and I was, in some cases, contributing to them, I knew something had to be done. I had to put an end to it. That's when I decided to start having my mood swings, becoming a little difficult at times and absentminded. Actually, I was laying the groundwork, so to speak. When Doctor Harrington became interested in my actions I knew the plan was going along well. Then the explosion. Connie, you can't imagine the personal hell I went through knowing that Wesley and Mr. Porter lost their lives because of me. It was unbearable. And our precious little Tonya almost lost her life as a result too. When I thought of Tonya lying in a coma not knowing when or if she might recover, it was enough to push anyone over the edge."

"But, Jake…Raymond. That was an accident. The fire marshal said so."

Raymond shook his head no, as he explained. "Connie…the truth is it was a fire bomb set for me. I was supposed to be in that truck, not Wesley. I have learned to live with the truth because I can't change it. Now, if you want to know the truth…here it is. That explosion was not an accident, it was deliberate and intended for me."

Connie lowered her head. "Oh my God," is all she whispered as she began to cry.

"Then the final straw, Connie. You were shot and almost killed by a bullet that was intended for me. It was too much for me to bear. I had to die…one way or the other."

Connie was crying hard now as the severity of his words bore deep in her heart. Cindy handed her the tissue box after saving a few for herself while Raymond paused to sip the wine before he continued with his confession.

Connie was visibly shaking now, as she was hearing things that were breaking her heart, but there would be no stopping or going back now. She had to know the whole story. She picked up her glass, controlling it with two hands and sipped at her wine as the mood in the room continued to turn somber.

"Actually, it was Alex here who unwittingly gave me the idea. We had left the hospital and Alex was giving me a ride home after a short visit to the Kramer building ruins. Do you remember this, Alex?"

"No…not really."

"Basically, I asked what you would do in my situation and you said among other things…'I know I would go crazy if someone hurt my Cindy or Becky because of me.' As we rode along for some reason I kept repeating those words over and over in my mind. That's when the idea hit me. I knew I was going to go crazy. So crazy in fact, that the whole world would see it and believe it. Everyone would know that Jake Kramer was a basket case and no threat to anyone any longer. However, there were one or two small factors in this little plan that I hadn't considered. Some people didn't care if Jake Kramer was nuts, they still wanted him dead. And two…I learned that by acting crazy for too long a period of time could actually drive a man there…crazy."

"Jake…" said Connie. "You were…"

"Raymond…please remember, I'm Raymond now."

"Okay, Raymond, but this is new to me, so bear with me. Are you telling me that you were only playing the part of being mentally disturbed?"

"Yes…crazy isn't it?"

Connie fell back into the couch in disbelief. "Do you know that you had Doctor Harrington completely believing you? OR…or, was she a part of your master plan too?"

"No. She wasn't part of the plan, but I did learn a great many things about your Doctor Harrington. I learned that she is dedicated, sensitive, concerned and a caring lady. I have a newfound respect for her and I do owe her an apology. I'm very sorry that she will never know that."

"Thank you for at least telling me," said Connie.

"Well, I admit that convincing Doctor Harrington was indeed encouraging to my plan," he continued. "But it was Connie Kramer that the world was watching. It would be she that would convince the world that her husband had a breakdown and was now mentally ill. That's why I agreed to return to Elliott's' program. My friends and family were in jeopardy because of me and I was desperate. It was on the ride home from visiting you in the hospital that I decided that I would go bananas on live television."

"Oh Lord," said Connie. "I'll never forget that program. Thank God Cindy and Linda were with me, because I couldn't have gotten through it alone. That man…the caller who accused you of taking money from their farm. He kept on and on, calling you a thief, making threats and terrible accusations. I wanted Elliott to hang up on him, to shut him up, but he just encouraged him to go on and on. I wanted to slap him …I hated him."

Alex broke out in soft laughter, causing Raymond to smile also.

"What?" asked Connie. "Why are you two laughing at me?"

"We're not laughing at you, honey," said Raymond as he pointed to Alex. "But if you'd really like to slap the caller he's sitting right over there."

"ALEX!"

"Yep, I was the angry caller."

"No. No way. I would have recognized your voice."

"I used a voice distorting cap over the mouth piece. They're not hard to get."

Connie leaned back in her chair and placed her hands over her eyes in disbelief. "I must be the most gullible person in the world," she said. "Cindy, you haven't said much. Were you in on this too?"

"Not this part. This is news to me too, and you're not alone because I didn't recognize Alex's voice either."

"Wait a minute here," she said as she once again took her position at the edge of the sofa. "I saw the close up of your eyes and your nose bleeding down your chin on Elliott's program. Your eyes were blood red and…"

"Did you see me remove my handkerchief from my pocket before that happened?"

"No. If I did I don't remember. Why?"

"I knew that movement would pass nonchalantly. No one took notice. Not even on the replays. My handkerchief was laced with pepper spray. When I rubbed my face with the cloth the results were immediate."

"And the nosebleed?" she asked. "That looked very real."

"Blood capsules from the *Good Time Novelty* store. I had them tucked in the handkerchief too. I simply pressed them in my nostrils and squeezed my nose," he explained. "The result that everyone saw was rather dramatic and very effective. The only thing I needed to do for a finale was prance around and make a scene. I knew Elliott's cameras would do their best to stay live and up close and personal with Jake Kramer losing his sanity."

Connie fell quiet for a moment and just stared at Raymond.

"What is it, Connie?" he asked.

"I was thinking about the time I found you in the den like that before. Do you remember?"

"Yes."

"Was that just a trick too? Just a test to see how I would react?"

Without hesitation Raymond leaned forward and answered, "No, Connie, no. The sad truth is that was very real. That was a very real and bad time for me."

"Does anyone besides me need a short break?" asked Alex. "I need to use the restroom and find more wine."

"No thanks," answered Connie and Raymond.

"I'll tag along," said Cindy, "but no fair continuing until we get back…agreed?"

"Agreed," said Raymond.

# Fifty-Nine

“We’re back bearing food and drink,” said Cindy. “Connie, I think you have the girls in the kitchen a little jealous of you.”

“Why’s that?”

“I believe they think you’ve stolen Raymond away from them.”

“And they better know it,” she replied. “What have you been doing to those poor women, Raymond?” she asked while slapping him on the arm.

“Nothing, honest. I think that’s why they’re upset.”

The glasses were refilled and the snack tray was passed around as the subject again grew serious.

“Where were we?” asked Raymond.

“You just walked off the Cameron Elliott show,” answered Connie.

“Yes, that’s right. I had the driver take me uptown and drop me off at the Easton Hotel. From there I made my way to White River State Park where I was found by the park rangers and sent to the hospital.”

“You were sent to the hospital with cracked ribs and a beaten body,” she corrected. “How did that come to be or were they self-inflicted too?”

“No…they were painfully real. Something I could have done without, but it could have been worse. Just a couple of kids who wanted to borrow some cash, that’s all.”

"Raymond, when the kids and I visited you in the hospital…each time we were there you never once responded to anything we said or did. When you and I were alone, not once did you react to my touch or anything I said to you, never. You just stared at that damn ceiling. How did you manage that if you were acting?"

Raymond paused before answering as he knew everyone wanted to know the answer to that. How could he blank out the people who loved him as they held his hand and cried at seeing him in such a state? Raymond went on to explain, "I stared at the ceiling tile for it was my image creator. When I looked there I saw the burning rubble of my truck and visualized Wesley inside. I saw his face looking out at me crying for help. Help that I couldn't give. I saw Mr. Porter and heard him tell me he wasn't afraid to die, but his biggest concern was for his wife who couldn't take care of herself.

As I looked up there I could see Tonya as she lay on the backboard with all her cuts and bruises. She would look at me and ask me to go and get her daddy for her because her daddy would make the hurt go away. I could see it all. And I could see you, Connie, as you lay in my arms bleeding from the head by a bullet that was intended for me. It was all in the tile and it wasn't hard to remember why I had to do this. It wasn't hard to know that if I failed the next innocent victim could be Margaret or JJ. I had to turn you away in order to keep you. No, even though I loved you with all my heart, I didn't have a hard time not responding. I had a hard time…not crying."

Alex was the first to break the long silence, "My God, I never knew. I can see how a man could go insane with daily thoughts like that. No wonder you wanted out. Who could blame you?"

"Honey, I'm sorry," said Connie as she placed her arm around his shoulder. "I'm so very sorry."

"Nothing for anybody to be sorry for," replied Raymond. "But I was glad when I finally had an opportunity to speak to Alex."

"You spoke to Alex? When? Alex, you didn't say anything about that."

"Alex, I guess it's your turn to fill in the blanks," said Raymond.

"Wait a minute. Alex…you were in on this from the beginning?" asked Connie.

"No. Not all of it. That is not until he asked me to become his fathom caller on Elliott's show. Up until that time, I was just grasping at pieces of his actions like everyone else. I had the impression that he was up to something and I tried to keep an eye on him in case he got into trouble, but as far as knowing his plan…no. Then I heard about your intentions, Connie, to transfer Jake to California. So that afternoon I stopped in to see him. He was sitting in a chair while the nurse changed his bed. When that was finished I carried Jake from the chair and placed him on the bed. That's when I knew."

"You knew what?' asked Connie.

"Well, as I leaned over to lower Jake in bed, his head was resting against my shoulder. That's when he whispered into my ear."

"Come on, Alex, don't just sit there smiling at us, what did he say?"

"He whispered, 'get me the hell out of here.'"

"No!" said Connie.

"It's true. The nurse couldn't have heard him and to tell you the truth, I wasn't sure that I did. I just stood there looking down at him watching for another sign, but old Jake didn't give one. He just lay there, staring at the ceiling tile. Once I snapped back to reality, I left immediately, went straight to Manny's Pub, sat alone in a corner booth, drank draft beer and devised a plan. But for my plan to work I needed a partner. Someone who was reliable, devoted, attractive and works cheap."

Connie immediately looked to Cindy. "You?"

Cindy nodded her head yes several time and blushed as she replied, "Me."

"I didn't feel that any part of my plan was dangerous, so I went home to Cindy and told her what happened at the hospital and asked if she would like to be a part of my plan to kidnap Jake Kramer from the hospital."

"Kidnap Jake?" repeated Connie. "You two kidnapped Jake from the hospital?"

"Yes we did," answered Cindy. "We really did. My God that was exciting. I was so nervous, but I knew exactly what I had to do and I did it," she continued with the biggest smile of the afternoon.

Connie grabbed her glass from the table and downed the last of grapes before quickly handing it off while saying, "More wine, Raymond. This is unbelievable."

As she accepted her refill, Connie exclaimed, "Hey …wait a minute…now wait a minute here. I just remembered something. You two were away when Jake was kidnapped. You were here in Cape Code looking for a place to buy. I looked after Becky for you."

"That's true. I wanted to give the impression that we were out of town during this caper so we caught a flight and had lunch at the Boston airport as we waited for our return flight home," confessed Alex. "We knew that we only had a few days to commandeer Jake before he was transferred from the hospital, so we had to act fast. Cindy rented the costumes and attended to the necessary travel schedules, as I leased the van, made badges and created paper work. All in all, things went along beautifully to this point."

"Alex, are you saying you took Jake out of the hospital?" asked Connie.

"We did. And as I said, things were going well up to the point that a third party was interested in having Jake vanish as well."

"Who was in that van with you, Alex? Who did I bury?" she asked with a cracking voice. "Please don't tell me that another innocent person died."

"No, Connie, answered Alex. The Jake Kramer that you buried was already dead. You buried a destitute homeless male who had become the responsibility of the county. I identified him as my stepbrother and signed the papers accepting final responsibility. I then rolled him into my EverCare van and went directly to the hospital to trade him in for Jake."

"This is unbelievable," said Connie.

"Believe it," said Raymond. "The best part is coming up. Go on, Alex."

Well…once at the hospital, I proceeded directly to the fourth floor where I ultimately convinced a very skeptical nurse named Susan that she should release Jake to me. Once she agreed to accept my papers, I moved quickly in and out of room 466, and then hurried Jake Kramer into the elevator."

"My God," said Connie, "and how did Cindy fit into all of this?"

"In the elevator. She was waiting with my adopted brother strapped in a wheel chair when I rolled Jake in."

"Cindy, you were pushing a dead man around in a wheelchair?"

Cindy smiled and nodded her head yes several times.

"That's right, she did," said Raymond who hadn't spoken for some time. "When the doors closed we had three floors to make the exchange. I got up then on rather shaky legs and with Cindy's help, I made it to the wheelchair, while Alex placed his brother onto the gurney. When we reached the ground floor, Nurse Cindy pushed me around the corner to her car while Alex rolled John into his EverCare van. Voila, the exchange was complete."

"Wait now…hold up for a minute," said Connie. "You referred to this homeless man as John. I never thought to ask his name. Who did I bury?"

"You buried John Doe, Connie. A generic name given to the nameless. The death certificate that I received stated that he died of a cerebral hemorrhage. Someone found him under a bridge in the city, lying on a cardboard box."

"It was a tragic end, but also a little eerie," added Cindy.

"That's true," said Alex. "But let's not forget that Mr. John Doe did receive a very nice family funeral service."

The conversation fell quiet while everyone took a moment to reflect. Raymond watched Connie tilt her head as her eyes began to roam back and forth across the ceiling trying to sort out some details of the drama.

"What is it, Connie?" he asked.

She then spoke softly, but to no one in peculiar. "I was just thinking about Inspector Pierson's visit to our house confirming Jake's death. He gave me your wedding ring while reassuring us that the evidence, which included dental records, was conclusive. I was just wondering how you managed to influence the FBI's investigation. Was the Inspector in on this too?"

"Alex, would you care to answer that for Connie?"

Alex slid to the edge of the sofa to set his glass on the table as he said, "Inspector Pierson is a good man and I must admit that at one time I had considered taking him into our confidence. But something told me that he had too many years on the side of justice to allow himself to falsify evidence or records. In reality, I happened to receive the dental x-rays of John Doe that were used by the county coroner in his search for a match that would possibility identify the deceased. When his personal effects were turned over to me as the next of kin, copies of the autopsy report and his dental x-rays were included. The end result was an identical match between Jake Kramer and John Doe."

"But they wouldn't have identically matched Jake's x-ray's on file at the dentist office," said Connie.

"They sure did," corrected Alex. "That's why the FBI's examination was conclusive."

"But how could that be?" insisted Connie. "Doctor Turner…"

"Connie…interrupted Raymond. "Let's just say that Alex has a special talent in record keeping and let it go at that…shall we?"

Everyone sat quietly as they watched Connie's expression change from confused to embarrassed, before saying, "Are you telling me he broke…oh no." she said before smiling and shaking her head in disbelief. "Well, I had to ask, didn't I?" she added."

Again the mood lightened as Raymond and Alex stood and moved about the room.

"Well," said Raymond, "I can't speak for Cindy and Alex, but I, for one, am glad that's off my chest." Cindy quickly agreed as Alex raised his glass and added, "I'll drink to that."

"Not so fast, everyone," said Connie. "You can drink to that if you want to, but we're not done here. I want to know what went wrong. What happened at the cemetery, and where in the hell did Jake go until you guys moved here?"

Raymond looked back at Alex, "Looks like you're on again, old friend."

As he stood and walked behind the sofa, Alex paced a few times before stopping behind Cindy and saying, "I was hoping that we could avoid this episode, but I guess you're all entitled to the truth." Alex collected his thoughts for a few moments before continuing.

"Looking back, I know that I should have locked the door of the van, but I didn't. I was in a hurry to get away. I really didn't see him open the rear door and climb inside the van before he directed me to the Calvary Cemetery at gunpoint."

"He? Who was he, Alex? Did he say who he was?" asked Connie.

"No. But I'm sure he was a paid assassin who went to the hospital to kill Jake Kramer."

"Thank God you were there first," she added as she shook with the thought.

Alex nodded in agreement as he continued, "Once at the cemetery he simply shot John Doe four times without hesitation or without looking to see if it was Jake Kramer he was shooting. It was just that simple."

"And the explosion?" asked Cindy this time.

"He carried a flower box, one that you'd expect to find long stem roses in. Well, there was no bed of roses in that box. It was packed with a fire bomb of some sort. At least that's what he told me. He said Jake missed his first one at the Kramer office, but he was not going to miss this one. That's when he set the timer and we struggled. I was the one who got away. End of story," he added as he returned to take his seat beside Cindy.

Connie met him standing and took him into her arms like she would never let him go. "How can I ever thank you?" she asked.

"Connie, that's what friends are for…you don't owe me anything."

"Listen," said Cindy, who had just finished drying her eyes once again, "Why don't we go out and sit at the bluff for awhile. I think we all could use some fresh air."

"Good suggestion," agreed Alex, as each gathered their glass and made their way through the atrium doors into the warm sun and clean smell of the sea breeze.

Cindy stopped and tugged at Alex's arm as she said, "Connie, you and Raymond go ahead. Alex and I will catch up with you shortly. Alex, I could use your help upstairs with you-know-what."

"No, I don't."

"Yes you do, now come on." Cindy pulled him close as she whispered, "I need your help upstairs …now do you want to help or not?"

"You bet." He then turned to Raymond saying, "Like she said, we'll catch up with you two shortly."

# Sixty

It was late afternoon as Connie and Raymond walked hand in hand across the lawn at the Sandman Inn toward the quaint setting at the ocean bluff. “We’re very fortunate to have friends like the Sanders, Raymond.”

“Yes, you can bet your life on it.”

“Can I ask you something else?”

“Why not?”

“Why in the hell did you choose the name Raymond?”

He laughed as he asked, “What would you prefer? I can change it you know.”

“Really? You can?”

“Sure. Why not? No one knows me but the few folks here around Barnstable. What would you prefer?”

“Well heck…I don’t know now. Let me think about it.”

“Okay, but until then I’m Raymond Baker. Jake Kramer is dead and buried.”

“Well…actually dead but not buried…I had you cremated.”

They reached the bluff and stood peacefully watching the waves break against the sand and rocks below. Connie was clinging tightly to his arm while looking across the horizon as she asked, “Where did they take you after the kidnapping, Raymond?”

"Washington. We flew out right away, all three of us, to Olympia. Alex somehow had made arrangements for a cabin in the mountains from an old Army friend who wasn't using it. It was very beautiful and very isolated there. I'd sit on the back porch and look out over the most stunning view of the lake and the surrounding mountains that returned an incredibly peaceful effect. Alex had struck up a deal with a man named Grady, who owned a little store at the foothills, to be my keeper. About twice a week ole Grady would drop in and bring me supplies. He must have grown to like me a little, because as the weeks wore on his visits lasted a little longer, which I welcomed. I think he was just a lonely old man too. Towards the middle of my confinement, he brought along his checker board and we'd play on the porch for hours. During one of our games, I must have mentioned something about the lake and that I had never fished or at least not seriously. So, on his next visit he came with his poles and tackle box and said something about, 'You can't learn to enjoy life if you don't know how to fish.' He was quite a colorful character. You'd like him. You want to know the most amazing thing about Grady?"

"What was the most amazing thing about Grady?" she repeated.

"He never once asked a single question as to who I was or why I was there. Not once. I don't believe, to this day, he knew my name. He just called me 'young fella'."

Raymond realized that he was rambling on as he turned to look at Connie who was facing the ocean breeze and crying her heart out.

"Oh Connie," he said while turning her towards him. "I'm so sorry. I didn't mean to go on like that."

"No, no. It's not that. I want to know."

"Well…what is it then?"

"I just don't want to lose you again. I don't want to go home without you, Jake, or Raymond…whatever you want to call yourself. I love you and I can't stand to think about leaving you again. I just can't," she sobbed.

"Oh, Connie honey…you're not going to lose me. We'll be together again."

"When?" she asked as she rubbed the tears from her cheek with the back of her hand.

"Here, allow me," he said as he removed his handkerchief and raised it to her face.

"Oh sure…it's probably full of pepper spray," she said forcing a laugh.

"Come. Let's sit and I'll tell you about the wonderful future in store for you and Raymond Baker.

They took a seat on the bench among the flowering hydrangeas and magnolia bushes as Connie regained her poise and waited for Raymond's predictions on their future.

"You will need to go back home without me, Connie. I'm sorry, but it's necessary and it's also temporary."

"NO!"

"Connie…let me finish. You're going to go back home and continue the charade as the grieving widow. You'll tell the kids that you had a wonderful time here and you have realized that getting away from Indianapolis is good therapy, so you have planned to take an extended cruise. Four months through the South Pacific. They probably won't believe you'll do it until they drop you off at the airport."

He could see Connie's mind catching up with him as her eyes began to stroll across the ocean's horizon.

"The kids also won't believe that while on this exotic cruise ship you met and fell in love with a very handsome, intelligent, witty, kind and wealthy widower by the name of Raymond Baker. And they'll go ballistic when you tell them that you're going to accept his proposal of marriage and live on his plantation on the island of Maui."

Raymond again paused as he saw her head slowly turning to him.

"You'll tell them," he continued, "that he wants to meet your children and he's sending first class transportation and expense money to get them there. I really miss them, Connie, but they can't know about me until we get them home on Maui and make it very clear to them the severity of our secrecy."

Connie shook her head and smiled at Raymond while asking, "Nice plan, but how are you going to come up with a Hawaiian plantation?"

"Did you forget the wealthy part of my credentials? I already have one. We own an incredible pineapple plantation and it will become our new home if you'll agree to be married at sea by the ship's captain. Will you, Connie…will you marry me?"

"Connie threw her arms around Raymond's neck and kissed him passionately before saying, "Oh Raymond, I never thought I could ever fall in love with another man, but you have made me forget all about what's-his-name. Yes, I will marry you."

"Good. I love you, Connie Kramer."

"And I love you, Raymond Baker."

The End

www.ingramcontent.com/pod-product-compliance
Lightning Source LLC
LaVergne TN
LVHW020515100826
845148LV00010B/1242

* 9 7 8 1 6 0 0 0 2 0 8 5 8 *